IT
CALLS
FROM
THE
VEIL

Dedicated to the ones that came before us. *Forgive us.*

EERIE RIVER PUBLISHING
HAMILTON, ONTARIO

IT CALLS FROM THE VEIL

ORIGINAL STORIES BY

RACHAEL BOUCKER
HOLLEY CORNETTO
HENRY BEN EDOM
DAVID-JACK FLETCHER
C.M. FOREST
RB KELLY
CONSTANTINE E. KIOUSIS
AMANDA CECELIA LANG
NIKKI R. LEIGH
COLIN LEONARD
CONNER MCALEESE
CA MCDONALD
R. L. MEZA
DANNY NICHOLAS
SHELBY SUDERMAN
ANGELA SYLVAINE
TRISH WILSON
NU YANG

IT CALLS FROM THE VEIL

Eerie River Publishing
www.EerieRiverPublishing.com
Hamilton, Ontario Canada

This book is a work of fiction. Names, characters, places, events,
organizations and incidents are either part of the author's
imagination or are used fictitiously. Any resemblance to actual
persons, living or dead, or actual events is purely coincidental.

Paperback ISBN: 978-1-990245-65-7
Hardcover ISBN: 978-1-990245-64-0
Digital ISBN: 978-1-990245-63-3

Edited by Lyndsey Smith
Compiled by Michelle River
Cover Design Michelle River

Special thanks to our Jr. Editors, Tim Mendees, David Green,
Chris Hewitt, Holley Cornetto, Rachael Boucker and S.O.
Green.

CONTENTS

FOREWORD
BY NICHI

Horror stalks us.

As kids, we enjoy being scared. We run around the house hunting ghosts in the dark, tell spooky stories by the campfire, stay up all hours watching movies like 'The Craft', playing 'light as a feather, stiff as a board' or 'Bloody Mary' during sleepovers. And let's not forget the shivering fear of that monster living under our beds, patiently waiting for one of our limbs to fall loose from the covers, ready to drag us under.

Many adults hold on to the love of being terrified, while some of us slowly lose that excitement. Sadly, I was one of the latter. I can't pinpoint the exact moment I stopped surrounding myself with all the dark, delicious, horrifying goodness, but what I do know is, I am happy it found me again, trapping me like some sort of witchcraft.

I have the horror community to thank for this. I may not be able to remember the moment I lost touch with my love of dark fiction, but one thing is certain: I can remember the exact moment I found my way back.

I called myself out one day, talking about the genres I could live without. Silly me, I mentioned horror as one of them. When a fellow book lover reached out, we had a great discussion on the options in the horror genre and the endless subgenres within. Jason White, also known as Jason's Weird Reads, author and fellow-book content creator said something to the effect of "You simply have to find your place within horror, explore all subgenres, find your favorites."

I followed this advice and immediately became completely devoured by horror again. I found my way home!

While exploring the depths of this addicting genre, it was clear how quickly supernatural horror became a favorite. The afterlife, death, good vs. evil—the exotic world of the unfamiliar is mesmerizing.

During my teen years, my friends and I would hide away trying to manifest a connection with the spirit world using the all-too familiar Ouija board, genuinely believing we were playing an innocent game. Yet now I sit here pondering if my chilling personal experiences after this were simply a coincidence, or our foolish mistake of forgetting to close the connection with the spirit side? Then there were the hours I spent watching paranormal investigators searching for proof of life after death firsthand.

Oddly enough, it never dawned on me how much I would enjoy consuming my obsession with the unknown through written stories. Eternity is perplexing! I find comfort, a warm feeling, with the thought of a passed loved one watching over us, sharing signs that they still surround us.

Although, how horrifying to think that the entity standing over us while we adore the dream world may not be familiar to us at all, nor have the kindest of intentions.

The afterlife is dangerous and eerie yet demands to be explored!

There are so many amazing, talented authors out there, with impeccable stories to tell. Anthologies and short story collections are some of the best ways to consume horror, especially if you are new to the genre or are trying to find your place in dark fiction again. These perfect, bite-sized stories are easily consumed.

However, you don't need me to tell you this. You must know already. I mean, you were drawn to this collection, right? It was whispering your name from the shadows, enticing you to pick up a copy.

So, what are you waiting for? Grab your favorite obnoxious mug, fill it full of your murky brew of choice and light that black-flamed candle while you open the everlasting pages of 'It Calls from The Veil'. Savor these arcane stories and be prepared to read into the dead of night.

Remember: Keep hands and feet inside the covers at all times!

Nichi aka DarkBetweenPages
July 2022

Few Small Repairs

By Holley Cornetto

Even the light from the sun couldn't undo the shadows hanging over Granny's old place. If anything, the house appeared more ominous for the details daylight revealed. Dead vines crept *from* the windows rather than toward them, like the veins of a diseased body. The walls of the garden where she'd grown herbs and remedies were now crumbling ruins. This was the house where Anne and I had spent most of our childhood summers, but I'd always gotten the impression the house liked Anne better. Though she and I were exactly the same physically, even it seemed to sense the darkness hanging over me—a darkness unable to penetrate the light of my sister's personality.

I grabbed my duffle from the back of Anne's car and lugged it to the half-caved front porch, stumbling over the rotted remains of the bottom stair. A faded red door loomed before us, ready to swallow us whole by way of welcome.

Anne produced a second set of keys from her jacket

pocket, and they jingled as she sifted through them. I wondered how long she'd give me the silent treatment this time.

We crossed the threshold and entered the parlor. The whole place was suspended in time. A museum, waiting patiently for Granny's return.

"You know I hate this place." I sat my ratty duffle on the floor and turned back to Anne. If I strained hard enough, I could see the shadow of the girl she once was, but the cold expression she wore when she looked at me was new. My hands trembled. I needed a glass of wine, bitter and red, to wash down memories of today and yesterday and all the days before.

Anne's eyes met mine. "This isn't supposed to be some happy family reunion. We're here so you can get your shit together."

It had always been the same—perfect Anne and her perfect fucking life. I'd been nothing but a burden to her since we were kids, a weeping stain on her otherwise flawless existence.

I stepped to the table in the center of the room. A Ouija board surrounded by candles lay spread over a black tablecloth with a box of matches in the center, relics from the days Granny had worked out of the parlor as a medium. I picked up the matchbox and turned it over in my hand. Anne and I had called her Granny Morticia behind her back.

"Lynne? Are you listening to me?"

"Yes, I get it. I'm a horrible person, and you've come to rescue me. Thank you. You're so benevolent."

"Don't give me that crap. You're the one who got kicked out of rehab. Again." She grabbed the matches from my hand. "Don't even think about smoking in here. The whole place is likely to burn down."

"Why are we here?" I tried to meet her gaze, but she stared at the mildew on the window.

"Mom and Dad said you can't stay there. They're done. You can't come to my house. You know Scott doesn't approve. We're going to stay as long as it takes. We'll get you clean."

Pressure rose in my chest, and I could taste the stale flavor of my own mouth. There's nothing like being told your own family doesn't approve. Not that any of them ever tried to understand, or even could have.

A shadow flitted across the wall, as if someone had passed outside the window. I drew back the heavy drapes, but there was nothing.

"Did you see that?"

"See what?" Anne asked.

"The shadow."

"There's nothing there, Lynne. There never has been."

Granny told me once that people never completely leave. A body dies, but a spirit doesn't just disappear. That energy had to go somewhere. She'd told me that when I'd seen my first ghost. I woke up screaming because a man stood at the foot of my bed. He'd looked solid, not at all how I'd thought a ghost would look. Granny said he'd wanted me to see him. Those are okay, she'd said.

It's the ones who don't want to be seen that you've got to watch out for.

I was still staring at the clock on the bedside table at three in the morning. Though the rest of the house was layered with decades of dust, Anne had cleaned and prepared the bedrooms for our visit. The room she'd made up for me was the same one I'd slept in when we were kids. It was smaller now, like the house had shriveled and shrank with old age and Granny's absence. The creaks and groans of settling wood whispered of how long it had been since a living soul had wandered these desolate halls.

I wondered if Mudder's Hole would still be open, could imagine Teeny in her tube top and tight jeans, standing behind the bar and flirting with every pretty girl who came in. We'd tried to make a go of it once and decided to get clean together. Even attended AA meetings at the First Methodist Church. It had been a beautiful, hurtful relationship with more downs than ups. When it ended, so did my brief stint of sobriety.

I sat up and put my slippers on. There was no point dwelling on the past and other things too broken to repair. My stomach rumbled. If Anne had gotten the bedrooms ready, she'd probably stocked the kitchen too.

I stepped out into the hallway and tiptoed past Anne's room. She'd left the door cracked open, probably so she could hear me if I tried to sneak out to do God knows what.

I took a deep breath and choked, inhaling thick layers of dust accumulated through years of emptiness. The fleur-de-lis paper hung from the wall in strips. The only things holding it in place were cobwebs strung like curtains along the ceiling. The musty odor was new. I could sense something deeper than memory, more concrete than the vague sense of unease I felt. It was as if the house had been sleeping since Granny's death, and now that Anne and I had returned, it had finally woken.

Three women sat at the kitchen table, heads bowed and hands locked together in prayer. Granny called them the praying sisters. Of all the ghosts in the house, these were the ones Anne had asked about the most. We'd always talked about ghosts before. She saw different ones from those I saw, so we traded stories. She'd even had nightmares. Then one day, it was like she stopped seeing them. She still asked about mine, though. At least for a while.

Granny tried explaining the mysteries of the afterlife to me once or twice. "Most of the ghosts are harmless enough," she'd said. "They just want to be seen and remembered. But some are drawn to the living. They want to possess, take over, and begin anew. Those are the ones that lurk unseen in corners and prey upon the vulnerable."

The praying sisters had always been the harmless sort, content to sit around the table in prayer. They hadn't changed in the years since I'd seen them last, still wearing their Sunday best, dresses at least a hundred years old.

"Hello, ladies." They never answered, but it felt rude to ignore them regardless.

The fridge's contents made me roll my eyes. Anne went vegan a year ago, convinced the diet would help her live forever. Almond milk, cashew cheese, and a big block of tofu sat on the main shelf. Going without booze was one thing, but going without bacon was a different matter entirely.

After taking a glass from the cabinet, I turned on the tap. The pipes gurgled and started, then spit out brown water. "Does nothing in this house work anymore?" I slammed the glass down on the counter. But it wasn't the house I was angry at.

I reached in the fridge for the almond milk, pouring a glass and emptying it in a few large swallows. Almond milk wasn't going to slake the kind of thirst I had. I replaced the carton and closed the fridge, leaning against the door.

The praying sisters stared straight at me. I bit my lip to stifle a yelp. They'd never moved before, never paid any attention to the living.

"Uhm, sorry if I disturbed you." My voice was shaking.

With their heads raised, I could see their faces clearly. In the kitchen's dim light, they looked older than I'd thought. Probably in their fifties.

"Beware the bottle."

I couldn't tell which spoke—none of their mouths moved. The hairs on my arms stood. The ghosts had never spoken. I gulped down oxygen in shallow, rapid breaths, processing the words she'd said. *Beware the bottle.* Jesus Christ, even the goddamned ghosts knew I was an alcoholic. My fear turned to anger. These people were dead. What right did they have to lecture me?

"Mind your own fucking business," I snapped before crossing the room and heading back down the hall. I hesitated in front of Anne's door. Part of me wanted to wake her and tell her what happened.

We were thirteen the first time she'd told me to stop talking about the ghosts, that it wasn't funny to make things up anymore, and it made me think maybe that was why her ghosts had always been different from mine. Maybe she hadn't actually seen them. She'd only made up stories, like she thought I'd been doing. After that, I'd only talked to Granny about ghosts.

I crept back to bed and pulled the blanket over my head, in case any of the house's other residents decided to lecture me about how I was living my life.

"It's time for a few small repairs," Anne said, placing a tool-box beside me as I finished my breakfast of avocado toast and black coffee and wished to God I had some whiskey.

I made one hell of an Irish coffee, so smooth and sweet it tasted like happiness and crisp fall evenings.

"What do you have in mind?" I asked.

"Fixing this place up. It's close to the lake. We could open up as a bed and breakfast."

"That would take a while. It needs a lot of work," I replied, sipping the last of my scalding coffee.

"We've got time." She looked away.

"What aren't you telling me?"

"I got laid off from the bank." Her fingers nervously edged over the hammer at the top of the toolbox. She'd been working there since before I'd flunked out of Auburn. It must've been a huge blow.

"Why didn't you tell me?" I asked.

"You've got your own shit to deal with. I wasn't going to drop more on you."

My face flushed. I'd been so angry I hadn't stopped to think maybe I wasn't the reason she was distant and upset. I'd been too shortsighted to see beyond my own problems. "What did Scott say?" I asked.

"Scott and I are taking a break."

It made sense now why she'd been willing to drop everything and bring me here, in the middle of nowhere, to Granny's old house.

"Shit, Anne. I'm sorry." I reached across the table and rested my hand on top of hers. It was strange to be the one providing comfort for once.

She pulled her hand away and took a sip from her mug. "It's fine. We'll get through it."

"Are you getting divorced?"

Silence answered the question for her. She'd always been the stronger of the two of us, had never been haunted as I'd been, whether by ghosts or bad decisions. It was as though something protected her from life's hardships. Or maybe she was lucky.

"Where do you want to start?" I asked, nodding to the toolbox.

"We'll start at the top and work our way down."

I cringed. The hanging man haunted the attic.

The attic's air wrapped around my shoulders like a blanket, heavy with summer's heat. Anne brought up a fan and set it to oscillate, but it only sent dust clouds spiraling through the cramped space. Boxes and crates overflowing with books and old receipts sat stacked in rows. Granny had kept records of every business transaction she'd ever made.

We placed a recycling bin in the corner. Beside it, the hanging man swayed from the rafters by his belt, his face blotted and swollen. Granny had never explained to me why some ghosts appeared as though they were going through the business of everyday life, while others, like the hanging man, appeared as they would have in death.

I sorted through a large chest of papers, keeping a wary eye on the swinging corpse. Anne paced under and through his dangling legs, never noticing him, and I winced. Near the bottom of the chest lay an old, worn-looking journal. I flipped through pages documenting Granny's elixirs, readings, and remedies. Curiosity got the better of me, and I turned the dated pages to 1989, the first year Anne and I had stayed with her. There was only one note that seemed to apply to us.

The twins have the sight.

Beneath the note was a recipe labeled *Witch Bottle*. Hadn't the praying sisters said something about a bottle?

I stared at the page, chewing at my bottom lip. It said twins, as in both of us, but Anne couldn't see the ghosts.

"What have you got?" Anne took a break from pacing to stand in front of the fan.

"One of Granny's old journals. There are a few of them here. I'd like to keep them, if you don't mind."

She shrugged. "Suit yourself."

I pulled out the rest of the matching set and stacked them on the desk in the corner.

By nightfall, we'd reclaimed the attic, clearing over half the space for new storage. Judging by the piles of paper garbage, we owed a forest somewhere an apology.

Anne yawned and stretched her arms overhead. "I guess we should start on dinner."

"I could go into town and grab some takeout if you don't want to cook," I offered. There was only so much tofu a girl could eat. "We worked hard today. You earned it."

She looked around the room, admiring our handiwork. "You didn't drive here."

"So, let me take your car."

Anne gave me a long glance, and I knew she was debating whether or not it was a good idea. "Okay," she said after a moment, then headed for the stairs. "I'll shower while you're out."

I grabbed the stack of journals from the desk and

reached for the cord hanging beside the attic's naked light-bulb. The hairs on the back of my neck rose. The hanging man was watching me.

A combination of horror and fury churned in my gut. What was it with these ghosts? His mouth was moving, but the sounds he made were like rusty garden tools scraping against each other. His hands groped for the leather belt at his neck, but his windpipe was crushed. I doubted he'd be able to speak, even if he managed to remove the belt.

"Goodnight," I said, clicking off the light and heading down the stairs after Anne.

The neon signs of Mudder's Hole blinked their welcome, inviting me in for a drink as I sat in the parking lot. This was the real test, I knew. It was easier to stay sober when someone was watching.

I could go in and say hello to Teeny and see how she'd been doing. It was a feeble excuse. Maybe I'd go inside and decide I didn't need a drink. Maybe if I could do that, I'd know I'd won. But nothing was ever so simple.

There was something wrong with the ghosts in Granny's house. They'd never tried to speak to me, not that I'd been aware of. It had never occurred to me they might be able to. A drink would help, but Anne might smell the booze on my breath or the cigarette smoke clinging to my clothes.

I turned the key in the ignition and left to pick up dinner.

The house had grown large in the darkness. There was no bulb in the porchlight, so the only illumination was a soft glow from the windows. It looked as though the house had eyes, as if it, or the ghosts inside, watched me the way everyone else watched me. I wondered if it was waiting for me to fuck up too.

I grabbed the bags and took them inside. Anne was sitting at the kitchen table, laptop open. The praying sisters sat beside her, watching.

After placing the Styrofoam takeout trays on the counter, I found mine—a bacon cheeseburger with sweet potato fries—and took a seat at the bar on the other side of the room.

"Why don't you sit here?" Anne asked, gesturing to the seat beside her.

I shook my head, looking at the sisters.

"Come on, Lynne. Not this crap again."

"I can't just sit on them," I answered, shifting to focus on my burger. It bothered me that they were staring at her, and she didn't know, like they were eavesdropping.

She sighed and ran a hand through her hair. "You said the therapy helped."

"I lied about therapy, okay? I told them what they wanted to hear, but it isn't true. The spirits are real. They—"

"Please, stop." She snapped the lid of her laptop shut.

Unsaid words died on my lips. I should've gotten that drink after all.

At one-thirty, I was still wide awake. I was one of *those* sleepers. The ones who lay in bed at night, questioning life decisions rather than falling asleep. It was worse sober. At least with the booze I could drink until my brain shut down—an off button for my mind. But tonight, there was no off switch, and the look on Anne's face played over and over on an infinite loop in my consciousness.

With a sigh, I rolled out from under the blanket. I flipped on the lamp and looked at the bedside table where I'd stashed Granny's journals. Maybe those would put me to sleep. I grabbed the one on top and flipped through the pages.

Most of the notes were about tarot card meanings and home remedies for common ailments. There were a few more risqué recipes in the book, like how to entice a lover or ward one away. I'd known Granny had a reputation in town, but I'd never known she sold love potions. Maybe I would have laughed if the whole thing hadn't been so depressing. She'd preyed on the desperate, a modern-day snake oil sales-man. I closed the book and placed it back on the stack.

The quiet boredom of the house was stifling. I couldn't take it anymore. I grabbed a sweater and jeans from my duf-fle that I hadn't bothered to unpack and slipped them on. I tiptoed to Anne's door and pushed it open a crack. "Anne?"

I waited.

Silence.

I crept to the dresser in the corner, where she kept her purse. She was a creature of habit, and I knew her keys would be on top. I slid my hand under the clasp and felt blindly inside.

"They aren't in there."

I almost pissed myself at the sound of her voice.

"I knew you'd come looking, so I hid them." Old and tired. When had we gotten old?

"I wasn't..."

"You were. You always do when you think about the ghosts."

"I don't know why you brought me here, Anne. You know what this place does to me. It's like you wanted me to fail." It wasn't fair of me to say, but once I started, I couldn't stop myself. "I mean, seriously, how about we bring the crazy alcoholic to a house full of ghosts? Because I'm sure *that* will go well."

"There are no ghosts." She sighed. "I need you to realize that."

"They have run every test and evaluation they could think of on me, and you know what it turned up? Jack-fuck-ing-squat. Has it ever occurred to you for one goddamned minute that I'm not hallucinating or imagining things or making shit up? Has it ever occurred to you that it might be real?"

"If they're real, why can't anyone see them but you?" she asked in a tone like her heart was breaking.

"Granny saw them."

"Granny was—"

"If you say crazy, I swear to God, I'm going to take a baseball bat to your windshield."

She flipped the switch on her lamp, flooding the room in incandescent light. "She had to do that, Lynne. She had to pretend. It was part of her business model. People came here because they wanted to believe in something. Some of them couldn't let go of the past, or of people they lost. She played the part."

"I need you to listen to me the way you did when we were kids. Something is seriously wrong with the ghosts in this house. They've been trying to talk to me, to tell me something. Will you just…believe me, just this once, and if I can't prove it to you, I'll shut the fuck up and never mention ghosts to you again."

"No more ghosts?" she asked. "You swear?"

My whole body trembled. I'd expected her to shout, or even worse, sigh and dismiss me. "Yeah. I swear."

"Alright, what are you suggesting?"

I led her to the parlor where Granny's dust-coated Ouija board still lay spread across the table.

She shivered and pulled her robe tight around her. This side of the house was drafty, somehow colder than the other rooms. "Are you kidding me?"

"You said you'd humor me."

She rolled her eyes.

I struck a match and lit the candles surrounding the board, then wiped the dust from the planchette with my sleeve. "If I'm right, and they are trying to tell me something, this might help."

"Or," she said, taking a seat in one of the old oak chairs, "you've gone stark raving mad like Granny Morticia. I can't believe Mom used to leave us here with her."

"Look, I need you to focus, okay?"

She nodded. "Fine, lets get this over with. You do know what you're doing, right?"

"Enough. There were notes in Granny's journals."

"Of course there were."

"I need you to concentrate on the ghosts we're trying to communicate with. Why don't we try the praying sisters? They were the first to try and talk to me, and they've been watching us."

She traced a line through the dust along the edge of the board. "They have?"

"Yes."

I placed my fingertips on the edge of the planchette and nodded for her to do the same. When her fingers touched the opposite side, I cleared my throat. "We are here because the spirits in this house have been trying to communicate with me. If you're here, spirits, please let your presence be known."

Silence covered the room like a blanket. The only sound I could hear was Anne's quiet exhalations.

The flame of the candle closest to me flickered.

"Anne," I whispered.

Her eyes snapped to the candle. "It's a draft," she answered, but her voice was no louder than mine had been.

"We're here to listen to what you would tell us, spirits. Are you willing to speak with us?"

The planchette slowly slid across the board. *YES*.

"Shit." I laughed with relief.

"You did that," Anne accused, her voice still a whisper.

"You tried to tell me something before," I continued, ignoring Anne's protest. "A warning?"

Anne and I watched as the planchette slid across the board, and slowly, letters became a word. S-P-I-R-I-T. I waited for the accusation that I'd moved the planchette, but Anne remained silent. Perhaps, finally, she was willing to believe.

"Beware of the spirit? What spirit? No, wait...does the spirit want something from us?"

YES.

"What does it want?" Anne asked.

Y-O-U.

The color drained from Anne's face. She glanced from the board to me, barely masking her horrified expression. "What the fuck are you trying to do? This shit isn't funny, Lynne!" She pushed back from the table and stormed out of the room.

I blew out the candles. If Anne was in danger, I needed to find out why. I wondered if the answer was somewhere in Granny's notes.

I retrieved the journals from my room and kept vigil outside Anne's door through the wee hours of morning.

She might not believe, but I wasn't taking any chances. Something in the house had changed since Granny died. Something felt off.

Nothing in the books directly mentioned our names, but there was another mention of a witch bottle sealed with a drop of blood. There was no explanation, and I could only guess what it meant.

I had already showered and made coffee when Anne emerged from her room. She opened the fridge and peered inside. "You having breakfast?"

I pointed to the plate on the counter. "Leftover burger."

To avoid the topic of ghosts, we chewed in silence.

"What room do you want to tackle next?" she asked, as if everything was perfectly normal and last night hadn't happened.

"I don't. I want to leave. You're in danger. They tried to warn us." I glanced at the praying sisters, who now constantly watched us, as if *we* put *them* on edge.

"Lynne...if you don't stop this, I'm going to call Dr. Patel."

Doctor Patel had held me in the psych ward for weeks. He was the reason I'd learned to lie to my therapists. Tears stung my eyes. I knew she thought she was helping, but she didn't realize the betrayal she threatened.

I grabbed my toolbox and brushed past her into the hallway. If we weren't going to leave, I needed an outlet for my anger, and that ugly-ass wallpaper was as good a target as any. I grabbed strip after strip of sagging paper and ripped them down.

Damn this house and its ghosts. Damn Anne for not believing me.

Tears slipped down my dirty cheeks as I worked. I grabbed another strip of paper, and as I pulled, the board beneath stuck and came loose in my hand. The panel had come out completely, exposing a hole in the wall behind it.

I clicked on the flashlight from the toolbox. If the wall panels were rotting or infested with termites, then fixing this place up was going to cost a fortune. I swept the beam inside the hole and reached in. Something roughly the size of my palm was wedged inside. I took a small screwdriver from the toolbox and tried to leverage whatever it was. The tool gave way.

The whole house shuddered as I pulled out a corked blue bottle that glittered despite its age. I blew off the layers of dust coating it.

Anne's quick steps echoed down the hallway. "Did you feel that? Was it an earthquake?"

I was torn between wanting to answer and not wanting to speak to her.

"What have you got there?" She was looking at the bottle in my hand. "Lynne, if you've brought any of your shit into this house—"

"I found it in the wall." I held the bottle up for her to inspect.

She crossed the distance and stood beside me, peering at the gap in the wall. "Why was it in there?"

I shrugged and turned it over in my hand. "There's something in it."

"More of Granny Morticia's junk?" Anne grabbed the bottle and pulled the cork free with a loud *pop!* She shook several pins and a rolled-up piece of paper with a rust-brown stain into her palm.

We reached for the paper at the same time, but she got there first. She unrolled it and stared.

"Well, what is it?"

"It looks like a spell or something. It has my name on it."

Even upside down, I recognized Granny's cramped handwriting.

Anne waded the paper into a ball. "I've had enough of this bullshit." She turned and stormed down the hallway. I followed at her heels.

"Wait, Anne! Don't!" I reached for her arm, but she shrugged out of my grip. "I saw something in Granny's journals. I think it's important."

She marched to the parlor and grabbed the box of matches off the table, striking one and lifting the flame to the paper until it folded and crisped into a pile of ash. "Hey, ghosts! Do you hear me? If you're here, why don't you come out, huh? Show yourselves, you dead fucks!"

The house shuddered again.

"What the hell was that?" she asked.

"I don't think they're happy about that."

"Who?"

"The ghosts."

"What a load of bullsh—" She stopped, staring at something over my left shoulder.

I turned, but nothing was there. "What are you looking at it?"

"You don't see him?" she whispered.

"See who?"

"The man with half a face?"

I looked behind me, but there was nothing between me and the wall.

"There's nothing there, Anne."

"I remember now. It came back when I destroyed the bottle." Anne hugged her knees to her chest and rocked back and forth in the corner. "I was like you. I saw them too. Do you remember that summer I got sick? I almost died."

I swallowed hard. "Yes."

A vague memory of a long-ago summer I'd spent mostly alone. A summer where I snuck into the bedroom to visit Anne, her face pale and her breathing labored. I remember whispering that if she became a ghost, I'd live with Granny so I could stay with her forever.

"Granny came to me that summer and pricked my finger. She said my sickness would mark me. She recited words and dropped my blood into a blue bottle. She kissed my forehead and told me I'd forget, and I did."

Somehow, Anne's sight *was* different from mine. She began seeing spirits I'd never seen before, spirits I hadn't known were in the house. A woman in the primary bathroom who sat naked and shriveled, with wounds on her wrist weeping blood. A girl covered in dark purple bruises given to her by her father. One ghost after another begged her to give them a day, a month, a year to find the ones who hurt them. To seek revenge. More than once, I'd entered a room to find Anne with her hands covering her ears, shouting, "Shut up! I'm not listening to you!"

I could feel the judgment-heavy eyes of the praying sisters following me each time I entered and left their presence. They'd tried to warn me, after all. *Beware the bottle*, as it turned out, had nothing to do with my drinking. Anne's name was in the bottle because, while we'd both inherited the sight, she'd gotten the worst of it.

When I was a girl, I'd thought of the sight as something good, something marking me as special. As I'd gotten older, and no one believed me, it had been a burden but bearable. Now, seeing the way it affected Anne, with her eyes sunk deep in their sockets, I knew I'd been the lucky one.

She nibbled at crumbs of dry toast and sipped black coffee, but she'd gone away from me. Increasingly, she stared wide-eyed and mumbled at nothing, ghosts I couldn't see. Part of me wanted to rage and say I told you so, but watching her wither beneath the weight of her new sight gave me newfound pity for my sister.

"They follow me," Anne confided in whispers. "They ask for things." Mascara-streaked tears ran down her cheeks.

I had to get her away from the house, but I had no idea where to go. I tried calling our parents, but they hadn't taken my calls in years. I even tried calling Scott. I left voicemails, but no one was listening anymore, if they ever had been.

Finally, I decided on a hotel. I could do that much at least. Though I didn't have any money, I found Anne's wallet with her credit cards inside. I could use her cards and cell phone number to make reservations in her name. It would have to do.

I brought a cup of coffee out onto the porch. She spent most of her time there now, unable to face the ghosts inside.

"Here you go."

She took the mug and held it, not drinking.

"Anne, I need you to tell me where the keys are so I can get us out of here, okay?"

"All this time, it was in the wall," she replied. "It was always in the wall. The house guards its secrets."

"Yes, but I need the keys."

"I thought the house liked you better, and that was why it let you see them when I couldn't," she confessed. "I was jealous. When you started drinking...I was finally better than you at something." She was speaking to me but looking through me.

"We'll do this later, okay? Once we're out of here. The keys, Anne? I need you to focus."

"I hid them." She laughed. The sound of it frightened me.

I opened every drawer in her room, searched under her mattress and pillows and in the kitchen cabinets. Leaning against the counter, I looked at the praying sisters. "I don't suppose *you* know where she hid them, do you?"

But they were done talking to me.

I found the keys stashed in the pocket of her slacks, folded and placed neatly in the top dresser drawer. It wasn't an imaginative hiding place, but it had been effective.

After throwing her clothes and mine into our bags, I loaded up the trunk. I locked the door to the house and offered Anne a hand up.

"I'm sorry. I'm so sorry," she whispered.

"Anne?" I squeezed her hand, but I knew she wasn't talking to me.

I climbed in the driver's seat and turned the key in the ignition. As I pulled away, I took a final look over my shoulder at the house. I had so many unanswered questions. Most people had written Granny off as a quack, but she'd seen the ghosts. She'd protected Anne from them.

Anne's terrified shriek pierced my eardrums. I slammed on the brakes and sent the car fishtailing. The car's backend slid, and I jerked the wheel to straighten. The airbags triggered as we slammed headlong into a tree.

The car's engine ticked. Steam rose from the under the ruined hood.

"Anne, are you okay?"

She groaned.

I unclipped my seatbelt and wriggled out of the car. It wasn't going anywhere anymore, at least not by itself. I looked around for a sign of what might've startled Anne but saw nothing. If it was a ghost, it had been one of hers. I crossed to the passenger's side and pulled her out, supporting her weight with my shoulder.

My leg ached, reminding me I hadn't checked for injuries. I limped to the porch and lowered her down. "Are you hurt anywhere?" I asked.

Anne sobbed. "They won't let me leave. Not until I help them."

"I'm going to call a tow truck right now. We're getting the hell out of here."

I called the first mechanic my search turned up. They could tow the wreck and drop us at the car rental place in town. When I walked back to the porch, Anne was gone.

"Anne?" I tried to keep the panic from my voice.

"In here," she called from inside. Somehow, I'd managed to miss the open front door.

Anne walked back onto the porch, mumbling to the ghosts surrounding her. Ghosts I couldn't see.

"We'll get out of here soon, okay? The tow truck is on its way."

"You don't understand," Anne explained, speaking as though I were a child. "I set them free when I broke the spell. They aren't going to let history repeat. They won't be abandoned and ignored again."

A sharp, metallic clang made me jump, and I noticed the gas can she'd dropped at her feet. She pulled Granny's matchbox from the pocket of her cardigan.

"Anne? Where'd you find that?"

She struck the match and a gout of flame rose between us. "Maybe I can set us all free."

The heat forced me off the porch. "Anne! Come on!"

I tried moving closer, shielding my face with my arm. Between the dry wood and the wind, the flames caught quickly. I couldn't get close enough to grab her.

"Anne, get out of there!"

She smiled at me, then walked into the burning house.

YOU TELL ME

By R. L. Meza

Have you ever ruined a life? Delivered the kind of bad news that makes you sick on contact? Like just by passing it on, you're contaminated. And after, you can't sleep through the night anymore. You can't even close your eyes without it playing on the backs of your eyelids, like a silent film with your voice laid over. You start wishing you were there—a witness and not just the messenger—because what really happened has got to be better than the versions you're drumming up in your imagination.

All those unwanted details scrolling through your brain.

That internal voice-over is stuck on repeat, like an echo that won't fade. It's getting louder by the day. Delivering that bad news is the soundtrack to your life now. You're thinking about what you said and how you said it, running through the dialogue and watching their face crumble every time, no matter how you reword it. And now your food tastes off, like paper and clay. It's all you can do to breathe most days. You can't look at your pets or your loved ones—not even the mailman—without a blanket of dread weighing you down. Because that bad news, it could happen to anyone.

So, have you ever ruined a life? Have you?

Because I've been doing it to poor Mrs. Abernathy for three years running.

Five days a week. Like it's my full-time job.

The best and worst part is, she never remembers. By the start of my shift, her mind's already been wiped clean. Yesterday's ghosts are dusty white smears, too faint to read. And so, I pick up the chalk. I do as I'm told.

I bring back the ghosts.

It goes like this: I clock in and make my rounds through Golden Acres Home for the Elderly. I usually save Mrs. Abernathy for last, to really take my time explaining the accident. But on the nights when the sundowning hits her hard and she starts screaming, I come running to administer the cruelest treatment our facility has to offer. One dose of reality later, and Mrs. Abernathy's weeping. I'm kissing yet another tiny shred of my humanity goodbye. I'm thinking of Eric. I'm turning the one-year sobriety chip over and over in my scrub pocket and swearing I'm going to quit this, not knowing if the quitting I mean is Golden Acres or just... everything. All of this.

Mrs. Abernathy sleeps.

She forgets.

And maybe I forget too, at least a little bit.

Enough to do it all over again.

The doctor who instituted this treatment is a real bastard. He tells me I have a talent for this sort of thing. Like it's a skillset, grinding down a human being. Tonight, he's waiting for me outside Mrs. Abernathy's room.

"Nurse, the patient is confused," Doctor Bastard says. He's trying for sympathy, but his eyes are drifting down the hall, already moving on to other things. "You'll take care of her?"

He doesn't remember our names. But he remembers to paste that dead rat of a toupee atop his head before every shift, so I know it's not a problem with his brain. I nod. It's the best I can manage with my teeth pinning my tongue in place. Like it or not, I need this job.

In my head, I'm still giving the doctor a piece of my mind when I enter Mrs. Abernathy's room and see the boy seated by her bedside. My white tennis shoes squeak a stutter-stop on the tile, and I lean back out into the hall. But the doctor's rounding the corner, gone before I can ask why there's a child in a patient's room long after visiting hours.

"You can see him," Abernathy says.

It's not a question.

Abernathy's hissing between her dentures, a slow leakage of air, like a balloon deflating. Her eyes are narrowed to slits. I follow her gaze to the chair in the corner. The boy flashes a sunny grin. He's missing a tooth. This boy, he can't be much older than six or seven—young enough to need parental supervision. With his knees tucked up to his chin, head rolling side to side, the boy starts humming a nursery rhyme.

Abernathy says it again. "You *can* see him."

And the boy giggles—a musical, broken-glass tinkling that raises gooseflesh on my arms.

"Mrs. Abernathy..." The rest is jammed up in my throat, blocked by this unexpected change in our evening routine. All those memorized lines thrown out the window by a last-minute script change.

Five days a week for three years running: *Your son was driving the RV. Joey was in the passenger's seat. The twins were playing cards at the table in the back. Your daughter-in-law was nursing the baby. It was quick—they didn't suffer. I'm sorry, Mrs. Abernathy, so sorry.*

A family of six leaves their campsite for a diner ten miles up the highway. If their RV is going sixty-five miles an hour in the pouring rain, and a brakeless semi-truck's doing eighty downhill when it veers into their lane...

How many family members does Mrs. Abernathy have left?

You can do the math.

So, who is this kid?

I clear my throat. "Excuse me, little—"

"Joey," the boy says.

And I feel anger stirring in my chest. His green eyes are glittering, and he's staring at Mrs. Abernathy's bewildered expression and laughing, as though her Alzheimer's is the best joke he's heard all week and not *the* most terrifying end I can imagine.

Losing your memories, your*self*, as your body forgets how to beat, how to breathe.

How to be.

"Joey." I'm trying to keep my voice level, but I'm going to strangle him if he doesn't quit giggling. "Please, come with me."

I extend an open hand, though the last thing I want to do is touch him. The boy unfolds from the chair, springing to his feet like a marionette on strings. He leans over Abernathy's bed and plants a noisy kiss on her cheek.

Except his lips don't come away.

They're puckered.

Suckling.

A runnel of saliva leaks from the corner of his mouth. Abernathy releases a miserable wail. The skin of her cheek tents outward as I grab the boy by the shoulders and try to pull him off.

There's a wet *pop!* as the suction releases.

And then I'm towing the boy through the door by the wrist, rushing him down the hall. My shoes are squeaking on the tile, drowning out the light patter of the boy's sneakers behind me—or maybe I'm just moving too fast for his feet to touch ground, too focused on reaching the nurses' station to look back at the child I'm dragging along.

Jessie's standing at the station with the phone pressed to her ear. She'll know what to do.

But I reach Jessie empty-handed, with my fingers still circled around...

Air and nothing.

He's back. Joey.

He brought the twins.

I've tried removing them twice already. It's well after midnight, and I've given up hope of ever finding their parents. Right now, I'd settle for anyone who could see them—just lay eyes on the three kids coiled in Mrs. Abernathy's bed—and confirm I'm *not* losing my goddamned mind.

Also, I'm not so sure they're children.

I'm outside smoking, cigarette cherry bobbing in the darkness as I nibble the filter between my teeth. I can't get that framed photograph out of my head—the one of them all together at the birthday party, the family members circled around Abernathy and her lopsided cake.

See, here's the problem. The kids in that photo don't match the ones in Abernathy's bed.

I inhale, dragging on the filter so hard the sucking sound makes me wince. I'm thinking of Joey's pink lips on Abernathy's liver-spotted skin. My stomach ties a knot around the slug of whiskey I pounded back at the start of my break—a quick nip from the bottle Jessie keeps hidden in the supply closet—just to get my hands to stop shaking. Something new to confess at my weekly meetings, though if

I'm being honest, I'm more worried about these maybe-hallucinations than my alcoholism. Twelve steps aren't going to solve the problem in Abernathy's room. If there's a higher power involved, He's taking the night off.

But I have a job to do.

Determined, I toss the unfinished smoke and grind it out with the tip of my shoe. I fold a stick of aggressively minty gum onto my tongue and push through the side door with my hands knotted into fists.

I can do this.

Only, once I'm back in Abernathy's room, my resolve splinters like a half-healed bone, following the old break lines easier than anything. Joey's perched on the metal headboard. His eyes shine like gold coins in the light from the television. The twin lumps under the blanket are twitching. They've moved up from Abernathy's calves to her thighs. I don't want to think about what that means.

I move to the bottom of the bed, anchoring my hands on the footboard to keep from running as Joey creeps across the blanket to join me. Or—no, he just wants a better view of the paunchy salesman selling knives on the television. Joey's pale hands curl over the footboard, and he cranes his neck, making a show of trying to see around me.

"Joey," I say, "it's time to go."

My voice is lost beneath the volume of the infomercial. The television is blaring. Joey's pounding on the buttons of the remote with his thumb, and I snatch it away. The plastic is cold against my palm. I switch off the set, and the room goes dark, save for the flickering rectangle of light falling across the bed from the fluorescent in the hall. A disconnected part of me is already chewing out Todd for not replacing the bulb.

Mrs. Abernathy stirs. She sits up and sighs. Her expression is wistful, her voice airy and dreamlike. "Can't they stay just a little while longer?"

She doesn't seem to be afraid of them anymore. Never mind that her neck and chest and limbs are covered with angry red splotches, hickeys left behind by the needy, greedy mouths rooting in her bed. I take her wrinkled hand in mine as I have countless times.

"Mrs. Abernathy, these are not your grandchildren," I say, speaking gently to cushion the blow. "Your grandchildren are gone."

There's a brief spark of recognition in her eyes, dim and distant. And then she shakes her head. Her whisper is so soft it could be the sheets swishing together. She squeezes my hand.

"I don't care," Abernathy says. Her frail chest rises, falls. "Please, let them stay. I don't want to be alone."

Movement from the lumps under the blanket.

Moist suckling sounds.

I fold back the blanket, then yank the sheet beneath down. I pull on gloves, snapping them at the wrists as a warning to the brats I'm coming for. The pointer finger of my right hand is still aching from the bite I earned earlier. I glance up at the responsible party, in case he's scuttling over to sink his teeth in again, but Joey's eyes remain fixed on the blank television screen. Like my reflection is entertainment enough.

He has no reflection of his own to watch.

The twins are battened onto Mrs. Abernathy, one to each shriveled leg. I grab the girl on the left by her ginger hair and wait until the flesh of Mrs. Abernathy's thigh is taut and straining to work my finger into the corner of the twin's mouth, breaking the suction. The twin on the right puts up a fight, so once he's detached, I throw the sheet over his head and twist it around him, winding his sister into the mess. With the pair of them bagged and thrashing like shark pups in a net, I haul them out into the hall.

Again.

Jessie passes by and does a double-take, saying, "Did she have *another* accident? You know, Penny, we put them in diapers for a reason."

I bundle up the sheet. It's lighter than air.

"Washer's still broke." Jessie sips coffee from a thermos and makes a face. "But that's the morning crew's problem."

I utter a shaky laugh.

Jessie nods as if I'm agreeing with her and not slip-sliding to the brink of insanity. She's examining her nails, saying something about finding Todd and making him clean up Abernathy—*it's his job, for Chrissakes*—and somehow I'm managing to decline the suggestion, insisting that I've got it. That I'm a nurse, sure, but this isn't beneath me.

If anything, I'm underqualified.

I'm not a medium or an exorcist. I can feel Joey behind me, grinning like he knows this.

By the time the sun peeks through Abernathy's window, there are two bulges under the blanket to either side of Abernathy's stomach. Joey's back to watching the blank screen of the television with Abernathy's thumb stuck in his cheek like a lollipop.

I do the only thing I can do at this hour.

I clock out.

Mrs. Abernathy's nursing the baby.

For just a second, I think of Eric, of how old he would be now if I'd managed to quit drinking while he was still inside me. If he'd had any other mother but the one he got. If...

And then the moment passes, and I'm pushing between the twins—they're more solid today, warm against my arms. Joey's fluttering his fingers in a wave, grinning with worm lips stained red by the raw patch he's worn away under Abernathy's clavicle. I want to scream at them, hurl furniture, slap their faces to give them a taste of the pure, blinding terror they've inspired in me just by existing.

But the sight of Abernathy's flaccid teat quivering between the baby's lips brings my breakfast—four fingers of whiskey, with a splash of black coffee for color—up in a rush. I barely make it to Abernathy's private bathroom. The light clicks on so I can see where to kneel and let go.

I'm bent over the toilet, thanking God for motion-sensors, when the light decides I've been slumped motionless long enough. Like maybe I've died and don't need to see my way out.

The light clicks off.

The door cracks open behind me, spilling a bar of yellow light across the floor. I'm still kneeling, face hidden inside the toilet bowl, because I'm too afraid to turn around. Because if I move, that light will click on…

The door swings closed. There's a snotty kind of mouth-breathing coming from the darkness over my left shoulder. The light is off, but *something's* in here with me, shuffling closer. Tapping its toes or heels or whatever, like it's getting excited.

Whatever it is, the motion sensor isn't picking it up.

Frigid fingers stroke the back of my neck.

I go straight from kneeling to standing, leap right up like you see in those martial arts movies, except the guys in those don't spend the next fifteen minutes holding their lower back and sobbing in fear. At least the light's back on, so I can watch my pitiful display in the mirror.

Bent over my new master, the sink, I wipe my mouth clean and splash water on my face. I'm trying to guess how many hours are standing between me and my lunch break. I just clocked in—forty minutes ago?—but the flask in my purse is calling my name.

By the time I'm finished cleaning up, my fear has retreated, beaten back into a corner by the pile of unpaid bills, the mortgage—the rest of the usual financial shit that keeps a person from turning tail to run, even when instinct is screaming at them. And I'm not crying anymore. No, I'm pissed. I'm done with these kids.

Mint gum, stern resolve, and I'm back at Abernathy's bedside. The baby goes in a plastic garbage bag. The twins go in the sheet. I throw Joey over my shoulder. I almost—*al-most!*—make it to the end of the hall with them before they dissipate or evaporate—up and fucking vanish, like they always do. But with every new attempt, they seem to last a little bit longer.

If I let them suckle until they've had their fill, I might be able to get them out of the building. Maybe they'll go on their own. They're able to move around the room without my help now. Maybe that's all they're really after...

Escape.

When they're strong enough.

There's no harm in taking a break.

That's the lie I tell myself as I leave them alone with her.

Big mistake.

Mrs. Abernathy is unresponsive.

Four hours ago, she was lucid. She was furious, pummeling the mattress with her bony fists and cursing me for taking away her grandchildren. She was screaming their names loud enough to wake every resident in Hall C.

I barely recognize the limp, drooling mannequin that's

taken her place. Abernathy's eyes are glazed. Her jaw hangs slack. Her skin dangles from her skinny frame in sweaty flaps. She's a monochrome version of her former self. Even the suck marks have lost their color, dappling her waxen skin like smudges of charcoal.

In contrast, the children lurking in Abernathy's bed could have crept right out from a Renaissance painting, like perfect little cherubs with their rosy apple cheeks and chubby limbs. Their reptilian eyes watch with cold intelligence as I edge around to check Abernathy's pulse. Their pouty mouths twist into slobbery grins, fat fingers plucking at my scrubs as they chortle, pretending to be human. I don't bother shooing them away.

I'm distracted just trying to *count* them.

A dozen, maybe more. The newcomers shiver like mirages in the corners of my eyes. Joey and the twins are bloated like ticks, throbbing with life—the baby too.

Joey's straddling Abernathy's stomach with his ear pressed to her heart. His lips are moving. I lean in to listen.

"Breathe out," Joey says. His breath smells like black mold and rust. Mrs. Abernathy's chest deflates, and Joey rides it down.

Seconds stretch into minutes.

Joey pinches Abernathy's eyelids and pulls them down like window shades. He giggles.

I reach over to shake Mrs. Abernathy awake, but Joey grabs my wrist. He's wearing the petulant scowl of a boy who's wrestling to keep his favorite toy, digging his pudgy fingers in. His head whips around. I jerk back as his jaws start snapping like a rabid dog's, taking oversized, clacking bites out of the empty air where my hand just was.

Joey smirks. He lowers his head to Abernathy's chest and whispers, "Breathe in."

Abernathy gasps like a diver surfacing from the deep. A tear leaks from her eye. One of the twins emerges from beneath the blanket, scuttling up Abernathy's left side to lick the tear away. The twin nuzzles into Abernathy's ear.

"Beat...beat...beat," the twin murmurs, snickering. She speeds up the chant as the others join in. "*Beat-beat-beat.*"

Abernathy's hand floats up, bumps against her chest like a water-logged corpse.

Joey grasps her thumb and pokes it into his mouth. He whispers into the meat of her palm, "Breathe out."

"Beat! Beat! Beat!"

"Breathe in."

"Penny?" My name is filtering through from somewhere...

Behind me, Jessie calls my name again. Her hand touches my shoulder, and I jump. I'm whirling around—not thinking—shouting at her for startling me.

"Jesus." Jessie wrinkles her nose. She takes a step back so I'm not breathing right into her face anymore. "Are you back off the wagon again, already?"

I give her a sharp look to remind her I know about the mint tin in her purse—the one that rattles with missing pills from the pharmacy—and Jessie takes another step back. Her face hardens. She crosses her arms and says, "Doctor

Harris wants you check in with a few of the residents. Seems they've been having some issues. He said you'd know how to handle it."

"Issues?"

"Yeah, like their condition is deteriorating." Jessie hooks her fingers into air quotes around the last word, waving her hands—*blah, blah, blah*—to fill in the details. She pulls her cell phone out of her pocket, taps the screen a few times, then looks up as if she's surprised I'm still here.

Of course, I am—she's blocking the door. I sidle past while she sends another text. Then, because I have to know, I turn and ask, "Jess, do you...hear anything?"

Beat! Beat! Beat!

Breathe out.

There's an emotion hiding under Jessie's pinched eyebrows. It's not quite sympathy.

Pity. It's pity.

Breathe in.

I don't wait for Jessie's answer. I say, "Which ones?"

"Huh?"

I snap my fingers over Jessie's screen. "Which residents?"

Jessie lists them off—three in Hall C, two in D—and then she pauses, chews her lip, and adds two more.

"All of them?"

Jessie shrugs.

"Since when does Gunderson have Alzheimer's? He was fine yesterday."

Jessie shrugs again.

Every room I visit is the same—a man or woman crying out in distress, pleading for me to tell them when their loved ones will visit again. The news I deliver takes me apart bit by bit, like bricks extracted from a wall. It's just a matter of time until I crumble.

Fall.

I almost called in sick.

Probably should have. If I look up from my shoes for too long, I start listing to one side of the hallway or the other, like a ship without a rudder. But you tell me—how am I supposed to stay dry when every room I visited last night, *every single one*, is now infested with children who don't belong?

The rooms are crawling with them.

The residents are thrilled. Splayed out like roasted pigs at a banquet, they moan and sigh. Over the suckling and giggling, I can hear the other residents calling out for the same attention. They've loved and lost, but their love is being returned to them.

At a price.

I'm not sure Mrs. Abernathy is still alive.

Joey sits atop the pile of writhing children on Abernathy's bed. He squints at me through rolls of fat, licking his lips. I doubt I could throw him over my shoulder now, even if I wanted to.

The children are chanting. The hallways echo with their simple commands.

Beat. Beat. Beat.

Breathe in.

Pump.

Squeeze.

Breathe out.

Release.

Listening, I realize my body is obeying them.

I've shit myself. My lungs are burning for my next breath.

I'm rushing to my car, fleeing. I burn out the worst of my fear with a long, breathless draught from the bottle that was full this morning. When I'm finished swallowing, it's nothing but bottom.

The rest of my shift passes in a blur.

Jessie's kicking my foot.

I must have dozed off. My spine creaks in protest as I try to sit up. I'm slouched in a chair I must've dragged out into the hall at some point...

"Penny?"

I blink and Jessie's gone.

Cold water splashes my face.

"Hey, asshole. Wake up. It's time to go."

I grumble as she helps me stand. Jessie touches my neck and smiles like I'm letting her in on a secret. She says, "You met somebody."

"Huh?"

"You've got a humongous hickey."

I can't breathe. I've forgotten how, like I can't do it anymore without being told. I'm listening for the chanting as Jessie says, "C'mon. Your kid's waiting."

"What?"

Beat...beat...

And then we round the corner, and I see him standing there—*my Eric*—and my heart...just...stops.

"He said your mom dropped him off?"

Eric cranes his neck to look up at me, blond hair falling back from his rosy cheeks. His chubby hand reaches for me.

"It's Saturday, Mommy," my son says. "We're going to the park."

But I don't have a son.

Not anymore.

Do I?

LITTLE FEET

BY RB KELLY

An eight-foot-tall inflatable Santa Claus beckons us through the snow to a petrol station forecourt that looks like it has long since closed for the night. I shoot a sideways glance at Ben. His eyes are narrowed in concern, but then, a moment later, we spot the light behind the side door. It's not late, barely 7:00 p.m., but we're well off the main roads now, and it's the day before Christmas Eve.

I realize we told Mr. Murtry we'd be here by 5:00 to pick up the keys, and Ben's clearly thinking the same thing because he says, "He must be holding on just for us."

I twist my head back over my shoulder to check on Mia, but she's fast asleep, head lolling on her chest. "We won't keep him long," I say, popping my seatbelt and opening the door.

The cold hits me like a slap, and I burrow deeply into my coat. It was raining when we left home. We might get a white Christmas for our little girl this year after all.

I knock on the frosted glass at the top of the side door. "Mr. Murtry? It's Alison McCullough. I'm sorry we're late—it was the snow."

I see a man's stooped figure moving toward the glass, shadowed by the soft glow from inside. The door opens onto a slight, shuffling man buried in thick cardigans and a woolen hat, a good fifteen years older than I'd have guessed from his voice on the phone.

"Mrs. McCullough," he says. "That's a bad night, all right. At least you've not too far to go now." He reaches a liver-spotted hand to a hook beside the door and pulls off a metal ring from which hang two chunky, old-fashioned keys and a laminated label reading *Knockeena Cottage*. "I went up and lit the boiler this afternoon, and the lights are on a timer. Should be good and cozy for you by now."

All I want is a warm bath and my child tucked up in bed. Gratitude spills across my face. "That's very kind of you. Thank you so much."

"Not at all." He hands the keys to me. They feel like they've been dipped in ice. "There's not too many folks these days prepared to make the journey this far up the mountains. Least we can do is make you comfortable."

I thank him again and hurry back to the car. My teeth are chattering as I fall into my seat, and Ben, without a word, turns the heating up full blast. As we pull away from the petrol station, I see the light go out behind the side door, but in minutes, it's all obscured by the snow.

LITTLE FEET

Mia grizzles awake at my touch and immediately wants Ben. "Where's Daddy?"

Daddy is fighting a battle with the iced-up keyhole of a thick, dark-wood door that looks like it's old enough to remember the vikings. But I only know this because I can hear him softly swearing behind the veil of snow bisecting the ten feet between the cottage and the car.

"He's opening up the house," I tell her. "Come on, sleepyhead. We're here."

I hope she can't hear the anxiety in my voice. She doesn't need to know how treacherous the road has been on the final thirty minutes of our drive.

"I want Daddy," she says, and I hear the sound of metal giving way to metal.

Light suddenly spills a path to the cottage door.

"Come on, then." I pop her seatbelt and zip up her coat as she shuffles off her booster seat. "Let's go and find him. Look at this snow, Mia! Isn't it Christmassy?"

She's five years old and hasn't seen enough brown-grey winters yet to understand why this is special. But her face lights up just the same. "Will Santa be able to get here if it's snowing, Mummy?" she asks, sliding her chilly hand into mine.

Santa has been the source of some concern ever since we announced we were going away for Christmas this year. "Yes, love," I say. "Santa lives in Lapland. It's always snowy there."

Our feet crunch on buried gravel as we pick our way

57

toward light and warmth. Ben meets us halfway to the cottage, heading back to the car for our bags.

"It's great in there, Ali," he calls over his shoulder, and I'm surprised at how the relief swamps me.

I don't know what I was expecting, but the trouble with the lock has made me feel...unwelcome.

"Can we make a snowman?" Mia wants to know. She tilts her head up to catch snowflakes in her mouth.

"In the morning, love," I say. "It's time for bed now."

I'm expecting an argument. Instead, I feel her hand pull on mine in the direction of a sprawling, snow-covered bush by the door.

"Look, Mummy! What's that?"

Before I can stop her, her hand has slid from mine, and she's wading through a drift that almost tops the fur trimming on her winter boots.

"Mia!" I call. I can hear the fear spiking my voice, making it angry. If she wanders out of sight in this weather...

"Look, Mummy! Look at this!" She's bending over by the bush, delighted with something she's found. Her little fingers scrape at snow, and I can't see what she's digging for, so I wade in after her. "How did she get out here? Can we bring her inside?"

She straightens, holding out her hands to me. The world tilts sideways. Fear spikes. Panic crackles my spine, and I barely even see the thing she's holding. All I know is, I need it to be out of my child's touch...right now. I swipe blindly, and it falls heavily to the snow, sinking into whiteness. Mia yells in outrage.

"No!" I hear myself shouting. "Don't touch that, Mia! That's dirty! You don't know where it's been!"

"It's not dirty!" She's hungry and overtired, and tears pour hot and fierce down her little face. "It's *mine*. I found it!"

"What's going on?" Ben has a clutch of wellies under one arm and overnight bags in either hand. Snow dusts his hair, and his breath mists in front of his face.

"Mummy hit my dolly!" wails Mia, and only now does it register with me that the thing I saw—the twisted, black-eyed, hairless thing—was once somebody's toy.

It glares up at me from its hole in the snow, naked and peeling paint, a hairline web of cracks skittering like veins across its ancient porcelain skin. I scoop up my child, like I'm protecting her from predators.

"It's *not* your dolly," I say. "It belongs to someone else, and it's been outside for too long. And it's time for bed."

Mia wriggles furiously in my arms, fighting to get free. Ben shrugs off the conflict, like a man who's been driving for the past four hours in treacherous conditions, and disappears inside, leaving me to flail against little vicious hands made wild by anger, flapping at my face. One glances against my cheek, and I feel something wet, oleaginous, ooze onto my skin.

At first, I think it must be blood. She must have cut herself on broken porcelain, and my mind whirls to thoughts of what diseases could be festering on the surface of such a thing and how far we are from the nearest hospital. I catch her hand and hold it firmly in front of my face, scooching us closer to the door, to the light, to see for myself what she's done.

It's not blood.

It's something black and viscous, like a kind of liquid jelly, and even Mia's horrified now.

I rush her inside to wash it off as my child's wails pick up pitch.

"God," says Ben, dropping onto the sofa beside me, "that took *ages*."

I hand him a glass of wine, and he accepts with one hand, the other shoveling a big fistful of crisps from the bowl on the coffee table. There's a frozen pizza in the oven, but I was too hungry to wait.

"Is she sleeping?"

"Just about. What the hell was that about before?"

The memory ripples in my bones like a cold breeze. "She found some kind of"—I can't bring myself to say *doll*—"thing by the door. I can't bear to think what was on it."

Ben munches on crisps by the glow of the multi-colored fairy lights on the tree the Murtrys have erected for us. I've stacked all our presents beneath it, and the house is starting to feel like it might allow us to stay.

"She kept saying it was *her* dolly," he says. "Even when she fell asleep. I was halfway out the door, and she said it again. Nearly gave me a heart attack."

"Oh God." I pinch the bridge of my nose. "Please don't tell me she's starting this again…"

He pats my knee. Cheese and onion dust scatters across my jeans. "She's just overtired. Here." He clinks his glass to mine. "Merry Christmas, love. We made it in one piece."

"Merry Christmas," I say.

But there's something twisting in my chest that makes the words taste hollow, even as I make myself smile around them.

I wake in the night to a small figure standing motionless beside my bed. Adrenaline spikes and quickly ebbs.

"Mia, love," I whisper, "go back to bed."

She doesn't move. I close my eyes. I'm just too tired for this.

"All right. Okay." I throw the duvet back, cold prickling goosebumps against my skin. "Let's get you all tucked up again."

She's solid, like a length of wood, but pliant as I put my hands to her narrow shoulders and gently guide her back toward the hallway. Mia's feet make no sound against the thin, threadbare rug on the floor, and Ben doesn't stir as I creak open our bedroom door and ease her gently toward her own little room at the front of the house. She hasn't had an episode of sleepwalking in almost six months now. I was starting to hope she'd grown out of it altogether.

"Come on, sweetie pie."

I pull back the covers on her bed, and she folds easily onto the mattress. Through the uncovered window, moonlight spills milky white across her small body, and I wonder why Ben didn't think to draw the curtains when he put her to bed. I cross to pull them now and see the world outside transformed. The snow has stopped falling at last, and the crisp, clear night opens onto the dark bulk of the trees surrounding us, the thick blanket of white draping our car and the forest, and the untouched carpet stretching from the cottage to the rough-surfaced lane and the open hillside beyond. The moon has risen high, and haloed stars prickle the deep navy blue above.

"Mummy?" whispers Mia behind me.

I snap the curtains closed.

"It's all right, love," I say. "Mummy's here."

"I had a bad dream."

"Oh, my pet." I cross to the little single bed, and it creaks as I perch beside her. "It's all right. You were walking in your sleep again."

"I thought I saw the dolly."

Ice crawls over my skin. I make myself smile and hope it doesn't look as frozen as I feel. "That was just a dream, love."

"It wasn't in my dream." She rolls over, tucking one little hand beneath her chin. Her eyes slide closed. "I thought I saw it going into your bedroom."

I make myself remember the night terrors that used to shudder our household awake when she was tiny. I make myself remember how she'd be pointing into a corner of the room, screaming and crying, and I knew…I *knew* it was a sleep disorder, nothing more, but it never felt less terrifying to watch. I make myself remember, and I make myself believe that's all this is too.

Even as I realize, with a sickly lurch, the thing she found was waiting beneath the bush that sits outside this bedroom window.

I stroke a strand of hair from her forehead. "Do you want Mummy to sleep beside you?"

She nods. Her eyes don't open.

"Okay," I say. I have no idea how I'm going to squeeze myself onto this narrow mattress beside her, but I know for sure I'm not going to leave her side until morning. "All right, my little love. You close your eyes and sleep. Mummy's here beside you."

I don't sleep well. Over and over, I'm woken from a fitful doze by the sound of little feet on the floorboards, but when I grind myself awake, Mia is tightly clutched beneath my outstretched arm. She doesn't stir again, but I'm awake to see dawn crawl through the gap beneath the curtain. The long night over at last, I haul myself out of bed and shuffle to the kitchen to make coffee.

Mia finds me there three quarters of an hour later, tousle-haired and yawning. She cuddles her way under my arm, and I kiss her hair and tell her we can make pancakes for breakfast, since it's Christmas Eve.

She animates brightly, like sun slicing through the clouds. "And then can we make a snowman, Mummy?"

"After you're washed and dressed." Her joy is contagious. It lifts the sleepless fog from my brain. "And then we can go for a walk, maybe, while Daddy gets the turkey ready for tomorrow."

"Did I hear somebody say pancakes?" says Ben from the kitchen door, and Mia, all Christmas-fueled and buzzing with excitement, squeals and leaps into his arms. He scoops her up and plants a kiss on my head as he passes by en route to the kettle. "Thanks for seeing to her last night, love," he says softly. More loudly to our daughter, he adds, "And, Mia-Muddle, if you need Mummy and Daddy in the night, just come and wake us up, all right? Don't be pulling the blankets off Daddy like that. You nearly scared me half to death."

My blood runs cold. Mia's face collapses in confusion.

"Mia, pet," I hear myself saying, "have you opened your advent calendar today? It's in the sitting room beside the Christmas tree. Better run and get your chocolate before the fairies eat it all up."

She wriggles free of her father's arms, confusion forgotten, and speeds out of the room. I hear her feet slapping on the bare tiles of the hallway, but I wait until the living room door whines open on its hinges before I turn to Ben. I see him register what's in my eyes, see his own eyes grow wide.

"What?" he says. "What's going on?"

"Ben." My voice sounds like it's coming from far away. "I was in with her all night. She didn't pull the covers off you."

His brow furrows. "Ali, I saw her..."

"You *couldn't* have. I hardly slept. She didn't wake up again."

He watches me carefully, like I'm an unknown quantity. An unexploded bomb. Then, he twitches his eyebrows and shrugs.

"Must have been dreaming then," he says. "You want another coffee?"

We build the snowman by the car, safely distant from the bush outside Mia's bedroom window. The evening's snowfall has covered over the little hollow where we left the thing she found last night, and I try to keep my eyes trained away from it—toward the trees, the ice-blue sky, the impassable, snowy lane.

"Did you know you were walking in your sleep again last night?" I ask Mia as we roll a ball for our snowman's head. I don't know why it's important to me that I know the answer to the question. I just know it is.

She considers for a moment, her little face puckered in concentration. "I don't think I was, Mummy," she says at last.

"Yes, pet, you were."

I don't look toward the bush. Not even when I think I see movement in my peripheral vision. It's the flight of a winter bird reflected in the mirror of her bedroom window, that's all.

"You came in and woke Mummy up."

"I thought I saw the dolly," she says, exactly what she told me in the middle of the night. And then she adds, "I was just trying to find her."

My hand stills in the act of patting snow onto an icy cranium. "What dolly?" I make myself ask, though I know. Of course, I know. "It can't have been Teddy. He was asleep in bed with us."

"No, not Teddy." She frowns up at me, as though she can't believe she has to explain it. "*My* dolly. The one you took away."

"Mia, love…" But I don't know what I'm supposed to say to that. "That's not yours, though." It's barely even a doll, I want to add, but I don't. *Barely* is not the right word anyway.

Mia's jaw sets in that obstinate way that reminds me of her father. "She's *mine*," she says. "I found her, and she's *mine*."

My breath is coming hard and fast. I can see it making little puffs in front of my face. "It's *not* yours," I say, and my voice is trembling with anger I can only just contain. "It's *not* yours, Mia, and I don't want to hear another word about it. Do you understand me?"

Mia glares at me, all ice and fire—a temper to match my own. "She told me you'd say that," she snaps, and before I can stop her, she's turned and is running for the house.

For a moment, a long and terrible moment, I think she's going to try to dig up the thing by the window, and I try to grab for her, sharp and swift enough to knock me off my balance. My gloved hands brush her coat, but she's gone before I can get purchase, and I tumble sideways into a drift of snow. Mia doesn't look back until she's at the door.

"I'm telling Daddy!" she shouts, and I start to scramble to my feet. I need to tell Ben to burn that thing, smash it into pieces and set fire to what's left. "I'm telling him you won't let me have the dolly when she's *mine*!"

I'm halfway into the cottage after her before I hear, really hear, the words she's just said.

She told me you'd say that.

Ben, predictably, blames my sleepless night.

"Ah, come on, Ali," he says. "She's five. You know what kids her age are like."

I blow on my coffee to cool it, watching through the sitting room window as my child wraps a scarf around her snowman's neck. "I know what Mia's like."

"It's a new place for her. We've never had Christmas away from home before."

"I wish we'd never come here," I say.

He sucks in a deep breath. I can hear the words churning in his head before he speaks them aloud. "It was your idea to..."

"I know it was my idea! But you chose this place!"

"I didn't exactly have to twist your arm, though, did I?" Ben's gone very still, the way he does when he's furious. "I'm going out to see Mia," he says, and he turns and stalks out of the room before I can say anything more.

I watch for him by the window, my fingers drumming against my cup, and when I see Mia run to him, I release the breath I've been holding. I watch her grab his hand and pull him toward her snowman, and I hear him, muffled through glass, tell her how great it looks and how clever she's been. And all I can think as I watch them admire my little girl's handiwork is that the coal of its black, sightless eyes seems to bore into me, into them, into the very fabric of this house.

We set out a mince pie for Santa and a carrot for the reindeer, and when Mia's in her pajamas, she hangs her stocking by the fireplace and snuggles into her dad on the sofa to read *The Night Before Christmas*, as we've done every Christmas Eve since she was born. I nuzzle my feet beneath her folded knees, and she grins a gap-toothed smile at me, and my heart contracts with the love I feel for her, my precious curly-haired child in her candy cane PJs, all cuddled up beneath my husband's arm. I sip a mug of mulled wine and gaze into the Christmas tree as the soft, familiar words wash over us, and I wish like hell I could feel something other than a chest-tightening, frigid fear.

It's hours before Mia finally falls asleep.

She hears bells jingling in the night sky. She thinks she

68

hears a crunch of boots on the snow-covered roof. She wants to be reassured, again and again, that Santa will *definitely* know how to find us here, and she's concerned she won't be able to fall asleep and that will mean her stocking won't get filled. It's after eleven o'clock when Ben closes the bedroom door behind us at last, and I submit to his sleepy hug, loose-limbed with fatigue and Christmas booze.

"Stocking and bed?" he suggests, and I'm too tired to even bring up the subject of the brie and crackers we've had sitting out, waiting for us on the kitchen table for the past three hours. I just nod, and he grins, and the tension that's hummed between us for the best part of the day melts away, and he's my Ben again. "You're dead on your feet, love," he says. "Tell you what. *I'll* do stocking. *You* do bed."

"Are you sure?" I don't want to sound like I'm discouraging him, but I also don't want to sound like I'm not.

"It'll only take me a minute," he says. "I'll stick my head in on Mia again quickly before I come in too."

I'm grateful he's heard the unspoken fear that's bubbled in my chest all evening. "You're a star."

"A Christmas star," he says, and the face he makes is so ridiculous I can't help laughing. This is what I need. This almost feels normal.

I don't think I'm going to get to sleep tonight, even though exhaustion is like lead in my bones. My nerves are strung tight, and my ears are straining for noises that shouldn't be there. My heart is hammering against my chest, and every bone in my body aches with the act of not running to my child and wrapping my arms around her. Keeping her safe from whatever lurks in the dark of this unquiet place.

But in the end, I pass out before Ben's even made it to bed.

I wake in the night to a small figure standing motionless beside my bed, and I can't bear it. I almost nudge Ben awake to deal with it because not again. Not tonight. She's going to be awake before dawn anyway, and I just need to sleep.

"Mia, love," I whisper. "Go back to bed."

She turns without a word and glides toward the door. Her little feet make no sound on the threadbare rug, and my eyes slide closed all by themselves. But I don't sleep. I nearly do, but something, some primal instinct, drags me back from the cusp of unconsciousness, and I'm suddenly very, very awake.

It takes me a second, two perhaps, to understand what's wrong, and then I'm scrambling, tumbling out of bed before I've even registered the source of my panic. The house is cold, freezing cold. I can see my breath in front of my face. Throwing back the covers is like stepping into a fridge. My brain is running on instinct, but my first thought—my only thought—is Mia.

I stagger blindly into the hallway, and then I understand what my gut was trying to tell me. The front door is lying wide open, and in the shadowy half-light of the winter moon, I can just see a small figure walking barefoot through the snow in the lane outside.

I hear myself scream her name. I see myself half run, half fall toward the door. I feel the scrape of my wellies against the bare skin of my calves as I force my feet inside them. I feel the vicious bite of frigid air scrabbling up beneath the fleece of my pajamas as I lurch out the door. Snow crunches beneath my feet, frozen treacherous as the temperature has dropped, and I almost lose my balance, but a strong arm catches mine just as I'm starting to fall.

"Jesus Christ, Alison!" cries Ben. "What the hell are you doing?"

"Mia!" I manage. My teeth are rattling so hard they've clenched my jaw, and the words will barely come out. "Mia! Look—*Mia*!"

He stares at me like he's looking through me. I grab his chin with trembling hands and force his gaze past me and into the frozen night.

"Mia's out there! She's sleepwalking! Ben, we have to get her!"

"Ali," he says. His eyes are bewildered, and for the first time since we got here, there's real fear behind them. "Ali, Mia's tucked up in her bed."

"She's out there!" My voice is rising to a scream, and I can't stop it. I'm struggling to free my arm from his grip, to run out away from him, after my little girl. "Ben, she's going to freeze to death! Help me! *Help me*!"

"Ali...," he says again, but there's movement in the hallway behind him.

Tousled hair, candy cane pajamas. Small fist rubbing sleep out of her eyes.

"Daddy?" says my child softly, and the last traces of my composure fall away.

"She woke up," says Ben. His arms are warm and solid around me as my knees sag toward the floor. "She came in to us, and you were asleep, so I brought her back to her bed. Ali, I've been sleeping beside her for hours. There's nobody outside."

But there is. There *is*. I can see it now—a small shape in the darkness, Mia-sized and very, very still against the shadows. I can feel it looking at me, at us. I can feel its black eyes waiting to see what we'll do.

"Ben," I say, "pack everything up. Do it *now*. We're leaving this house tonight."

Dawn is shading the eastern sky a watery gray as the car pulls up in front of our house. The journey has taken six hours, but most of those were eaten up in trying to navigate impassable roads of snow and ice. I'm curled up in the back seat beside my sleeping daughter, and I know I won't be letting her out of my sight for days, for weeks, for months. Maybe years. Not for as long as it takes for this fear to subside. I may never leave her side again.

"Home sweet home," says Ben. There's a tone to his voice, a kind of exhausted anger, that tells me we're going to be having this fight for a long time to come, but I don't care.

All that matters is we're here. We're safe. We're away from that place.

Mia doesn't wake as Ben lifts her from the car and carries her, without a word, toward our cold, dark home. I watch them disappear inside, and then, with limbs that feel a hundred years old, I heave myself upright and move around to the back of the car to start emptying the boot. It's a mess of Christmas presents, wellies, coats, and bags. We left the Christmas dinner in the cottage kitchen. It'll be a takeaway for our festive feast this year.

I grab a handful of presents, pull them free, arrange them under one arm, then sling a couple of coats on top. Mia's bag has been pushed right to the back of the boot, but she'll want it if she wakes, so I find my balance and reach for it, tugging it clear of the tire iron that's wedged into one corner. I stagger backward as it jerks free, and a scream erupts from my mouth before I can stop it.

"Ali?"

Ben's suddenly at my side, anger driven from his eyes by an agony of concern, but I can't speak. I can't say anything. I can only point.

He follows my gaze, and I hear him whisper, "What the hell...?"

It glares up at us from a nest of Christmas presents, naked and peeling paint, a hairline web of cracks skittering like veins across its ancient porcelain skin.

But I know what it's doing there. And now, I think Ben does too.

I look up at the house, toward the curtained window of my daughter's bedroom. And I swear I see a pair of black eyes looking back at me from behind the shadowed glass.

SHE IS SOMEWHERE IN THIS HOUSE

BY NIKKI R. LEIGH

hen you find her, don't let her go.

The memory of my mom's words, uttered through ragged breaths, rushes through my mind. She had held my hand while looking out the window from her hospice bed in my living room, taking in the sun on her face, filling my body with comfort only a mother can provide. I think she knew she only had another day or so, and she wanted to impart all of the encouraging words she could.

Acceptance. Yearning for my happiness. Hope I would be as fulfilled in my life as she had been in hers.

Those words beat in my chest now, alongside the throbbing of my heart. Already, I feel unsettled, taking in the black grime coating the front door of the rickety structure looming over me. For just a moment, I hesitate to touch the doorknob, noting the same raised stain on its metal finish. I place a hand on the oak door—the last place Tasha touched outside the walls of this house. The mold on its surface feels unlike anything I've felt before, and I shiver at the sensation. Like flesh, almost.

I push thoughts of mottled skin from my mind, take a deep breath, and press on. I grip the door firmly, knowing she held this thick metal doorknob in her hand, turned it just so, and let herself in. I swear, I can feel her already through the thick wood.

A month ago, I broke my promise to my mother. Somehow, even though Tasha and I were as close as we'd ever been, ready to buy our first home together in the quiet neighborhood against the forest, I lost her.

I let her go.

And I didn't even mean to.

I'm sorry, Mom. I break the door open and push. *I'm sorry, Tasha.*

The smell of musty air hits me first. Then, beneath that, something earthier. *Mold.* I hope I don't have to spend too many days in this house before I find her. Don't have to inhale the spores for too long. A morbid thought crosses my mind—*perhaps that earthy smell is her*—and a shudder ripples through me so fast I imagine a child chucking a basket of rocks into the pond that is my stomach. I feel just as heavy.

The house is nearly empty. We'd signed the paperwork, and it was ours. But once she went missing, I barely had a moment in the day to finalize and move our things. People kept telling me I should so she'd have a place all ready for her when we found her. My heart knew, though, there wouldn't really be an "our." Not for us.

The gnawing in my stomach confirmed.

The search parties droned on for days, like bees gathering materials for their hive. Searching for any nugget, any treasure, any sign of her. It's funny, we act so happy to have found a trace of a missing person, when, in all likelihood, it leads us to a cold, rigid body.

I know I won't find *her*. Just a discarded shell.

But I can feel her here, and for a moment, I hope. I let my mind wonder and wander.

The police swear they searched this house. Turned over every corner, searched with blacklights and dogs. Despite her car parked in the driveway, they concluded she wasn't in the structure. They began to tirelessly search the surrounding woods, never returning to the empty house.

I had to try again. I had to know. The intensity of their search had waned over the month, but they couldn't feel the tugging in their chests, the thread I felt being pulled through my throat and out my mouth as a pained sigh. A sign she was close.

She always had a way of tying a rope around my heart and fishing out the love.

I take my first step inside. The air is still, but her presence hangs heavy.

She is somewhere in this house.

The previous owners had left a few things behind in their haste to move away. A heavy oak dresser in the master bedroom, a couple of the drawers askew. An old coffee maker, grounds caked in its body. A pockmarked couch, its back ripped open like it had lost a battle with a pair of shears. Some scattered clothes and towels, old utensils, and plenty of dust.

We bought the house because we loved its bones, the sturdy structure. *A place to build*, we thought, picturing rooms for future children, reading nooks, and craft corners.

If only I'd known I'd be hunting for bones left behind as well.

I walk the house, my hands brushing the wallpaper stained yellow by cigarettes. My eyes find the staircase but dart back to the wall when my hand touches something wet and thick, jerking away as I recognize the black, foamy dirt.

My heart pounds, and I almost sob when I lose connection with the mold. Though the touch had been brief, for just a moment—one single moment, for the first time in a month—I felt like I had touched her. I remember the smoothness of Tasha's skin and reach out again.

My fingertips press into the black mold, and my breath hitches. God, it feels just like her, just like the way her skin would surrender to goosebumps when we kissed.

I know I shouldn't, but I do—I lean in, sniff the wall, and am sent to my knees when I catch the faint smell of lavender.

The tears come fast, finding the scent of my wife working its way through my senses, sending them to a frenzy. I've long run out of shirts of hers to smell, and with a wetness on my face, I fight the urge to caress the wall.

I'm certain now. I will find her.

She is somewhere in this house.

I spend the next few hours navigating rickety floorboards and dusty closets, inspecting every one of the three bedrooms upstairs, the kitchen downstairs, the cold dark basement. My flashlight illuminates every corner of this house that ate my wife, finding no crumbs. No pieces of her left between its teeth. Just dust, the discarded furniture and appliances, and that black stain in the living room.

I return to the couch, nestled in the corner of the room where I encountered the mold, and sit on the worn fabric, in the place I feel her everywhere but see her nowhere.

Before my eyes, the mold transforms. It grows, doubling at least another yard in all directions. A blast of lavender strikes my nose, pulling me to my feet, dragging me back to the wall while the darkness continues to expand.

My hands seek refuge in the dampness of the mold, grabbing fistfuls of it from the plaster, pulling it to my face and deeply inhaling her scent. My fingers cut ravines in its mess, only to have it fill in the space again, like sand collapsing into a moat dug around a castle.

I know I should care about this impossible thing, this sequence of events which shouldn't be happening but is. I know I shouldn't be caressing this mold like it was the first fistful of land a sea-wrecked sailor has grasped. But I can't stop myself.

The more I touch, the more real she becomes, no longer just a scent and a touch but now a *sound*. A voice. Her voice.

"You're here, Nessa." A whisper through the halls.

Black spots before my eyes. Not just the mold, but my vision blurring, spiraling away from it all when I want nothing more but to sink deeper in.

"You've made it," she whispers again, wind touching the tips of my ears as I crumple to the floor.

I hear her speak one more time before the darkness finds me and tucks me into her folds.

"Our house, Nessa. Our house."

I wake up sometime later. By the sun filtering into the windows, it must have been hours. My eyes adjust to the light, and the first thing I see is a bare wall, the mold gone, no traces left behind. Except...

Under my fingernails, marred as though I'd been digging through soil.

God knows this house to be dusty enough, but maybe... maybe it wasn't just a grief-fueled dream.

I head to the hallway bathroom next to the living room to wash my hands.

Inside, a dampness hangs heavy, tinged with lavender. I shake my head, trying to clear away the nightmare I must have had.

I grip the sink and stare into my bloodshot eyes, remembering how Tasha used to do the same when she was overwhelmed and needed centering. She'd eventually crack a smile.

"The bathroom, such a sacred space, you know?" she would joke, letting me know she was okay.

Her easy humor, even in the throes of stress, was just one of a thousand reasons I loved her. You'd have thought her making a joke in the months leading to my mother's death would feel off limits. But without her and a reason to laugh, I think I would have folded in on myself, like a broken poolside chair.

I miss her. She'd have the right thing to say to make me whole again. To keep me from losing myself in this god awful house that has swallowed her whole.

The sun dips behind the clouds, a storm rolling in. I remember when we first toured with the realtor—it was raining, and the house was filtered through streaks of falling gray. Just like then, the thunder begins, slow and deep, and it echoes off the bare walls.

My ears perk at the noise stirring just under the deep sounds of the impending storm—a faint scratching, a tinny tap from the vents. I follow the sound and get to my knees, the linoleum cold on my skin. Lightly, gently, a tap which could be the sound of rain falling on rooftop apparatuses but sounds so much less wet. Not so much a plink, but more of a scratch.

I strain my ears and hear a whisper underneath it all.

"*The rain...*" Faint, from the vents. Tasha, her voice. Louder now. "The rain always clears the shit away, no matter how big the pile."

Then nothing. I smile, my heart pounding, knowing what I'd heard last night was not a dream, but a sign.

A most beautiful sign she is somewhere in this house, and she still knows just what to say.

A few days pass, and I continue moving into our home. I order some groceries and pick up some clothes from our old apartment.

I whip the house into shape—patching holes in wall plaster, sweeping dusty floors, shining windows and scrubbing toilets. My heart weighs heavy, wishing I was laboring with Tasha, that we were prepping a home for our future children. We always dreamed of being fun moms to weird kids.

Every step, every movement and noise, I stop and wipe the sweat from my brow, hoping it's her again. That her voice will call from the vents, her soft touch will sprout from the walls, and I'll catch a whiff of her lavender shampoo.

She's quiet though. Tasha says nothing while the house gets louder and louder. Groans under my feet and cries against the wind, windowpanes plinking under the raindrops continuing to spill over the days.

I don't know what I'm waiting for, if she'll speak again, or if I'm cleaning this house in solitude for God knows what reason.

On the fourth day of her silence, I'm bundled up on the ragged couch, reading a book by the living room fireplace. I'm turning the page, my mind anywhere but on the contents of the paragraph I've restarted five times, when I feel it.

The gentle breeze on the hairs of my neck, the chill in the air biting the tip of my ear, warmth flowing through my body.

"*Nessa...,*" the wind whispers with her voice.

My spine stiffens even as my body relaxes under her touch.

"Between. I'm between," she says, louder, tinged with confusion.

"Tasha?" I hate how shrill my voice sounds. "I hear you," I say, almost a whisper to myself.

A rustling on the wall by the couch, and my eyes dart to track the sound. Black mold appears, like earlier in the week—a sprinkling first, then an infestation.

It reeks of earth, but the scent levels out as *her* scent filters through.

I reach my hand out, my palm hovering over the stagnant spores.

"Not now, Nessa."

Her voice startles me, and my hand retreats.

"Then when?"

As quickly as it comes, the mold dissipates, only to reappear on the floor in the shape of footprints. One after another, they stain the ground, a twisted trail of rot leading to the basement.

"Follow," Tasha's voice croons over the staticky air.

So, I do, to the basement, where the footprints cascade down the cement stairs and to the corner of the room under the laundry chute.

"Between."

I watch as the footprints step vacantly across the floor, and I swear I can spot Tasha's swagger in their stride. A yard left until they reach the wall nearest the laundry chute...a few inches...then, before my eyes go vertical, up the y-axis of the wall, only to disappear into the ceiling above.

I race back up the stairs, approximate where the trail ended into the ceiling, and mark the floor with a sock I rip from my foot.

"Between," she says again, her voice trailing off into the night.

The atmosphere stills, and the sound of rain is soon all I can hear as her presence disappears again.

I howl in frustration, feeling her leave. My chest heaves as the sobs fight their way through my tight throat.

I have a little more than nothing, though, which is better than how I started the night. So, I gather myself and head to the living room, where I've stored a small toolkit to repair things in the house. I glance at the wall where the mold has returned. It has clumped itself in two mounds and a long, curved line. A black smile on the wall. It almost has her dimples.

Hefting the hammer, feeling its weight in my hands, I return the grin. I march back to the spot I've marked with my discarded sock, raise my arm, and bring the hammer down, claws first into the floorboard, cracking the brittle material with my blow.

Again and again, I smash the floor, hoping I'll find my sweet Tasha underneath. A frenzy of swings, my mind racing to understand how she could have gotten there. After slamming and cracking the wood, I toss the hammer aside and begin to rip the planks from their spot. I peer into the sizable hole and sob again at what's inside.

Nothing but dust.

Nothing but darkness. Empty.

"No," Tasha says, as if she's standing in front of me, and in my mind, I can see her shaking her head, a coy smile on her face. "Between."

"I am! This is...Isn't it?"

The sound of feet beating the ground pulsates around me, thumping like a demonic drum, up and down, to the basement, up the stairs to the second floor. I squeeze my eyes shut at the monstrous beating. Lightning fills the house, thunder screaming into the night.

"Please, Tasha. Where are you?"

My body coils in frustration, feeling her, smelling her, knowing she's here but still so far away.

I make a choice, rushing in the direction of the moldy footprints heading to the second floor, shouting as they stop abruptly in front of a set of cabinets. Handprints appear on the wood panels, Tasha's delicate fingers outlined by black spores, gripping the center door.

I place my hand atop her absent one, feel her strong fingers in mine for just a moment as I hold her spectral hand. Gripping the handle, I swing the cabinet open, expecting to find her bones within.

But again, nothing. Nothing but the laundry chute.

Realization grips my core, like the hand of a god reaching through my flesh and puppeteering my spine. I lean in, trying to peer down the chute, and can only make out a dark shape the worst part of me knows isn't some trapped clothes the previous owner left behind. I can't see well enough though, and I don't want to fall in myself, so I rush back to the living room, grabbing a flashlight this time.

I follow the set of footprints back down to the basement, head right to the chute exit overhead, and shine the light up.

The strangest thing overcomes me, surrounded by Tasha's scent and the comfort of her presence. I know seeing her body, twisted and bent in the metal confines of the chute, should paralyze me with despair. It's there. I can't deny that. But relief, relief I've found her at last overcomes the sadness.

"What happened?" I ask. A death that shouldn't have transpired. An accident. A mistake.

"Life, Nessa," she sighs. "Just life."

In a big, big way, I think. A darkness crawls up my legs, spreading across my skin and clothes.

"I love you, Tasha."

I feel her arms embrace me, see the mold dot my forearms.

"You can stay here, you know," her voice wheezes into my ear.

"I can, and I will," I say, panic setting in as the mold smothers my pores and creeps up my neck. "But please, not like this."

The mold hesitates, pausing just centimeters from my lips.

"Stay," she pleads.

"I will."

The mold climbs, my breathing slows, my heart pounds, and I see black.

For the second time this week, I wake up on the floor. The cold cement of the basement bites into my back, and my eyes adjust to the near dark of the room.

The first thing I see is the bundle of clothes and bones and decayed flesh that is Tasha, suspended and stuck in the laundry chute above my head.

The unpleasant sensation of water pooling in my ear canal indicates my tears. I lie like that for some amount of uncountable time, sobbing at the sight of my wife above me.

She is somewhere in this house, and I finally know where that is.

Weeks have passed, and Tasha's body has been removed from the house. An accident, the police ruled it. A bit of curiosity gone too far.

86

The house swallowed her up.

I've almost moved in completely now, though my friends and Tasha's family think I'm a bit unhinged for doing so. They're right—I've become dislocated from who I once was, but it's not the move that did it. As soon as Tasha died, I was changed, but at least here, I can be changed with her.

I'll take care of her, of this house.

I've painted her body, scrubbed the soles of her feet. Her garden is beautiful now, just like her, the way the sun shone on her hair and lit a fiery halo of warmth around her.

This house, this woman, I'm with her. And I'll stay with her.

I run my hand along the smooth living room wall. I let a smile slip through, happy to finally be able to heed my mom's advice and hold Tasha tight to me, for as long as I can.

When you find her, don't let her go.

She is somewhere in this house, everywhere at once.

And so am I.

DONE DEAL

BY COLIN LEONARD

"What are you looking at, Owen?"

Owen Mathis raised his head from his tapping and scrolling and placed the phone beside his neglected cup of coffee. For a moment, he wasn't sure which of his work colleagues had addressed him. The canteen in the insurance brokers was too poky, even for their small office. A busy coffee break could leave some people standing. The question might have been inferring that if he was just reading shit on his phone, he could do it at his desk instead of taking up a seat.

"Beds," he said.

"Beds?" It was Sinclair who was speaking. He was standing by the sink, which meant his previous words probably were laden with the suspected inference.

Owen didn't much care.

"Yeah, for the boy. I'm looking for one of those beds with the desks underneath. You know them? Fucking expensive."

"Where are you looking?" Gemma was sitting at the only other table.

"All the big stores. You'd think one of them would have a sale on."

"They all have their sales at the same times. What one does, they all do," Gemma said in the same tone she used to let customers know they weren't going to get any further help from her.

Sinclair was going to help, though. Sinclair always had some advice. He sidled over, dipped his nose toward Owen's phone.

"Jesus Christ. How much? You want to check on DoneDeal, my man. Great website. Get yourself a bargain."

"Dunno. A secondhand bed? Is that not a bit scummy?"

"What are you talking about? It's just wood and metal. Wouldn't you sit on a secondhand chair? What age is your boy?"

"Eight."

Owen thought of his wavy-haired son's pleasant nature. Cian wouldn't know or care if a bed was new or not. He just cared about football and computer games.

"Eight," repeated Sinclair. "He'll probably have grown out of it in a few years. So, you can pay a fortune for a piece of shit from one of those shops, or else get a quality one for half the price on DoneDeal. And don't offer the asking price. Ever. Once you're in front of them with cash in your hand, they'll take any reasonable amount. They just want to get the deal done and move on."

"Yeah, I know that. I've bought stuff on DoneDeal before."

Owen had bought a lot of things secondhand. The whole of the first decade of their family life had been inhabited by used goods. He and Melissa had hoped they'd be past that by now, but mortgage rates and bills weren't coming down, and his salary wasn't going up.

"Have a search. Go on." Once Sinclair had his teeth around something, he wouldn't let go until he'd bitten it off and had a nice chew on it. He was the same with his customers—a pushy fucker.

"Gimme a chance." Owen swatted him away.

The man had no sense of personal space.

"Bet there's some real bargains."

"Half eleven now, boys and girls." Gemma stood up to leave and waited for others to move, jealous they might steal a bit more unentitled break time than her.

"What's there? Anything good?" Sinclair leaned over Owen again, exuding an odor pungent from cheese and onion crisps, and licked his fingers.

Owen noted the prices under the thumbnail pictures on the first page and knew he'd be buying from there.

"Yeah, there could be a few suitable. I suppose, if I get the mattress new, it'll be okay."

"The mattress is as dear as the bed, man. Kids don't wear out mattresses. Just give it a good wash. Trust me. You can buy me a pint with the money you save."

Owen threw the cold dregs of his coffee down the sink at the same time as clicking an ad near the top of the list.

At four o'clock in the afternoon, Owen pulled up outside a handsome house in the countryside with scruffy lawns and an advancement of weeds invading the driveway. He had disappeared early from work, hoping he'd snag this bargain before anyone else. A man in tennis shorts and a tan polo shirt stood outside the front door, wearing tinted glasses like he was caught in a Polaroid photograph from forty years ago. Owen exited the car.

"Hi, I rang earlier about the bed on DoneDeal."

"Which one are you?"

"Owen. Why? Are there others coming to see it?"

"Others? Oh, yes, there's a good bit of interest, but you're first in line. Don't worry. Come on in and have a look."

The man guided Owen inside and led him up a polished wooden staircase. This was one of those houses whose first requirement was to be large, puffing out its chest to the outside world, and spacious enough inside to hold a lifetime of possessions. It didn't seem like the sort of house whose owners would bother to sell unwanted items. They could just have them dumped or get a local charity to take them away. But the air inside was still and undisturbed. Maybe the place was being sold, and they were clearing it out. Maybe they were desperate for cash, despite the size of the house. Who knew what anyone's real financial situation was these days.

"How come you're selling it?" asked Owen, primarily for something to say that would fill the void of silence.

"Oh, it's not mine. I'm just the neighbor. The owners are away at the moment. I'm merely doing them a favor. Helping them get rid of a few things."

The man waved Owen toward a child's bedroom—one wall painted deep blue with decorative stars and planets, a telescope on a stand by the window, a full untidy bookcase, and the bed.

"There it is," said the neighbor.

He hadn't taken off his sunglasses since they'd come inside. Owen wondered whether they were for some kind of eye condition. They were clunky and amber. The man's age was hard to gauge. He must have been in his forties, but he had a 1980s style about him that spoke of cigarettes and loafers, VHS tapes and sports cars. It was hard to tell if he had a faint moustache or a shadow under his nose. Maybe some rich guys were stuck in a time warp of the era their money came from.

"It seems to be in an all right condition." Owen put a hand to the thick wooden frame. It was of much greater quality than anything he could afford new. The advertised price was substantially less than it should have been. Still, no point in coming across as too eager.

"Some wear and tear," he added slyly, but the neighbor ignored his ruse.

"So, do you want it? You'll have to dismantle it yourself, I'm afraid, but I'll help you carry the pieces down to your car. There are tools here somewhere. It should fit in that... that...What is it you drive? A Japanese car of some sort?"

"Yeah, the seats fold down."

Owen debated whether or not to haggle with the guy. It was ridiculously cheap for what it was. A beautiful finish to the solid oak, the desk was curved and neat on cool black steel legs with a matching stool. It was usually expected there'd be a bit of bargaining, but perhaps that was alien to this class of person. Maybe he'd take offense and ask Owen to leave. Fuck it, he'd just pay the asking price.

"Um, yeah, cool. I'll take it. I don't need the mattress, though."

"Oh. I'm afraid you'll have to take the mattress. It will fold over and fit in your car, I'm sure. I'll find you something to tie it up with."

"Well, I was going to buy a new mattress to go with it."

"But then I'll have to get rid of this one myself somehow. Or else leave it in here to gather dust. They won't be pleased with that at all. Perhaps I should wait for somebody who'll take both."

The neighbor seemed bothered by this mattress situation, as if he had agreed to something that had turned out to be more hassle than he'd expected. Nothing else in the ads had been as nice as this for such a good price. This bed would cost well over a grand if it was new. Owen couldn't let it slip away.

"Hey, no. Look, if it's a deal breaker, then I'll take the mattress."

"Oh good. I don't think it was used very much anyway. I'm sure it's fine to use it if you want. Different sheets and all that. Ah, there's the tools."

The neighbor pointed to a small spanner and a pair of Allen keys under the desk.

"I'm sure it's fine if you want to keep them as well. They probably came with the bed. You may need them to put it back together at your house. What age is your child?"

Owen picked up the tools and sized up where to begin. "He's just turned eight."

The car was crammed. Owen found it awkward to reverse into his driveway when he got home because the mattress was blocking most of the back window and the stool in the passenger seat was obstructing his view of the wing mirror. If he had been stopped by the cops on the way back, he could have been in trouble.

He went through the house and out to their back garden.

"Guess what I got," he teased Melissa.

She was weeding the flower beds. Cian was kicking a ball against the wall at the end of the short lawn.

"The bed? Great. Which one did you get?"

"I got a deal."

"Owen." She frowned with mistrust.

"No, no. Wait until you see it. It's amazing quality, and I got it for a song. Come on, I'll need a hand to bring it in."

She was impressed when she saw it, even just in its constituent parts.

"Oh, yes, that wood is gorgeous," she said. "How much was it?"

"A hundred cash."

"No way."

"Yup."

He presented her with an armful of slats to carry inside.

"How come it was so cheap?"

"Some rich family. They just wanted rid of it. They weren't even there. They had their neighbor selling it for them."

He followed her in with the bedrails. They hefted their loads upstairs and put them down inside their son's room.

Cian appeared, hopping his football on the carpet, and checked out the bits of his new bed.

"Cian, not in the house," said Melissa.

The boy bounced his way back downstairs, and they heard the hard repetitive slap of the ball on the kitchen tiles.

"Outside, Cian," she yelled. At the sound of the door closing behind him, she put her hand to her mouth.

"Wait. You don't think...?" She gripped her husband's arm.

"What?"

"Did you ask why they were selling it?"

"Yeah, sort of. I didn't ask too many questions. I don't think he knew. He was just doing them a favor. Weird sort of a guy."

Melissa didn't say anything for a minute. She just kept staring at the bed parts and holding his arm. Owen wished he hadn't said anything about the guy being weird. Melissa was searching for a fault with his bargain purchase somehow. He knew it. She wanted a brand new bed, no matter how nice this one was. But he wasn't expecting her to say what she said next.

"Did the child die?"

"What?"

Her mouth moved as if she were sucking a sour confectionery.

"Why else would they sell the bed? Why were they not there? Was it too painful for them? Maybe they can't bear to go back to the house until all the reminders are gone."

"Jesus Christ, Melissa. Don't be so morbid. It was nothing like that."

He had to play this right, or it was a hundred dollars down the drain and a chunk of change going on a new bed. "Kids grow out of these things all the time. He's probably a teenager now. He's probably off to some posh boarding school, by the look of the house."

"So, why weren't they there themselves to sell it?"

"I dunno. Maybe they were on holiday."

"Why didn't you ask?"

"I didn't think to. I was just concerned with making sure there was nothing wrong with the bed. And there isn't. I've priced this type. They're a grand and a half new, two grand sometimes. C'mon." He took her into an apologetic hug. "I know you're sick of secondhand stuff, but this was too good to pass up. Wait till you see it when it's built."

The best thing about the bed was that reassembly didn't involve a multitude of annoying, fiddly screws and receivers and dowels, connecting together with chunky nuts and bolts of just two types. It took as long to dismantle Cian's old bed and gather up its pieces as it did to put the new one together. He offered the old bed's mattress up to see if it would fit on the new arrival, but it slid around within the bigger frame. Owen considered stuffing blankets around it but instead hoisted up the used mattress that was designed for it. It looked right and proper there. Comfortable and firm.

Should he lie to Melissa and tell her he had bought it new on the way home? No, she'd never believe him. Fuck it. Even if he had to dispose of this mattress and source a new one of the same size, he was still on a winner financially.

"You're right. It's really nice." She appeared at the door of the room, having spent the last hour keeping their son from getting underfoot with the distraction of a flashy TV game show.

"Cian, come and look at your new bed."

She needn't have hollered. He had followed her up from the sitting room.

"Wow, cool," he said, excitement in his eyes.

"What about the mattress?" Melissa asked.

"It came with the bed," Owen admitted.

"Is it clean?" She stepped up on the ladder to inspect.

"Yeah, seems to be," said Owen. "His old one doesn't fit too well on it."

"I'll get some sheets. It looks as if it was washed well.

Doesn't appear to be too worn, but I think we should try to get a new one that will fit it. It'll do for tonight, though. I'll just fit two layers of undersheets."

Cian dived straight for the desk and arranged his pencils, his football magazines, and an old Arsenal alarm clock he loved but which his parents had been forced to remove the batteries from by bitter experience. Owen ruffled the boy's already messy hair and kissed his forehead.

"You'll get loads of schoolwork done in there, won't you, little guy?"

The most pleasant thing about Owen's start time at work, and the fact his commute wasn't overly long, was he got to have breakfast with Melissa and Cian before they embarked on the school run. He had a routine where he rose, showered, dressed, and got some coffee brewing before rousing his son.

Melissa was tumbling cereal into three bowls when he pushed open the door of Cian's bedroom and took a moment to admire the fruits of his bargain hunting. Cian was fast asleep in the bunk, wrapped up in the red and white of his official Arsenal duvet with footballs, cannons and crests all over it. His head was covered over like he was snuggled up in a cocoon. There wasn't any motion from him.

"Rise and shine, Cian," called Owen.

Just before he made a move toward the bed, he became aware of a presence behind him. He turned. Cian stood there in his pajamas, yawning and squinting up at him.

"I had to go to the toilet," he said. "Is it morning?"

"I thought you were still in bed. You left a shape. Look." Owen pointed toward the duvet. "How was your new bed? Comfy?"

The boy made a gesture that could have meant anything but turned into another yawn.

"Time to get dressed anyway. Where's your uniform?"

During the bed assembly, Owen had stuffed bundles of clothes into the wardrobe from where they'd been strewn on the old bed. He rooted around for them now, while Cian sat on the stool under the bunk.

"Here we go." Owen sniffed the navy blue school jumper. It smelled of cut grass. "Were you playing football in your uniform again?"

The shape in the bed unnerved him now that he could see his son sitting down below it. For a moment, he had a flash of what it would be like to have two kids. He reached up and was about to shake out the duvet, but something made him hesitate, and he prodded the shape first.

It was firm.

"Cian, did you put something under the covers? Did you make a body out of teddies?" But it felt too hard to be constructed from soft toys. "Or footballs? You playing a trick on me and your mother?"

Owen knew he should just pull back the duvet, but for some reason, he didn't want to. He didn't want to see what was underneath it.

"Hmmm?" said Cian. "I'm too big to bring teddies to bed now that I'm eight. I only do it when there's nightmares."

"Were you playing a trick on us, Cian?"

The boy mopingly pulled on his trousers and then his socks.

"No, Daddy."

Melissa appeared at the door.

"Everyone up? How was your new bed Cian?"

"Fine."

"What's that?" she asked.

Owen didn't say anything. He spidered his fingers against Cian's shoulder to try and get him dressed quicker, stood the boy up, and ushered him toward the door.

"What's under the sheets, Cian?" said his mother. "Owen? What's going on in here?"

He twisted his lips into a tight, pursed shape and stood blocking her path to the bed.

"I dunno. It's nothing. I just got a funny feeling, that's all."

"Is there something underneath the covers?"

"I don't know. I haven't checked."

"Why not? Owen? Why haven't you checked?"

But she wasn't making any movement in that direction either.

"Come on. We'd better have breakfast, or we'll be late."

He closed the door behind them.

Cian ate his cereal in sleepy silence, while his parents stared at each other over untouched coffee.

"What is it, Owen? Is there something under Cian's duvet?"

"Cian," said Owen. "What time did you get up to go to the toilet?"

"Not sure."

"And was there anything in the bed with you when you woke up?"

"Oh God," said Melissa. "Why don't you just look under it?"

Owen stood up and slung on his jacket.

"I have to go. I'll be late for work."

"But what's under it?"

"I'll ring you later."

He kissed her bemused face goodbye.

On the drive into work, Owen couldn't settle on music or talk radio, so by the time he arrived at the office, he was still listening to silence. There was a black piece of rubber on the floor of the passenger seat, and he recognized it as being off one of the legs of the stool that went with Cian's desk. He'd been momentarily annoyed last night, thinking it was missing, a slight wobble in the stool being a reminder of its secondhand status. At least he had found it. But he didn't pick it up. He wondered if he would ever bother reaffixing it. That seemed so far away from something he would do now.

Owen couldn't align his thoughts about this morning

clearly, and he didn't want to get out of the car until he had done so. There was something wrong, that was certain. What? A bump under Cian's duvet. A solid shape. It had to be something Cian had put under there. But why had it unnerved him so much? Why had he not been able to look under it? Why hadn't Melissa just thrown back the sheets either? The image of that action made him shudder. What the fuck did he expect he would see?

Sinclair opened the front door to the offices and frowned over at him. Owen checked the time. He had been sitting in his car for fifteen minutes, trying to catch hold of rampant thoughts.

"Forget about it," he told himself and got out of the car.

"What are you doing, sitting out there?" asked Sinclair. "Hey, did you manage to get that bed yesterday?"

At eleven o'clock, he rang Melissa. He called her from beside his car, away from the posse of smokers he worked with who were fumigating the side of the building, far away from Sinclair and the cramped canteen. He hadn't been able to concentrate on work at all. Once, he had let the desk phone ring out in front of him while Gemma nagged, "Owen, Owen, Owen, are you going to get that? Owen?"

When his wife answered his call, he could hear the sounds of the outside world from her end.

"Where are you?"

"I'm in the park," she replied. "I haven't gone back to

the house after dropping Cian to school."

"Why not?"

"What's in his bed, Owen?"

"I don't know."

"How can I go back to the house when there's something there? How can I stay inside with whatever it is?"

"It isn't anything."

"Then why wouldn't you look?"

"I don't know."

"Did their boy die?"

That was a question he didn't want to ask, never mind answer. If they were asking that question, then that meant they believed something terrible was under that duvet. That meant they were admitting to a different reality than the one in which they loved and lived and learned on solid ground with firm rules and expectations.

"I don't know."

"I can't stay there."

After work, he got home to find the house unoccupied, by his wife and son at least. He didn't go into Cian's room to see if it was empty. When he rang Melissa, she told him she had taken Cian to stay in her parents' house. She asked Owen to pack some clothes for them and drop them round.

"How long are you planning to stay there for?" he asked.

"Until you get the problem sorted out."

"It's not like it's a leaking pipe. I can't call a plumber to come out and have a look at it. What am I supposed to do?"

"You brought it into the house, you can get rid of it. I mean, we can't let Cian sleep in it, so we have to stay here until you fix it."

"He could sleep with us in our bed tonight. Just come home, Melissa."

She wouldn't. He dropped the clothes over and stayed there, drinking tea and chatting with his parents-in-law, supporting Melissa's lies to them about a wasp infestation in the attic. They said he should stay the night with them too, that it surely wasn't safe for him to go back until the pest control people became available.

Owen had no change of clothes with him, no toothbrush. He hated squeezing into the uncomfortable spare single bed with his wife, nudging each other to an unromantic sleeplessness. But he agreed to stay.

"You'll sort out the problem tomorrow, though, won't you?" warned Melissa. "You should take the day off work and go home and make sure that the wasp nest gets removed."

"I will," he promised.

Going back there didn't seem as daunting the next morning. Owen's body ached from the spare bed, but he knew that had he spent the night in his own house, he wouldn't have slept for even a single second. The morning cast a comforting light on the situation, and he felt he could deal with it now. He ate a slice of toast standing up, drank an orange juice, pretended to take a phone call from the pest control company, and drove back home.

His confidence dissipated as soon as he opened the front door to the house and felt the sinister stillness waft through the hallway. The door to Cian's room hadn't been opened since he'd shut it behind him the previous morning. He stood staring at it like it was a gateway to another world, as if on the other side of that cheap, painted wood, there were no walls or floor or ceiling, just an evil blackness he couldn't comprehend, that his mind wasn't developed enough to understand. That nobody's was.

Owen stood there, going through all the possibilities of who he might ring to help him—police, priest, friends, colleagues—until he came to the conclusion there was nobody he could conceivably bring into this dizzying fold, and he took himself to the kitchen. Coffee was too complicated to make. He drank a glass of water, emptied his mind, went back upstairs, and flung open the door.

The shape was still there.

Same size. Same position.

He almost wished it would move. His worst dreads were projected onto its inertia. Owen stayed just outside the threshold of the room, staring in. The lie to his wife's family congealed with reality for a moment, and he considered trying to buy poison or a spray or setting the bed on fire with a flaming stick and shutting the door.

He visualized that last scenario. The house would surely burn down unless he timed an intervention with a fire extinguisher for just that moment after destroying the wasps before the flames spread from the duvet to the curtains.

"No," he said under his breath, laughing at his own idiocy. "It's not wasps. It's not wasps."

The shape didn't move.

"It's nothing. Just go in and rip away the sheets."

Owen didn't move.

He knew he had to speak to somebody, or this standoff would last until he abandoned the house forever. The number was still in his phone's recently dialed list. He'd appear a fool, but maybe that's exactly what was needed to snap him out of this stupor. Maybe then he could take some action. Maybe then he could investigate the phenomenon with a healthy skepticism, whip away the duvet, and laugh with his wife about how childish they'd been, cowardly fools scared of a crumpled sheet.

He raised the phone to his ear. The man would probably think he was trying to pull a fast one, looking for a refund.

"Hello, is this concerning the bed?" The neighbor's well-spoken voice, clear and friendly, like a toastmaster or a gracious host.

"Um, yeah," said Owen. "I don't know how to explain. We can't use it. There's something in it." Other voices whittered in the background. "I'm not looking for the money back. I don't care about the money. But I can't bring it back to you. I can't dismantle it."

"No, of course you can't," said the neighbor. "Give me

your address, and I'll be right over."

After slowly imparting his address, Owen hung up. He shut the bedroom door again, went downstairs, and stepped into the kitchen. This time, he was able to extend his concentration to preparing a coffee. He would have liked to have listened to the radio or put on the television, but that might have disturbed whatever was up in the bed. The neighbor hadn't laughed at him or fobbed him off. He was coming over.

What did he know about it? He obviously knew something. Unless he had been lying. Maybe he was just humoring him while he was on the other end of the line. Maybe he had now blocked Owen's number and reported his name and address to the police as a prank caller. Maybe the next knock on the door would be a pair of patrolmen instead of the neighbor. That would be okay too. That would be just fine. They could look at the bed with him.

But half an hour later, a knock on the door startled him off his chair, and when he opened it, he wasn't confronted by law enforcement. It was the neighbor. A man and a woman, a decade or so more haggard than Owen, were with him.

"May we come in?" the neighbor asked reverentially.

Owen made some rapid assumptions. He guessed the neighbor had some other business involving these people and had just brought them along for expedience. Owen assumed from the distressed expressions the couple wore, the neighbor hadn't wanted to leave them sitting in his car on their own. They looked as if they needed to be taken care of.

Surely there wouldn't be any danger in letting three people like this into his house. They didn't seem dangerous. They were respectable looking people, just emotionally fraught about something.

He stepped back to allow them inside.

The woman was particularly fretful. Her hands were up at prayer height, with trembling fingers. The man was obviously her husband, from the way he kept a protective hold of her narrow shoulders as he hovered behind.

"Owen Mathis," he introduced himself.

They didn't reciprocate or even acknowledge him. Both peered around the place, then stretched their necks toward the stairs.

The neighbor was attending to them as if he were terribly concerned with their welfare and didn't pay any heed to Owen. He took the woman's butterflying hands in his, fixed his eyes on the man, and made a soothing hush to them both. The woman took a deep breath, as if she were about to swoon. The man gave a firm nod to the neighbor.

"Whereabouts is the bed?" the neighbor asked Owen with deliberation, as if one misunderstood word could bring the roof crashing down upon them all.

"Upstairs. Who are these people?"

"Lead the way."

He started up the stairs, turning a wary eye behind him. A visible glimmer of excitement surged through the woman as they followed him. He brought them to the door of the bedroom.

"I feel silly," Owen said. "But I had to call someone. It's hard for me to explain."

"Don't worry about it," said the neighbor.

"May I?" chirped the woman, bright tears making their way down toward her emerging smile. The man hugged her and let his hand trail away from hers while she stepped forward.

Owen didn't feel it was his right to either give or deny permission.

She turned the handle and pushed open the door. The curtains were still closed. There was the faint, trapped scent of a young boy's discarded clothes. Not sweaty or heavy, just the slight tang of a day's young energy. She turned back to her husband and put her thin fingers to her mouth.

"Go on." The neighbor smiled.

She stepped up on the halfway rung of the bed's ladder and leaned in across the mattress. Owen saw the movement of the duvet where she pulled at it. She peeked underneath and gasped.

"No," she said. "It's not him. Where is he?"

The neighbor and the man both barged into the room. The neighbor pulled the duvet off completely and turned to Owen with accusation undisguised in his voice.

Six eyes stared at him with determination and malice.

"That's just the shell. Where is the boy? Where is the live boy that got out of the bed?"

COLD BAPTISM
BY CA MCDONALD

Detective Roland Carney pulled the car into the driveway of 600 Hollow Lane and killed the engine. He'd been silent since the start of the drive, and Julietta wondered if he was going to continue the trend indefinitely. She nearly jumped out of her skin when he cleared his throat.

"So, how's this work?" He didn't look at her, but stared straight out the rain-spattered windshield to the dark silhouette of the house beyond.

"We go in. I walk around, tell you if I sense anything."

A pause. "Right."

So that's what it was. He was a non-believer. Once, she would have launched into a tirade of self-defense, but after twenty five years of being neck-deep in the supernatural, she couldn't give two shits if he believed she was really psychic or not. She was here to do a job.

Julietta got out of the car and let the icy rain wash over

her, clearing her head for the work in front of her. Going in with compromised emotions could make the scene hard to read—much like trying to detect a smell in the air if you were already wearing perfume. She needed to be neutral and centered to do her best work.

Her mind settled into the familiar assessment ritual required at crime scenes. See the facts first and then let the ethereal qualities come second. An older home, though well maintained. Built in the early twentieth century. Roses out front, battered to limp corpses by the assailing rain. A little moss in the gutter but no obvious maintenance issues.

"You in a hurry, Miss Wander?" the detective asked, rushing through the rain to join her under the relative safety of the front porch. He pulled out a key and unlocked the door.

"I'm missing my shows." Maybe his disbelief bothered her more than she was willing to admit.

He gave a dry chuckle. "No Netflix?"

She didn't laugh. "Can I see the pictures?"

Bless him, Detective Carney looked a little sheepish. He pulled out a file from under his jacket and opened it, flipping through it as she fished for a light switch on the wall. Urine-yellow incandescent light flooded the living room when she found it. A sofa with cushions worn flat. An older TV. A recliner, complete with knit remote holder draped over the arm.

"So, uh, they didn't find anyone in this room. Just blood on the wall there." He held up a glossy five-by-seven of a bloody streak, deep brownish-crimson against wallpaper—the shade of nicotine-stained fingernails.

Julietta stepped away from him a little. She took a breath and focused on the feeling of her feet on the floor and the stillness of the room.

"Are you—"

"Yeah, quiet, please."

She heard the photo rejoin the others in the file. Tried to forget about him, let her thoughts settle. She became quiet. Small. Then nothing. Let what was beyond reach in. Let it find her open and willing to listen.

Anger hit her at ninety miles an hour. Her fists curled. Breath held. She rocked on her heels with it, letting out an explosive sigh that made the detective visibly jump.

"What the fuck!"

She released the rage before she tried to punch him in his face. Her own thoughts and feelings returned in a soft rush, soothing where the scorching anger had singed.

"He was pissed," she said. "The killer."

"Are you going to do that again? Can you warn me next time?"

She looked at him. "I don't know what I'll find. I never do."

"Great."

"Did you hear what I said? I said the guy was mad."

"Okay. Anything else?"

I was too distracted by the sound of you shitting your pants, she wanted to say but held her tongue. Fuck, the anger was the sticky kind, hard to wash off, even when she came back to herself. She took a breath. Made sure her feelings were her own before she spoke again. "No, nothing else yet. It takes a minute sometimes."

"Okay."

She blew out a tight breath and looked away from him. Let her gaze fall softly on the peeling paint around the window behind the sofa. Movement, in the past, stirred like a foul wind. Someone in the room, moving quickly. So angry. So fucking angry it ate every thought, consumed every shred of their energy. Julietta began to walk the room, unable to stay still with such toxic wrath boiling inside of her. He'd hated this chair, the sagging couch, the old shitty carpet. He'd hated himself and everyone in this house with such shameless vehemence she felt sick.

"The husband was a regular guy on the surface, wasn't he? Quiet. Polite. Office-type."

"He was an accountant." Carney's voice was neutral.

"Everyone thought he loved his wife, his kids?"

"They said he was a model father, a good neighbor, solid worker. No history of violence, no priors."

Her throat felt so dry her voice came out sounding like someone else's. "He was rotten on the inside, Detective. I've never felt anger like this before."

"I mean, you gotta be pretty pissed to off your whole family and run, right?"

"Homicidal anger is one thing. This was..." She shook herself as a snarl began to form in her mouth that didn't belong to her. "This was something different. Can we see the backyard?"

"In this?" He jerked his chin at the storm raging behind the four walls of the house.

"He killed the dog back there. It could be helpful to see how he felt about it."

"Be my guest," he said with a shrug. "Here's what the crime scene out there looked like."

He handed her another picture. An old Australian Shepherd, face eerily peaceful, with its insides spilling out its open ribs like a bucket of big, glossy brown worms. She winced. Fuck people who killed animals and kids.

She passed the picture to the detective and found the back door just off the living room. A flickering floodlight did little more than turn the rain into a reflective soup. Hitching up her collar, she stepped out, ignoring the wet drops that managed to penetrate her clothes.

He'd left the body of the dog out in the open, nearly right between the house and a big oak tree about fifty feet away. When she was about where the dog had been found, she opened her mind again. It was hard. The wind whipped at her hair and sent cold gusts down her collar. The night smelled strongly of wet earth and rot. The flash of the dying floodlight made her dizzy as it cast her shadow into tortured shapes across the muddy grass.

She closed her eyes for a moment. Let everything recede. Let go of her own thoughts. Sadness, like a cloud passing over the blazing sun of rage. Uncertainty. She felt the detective join her, sensing a presence. Something cold pressed into her hand.

Her eyes flashed open, and there was nothing. No detective, no other feelings, just her hand still tingling where something cold and wet had gently pressed into it. She resisted the urge to pat the grass and tell the spirit lingering here that he hadn't deserved what had happened to him. He'd been a good boy.

"Find anything?" Carney asked.

Julietta shook her head.

"Kitchen?"

"No bodies there, just blood."

She opened her senses and found the current of anger, like a familiar stream of lava and filth. Julietta grimaced, letting it pull her physically through the space.

"There is more motion here. Like he rushed through. He hated everything here too. The curtains, the sink." Only the rug on the floor was humbled enough to escape his ire. She released the foul emotions and shook herself, wishing there was the spiritual equivalent of a shower.

"We think the order of the killings took him from the backyard first, through here, to the back of the house."

"Dog first to avoid noise."

Carney nodded. "Yeah, exactly."

"Is there anything about why he was so angry?"

"You read the file, right? Everyone thought the guy was fine, if a little quiet."

"Anything not in the file?"

"You asking me for some cop-gut-hunch-shit?" He snorted. "I don't play that way. I like facts and science and things that hold up in court. All that...other stuff is a Ramirez thing."

Ramirez, the detective who was missing out on this haunted house tour because he was sick as a dog, leaving Carney to escort Julietta around instead.

"I see," was all she said. "Bedroom?"

He fiddled in the folder again and passed her a photograph. "The wife was found there." His brow tightened subtly, and the corners of his jowly mouth pulled down.

Julietta felt like she had been kicked in the stomach. A middle-aged woman lay in her bed, dressed in a white, blood-soaked nightgown. She handed him back the picture, only letting her eyes float over the details. Julietta didn't need to see every slice of the knife, just get a general impression of the scene.

As she stepped into the bedroom, a chill ran down her spine, the air a good ten degrees lower than the hall. The bed lay stripped, the mattress taken for evidence. Every breath smelled like cleaner, but under it was the psychic stench of death.

His rage had poured white hot into this room. Sublime, impossible, transcendent rage. *His palm, on the wife's brow. She didn't know him when he touched her, when he forced her to obey. The knife in his hand, slicing, carving. Her flesh as soft as a sculptor's clay beneath his blade.*

"Julietta?"

She stumbled, legs hitting the edge of the bed. "Fuck." She jerked back to reality with a gasp. To say nothing like that had ever happened before was a horrifying underestimation. She had always been in charge of her faculties before, never swept up in the emotions, let alone the memories of victims.

"Are you okay?"

Julietta backed away from the bed in horror. "Yes, and no. Did he cut her up? Did he...carve something onto her?" Her hands were gripping her sweater of their own accord, feeling the warmth of her soft belly beneath. Flesh was easy to carve under the right hands.

Detective Carney's face went bloodless. "What are you talking about?"

"He cut her up. He did something to her. Put a mark on her."

She was too shaken to take any satisfaction from the tremble in his hand as he opened the folder again and, from the bottom, pulled out another photo. Julietta took it and nearly dropped it immediately.

"Christ."

"Did you talk to Ramirez about this?" Carney's voice was low.

"No! Were you testing me?" She looked at him, incredulous and angry. "You kept this back on purpose."

"I wanted to see if it was just the pictures you were cuing off of."

"Fuck, do you know what this is? It's an occult symbol. Was he into the occult?" Her skin had erupted into such shivers it was starting to ache. She had to get out of this room.

"We have no evidence of that, no."

Julietta closed the door behind them and rubbed her forehead, unable to shake the feeling of dread growing in her gut. "Detective, it's important you don't hide anything from me."

"I was trying to be scientific—"

She cut him off with her stare. "No, you were trying to pull one over on me. I get it. You don't believe in this shit, but if this guy was messing around with...with dark things, I can't be here. That's outside of my job description."

"Dark things?" He sounded incredulous. "Like what, I'm supposed to call an exorcist? Was this guy some kind of Satanist?"

There was a little shake in his voice, revealing he was neither totally skeptical nor immune from whatever happened in the bedroom. Maybe it had just been watching her. Who knew what her face had looked like. She had walked unconsciously to the bed.

"There are degrees of supernatural activity. Most are harmless. But for the ones that aren't, it's one thing to be able to sense them, and another to be able to deal with them."

"Why do you sound afraid?"

"Because whatever energy he left here just slipped into my mind and took me for a little ride."

"Look, we gotta finish this, Miss Wander. Ramirez is going to kill me if we don't."

"I'm not saying I want to quit, and I certainly don't want to leave him out on a limb." She blew out a slow breath, nerves somewhat returning to normal. "Just be honest with me. Was there anything else like that here? Symbols? Occult paraphernalia? Books?"

"Let me see." He opened the folder with its pictures, and without warning, every light in the house went out, plunging them into darkness.

"Fuck," she breathed.

"Let me see here," Carney murmured, and she heard him paw at this jacket. "Goddamn it. Left my flashlight in the car. Hold on. I'll go get it and check the breaker."

Her phone was in the car too. Behind her, she swore she could feel the cold air of the bedroom begin to bleed from beneath the door and start to lap at her ankles.

It took all of her professional discipline to keep her voice calm. "All right."

Spirits didn't interfere with the material world. They couldn't. They could only interact with other things with souls, so the lights failing *was* bad luck and nothing else. Yet she couldn't stop the fear bubbling up inside of her, thick and choking, making her chest so tight it was hard to breathe.

Her adjusting eyes registered Carney's muddy silhouette as he retreated down the hall. She made to follow him, if just to the light of the hall window. Her hip bumped some piece of furniture hard, and she stopped, gripping the top of a slim shelf as it wobbled from the blow.

A bookshelf, about a two-feet height, with a bum leg. Carney's boots crunched on the gravel outside. She pulled on the shelf, dragging it back into the light of the window. Bleary gray light caught silver and gold on the spines of old classics. Nothing incriminating. Dust coated everything.

The headlights of the car turned on, and light flooded through the glass. A dark rectangle lay against the wall beyond the shelf—a book dislodged from the collision.

She picked it up, the cover so cold it made the bones in her hands instantly cramp.

The headlights went off, plunging her into darkness, but not before she had read the cover.

"Carney," she whispered, voice suddenly no louder than a breath. "Carney." She rose as in a nightmare, her body feeling too clumsy, too slow.

He didn't reply. No sound outside. No sound inside but the rapid hiss of her breathing and the drone of the rain. She dropped the book, and the bedroom door opened.

The air rushing out smelled like ice and old blood and something else, a psychic stench that clogged her throat with bitter, burning bile the instant it touched her nose. Wrath like winter, like death.

It was hard to move, like the presence in the house was muting her ability to control her body. She limped forward, sagging to her knees, whimpering as the cold air rushed from behind, creeping up the naked skin of her ankles. Carney didn't answer. Julietta was alone in this house, with whatever evil the killer had unleashed. Even now, it tried to unseal the gateways of her mind. It was relentless. Like a machine with one terrible, unfathomable purpose. If she stayed here, it was going to win.

Julietta barely held back her panic as she prayed the demon would leave her be.

A sound from the front door brought her head up. "Carney?" she whispered.

A thick shadow in the shape of a man unfolded in the doorway. She couldn't see anything besides darkness on darkness. It moved toward her.

Her hands hit the rug on the hallway floor as she crawled, snagging something hard and round. A handle. She acted without thinking, one hand jerking the carpet aside, the other lifting the trapdoor instantly. Yellow light flooded up into her face. She didn't pause to see what it was—she just flung herself down on instinct. Julietta hit the stairs awkwardly, facedown, but able to save herself by sacrificing her shins and palms, which screamed with splinters. The trapdoor closed loudly behind her, and the shadow-shaped thing thumped right over where she had been before.

Silence. She lay in a puddle of light on the dirt floor for a moment, trying to catch her breath. The presence wasn't as strong here. She neither felt its cold on her skin or its tendrils creeping into her mind. The fog of slowness began to lift, the stinging pain in her hands and knees growing more pronounced, and her senses returned to her.

"Fuck." Julietta breathed softly to the cobwebs above. She sat. An emergency lantern on a worktable spilled sulfurous light across a single large basement roughly equal to the area of the living room above. Shelves lined the walls, stacked with books and bundles of what looked like notes and dozens of glass containers in varying shapes and sizes. The worktable was huge, and on it, a large sheet of paper took up most of the space. Someone had inscribed a whole mess of occult symbolism she couldn't even begin to decipher.

Above, she heard a noise. She froze, terror cold in her gut. Then nothing. She breathed out.

"What the hell did you do?" Julietta stared at the table, wishing she had more than passing knowledge of sorcery. It wasn't pertinent to her job. Most people either were unsuccessful at summoning demons or, go figure, were smart enough to never try in the first place. Had this man intended to call upon this demon, or had he been trying for something else?

She imagined the scenario—an idiot occultist biting off more than his dumbass could handle and ending up possessed, broken to the creature's whim. Who knows what it might have made him do.

Kill his family, perhaps?

The floor creaked overhead, and Julietta stared up at it.

"I'm not going to die in this basement," she whispered, hands balling into fists at her sides as she watched dust fall like ashen rain from the edges of the closed trapdoor. Fuck this guy and whatever he'd summoned from Hell. He wasn't going to get to add her to his list of victims.

The floor strained again, in rhythm. Footfalls. Someone walking back and forth down the hall quickly. Not a ghost. A real live, flesh and blood person.

"Carney?" she yelled.

"Julietta?" The pacing stopped.

"Oh, Christ." Relief crashed through her, so powerful it made her eyes sting.

"Are you...Where the hell..." Fumbling on the floor, thumping, then the trapdoor lifted. The light was on behind him, framing him in a halo. "Hot shit, what in the fucking... We missed this..."

Julietta felt a smile forming. "Where did you go?"

"The garage. Threw the breaker." He eyed the steep steps wearily. "I'm gonna need you to come out of there, I'm going to need to call the crime scene folks back, have them search this place—"

A shape moved behind him, like a clotted, seeping shadow, blotting out the light.

"Carney!"

"What—"

The detective jerked forward, startled even as he lost his balance. The force sent him rolling over himself in a terrible tangle of limbs, skidding down the final steps on his back. The trapdoor closed so loudly Julietta felt the air in the room shift with the violence of it.

She moved toward him, and he was already starting to pull himself up, hissing in pain and reaching for his ankle. He snapped out of it, and his hands jerked to his jacket and pulled out his gun.

123

"You see who did that?"

Julietta wished she hadn't. "It's him. He's here."

"You saw him?" Carney's thick face was almost bloodless.

"He's not...He's not himself anymore." She gestured to the table, the jars. "Something has taken him. I saw it. I can feel it."

"Like a spirit?" No rudeness now.

"A demon." She watched the muscles in his jaw twitch. "It doesn't matter if you believe in them or not. That's what's in this house. That's probably what killed the family. Demons grow because of the souls they consume—with each death, he's been getting stronger."

"Fuck!" He spat venomously, rising shakily to his feet. "I've had it with this demons and ghosts bullshit. Someone pushed me down the goddamn stairs." He limped up the steps, gun in one hand, fist clenching the shoddy safety rail in the other.

"Carney, this isn't going to do anything but maybe piss it off."

Ignoring her, he pushed on the door. Heaved with one arm. Put his shoulder against it and thrust all of his considerable weight at it. Nothing happened.

"This is the goddamn police! You listen and do as I say. Let us out, or I swear every cop in this town is going to show up at this door to break your legs!" He knocked with the side of his hand, smashing loud, furious pops against the wood. "What is this fuck planning on doing? Dispatch is going to notice I didn't check in in an hour or two. Someone is going

124

to come out here and rip this sicko a new one." There was sweat on his hairline, maybe from his injuries, maybe from exertion, maybe both. "Did you get a good look at his face?"

"Yes," she said coolly. His rant infuriated her beyond words. Skepticism was a privilege of those who didn't know how the world worked. "He was wrapped in shadow. He didn't even look like a human."

Carney stared at her. "You've lost your mind."

She licked her lips, tasting cruel words before they even formed and swallowing them down. "Come here."

"What?"

"You want some proof, Detective?"

Carney regarded her with suspicion for a moment before giving the trapdoor another shove for good measure. Dust fell, but nothing happened. He half wilted down the stairs, favoring his hurt ankle.

When he stood in front of her, she held her hands open. "What?"

"Give me your hand."

He did. Julietta grasped it, ignoring its clammy coolness against her fingers. She couldn't believe she was doing this. It would make her a pariah all over again if anyone knew what she was doing, but she couldn't hope to get out of here if this twat didn't believe her. Julietta took a deep breath, calmed her thoughts, then thought back to the pictures he had shown her. Pictures of bodies, of violence and death. Let them fill her mind and spill out through her hands and into his.

Carney gasped like he'd been dunked in a winter stream

and jerked right out of her grip.

"What in the hell!"

"Happy?" she growled.

"How did you do that?"

"I put pictures in your mind. It's a basic trick people like me learn when we're kids."

He gaped at her. She could see the disbelief desperately trying to take root again, flowering and wilting a thousand times as each seed couldn't overcome the poison of the truth. Eventually, he turned away from her, pinching his brows.

"Goddamn."

She let him stand in silence for a moment. "Now you see? It's not insanity or trickery. It's real. What I do is as real as the thing in this house."

"How come everyone doesn't know about this...?"

"It's complicated."

"Does Ramirez know?"

"Of course, he does. It's why he asks me to look at these dead-end cases! But are those the kind of questions you want to focus on, or do we want to figure out how to get out of here?"

He sighed, then nodded. The detective still looked dazed and bewildered, but his professionalism seemed enough to keep him going. Begrudgingly, she respected that.

"Okay. So, you're serious. This demon thing, it's here, and it wants to hurt us."

"I don't know what it wants, but I don't want to find out."

"How do we fight it? Can I shoot him?"

"That might kill the man, but it won't stop the evil here from hurting us, or hurting more people."

A flicker of horror passed through his eyes. "Then how?"

Julietta felt sick. In a different life, she would be able to fight this thing, to go toe-to-toe with it and win. But decades ago, she'd made different choices, chosen a life of her own, and ended up here, walking this fine line between two worlds where she was powerful in neither.

"We can't fight it," she said softly. "Nothing we can do will harm it."

"So, we're fucked."

She shook her head furiously, as much at him as at the doubts forming in her own mind. "No. We just have to be smart. If we can't kill it, we can still get out of this house and go get people who can." What she left unsaid was that those people were lost to her now. She had left them long ago, so even if they escaped, who knew if she'd be able to find anyone who could help them. And even that was a fantasy. They'd have to escape first, and she knew, deep down, the odds were slim either of them would step outside again.

Julietta wasn't afraid to die in normal circumstances. But if she died here where the demon could get to her, it wouldn't leave her behind like the spirit of the poor dog. It would most likely consume her, in which case there would be no Heaven, no Hell. She'd be erased from all existence.

Fearing Carney would see how terrified she was, she

averted her face from him, pretending to study the table once more.

"Okay," the detective whispered to himself and ran a meaty hand through his thinning hair. "Okay, you know what you're doing here. If we can't kill it, what can we do?"

She stared at the symbols on the table, wondering with distant dread what had been burned to make the charcoal they had been etched with.

"I don't have a fucking clue."

She wished she knew the time. Carney sat on the bottom step of the stairs, panting after his umpteenth attempt to open the trapdoor. Dispatch would figure out what had happened, he kept saying. They'd been there long enough, officers would show up any moment to set them free. And yet they didn't, or if they did, they heard nothing. Nothing changed.

Julietta didn't want to imagine the cops showing up and then giving up, leaving, not finding the trapdoor. What if it was the product of demonic power and couldn't be found unless the demon wanted you to see it? The thought made her heart beat too quickly. She tried to distract herself by going through shelves on the walls, performing a deliberate inventory of suspect utility. Jars of plants, bones, powders. Boxes of plants, bones, and powders. A sack of stones. All of it was carefully maintained, clean. Not a speck of dust on the containers. Everything had been placed with such precision—just as the marks on the table had been made, sweeping and crisp and deliberate.

He had been so careful, and yet the demon consumed him anyway.

"I wish this fucker would just come down and try whatever it was going to try," Carney murmured. "What the hell does it want from us?"

"Maybe it's gathering its strength. It takes a lot out of it to affect the physical world."

Carney's bloodshot eyes flicked to the trapdoor, and he gave it a half-hearted thump with his fist. "Where did you learn about this shit? *Ghost Hunters* is off debating if ghosts are real, and you got, like, what, a spook PhD?"

A half-strangled laugh escaped her. "I dropped out of spook PhD school. Couldn't hack it."

"Why?"

He'd cut right to her juggler without even realizing it, and yet she didn't try to stop the bleeding.

"The price was too high. You don't fight demons with holy water and rosaries. It's more of a fight-fire-with-fire situation."

"I don't follow."

She sighed. "To fight evil on its turf, you have to be a little evil yourself."

"Like black magic?"

"I would have had to kill a man, Detective," she said, meeting his suddenly shocked gaze relentlessly. Was he a little scared of her? It seemed he was. "You can't just control evil entities. You have to bargain with them. Make a sacrifice that they will accept, and then you battle your wills against one another for control." She paused. "You have to become the very thing you're trying to stop. Most people like me think the ends justify the means. Someone had to be able to clean up things like this, right? I used to believe that, but when it came down to brass tacks, I just...couldn't stomach it."

She didn't know what she expected out of him, but it wasn't the slow, thoughtful nod he gave her. "Not everyone is cut out for their dream job."

"Yeah."

"My kid, he joined the Marines, thinking he'd be some Captain America badass, and ended up quitting. Went through something like that. Just couldn't handle the violence when it came down to it. I was pissed for a long time, but I saw how he hated himself for it, how much he wanted to be different than he was." He shook his head. "There's gotta be room for all types, right?"

Julietta laughed mirthlessly once more. "I hope so. It's how I can live with myself."

Carney fell into silence, his brow tightening in pain. "I've got to get out of here soon. My ankle is fucked up."

Something loud thumped against the trapdoor.

"Maybe this is our chance."

He hobbled down away from the staircase, gun drawn, and pointed at the entrance in a breath. "What do we do?"

"If we get the chance, we run," she whispered. The wood

creaked as if something very heavy was pushing down on it above their heads. Julietta's heart beat so fast she wondered if it was possible to die at thirty-five of cardiac failure. The fear sent electricity down her arms and legs, shaking her wide awake after interminable hours of doing nothing.

The staircase shuddered as a violent rain of dust showered down from above. The shriek of metal and old wood made her grit her teeth. Was it going to pull the house down around them? Cave it in and bury them?

The temperature of the air fell so sharply she gasped, her breath pluming instantly. With the cold came the now-familiar river of wrath, lapping against the edges of her mind like a rising poison tide. She pushed it away, refusing to open herself to it. It pushed harder, creeping between the cracks of her thoughts, seeping into her blood. It was so powerful now, having rested for a while. It was beyond a mere demonic presence sensed from far away—it was here, with her, demanding to be acknowledged.

Julietta hated herself for having nothing but the simplest of defenses, and her self-hate flared white hot with the demon's invasive rage. She imagined clawing out her own eyes. Shooting herself with Carney's gun.

"No," she spat, shaking herself. "No!"

The trapdoor blasted downward, shredding its hinges, and something gray and shapeless plummeted like a stone onto the top of the stairs. It rose on backward, broken legs, dragging one arm behind, the other reaching out toward them with a contorted hand.

The killer. The husband. The man they had come to search for.

His face was frozen in a grotesque cry, mouth wide-open and eyes rolled upward toward the heavens. White frost bloomed over bluish skin and on the stiff, blood-splattered remnants of his clothes.

Julietta knew, without a doubt, he had summoned the demon, tried to control it, and been consumed by it instead. All that was left of him was this husk—the soul devoured, the body nothing more than a puppet for the diabolical creature within.

Gunfire split the air. Her ears shrieked. Instinctively, she covered her face. Carney was shouting something, eyes as blazing as the tip of his weapon.

She couldn't hear him well, the splitting pain in her head drowning near everything out.

"Julietta, I said run!"

There was nowhere to go but up the stairs and straight at the demon. She couldn't make herself move toward it, like every shred of her survival instincts knew that if she did, she'd die. Panic rose inside her, choking her, boiling together with the bubbling tide of rage until she heard herself screaming, insane with frustration and hopelessness and fear.

The demon reached Carney and grabbed him by the throat, pulling him off his feet as if he was a child. The dead-white eyes stared up into his terrified face, impassive as Carney choked in his grip.

The gun clattered to the ground.

Julietta saw it and, somewhere far away, heard herself stop screaming.

She couldn't run away. But she couldn't die here. She'd do anything to survive. Anything. The part of her that had turned down power because she didn't like the price had been as naive as an innocent child. So idealistic and so stupid. She felt reborn in this moment, baptized by death and the cold ocean of primal terror.

Ideals were little comfort to the damned.

The gun shook her in her hand, but she held it steady.

"Accept my sacrifice!" she said, voice breaking. She fired.

The bullet smashed through the back of Carney's head. Blood and bone and brain matter ejaculated across the demon's face. It released Carney and turned toward her where she knelt behind him. She tried to speak, but the words were broken.

"I give him to you, as tribute."

He was mine to take, Witch.

The voice was like acid in her bones, each syllable agony to endure.

You have no sacrifice worthy of me.

She scrambled back from it, panic returning, stealing all rational thought away. A low keening note resounded in her throat, a harbinger of the mad scream to come. She choked it back.

"I do have something you want!" she shouted, desperate. "You know what I am. The man before you was a mere mortal. You could use me. I can help you, with my power and with the connections I have."

It paused.

"Spare my soul, and I'll help you. I'll swear it."

She hated herself as she said the words. But it didn't matter. Hating herself was a small price to pay if she could live. The new, reborn Julietta knew this. Nothing was worth death and oblivion, no matter how precious it might be otherwise.

You swear this? A bargain? Your soul for your service?

Her fate, sealed in icy darkness, with the taste of Carney's blood on her lips.

"I swear it."

She felt its power rise up around her and in her mind, like a blizzard of destruction, eager to consume all it touched.

So be it.

GOODBYE
BY SHELBY SUDERMAN

JULY 19, 2020 – LATE EVENING

T he paramedic aims a light in my eyes, and I try not to squint, training my gaze where he tells me to look while he searches my vision for signs of a concussion. My short legs dangle off the back of the parked ambulance as I wait out the dull ache on the side of my skull. He turns my head, and my skin crawls at every prod and touch. I hate to be touched, but I know better than to resist after our neighbor called 911.

The pen light flickers in his hand. I expect him to lower it, but he hesitates. He leans in and peers closely at my eyes, his brow furrowed. I turn to stone.

I resist the urge to blink so this can be done as soon as possible. My eyes are striking. It's the thing people can't stop telling me about myself, second only to asking how short I am. Even after all this time, I still catch Livia staring...

I shy away from the thought before it can complete itself.

The medic frowns, shakes his head, and straightens. "I expect you'll have a headache, but otherwise, you appear to be fine, Miss Byers."

Relieved, I slip off the ambulance and land on my feet.

"Just take an ibuprofen for the pain if you need to," he adds before gesturing to the cop waiting nearby. "Detective Sanders has some questions for you."

I'll bet he does.

I shuffle across the front lawn, accompanied by the night songs of crickets hiding in the grass. When I reach him, I catch the briefest glimpse of a badge before he switches it out for a notebook and flips through it.

"I just need to follow up on your initial statement. Can you tell me in your own words what happened?"

In my own words. If only it was as simple as telling the truth.

The truth is, Livia is gone. She could be hurt or worse, and I don't know how to help her.

The truth is, Livia normally hangs out with her friends to perform séances and Ouija sessions, but the world's on lockdown because of a pandemic and doing it virtually just isn't the same.

The truth is, Livia lights up a room when she's really excited about something she loves. It's as if the whole world falls away, and it's hard to say no to her.

The truth is, Livia promised me it would be safe.

But the truth is, Livia was very wrong this time. The spirit we reached out to did not leave like she promised. Instead, it fixated on her. It drained her all day and tormented her at night, and all that time, I couldn't help her.

The cop shivers, drawing my attention back to him. I still have to tell him something.

My vision blurs, then darkens, and I blink at the tears of frustration. I still don't know what to do, but if some anonymous caller hadn't dialed 911, I could be out there trying to help her instead of stuck here with a parade of officials who will never believe my partner was viciously attacked by a ghost.

"I was upstairs," I say, my voice choking. I work to clear it. "Tonight was supposed to be movie night. Livia was down on the main floor, and I heard the door open."

"Which door?"

"The back." Tears threaten, but this time I can't blink them away. "I heard Livia say something, and then there was a crash. She was in pain. She screamed for me. She needed me." My voice shakes, and I'm having trouble forcing the words out. "The next thing I know, I'm hurtling down the stairs, but the house is empty."

"When did you hit your head?"

"Against the wall. I tripped when I was going down the stairs." The ache in my head is worsening. How much more of this?

The cop suddenly leans in close, his brow furrowed as

he stares me in the eye. I blink, drawing back.

"You all right?" he asks.

I shake my head. "Of course not." And this new crick in my neck from having to look up at him isn't going to help.

"I'm gonna be honest here, Miss Byers, there's things in this case that aren't adding up. The woman who called 911 said she heard a crash." He nods toward the front left side of the house, where the corpse of our coffee table rests on the living room floor. "Followed by Miss Wells screaming your name. The back door was open when we arrived. We have no evidence of forced entry, and there's plenty about the scene of the...attack...that doesn't make any sense. Plenty of blood, but no trail. On top of that, Miss Wells is just, well, gone."

I wait.

"And yet, you say you didn't even get a glimpse of the person, or you somehow don't remember."

"So, you think that I, a woman barely five-three, must've attacked my much taller and stronger partner?" I bite out.

He holds out his hands. "Granted, I can't explain how you could've done the damage that I saw in there, but... someone did do it. I noticed you used the word *partner* just now. We're in the 2020's, Miss Byers. You can call Miss Wells your girlfriend. I understand."

"We still prefer *partner*," I answer stiffly.

Livia had never been comfortable with the romantic and sexual implications of *girlfriend* when talking about our queerplatonic relationship. But I wasn't about to offer him more about us to microanalyze.

"And," he continues, as though he didn't hear me, "while we were looking through your rental house to see how the intruder got in, we couldn't help noticing two separate beds in the primary bedroom instead of one big bed." From his expression, he clearly thinks he's hit paydirt. "Now, speaking from experience, if my wife kept me at arm's length, so to speak—"

"You'd attack her?" I demand.

He blinks, stalled by my interruption, and quickly shrugs it off. "All I'm saying is, I've only ever seen couples living with one big bed. That's kinda the whole purpose, isn't it? One big bed. For two people." He pauses before quickly adding, "My wife and I have only one bed." When I don't answer, he speaks even slower, as though to a child. "So, what do you say about that?"

"I say that you and your wife clearly have different wants and comforts than I do with Livia." I hate this topic. This isn't a competition. "Is that everything?"

Another pause before he reluctantly produces a business card and hands it to me. "In case you remember anything else."

Right.

"Is there someone you can stay with for the time being?"

"No," I answer immediately. "I need to be here for Livia when she finds her way home."

I can tell he disagrees, but he doesn't push it.

It's another very long hour before they leave. The whole

time, I'm itching to know if they've found what I hid under my mattress in the moments before they arrived. There wasn't time for a better hiding place, and it all happened so fast, the memory is a blur. I'm not even positive what I needed so badly to hide. The only explanation I can come up with is the Ouija board that set this whole nightmare in motion. Maybe they'll think it's the murder weapon.

Maybe it is. I cringe back from the thought, so detached and clinical.

I go inside. If I have to look at that shattered coffee table again, I'll start screaming. The living room is on the immediate left, so I avert my eyes to the right. It does nothing for the intense coppery scent hanging heavily in the air, so I take shallow breaths, trying to breathe it in as little as possible.

I work to focus on the right side of the house, making my way to the back. First is the dining room and, directly behind it, our kitchen. My vision darkens at the sight of it, and I look away quickly, navigating to the left around the stairwell splitting the back half of the house down the middle.

Behind the living room is the hallway leading to two bedrooms. The first door appears on the left—the smaller one Livia uses as her paint studio. At the end of the hall is the primary bedroom.

I open the door. My bed is on the immediate right against the inside wall. Livia's is on the other side of the room next to the back window.

I'm both surprised and relieved to see my bed looks untouched. At the same time, it's strange how easy it is for me to be this close to the board. Usually, I can't get far enough from it without being sick. My skin crawls at the idea of touching it again, but maybe there's something in the box that can help me fix this?

I toss the covers aside.

But when I lift the mattress, the board's not there. Instead, I'm left holding something else.

I'm not sure how long I stare at it, my mind completely blank.

I try starting small. This is my shirt. Specifically, it's the shirt Livia got me for my birthday years ago. I'd know it anywhere because the lettering of "My Kitchen, My Rules" is fading from overuse.

Worse, I'd hid it from the cops. I don't remember the details, but it's the only explanation. It certainly made more sense than the Ouija board.

Worst of all is the blood. The shirt's soaked stiff with it. Whose is it? It couldn't be mine. I yank off my current shirt to search for cuts, for anything, but there isn't so much as a bruise on me. It's then I notice I'm wearing a fresh bra.

My head is spinning, and I slowly pull the clean shirt back on. I remember the cop. Not convinced by my story about an intruder, he'd suggested that somehow I'd picked Livia up and slammed her down into the coffee table so hard the glass top shattered and sliced her open. I squeeze my eyes shut at the thought. I can almost hear the crash, feel the bloom of pain as shards slice deep into my gut.

But that's impossible, just as I'd pointed out to him. Livia is tall and athletic and could certainly overpower my slim, petite frame. She's more than a foot taller than me, for god's sake. I can barely reach our lowest cupboards! There's no way I had the strength to cause the destruction in the living room.

And yet, my shirt was drenched in blood, and I must've hidden it before the police and paramedics got here without understanding what I was doing. The blood on it matches the amount on the coffee table, but there isn't a scratch on me.

My eyes go to the window. There's a handprint on the glass that's too big to be mine or Livia's. To me, it looks like a sign the spirit was stalking Livia, but what if there was another explanation? Maybe Livia made it as a decoration for Halloween or something. Maybe it was there when we moved in, and I somehow never noticed. Maybe it's like the shirt—I just don't remember doing it.

I'm shaking. My mind rebels against the conclusion, but I arrive there anyway.

What if there was never a ghost? What if this is all me?

I bolt back to the living room, bloody shirt in hand, and stare down at the remains of the coffee table. It's still coated a dark, dried red that's trailed onto the cheap carpet.

The cops saw it. And probably the paramedic. None of them thought for a moment the blood was mine, and the medic didn't find anything on me but a slight head injury.

The blood is Livia's. It has to be. There's no way it could

be mine when I don't even have a scratch on me. And yet, now that I'm staring right at it, I remember the glass, the exact sensation when it sliced into me. Just the thought of it is enough to make me shrink back.

What else isn't how I remember it?

Tonight had been movie night. It was Livia's turn to pick, so we were going to watch *The Babadook*. She left it sitting on the TV stand.

My pulse throbs in my throat as I stagger around the broken glass and pick up the case.

But no. The Blu-Ray in my hands is black and white on the front. A man with a briefcase stares into a white light blazing from a second story window.

Something in my mind unlocks.

A door swings open.

July 13, 2020 – Evening

"Rachel, the *goodbye* is on the board for a reason," Livia assures me, although she doesn't argue. It's enough that I'm agreeing to do this with her at all. "We'll be perfectly safe." When I don't answer, she grins at me. "Nothing's ever followed me home, and that's not about to start now. Just follow the rules, and we'll be fine."

All the same, I can tell she really doesn't mind using the

board elsewhere. Yesterday, she'd searched for secluded areas online before settling on a small local historic site that's currently closed due to the lockdown.

The parking lot is empty when we pull in on a clear evening an hour after sunset. We climb out of the sedan, and I survey the empty lot while Livia retrieves the board from the back. We can't go in, but there are picnic tables standing out front. Livia picks the one closest to the building in case the artifacts inside have spirits attached to them.

I sit down directly across from her and watch as she sets up the board with practiced ease.

"Now..." Her voice is soft, but the spark in her eye betrays her excitement. "We both need to put our hands on the planchette, like this."

I do as she instructs, copying the way she settles her fingers over the triangular wooden disk. Her enthusiasm helps to soothe my nerves as I follow her lead. Our hands carefully avoid each other, neither one of us wanting to make the other uncomfortable with our mutual touch-aversion. In a larger group, I wonder if she wears gloves or perhaps stands back and asks the questions. Not this time, though. The planchette needs at least two people.

I eye her. "How do we start?"

"We could introduce ourselves," she suggests.

We read the letters aloud as we direct the glass circle— what Livia calls the *window*—over the corresponding letters to spell out our names.

"We'd like to speak to anyone here who might be

willing to communicate with us." Livia's voice is rock-steady, and I try to let that comfort me enough to stop toeing the dirt with my shoe.

Livia lets the answering silence hang over us undisturbed for a full minute before she says, "Is anyone here with us tonight?"

I listen to the night breeze, letting it distract me, until suddenly...the planchette moves.

My foot drops to the solid earth, the hair on the back of my neck standing up. My muscles clench, tension invading my limbs as the planchette tugs our fingers across the board to *yes*.

I meet Livia's gaze, wondering if this is enough for her, knowing deep down that it isn't.

"It's all right, Rachel," she soothes, her face alight with excitement. "We're perfectly safe."

Seeing her this way is the entire reason I agreed to this, and it helps mollify some of my unease. I make myself smile back and try again to relax.

But then she asks the next question.

"Are you a good spirit or bad?" She hasn't even finished before the planchette darts to the moon symbol, and my apprehension returns with force.

"Liv..."

"We're all right," she answers evenly.

"I really don't like this."

"I know." Her expression is sober. "Not much longer, I promise."

My hands are shaking, but I manage to keep them on the planchette.

"Why are you here?" she asks it.

The planchette spells out B-O-R-E-D.

Okay.

"Did you die here?"

B-O-R-E-D.

Livia shifts uncomfortably. "What is this place?"

B-O-R-E-D.

"What's your name?"

This time the letters are different.

S-T-O-P-B-O-R-I-N-G-M-E.

I let go. Livia looks up as I climb off the table and back away.

"Come on, we have to close the door."

I just shake my head, my arms covered in gooseflesh. A panicking, shuddering dread has sealed over me, and I can't stop shivering.

Livia stares at me. "It's going to take both of us, Rachel. Just put your hands on the planchette so we can go."

"I can't do that," I manage. It feels like if I touch it again, I'll cease to exist.

"Rachel—"

"Please, Liv," I whisper. "I can't touch it again. Don't ask me to."

For a moment, she just watches me, her eyes full of concern. "I guess I can do it alone," she decides with reluctance.

I hover nearby as she slides the window of the planchette over to the *goodbye*. Only once it's done am I able to take a slow, steadying breath.

Neither of us say much on the way back home. I want to feel relieved, and mostly I do, but knowing the Ouija board is resting on the back seat behind us makes me ill. I can't even look at it. I won't touch it again. This is the last time Livia will ever talk me into trying to contact something.

When I finally shut the door to the house, Livia turns to me. "I'm sure it's fine. We closed the door."

I don't know if she's trying to convince me or herself.

"I'm fine, Liv, really. I'm just..." I shake my head. "I'm never touching that thing again."

I don't hear her response, because at that moment, the sound of something scratching across the hallway on the second floor makes me look up.

"Probably the neighbor's cat again," Livia murmurs.

I start for the stairs, but the noise stops just as I reach the first step. I hesitate before calling up, "Titus?"

Nothing. Not a sound. The house sits empty.

When I glance back at Livia, she just shakes her head.

"Whatever," I say. "I'm beat. I'm going to bed." I can hear Livia starting up the stairs as I make my way to our bedroom.

July 14, 2020 – Morning

When I wake up, Livia is still asleep in her bed across from me. I sit up, my hand automatically reaching for the night-stand, only to find an empty space. With a yawn, I glance at the table, expecting to see my ring stand where I always keep my black band during the night.

The table is bare, except for lamp. My ring isn't there, and neither is the stand Livia gave me. I blink in confusion before throwing off the covers and standing in one fluid motion, meaning to look under the bed for it, but the shock of cold air in the room makes me stagger, and I sit down heavily.

"Liv?" I croak, wrapping myself in my blanket before checking under the bed more successfully. As I do, she groans and rolls over to face me.

"Whuh?" she mumbles.

"Have you seen my ring?"

Her eyes open, and she cranes her neck to look at my nightstand, where she knows as well as I it's supposed to be. "Mmmno."

I frown. Where could I have left it? I'll need coffee if I'm going to remember that. Still robed in my blanket, I stagger out to the kitchen to fix some.

I find the ring when I go to add the filter. It's nestled inside the coffee maker, the black band gleaming up at me. Nearly miss it entirely in my pre-coffee stupor. I slide it onto my finger where it belongs, then with a sense of unreality, I search the kitchen to see if the stand is somehow hidden nearby while the coffee filters into my mug. No ring stand in the kitchen.

Using the mug to warm my hands in the freezing house, and with my brain now awake, I return to the bedroom and sit down on my bed.

Something on the other side of the room catches my eye as I set the mug down on my nightstand. Underneath Livia's bed and opposite me is a familiar-looking box.

I snort. "You're fucking crazy, you know that?"

"You're the one who got up before you had to," Livia murmurs, a smile playing on her lips.

I shake my head, taking another sip to warm my throat. "I don't know how you can sleep with the board tucked under your bed like that. Especially after last night."

Livia moves so fast I almost spill my coffee. She's up, her eyes wide. "What?"

"You've got the Ouija board under your bed," I repeat, but she's already knelt and torn back the covers to see for herself.

Her blond hair cascades off her shoulders, obstructing my view. When she glances back at me in confusion, the spot is empty.

"There's nothing there."

Before I can answer, a scratching noise from the second floor makes us both look up. The definite sounds of little claws scrabbling against the hardwood make their way against the upstairs hallway.

"I've got it," I say.

"I'll come with you."

I take a deep breath and let it out. "No, you've got commissions to work on. The neighbor's cat probably came in through the flap on the back door again."

"There's not much up there," she points out. "It shouldn't take long."

Can't argue with that. We make quick work of it. The upstairs hallway is empty, the whole floor dark aside from the early sunlight streaming in through the window at the end of the hall. There isn't much on the second floor—just the bathroom, laundry, and a large closet. Not a lot of places for a striped, chonky ginger to hide, but by now I know the drill. I open the laundry room door to the immediate right while Livia goes down the hall, past the window, to check the bathroom.

"Home time, your majesty. C'mon. Your mom's proba-bly—" I stop as I switch the light on to reveal an empty room with absolutely no giant purring orange tomcat splayed out on top of our dryer.

"Is he in there?" Livia asks, coming to join me. She takes in the empty room. "Huh."

"Maybe he's found another way in and out of the house."

"I guess," she agrees. "Well, now that I'm up anyway, I should get to work."

July 16, 2020 – Afternoon

"Did you just turn the air conditioning off?"

I glance up from my phone, distracted from the recipe I'm reading on my bed, when Livia speaks. "What?"

"It's freezing in here, but the A/C isn't even on."

I take in the alarm on her face and cautiously set down my cell. "No. I haven't touched it."

She hesitates. "Rachel, I think maybe we didn't do it right." When I don't respond, she adds, "The goodbye, I mean."

I shudder. "Of course, we did. I watched you do it. I was there. We did it right."

"The house is always freezing. Stuff keeps going missing and turning up in random places. All the scratching sounds upstairs when there's nothing there, and…"

"And what?" I demand.

"You've been acting weird."

"I've been acting weird?" I can't believe what I'm hearing. "You want me to use the board again, but *I'm* acting weird."

Before she can respond, the scratching noise from the floor above starts again.

"I got him," I say, welcoming the interruption. I've left the bedroom before she has a chance to answer.

If I'm quick enough, maybe I'll finally see how else he's coming in the house. I cut down the hall and head for the stairs.

"Titus?" Do cats come when you call them? Not in my experience, but it's worth a try.

I'm about to start up when a soft *meow* from behind

brings me up short. I turn to find Titus sitting perched on the arm of our couch.

I let out a breath. "*There* you are! What happened? You get sick of the second floor?" His bright yellow eyes stare past me intently, but he doesn't protest when I pick him up. "Let's get you back to Frieda."

I set him against my shoulder and reach for the front door with my free hand when I hear the unmistakable creak of hinges from the door to the laundry room, followed by a quick and lurching *thump-thump, thump-thump,* as though something huge is coming down the staircase directly behind me.

I don't move. All my attention is on the way Titus's fur puffs up, nearly doubling him in size in my arms.

A heavy footstep lands on the wood floor, followed by another, then another. There's a slight pause, and now I can hear labored breathing. Titus begins to growl. I've never heard a cat growl like that before. The steps end within easy reach, and then the only sound is Titus's snarls.

My throat is bone-dry, making it hard to swallow. I wait for whatever it is to do something—grab me, maybe—but the seconds crawl by, and Titus keeps growling. My dread frays, then snaps. I whirl around.

The house stands empty. Titus quiets. I stare in disbelief until the cat makes an impatient noise, and I reluctantly turn back to the front door. The moment I have it open, he springs from my grasp and is off our porch, streaking for Frieda's house next door.

I stare after him in surprise, my arms still bent to hold a chubby cat-sized nothing, before the front door slams shut in my face. I'm shoved roughly into the door so quickly that if I hadn't already had my arms up, I wouldn't have had time to protect my face.

A shriek dies on my lips as something colder than ice sears me in the side. I hit the floor in a heap.

When I can move, I pull up my shirt to find three parallel slashes. They knit together before my eyes and fade into unblemished skin, as though it never happened.

July 17, 2020 – Afternoon

I don't tell Livia about being pushed, or the scratches. I know she'll just take it as another excuse to use the board, and I don't want to argue with her. Besides, there's something that feels so personal about those scratches in a way that's hard to describe, even to myself. It feels wrong to share their existence with anyone.

All the same, I catch Livia watching me a few times after the incident with Titus, as if she can just tell something's different. That's why I decide to take some time for myself by trying a new lasagna recipe I found recently. While Livia has her art studio, my skills are in the kitchen.

I round the staircase dividing the main floor in half and stop dead.

The kitchen's already occupied.

A figure stands in the center of the room, their back to me, towering over me and standing unnaturally erect, their head angled at the ceiling.

I blink once, twice. They're still there. I'm rooted to the spot, unable to speak as my breaths grow quick and shallow.

There's a person in our house.

I don't know how long it is before the figure begins to move. As I watch, the stiff spine bows in, the movement smooth, easy, deliberate. Like a marionette coming to life at the start of a performance.

The figure hunches lower and lower until their height is as petite as mine, almost halved what I first saw.

They sway for a moment, leaning slightly to their right, where I can't see. They're wearing a long skirt that swishes against the tile. There's a soft *thunk* sound before the figure turns to face me.

The chill coming from the kitchen makes the hairs on my arm stand up. It cools the hot, silent tears trailing down my cheeks, and only then do I realize I've been crying.

The old woman lowers her head as she turns to face me. She was staring directly where the scratching noises— that aren't from the cat—keep coming from. I hear that noise again as she moves, as though the sound comes from whatever she really uses for legs. Whatever's hidden by that floor-length skirt.

Her right arm is threaded through a single crutch. That's where the *thunk* sound comes from. The crutch should be familiar, but the texture along its surface is off. Instead of wood or metal, it looks more like it's held together with skin. When she moves her arm, the crutch seems more like it's attached to her than she's holding it.

My heart is beating so hard, it's a surprise it hasn't cracked my ribs. The heart is a muscle. Can't muscle break bone?

I shudder at the cold, still unable to move.

Her eyes are open unnaturally wide. I can feel her gaze on me, though it's hard to be sure she's seeing anything because there's something swimming in her eyes.

A filmy, translucent substance drizzles from her mouth, coating her lips a red befitting some predatory jungle bird.

"I'm lost," she says once she's faced me. "I wandered into the wrong house by mistake." Her voice is soothing, a blanket of calm over the unreality and the chill.

When I can't answer, she starts toward me. Her skirt swishes. The sound of unseen claws scratch the linoleum. The hideous crutch *thunks* after her like a deadweight. Like a prop.

"Can you lend an old crone a hand, my dear?" she goes on in a saccharine voice. "You and your partner were already so kind to me."

Swish! Scuttle-scratch-scratch! Thunk-thunk!

I want to back away, but my body refuses to cooperate. Everything aches with the need to do something as she gets closer. Even to say something.

She repeats herself, "I'm lost."

"You're lost," I say. The hidden scratches on my side throb.

"I wandered in by mistake."

"You wandered in by mistake."

She stops when her face is a foot from mine, lifts a hand, and presses a clammy palm over my racing heart. My skin crawls as my touch-aversion kicks in. My muscles clench with the need to draw back. It's oddly comforting, in a way, one familiar thing I can cling to.

"You're so afraid all the time." The old woman beams at me. "But you don't have to be afraid, just like I don't have to be bored."

I'm shaking. It's a mistake to look into her—no, *its*—eyes. Tendrils strain from the black substance, shifting it under the cornea. The sight of it makes my eyes sting.

She wraps her other arm around my shoulders, and the crutch that isn't a crutch trails limply down my throbbing side like an afterthought.

"I know you've been looking for me, Rachel." I'm powerless to stop her as she guides me back into the kitchen, to the very spot I found her standing. "It's all right, dear. You just weren't searching in the right place, but I'll show you just the spot."

Her lips pull back into a ghastly grin, revealing a mouthful of the horrible, translucent substance. Sickly yellowish, it trails down her chin to splatter on the floor.

The hand over my heart takes my chin and guides my gaze up to the kitchen ceiling. "*Look!*"

I see it now.

Standing out on the pale ceiling is a dark stain about

the size of a quarter. Shiny black, its surface appears to shift. It looks familiar. I watch, still frozen but somehow fascinated, before the ceiling releases the stain and it drops, landing silently on my forehead before splitting in two and running into my eyes.

I'm on the brink of collapse when Livia finds me. Her voice is muffled, like I'm hearing her from far away. I'm aware of her shaking me, but I can't see her. I can only look to the ceiling.

Without warning, I come back to myself, and my legs buckle. Livia cries out, doing her best to support my weight.

I'm shaking, my skin burning up. My hands grasp at empty air. I brush them against my eyes, but I can't remember why.

"You're feverish!" Livia says, hauling me toward our bedroom. It's an unpleasant few minutes for both of us. While my skin crawls from physical contact, Livia's touch-aversion makes her nauseous. Somehow, she makes it, hauling me to my bed.

It's only when I'm lying against the covers that she glances back toward the living room, as though realizing the couch would've been closer. Her shoulders slump.

I think she's asking me what happened when I black out.

It's well after midnight when I wake up. At least, I think I'm awake. A hint of moonlight is outlined around the shut curtains, the faintest glow in the otherwise pitch-black of the room. Soft breaths come from Livia's bed, and my eyes follow the sound. She's slumped across it in her day clothes. Livia hadn't planned to fall asleep, then, but I must've gotten better while I was out.

I think I'm better. I feel much better.

Livia doesn't stir when the mattress creaks under my weight. The poor dear. She must be exhausted.

I'm aware of standing up, and then between one blink and the next, I find myself in the laundry room. My thoughts are thick, like they have to travel through a swamp to reach me.

Why am I in the laundry room?

Because it's upstairs.

As soon as the thought occurs to me, I know it's the truth. I'm not afraid. Instead, I feel utterly calm. Serene, even. I stand with my gaze focused on the floor, elated by this new sense of tranquility.

"Rachel?"

I turn at Livia's shout of alarm from the bedroom.

I know I should answer, but I'm not ready for the peace to be interrupted yet. So instead, I stand and listen as she searches the main floor. It doesn't take long. She starts up the stairs. I know when she's spotted the light on because she races up the rest of the way.

Livia jerks to a stop in the doorway when she sees me

waiting for her. "Rachel! What the hell?"

I don't have an answer for that.

"What happened?" she insists.

"I got lost," I say. "I wandered in by mistake."

I watch the panic ease from her face, taking in that I'm on my feet again. "Are you hurt?"

For the first time, I realize I'm leaning heavily on the dryer, favoring my right leg. I straighten, distributing my weight evenly without effort.

"No."

She's already caught her breath, and she hesitates. "You're feeling better?"

"Yes. Much."

"Because I kept thinking I was going to have to bring you to the emergency room, over-packed hospitals be damned."

"Well, I'm better now," I say with a smile. "Better than ever. Nothing to worry about."

JULY 18, 2020 - AFTERNOON

It's as if I'm stuck in some permanent haze. At times, my thoughts feel like nothing more than whisps, brief gasps of an idea that are gone just as quick. My senses are similar—an indistinct blur, aware of nothing. Other times, the contrast sharpens in moments, and the world feels rich and crisp. Nothing escapes my notice. It's terrifying but exhilarating.

The normal in-between moments are harder to find.

One of them happens on a dreary Saturday afternoon.

I find myself in the laundry room above the kitchen. How strange. I have no more reason to go looking.

A scream from below jars me from this reverie.

I'm out the door and down the stairs in an instant. "Liv?"

There's a familiar whiff of fresh paint from Livia's studio. The cloudy day outside renders the room darker than usual, and it takes me a moment to spot her on the floor, pressed into the far corner. I start toward her, only to draw up short when I notice the Ouija board and the planchette scattered next to her.

"What did you do?" My voice is flat, at odds with Livia's shallow breaths. Her wide eyes lock onto me, and it's like she's only half aware that she's picking up the board with paint-stained hands and holding it in front of her chest like a shield.

"M-my paintings!" she chokes out.

Hovering by the doorway, I glance at the nearest one resting against a wall, and my breath catches.

The canvas is riddled with holes. My first thought is it looks like someone used it for target practice. There're more than two dozen tears. It's then that I realize the tearing is facing out, as though something small hatched out of it. Lots of somethings.

I turn to the next painting, and the next. All of them are pockmarked. I count eight—three hanging to decorate the room, another four against the wall, waiting to go to clients, and another on her easel, recently started. They are utterly destroyed.

"I came in," Livia manages, "t-to get some work done, and then they started bursting out of the paintings." She shudders. "Roaches."

I wait for the fear to come, but instead, there's nothing. I'm almost as terrified of bugs as Livia is, but all I feel is a vague disinterest as I survey the room. Livia's fine. Scared, but fine. The bugs are gone now. They must've found an open window.

"Liv, what are you doing with the board?"

She takes a long look at it before her eyes turn pleadingly back to me. "You were so sick last night. And then this...I stored it in here so you wouldn't be upset, but now..." She takes a steadying breath. "All we have to do is put our hands on the planchette over the goodbye—"

"No."

"I swear, it'll be..." She trails off, her eyes huge as her gaze shifts from me to something just past me. She swallows. "R-Rachel...I...I need you to come over to me. Carefully."

On some instinct, I take a step further into the room before my stomach squeezes so suddenly and so painfully that my legs give out.

"Rachel!"

"I c-can't," I choke out. My chest heaves, and something warm and slimy climbs up my throat, cutting off my air. I gurgle, nearly blacking out. Painful tears fill my eyes as I begin to choke. "Can't," I repeat, and then my body starts to convulse. My limbs are like ice. My heart thunders in my chest, saliva bubbles and dribbles down my chin, and I shake like I'm having a seizure.

I can't breathe. My eyes cloud over.

I'm dimly aware of Livia screaming. The sound is distorted, like I'm underwater.

"I did what you wanted! I put it away. Now, let go of her!"

I don't know how long it is before the convulsions stop, the blockage in my throat vanishing along with it. The cold air is painful against my raw throat as I gasp in a breath, but nothing compared to moments ago.

My wild eyes settle on Livia crouched next to me. Tears trail down her cheeks. Her earlier terror has returned with force.

"I'm sorry," she whispers. "I'm so sorry."

July 19, 2020 – Evening

I've never felt so minimal in my own body. I'm a speck, blotted out by something bigger and so much older. As inconsequential as a fly.

Awareness comes and goes. I know it's wearing my favorite shirt today. Not because it's trying to appease Livia. It's no longer hiding inside my head.

It wants to play house. If Livia goes for the board, it starts killing me.

I only catch moments, trapped like a fly on the wall of my own mind. Livia's remorse bores it, and there's a terrible moment where it grabs a knife out of the block. I rail against it, and it relents. Just like a fly, it seems I'm easier swatted but harder to get rid of.

We're on the couch for movie night. Livia's on her end, a blanket curled around her. She gets cold so easily whenever I'm around now. I keep to the opposite side.

The voice in my throat is scratchy and distorted. Its laugh is so suffocating I almost wish I could pass out.

"Are you so desperate so soon?" it sneers. "You think if I watch the right scene, the priest will say the right words, and this'll all be over?"

Livia's face flushes, though her grip on *The Exorcist* tightens. "I thought maybe it would entertain you." But the index finger of her free hand twists absently around strands of her blond hair.

I know her tells after four years together.

"It would. In fact, I'm already entertained. Well, go on," it says when she doesn't move. The TV lights up, making her jump, and it cackles.

Livia goes and sets the disk in the player with shaking hands. With her back turned, my eyes go to the nest of blankets on her side of the couch.

Livia sits and starts the movie, pointedly ignoring the amused way it watches her.

I'm only aware of fragments as the movie plays. On the screen, the characters are having a party, but I barely notice.

The moments I can tell what's happening around me are for checking on Livia. She keeps shifting, as though trying to get comfortable. It's not until the priest shows up in the movie that I realize she's inched over to my side of the couch.

"And here I thought you were touch-averse," it says abruptly, turning from the screen to stare coldly up at her.

Livia doesn't move other than to meet its gaze. "I miss her. You're keeping her from me. If I can't be with her our way, maybe this can still work." Swallowing, she offers her hand.

There's a horrible moment of stillness. The only sound is the TV in the background while it considers her.

"That's a good answer," it concedes, "and yet..." It flings the blanket aside to reveal the Ouija board nestled between us. In her other hand is the planchette.

The TV shuts off.

"Livia..." It sighs, and my dread is so immediate that it nearly takes me out. Crushed to the side as I am, there's no avoiding the raw, arctic chill of its fury. It overtakes everything, and some part of me knows that if I can't stave off the enveloping numbness, I'll never wake up again.

I push back, resisting with everything I have left. I don't care what happens to me, but I need to give Livia a chance to escape. It's the best I can do for her now. I fight, and I keep fighting it. I'm going to freeze here, trapped in my own mind.

It stands in one fluid motion, as though my limbs were made for it and not me. Livia scrambles back, and it heaves the board away.

And then suddenly, the cold is gone. In that same instant, it staggers, pitching to the side, with a hand on the couch for support. I'm dazed by the effort. I can't believe I've taken back control.

"Liv?" My voice comes out hollow after the distorted snarl my throat's used to. "Liv...I can't...It's too strong."

"Rachel!" Livia's on her feet.

"It's killing me." My voice is barely a whisper. "Liv, why did you make me do this?"

For a moment, I'm too shocked to think. It's my voice, without a doubt, but I'm not speaking.

"It's coming back!" it wails with my voice.

I hear Livia's scream right as it flings me into the glass coffee table. I'm lifted like a marionette, before I slam back into the shards, over and over again. Pain rips through me. My skin is sliced, my organs torn open.

It lets her stew in her panic before it hauls me back to my feet, nonchalantly plucking the shards of glass out of my skin. There's a gash on my forehead, and blood trails into my eye as I turn to face her. Her look of terror is warped through my bloody vision.

"Just kidding," it reveals, breaking into a wide grin. The wounds are already knitting together, as though they were never there.

It stops to examine my shirt—almost as ruined as the coffee table.

The wail of sirens makes it look up, followed by a thunder of footsteps. It turns just in time to glimpse Livia disappearing out the back door.

There's only time to clean up or go get her before the cops arrive. Not both. After a moment's reluctance, it retreats to our bedroom, already pulling off the soiled shirt.

April 9, 2016 – Four Years Ago

"They tend to disguise themselves as children."

"Why children?" I ask as one lumbers past our booth. In the warm glow of the pendant lamp, I'd nearly forgotten we weren't the only ones in the restaurant. "Even I know scary kids are cliché."

When Livia doesn't answer, I catch her studying my eyes.

I grin. If she's the one looking, I don't mind. "People always say my eyes make me look like a petite Alexandra Deddario."

"*That's* who I was thinking of!" Livia says. "Seriously, it was driving me nuts!"

"So, why kids?"

Livia's eyes are alight. I wouldn't dare interrupt her when she looks at me like that.

"It's about appearing as non-threatening as possible," she says. "Sometimes they'll present themselves as someone else, but you're right. We know what's up when a scary kid appears."

"You and your friends ever come across one using the board?" I ask.

Livia hesitates for the first time. "Once or twice, maybe."

"Really? It seems like you can't go looking for a story with a Ouija board without one showing up."

A server hurries past us with fresh garlic bread, distracting us both with the aroma. Livia watches wistfully as it disappears, and I make a mental note to bake it for her sometime. She sighs.

"We have at least one prankster in the group. You know, moving the planchette on purpose to mess with the rest of us. There was one time, though." The excitement is gone now, replaced with unease, and I'm sorry for it. "There's a girl, Marnie. I didn't know her well. She only showed up once or twice. The last time we saw her, we were using the board inside this abandoned old house. We stopped early because she freaked out. She kept insisting something had scratched her, but when we looked, there was nothing there."

I grimace at the thought. "I didn't know they scratch people."

Livia laughs. "You really don't know much about this stuff, do you?"

"Nope. I think I'm going to need you to tell me all about it." I match her smile with one of my own.

She lifts her wrist and traces her first three fingers down her inner forearm. "Three scratches. They like that number. That's how you know a demon's marked you."

JULY 19, 2020 – LATE EVENING

I'm jolted back to reality to find my hands still clutching *The Exorcist*.

There was never a ghost. It's something much worse.

I set the movie back on the TV stand. I've just managed to stand on shaking legs when a horrible scream from our bedroom nearly makes them give out.

"Livia?" I lurch around the broken table and stumble down the hallway.

An answering scream cuts off abruptly the moment I stagger into the room.

It's untouched. More importantly, Livia is nowhere to be found.

Another scream. This one comes from the second floor.

I don't move. Now I know why it's let me take control again. It must get boring when there's no one to mess with. Might explain the headache too. I sit down on the edge of my bed, trying to think. I shut my eyes tight and cover my ears as more wails fill the house.

It isn't Livia's blood on the coffee table. It's a small relief, but where is she? Is she safe? My fists clench. If I could just be sure of that much. But I can't be trusted. If I do find Livia, I'd only be bringing the demon straight to her, and I refuse to put her back in danger.

So, then what? The screams die off, and I wonder dimly if the neighbors can hear those too.

As long as I'm possessed, I can't get near Livia.

So, get rid of the demon. The answer comes to me so suddenly I almost laugh. Livia's already told me how.

If I never hid the board under my mattress, that means it's still in the living room.

That's my final thought before a dark nothingness engulfs my sight.

I finally understand why. First, it made me afraid of the board, then it made me sick, now this. It needs to keep me from the board so I can't close the door and banish it.

My hands reach blindly for familiar surfaces as I stagger back to the hallway. I've just made it out the door when a low growl stops me cold. I hesitate, but when there's nothing more, I reach out a hand for the nearest wall. My palm slides against the surface. A thick, slimy substance coats the wall, and I nearly slip to the floor. I think of the old woman and her viscus saliva and nearly throw up. I'm able to brush the worst of it off my hands as I reach the end of the hall.

The darkness covering my eyes shifts, tricking my brain into finding grotesque patterns. I do my best to ignore them.

I don't get far into the room before I'm forced onto my hands and knees in order to make my way around the couch without slicing my hands on broken glass.

Something large moving nearby sends my heart in my throat, and I freeze. Sulfur hangs thick in the air. I shudder. Something is in the house with me now, something moving, letting me know it's there and it's watching me.

I close the distance to the couch. My hands search it frantically for what feels like hours before I locate the box. Finally, I find its smooth surface and wrench it open.

But when I feel around the inside of the box, it's empty.

It's only then that I remember the demon throwing it. It could be anywhere now, and I'd never know.

I don't move. It's hard to tell, but it feels like there's more than one of those huge creatures in the house with me now. They shuffle around, making me aware of their presence, and I feel like I'm gonna choke on the stench of sulfur.

I'm out of options. With those things crowding in around me, I can't search the house blindly, hoping I find the Ouija board. I scramble back from the couch and loop back around the table to make for the exit.

I reach for where the front door is supposed to be, only to discover I'm in a completely different part of the house. In my panic, I'm lost without my sight. I struggle to my feet, just as the definite footsteps of something coming right for me sends me into a run.

I barely have a chance to move before I fall forward and land on the stairs. The pain from hitting them hardly registers because the thing is at my side. It seizes my hand, and I let out a scream. My hand is pressed onto something...I don't know what.

"Goodbye!" Livia shouts.

I'm frozen. Icy tears trail from my eyes, so cold I don't know how they don't freeze to my skin. The darkness over my vision slowly recedes. Thick, black tears slide down my face in a solid line, trailing down to stain the wood floor a hideous grayish brown. It stings with cold, and I shiver violently.

"Oh my god!" There's fresh panic in Livia's voice, and I

realize she thinks it's making me seize again. "It's not working?"

"No," I manage. "It's just...c-cold."

Finally, the last of the black substance trails off into the grotesque stain on the floor. I breathe in deeply as my vision clears.

The first thing I see is Livia's anxious gaze.

"Hey," I say, distracted again by that face.

Her laugh comes out as an exasperated bark. She takes the planchette from me and pushes the board aside.

"Hi."

HIDE AND SEEK

By Nu Yang

I was it.

The setting June sun beat down on me while I searched for my little brother in the cornfield behind our house. I swatted away the mosquitoes, slapping one on my bare arm, but not before it left me an itchy present. I turned into another row, scratching the red bump.

No Carter.

We had been playing hide and seek for about thirty minutes. Mom didn't like us going off into the cornfield by ourselves, but we had begged her to let us play there. It wasn't like we were little kids. I was twelve. Carter was eleven. We would be all right.

"Okay, but be back before it gets dark," she had told us, hanging Dad's Iowa Hawkeyes T-shirt on the clothesline to dry.

Now, it *was* getting dark, and I couldn't find my brother.

"Carter!" I stomped through the dirt, splattering mud on my pink sneakers. "Come out! I give up!"

Nothing but tall green stalks of corn moved. I pushed past another row until I made it to a small clearing. My stomach knotted, knowing what waited for me inside. I almost wanted to turn back around, but that was probably what Carter wanted me to do.

I walked further into the clearing, and my insides clenched. A moment ago, I was sweating like a pig. Now, I shivered in the shade cast by the large wooden cross. But it wasn't just the missing sun causing goosebumps on my arms.

Barry rested with his straw-filled arms stretched out into a T. He wore one of Dad's red flannel shirts, tattered after being outside for almost a year.

I remembered when Dad had brought him home the previous summer. Carter claimed him immediately, naming the scarecrow after an imaginary friend he had when he was little. When Barry was invisible, they used to play the meanest jokes on me, like locking me inside the basement and cutting my hair when I was asleep. I was glad when Carter grew out of Barry, but now his friend had come back to life in a new way.

Carter had glued black buttons for Barry's eyes and used a marker to draw dotted freckles on Barry's nose, then he drew Barry a creepy smile, complete with a front gap tooth. That smile always gave me the creeps.

I pushed down my fear, reminding myself Barry was just made of old clothes and straw. "Hey, Barry, have you seen Carter?" I fixed my ponytail, pulling my blond hair through the elastic band.

Barry kept smiling.

"Okay, fine. Take his side." I put my hands on my hips. "I know you saw him." I cupped my hands over my mouth and shouted again. "Carter! You better come out before we get in trouble!"

When I dropped my arms, something black darted toward my face. I jumped back as a large crow landed on Barry's left shoulder. The crow stared down at me, not even the least bit afraid of me or Barry.

I clutched my chest, waiting for my heartbeat to slow, and narrowed my eyes at the scarecrow. "You are totally fired."

Just as my breathing returned to normal, I heard giggling behind me. I turned to see a shadowy figure crouched down behind a wall of corn.

Gotcha.

I tip-toed to Carter. Before I made it to him, someone grabbed me from behind. I yelped and spun around.

Carter doubled-over in laughter. "Haha! Emily's a scaredy cat!"

"How did you..."

I looked back to the spot where I thought Carter had been hiding. The shadow was gone.

Carter circled around me. "Scaredy cat, scaredy cat."

I hit his arm. "Shut up!"

He ran into a row covered in green corn stalks. I chased him, focused on the back of his white T-shirt. I finally caught up with him as we both emerged from the cornfield.

I punched him in the arm again. Hard.

"Ow!" He rubbed the spot. "I'm telling Mom you hit me!"

I followed him past the red barn and into the yard, where Mom had been hanging laundry. She wasn't there. I looked past my purple bedsheets blowing in the wind. The air smelled like spring rain fabric softener. Our parents stood in the driveway next to Dad's blue pick-up truck.

"Dad's home," I said.

"Good. I'm telling both of them you hit me."

"Whatever." I gave him a small shove, and we ran to our parents.

As soon as we made it to them, Carter blurted out, "Emily hit me when we were playing hide and seek."

Dad frowned and put an arm around him. "Why would she do that?"

"Because he was being an annoying brat." I shot him a dirty look, and he stuck his tongue out at me.

"That's it," Mom said. "No more playing in the corn-field today."

"But Mom—" Carter and I both said.

She dismissed us with a wave of her hand. "Emily, help me with the groceries, will you?" She pulled open the door to the back of Dad's truck.

"Wait, Maddie." Dad stepped forward, but it was too late.

Mom shrieked as a head fell into her hands. The tan, round object was the size of a volleyball. The new scarecrow didn't have a face or clothes, but it was large and bulky, just like Barry.

"Cool," I said, peering into the back. "Where did you get this, Dad?"

Dad pulled the scarecrow out. It was as big as him, and my dad was almost six feet.

"I ran into Mr. Peterson at the store, and he said he had an extra one. All I had to do was pick it up from his place." He kissed Mom on the cheek. "Sorry, sweetie. Hope our new friend didn't scare you."

She crossed her arms. "Very funny, Jack."

I touched the scarecrow's arm. The fabric felt soft and strong underneath my fingertips. "Well, at least we know it works."

"See, Emily understands," Dad said.

"Does that mean we're getting rid of Barry?" Carter asked.

"Well, we kind of have to," Dad said. "Barry's getting old. He's going to have to retire."

I thought about Barry's torn flannel shirt and the faded marker on his face. Even the crows didn't seem to care for Barry anymore.

"When can we put up the new one?" I asked.

Mom ruffled her fingers through my hair. "Not until tomorrow, honey. Sun's going down."

"Mom's right." Dad wrapped his arms around the face-less, naked scarecrow. "Carter, wanna help me put him in the barn?"

"No." My brother pouted. "I hate that stupid thing."

Mom put her hands on her hips. "Watch your attitude, young man."

"But I don't want a new scarecrow."

"Didn't you hear Dad?" I said. "Barry's old and gross now."

Carter took a swing at me, but I ducked behind Mom. A small smile touched my lips. I was a little happy he was mad. Payback for scaring me in the cornfield earlier.

"Whoa." Dad dropped the scarecrow and wrapped an arm around Carter's waist, lifting him off the ground. Carter kicked his legs in protest. "Calm down, you hear me?"

My brother narrowed his eyes, but he stopped kicking.

"Can you say sorry to Emily?" Dad asked.

"No."

"Well, I'm not going to let you go until you say you are."

Carter remained silent.

"Fine, have it your way."

Dad kept one arm wrapped around Carter and used his other hand to grab the scarecrow. They headed to the barn together.

"What's gotten into your brother?" Mom asked with a frown.

I shrugged, but I knew he was mad about Dad getting rid of Barry—and I was glad.

The next morning, I spent time inside the barn with the new

scarecrow, sitting on the ground, surrounded by markers. I drew green eyes on the tan face, then used a black marker to create a smile. A nice, normal smile. I added a tongue sticking out of its mouth, then stood and smiled back at him.

"How's it going in here?" Mom entered the barn, carrying a black T-shirt. She looked down at my work and rubbed my back in approval. "Looks great, Em, and I think I found the perfect shirt for him. Your dad used to love these guys."

I held the scarecrow's arms up, and Mom slipped the shirt over his head.

"See?" she said. "It fits perfectly."

"And that kind of looks like him," I said, pointing at the yellow smiley face with X's for eyes and a squiggly smile with a tongue sticking out. I tilted my head, reading the words on Dad's shirt. "But, what's *Nirvana*?"

Before dinner, I returned to the cornfield, this time with Dad and the new scarecrow. My parents had grounded Carter for the rest of the week. He couldn't leave the house unless it was with one of them. Good, he deserved it for being a brat.

I watched as Dad took Barry down from his stand. He smelled like earthworms, and his face was smudged with dirt. White bird poop smeared the back of his shirt. The gray cloth making up his skin was so worn down we could see the straw inside. Once Barry was off the stand, I grabbed his legs and helped Dad move him to the ground.

"Any last words?" Dad asked.

I stared at the gap in Barry's smile. "Not really."

Dad might have considered this moment a retirement party for Barry, but I had already fired him yesterday.

He picked up Barry's replacement and hauled him to the cross. I pushed from the bottom up, and Dad draped the arms around the crossbeam. Once the scarecrow was secure, Dad dropped back to the ground. He placed his hands on his hips and looked up.

"Looks good," Dad said. "So, since Carter got to name Barry, why don't you give our new friend a name?"

I looked at Barry, lying on the ground in a gross pile of old straw and bird poop, then I looked up at the new scarecrow, with his clean T-shirt and freshly-made marker smile.

"Nirvana," I said, reading the bright yellow word.

Dad smiled. "Perfect."

We left Nirvana alone to get used to his new place and picked up Barry—Dad up front, and me in back. As soon as we got back to the barn, I couldn't wait to let go of Barry. He was wet and musty. I felt sort of guilty for taking him away from his home, but when I glanced at his tattered face and his gap-toothed smile, I thought, *Good riddance.*

After we dropped him off, I wiped my hands down the front of my jeans, but my palms still felt grimy. I probably had to wash my hands a hundred times to get rid of the feeling.

"I can smell your mom's pot roast from here," Dad said. "Come on. Let's go eat."

We headed back to the house, and I glanced up at

Carter's window on the second floor. He stared down at us, his lips in a straight line. I gave him a smug smile, and in response, he flashed me his middle finger.

My eyes widened, and I pulled Dad's arm. "Look at Carter."

He lifted his gaze to the window, but my brother was already gone.

When I came downstairs for breakfast the next day, Mom and Dad were arguing in the living room. Mom stood with her arms crossed, while Dad paced the floor.

"Who would want to take that thing?" she asked.

"Maybe it was a bunch of kids," Dad said.

"And why would they take it?"

"I don't know. To mess with us."

I frowned and continued into the kitchen, where Carter sat at the dining table, eating Cheerios.

I poured myself a bowl and asked, "What happened?"

"Someone took your new friend," he said in between mouthfuls of cereal and milk.

"Nirvana?" I used a stool to look out the window above the kitchen sink, and sure enough, there was an empty wooden cross in the middle of the cornfield.

"Do Mom and Dad know who took it?" I asked Carter.

He shrugged. "Dad thinks some kids took it as a prank."

He wasn't looking at me, probably happy Nirvana was gone.

Our parents entered the kitchen, and Dad went right to the phone on the wall.

"What are you going to do, Jack?" Mom said. "Tell the cops someone took our scarecrow for the fun of it?"

"I'm going to tell them someone came on to our property last night and stole something that belongs to us."

"Come on," Mom said. "Don't you think you're over-acting?" She touched Dad's shoulder. "Wait one more night. If whoever took the scarecrow doesn't return him, then go ahead, call the cops."

Dad sighed and placed the phone back on the receiver.

In the morning, a scarecrow had returned to the cornfield.

I shielded my eyes from the sun and stared up at Barry. Everything about him looked the same except for two things—he was wearing Dad's Nirvana T-shirt, and I swore he had a bigger smile on his face. Behind me, Dad kicked the dirt.

"Those damn kids. I swear, if I catch whoever is doing this, they're going to pay."

I stepped back with my hands folded in front of me.

He took in a deep breath. "I'm sorry, honey. I didn't mean to lose my temper."

I nodded. "It's okay."

"Can you help me take Barry down?" he asked.

"Sure."

Dad climbed up to the top to remove Barry's arms from

the stand, but he struggled to free the scarecrow. "It's like he doesn't want to come down."

Despite the morning heat, I shivered.

Dad took a pocketknife out from his back pocket and cut through Barry's arms until he dropped to the ground. We carried him back to the barn and placed him in a corner. This time, Dad covered him with a large fleece blanket.

"I don't want those kids to find him," he said.

"Do you think they'll come back?"

"Not if I stay up all night." Dad wrapped an arm around me, and we walked back to the house.

I couldn't help but look back at Barry underneath the blanket.

A loud thud woke me up in the middle of the night. The red numbers next to my bed said it was 2:36. I lay still and pulled the covers up to my chin. At my age, I didn't believe in the Boogeyman, but for a second, I imagined Barry would jump out of my closet at any moment.

Squinting in the pale moonlight streaming in through the window, I scanned my dark room. I heard the thud again and gasped.

Outside my window, a big black crow jumped around on the roof. Had it flown into the glass by mistake? I crept out of bed, wrapping my blanket around my pajama shorts and T-shirt. My feet touched the cool wooden floor.

I peeked outside my window just in time to see the crow

spread its wings and disappear into the night. As I watched it go, I noticed a large figure hanging from the cross in the middle of the cornfield. The kids had either returned with Nirvana, or Barry was back on the stand.

I hurried to tell Dad, but before I made it to the door, another loud thud came from the window. Expecting to see another bird, I slowly turned.

But it wasn't.

It was Nirvana's head.

Just his head.

He smiled back at me, his tongue sticking out like a dog happy to see its master. I dropped my blanket and ran to my parents' room.

"Dad, wake up! The kids are outside!"

But as I pushed their door open, I found an empty bed filled with tangled sheets and pillows. Mom's purse still sat on the nightstand. I looked out their window and saw Dad's pick-up truck still parked out front.

Then, I saw the light from the barn.

I raced into Carter's bedroom. He was still sleeping, so I shook him until he woke up.

"What is it?" he asked, rubbing his eyes.

"Mom and Dad are gone. I think they went after the kids who took Nirvana." I left out the part about his head sitting on the roof.

Carter's eyes widened. "We need to check on Barry!" He slipped into his sneakers and threw on a jacket before running out of his room.

"Wait, Carter." I hurried after him. "We need to stay inside. Mom and Dad might—"

We stopped at the top of the stairs when we heard glass shatter down below.

I motioned for Carter to be quiet and looked over the banister. A large, shadowy figure appeared in the living room. I couldn't see the person's face, but I recognized the smell of earthworms and dirt.

Barry.

My stomach dropped, and I grabbed Carter's arm, pulling him into our parents' room and shutting the door behind us.

"Someone's in the house," I whispered.

Carter pulled away from me. "What if it's Mom or Dad?" He turned the door knob, but I moved in front of him.

"It's not them." I grabbed my brother again and opened the window. It was probably only a couple feet from the roof to the ground. "We have to jump."

"No way."

"Listen to me. We have to go find Mom and Dad." I pushed him toward the window.

He climbed out and stood on the roof to wait for me.

The stairs creaked from the other side of the bedroom door.

"Hurry!" Carter reached out for me, but I turned away. "Where are you going?"

I grabbed Mom's purse and rummaged inside. Lipstick.

Her planner. Her wallet. Hand lotion. Finally, I found the cell phone. Since I was only wearing my pajamas, I handed the phone to Carter. "Here, put it in your pocket."

He placed it inside his jacket.

The door knob clicked open as Barry—or whoever was in the house—made it to the bedroom. Carter and I didn't wait to see who it was. We rushed to the edge of the roof and jumped down to the grass. My bare feet slipped on the early morning dew, and I groaned as the pain shot up by back.

Carter helped me up. "Come on, Emily!"

We rushed past the house, and I turned to see what had caused the crash downstairs. Nirvana's naked bottom half was sticking out of the living room window.

I looked around the quiet, dark land. The cornfield looked like a massive black wall, but the light was still on in the barn. Maybe Mom and Dad were there.

I limped in that direction with Carter right behind me. We rolled the wooden door to the side. Inside, the dangling bulb created a dim yellow light, revealing Dad's farming equipment, tools, and John Deere tractor.

"Mom? Dad?" I whispered as loud as I could. "Are you in here?"

We walked further inside until we came across a figure sitting up against a wall, covered in the fleece blanket Dad and I had put over Barry. But I didn't smell earthworms and dirt.

I held my breath as I pulled the blanket back.

Mom stared at us with blank eyes. She wore a pale blue

nightgown, and her hands were folded on her lap. Bruises covered her neck. I reached out to touch her, but Carter grabbed my arm.

"Don't," he said.

I pulled myself free. Even though there was nothing behind Mom's blue eyes, I had to make sure. When I touched her cheek, her skin felt icy cold. I covered my mouth to stop my screams.

"No!" Carter burst into tears and fell to his knees beside her. "Mom? Mom! Wake up!" He shook her body, but there was no response.

Something sour started to come up my throat. I turned away, swallowed, and squeezed my eyes shut. This had to be a bad dream. Just a dream. But when I opened my eyes, I saw the shadowy man making his way to the barn.

"Carter, we have to go!"

He was still sobbing next to Mom.

"Let's go!"

I grabbed the closest tool from Dad's table. A pitchfork with a handle the size of my arm. My back still throbbed with pain, so I could only limp along with Carter as we ran out of the barn.

The man charged toward us. The only way out was the cornfield.

We vanished into the field, corn stalks slapping my face and gravel digging into the bottom of my feet. Carter zoomed out in front of me, but I couldn't keep up, not with my limp.

"Carter, wait!"

I paused as jolts of pain shot up my spine, like someone was pushing needles inside me. Hoping it would help, I rubbed my lower back, but when I lifted my head, he was gone.

"Carter!" I didn't want the shadow man to find me, so I called out my brother's name in a loud whisper. "Carter, where are you?"

I held the pitchfork close to my chest, ready for anything. My teeth chattered, and the hair on my arms stood. I wished I had taken a jacket and shoes with me.

Each step I took, my mom's empty expression flashed in my mind. Just a couple hours ago, she had tucked me into bed, kissed my forehead, and wished me sweet dreams. Now, she was dead. I wiped away my tears and continued to look for Carter in between the rows.

I called out his name again. Instead of Carter's voice, a loud grunt responded. The shadowy man was making his way to me. Turning back around, I screamed and ran as fast as I could, even though my body still hurt. Breathless, I stopped in the small clearing in the middle of the field. Tears fell down my cheeks, and snot dripped from my nose. Even though I held a pitchfork, I still trembled.

Scaredy cat, scaredy cat...

I dropped my weapon and held my head in between my hands to block out Carter's taunts. Walking backward, I hit the bottom of the wooden cross. I looked up and screamed.

Dad hung from the stand, wearing jeans and a red

flannel shirt, his arms outstretched into a T with his wrists bound to the wooden beam with rope. His eyes were closed, and when I grabbed his legs to shake him, he didn't open them.

"No...no..." I grabbed my head again. "This can't be happening. Please, this can't be happening."

The corn stalks parted in front of me, and the shadow stepped into the moonlight.

It *was* Barry, and he was alive.

The black Nirvana T-shirt covered his chest. Straw still stuffed his gray cloth skin, but he now had a muscular form like a bodybuilder. Even though his dark eyes narrowed at me, his creepy smile was still plastered on his face.

I picked up the pitchfork and swung it at him. "Get away from me!"

I stabbed the weapon into his stomach. The sharp edges slid into hard muscles like a knife into butter, but as I pulled the pitchfork out, Barry showed no reaction.

He towered over me. With an open palm, he swatted my weapon away and grabbed me by my neck with both hands. My feet left the ground, and warm pee trickled down my legs. I thought about Mom's bruises.

Is this how Barry had killed her?

I gasped for air and hit him with my small fists. It didn't do anything. He only squeezed harder. Back spots danced in front of me.

"Let her go, Barry." Carter appeared in the clearing, holding the pitchfork.

I waved my hands, telling him to run for help, but he stayed put.

"Let her go, Barry," Carter said again. "The joke's over." His voice sounded off, cold.

This time, the scarecrow listened and dropped me to the ground. I coughed and gasped for air. As I rubbed my sore neck, I stared at Carter, but he kept his attention on Barry. There was Dad, pinned to the cross, not breathing, and Barry, who had been seconds away from killing me—and Carter wasn't freaking out about any of it.

I looked from Barry to Carter.

"What joke?" My voice was raspy from having my windpipes nearly crushed. "Are Mom and Dad really—"

"Dead? Yes, they are." He said it with no emotion at all.

I realized the tears he shed for Mom earlier had all been an act.

"Did you do all of this?" I asked, crying.

Carter moved to Barry's side. "*We* did."

I stared at him. How could this be my little brother?

"You guys made me!" He pointed to Dad. "He brought home a new scarecrow. I hated Nirvana. What a stupid name. Barry is *my* friend, and I didn't want to get rid of him." Carter looked up at Barry's menacing face. "And Barry didn't like the idea of being replaced either."

I thought about Nirvana's ripped-up body back at the house. Now I knew who had taken him down from his post and why.

Carter sniffed the air. "Did you piss yourself?" When I

didn't answer, he cackled. "Scaredy cat, scaredy cat, Emily's a scaredy cat..."

"Please, Carter, you have to stop this!"

He handed Barry the pitchfork. "It will stop, but first, I want to play hide and seek."

"No..." I shook my head, tears running down my face.

"Come on," he said. "I'll be it first. That's fair, right?" He covered his eyes and turned around. "One, two, three, four..."

I didn't wait for five. I limped out of the clearing, desperate to find a way out of the cornfield. Instead, I found myself deeper in between the tall stalks. Each one slapped my face like a slimy fish out of water. Dirt rubbed in between my toes. I turned a corner and tripped over a rock, landing flat on my stomach. I hissed when I saw my bloody knees.

If only I hadn't given Carter the phone. I looked up into the black sky. "Help! Somebody help me!"

A black crow squawked above me and flew to the left. Maybe it was the same one who had come to my window. I hobbled on my legs, moving as fast as I could, hoping the bird would lead me to safety. But then, the crow descended—landing right on Barry's shoulder. He stood only a few feet away from me, still holding the pitchfork.

Still smiling.

When I tried to scream, my voice was gone. I stumbled back, colliding with another body.

"Tag," Carter said in my ear. "You're it."

THE END

HARROW HEARTS

BY HENRY BEN EDOM

T he baby wrestles in Serena's gut, and she presses her palm against her stomach, already the size of a football. "Okay now, I hear you." She sits down on the corner of the motel room's double bed. *O'Christ, goddamn.*

Serena tries to lie down on the bed, but her back is mangled from several hours of driving. She grins, huffs, and pushes herself back up onto the bedside.

William sits by the TV desk with his laptop. "Qliphot, Klifot...," he mumbles. "How do they say that?"

"I don't fucking know and don't care right now," Serena gasps. "I'm done with these trips." She lies down again and tries to see if lounging sideways is better. *It is.* The pressure of sitting eight hours in the car relieves immediately. She gasps from the pleasure of it and closes her eyes for a second.

William turns toward her, and they look at each other. He stands up and comes to sit by her side, tapping his lap with his hands.

"Yes, please." Serena smiles and moves her legs to his hands.

William starts to work his way up from her ankles, massaging her shins and up to her knees. Then, he returns back down. "There's so many variations of that single word alone. Let alone the doctrine. The Jewish history, Kabbalah, Jacob Frank, and then all this modern stuff...Crowley, Grant," he memorizes the wealth of material he's been researching for the upcoming episode of their paranormal series.

"Can't we just say they're trying to open the gates of Hell?" Serena asks. "Because honestly, they wanna dive deep. And we're wanting to find out what they're gonna do about it. It's quite far from academias and, you know, dogmas. Opening Hell's gates is sexy."

"Huh, yeah." William laughs a little. "I really think we're onto something. Just think about it already, that black figure in the photo and that whisper you heard."

"Please! Don't wanna remember that."

William pulls his phone out of his pocket and opens the selfie he took. They stood together by a little meadow, about mid-drive here. They had stopped for a leak.

Cropped from about their shoulder lines, they stand in the lower left corner and smile to the camera. The meadow behind them opens toward the treeline, its waist-high grass filling most of the middle until the shady population of spruces in the upper fourth.

There, nothing at first glance.

One gap between the tree trunks stands blacker than the others, with the darkness cutting across the trunks like a pair of arms.

They might have hit the jackpot for real.

William zooms the photo back and forth. "This is real. I mean, seriously, depending on what else we get, there's so many possibilities for the episode. We could go for the fact-based thing, like a lot of history, and fill it up with this stuff, or just blaze the trail like crazy into the dark, like as our own account too."

"I definitely hope for the fact-based stuff. I'm done with getting my heart rates running." She looks down at her stomach, and the baby kicks her again.

William rests the phone on the bed and continues to massage her legs. "As long as the views are gonna rocket, I'm fine. He's gonna have to eat."

"Who said it's *he*?" Serena laughs and slaps William's shoulder gently.

The phone beeps. William opens the message and stops to stare at the screen with wide eyes. He double taps it and zooms onto something. His mouth opens, but he doesn't say a thing.

"What is it?" Serena pushes herself into a half-sitting position.

William gives her the phone. A photo is opened on full screen and zoomed to the max. A brown, pixelated mass has something dark and dirty showing from it. Serena zooms out a little. It is a pit, dug into the earth. As she continues to zoom out, greenery comes out from the sides. Then, something gray.

A headstone...It is an open grave.

Violated. Serena gasps, realizing the exhumed remains in the center. The text says: *Preparing. Tomorrow.*

"It seems we're going straight into the dark," William finally speaks out.

What did you expect? We knew they were serious. Serena stares at the dark ceiling and recounts their argument. It lasted until they lay down in bed, and William went to sleep with his back turned to her.

He or she or they are fucking grave robbers. She should report this right now. But what a mess that would make. The trip would be ruined. The possibly sensational rise of the channel they really needed.

Are we safe? She stares at the camera bag lying by a main door. Who would harm the media? We're allies. They want to be heard, and they trust us.

She will report this. After the episode. After they'd read the legislations, understood everything exactly, and secured their footage. After all, nobody was going to get hurt, at least for now. As disgusting as this is, it is still far from an assault or murder.

Bright headlights sweep across the ceiling, coming through the blinders, as a truck rams past the motel. Serena closes her eyes until she hears quiet gasps coming through the wall. Then, a cry that blows her half-shut eyes wide awake again.

She raises her head from the pillow. The rhythmic moaning of a woman continues, coming from some of the neighboring rooms. Serena lets her head fall back down and shuts her eyes. Somebody, somewhere near, is having a far better Friday night than theirs have been in a long time. Before she falls asleep, she doesn't worry about the fact she hasn't heard or seen anyone else in the motel during the whole evening. People come and go quietly when it comes to casual sex.

Sometime later, she feels a soft touch. The fingertips glide up past her knee, moving slowly across her inner thigh. She keeps her eyes closed and takes a deep breath.

William's warm breath passes by her cheek. Coming from so close, she knows he's watching, waiting to see her first gasp as his fingers approach her genitals and touch her through her undies.

She presses against the sheets. His fingers go around her pelvis in a wide circle and return back down, this time with added pressure. Her hips tighten, and she raises her head up from the pillow. The brushes continue, now staying about her clitoris, and a single moan escapes her lips. She opens her thighs and reaches toward William. Serena tries to kiss him, but William evades. Plays with her. She opens her eyes a little. The last stroke burns her.

William? She snaps up, lightning struck, and struggles to escape the empty bedside.

The room is quiet. A narrow ray of light hits the floor by a bathroom door at the room's other end. Serena stands up, shaking, and approaches the slightly ajar doorway, shielding herself with her tightly wound arms. She stops by the door and sees movement through a narrow split.

William stands there with his back toward the door. His head tilts a little to the side, and he focuses on something on his front. She reaches to open the door but realizes steady throbbing sounds are coming from inside. William works his front with his left hand.

She turns away and returns to bed, ramming it in protest. The throbbing sound stops. William knows that she knows. That is enough for her for now.

Serena wakes up when William comes in, holding a paper bag and two large take-away coffees on a carton tray. "You were out already?"

"Yeah, got us breakfast." He rests the paper bag and coffees on the desk and fetches his laptop.

Serena stands up and walks to the desk. "Donuts. Seriously?"

"The best I came up with. We're in the middle of nowhere," William huffs. "The manager wasn't up for much help either."

Serena shrugs, takes two donuts, and places them on a napkin. "How did you come up with that...guy, I assume?"

"Richard knows him from somewhere." William sits down by the desk and begins to open the files on his laptop. "He passed the message."

"Quite friends he has…" Serena sighs and takes a sip of her coffee. "Holy shit." She looks into the cup and grins.

William gives her the lazy look that usually means she should let up a little. "Like I said, the best I came up with. By the way, I think we're gonna find out soon where we're heading."

"You don't know yet?" Serena frowns. They're trusting their success on this illegal secrecy?

"The only time we talked on the phone, the guy just told us to be here today. He will tell us soon what's gonna happen."

"Well, that's nice." Serena's tone doesn't let her sarcasm go unnoticed. She reaches the blinds and opens the view to the parking lot and the woods behind the overgrown thickets of the roadside.

"Richard knows the guy. Why would he take us in if he didn't trust us or want us to?"

Serena looks beyond the thickets, messy enough to keep any living soul from entering the woods. "Yeah, guess you're right."

They work past the midday, lying on the bed, writing speeches and looking at their online sources. Traditions of sorcery, dark magic, numerous works growing into various directions from the same concepts and turning into a many-headed, sorcerous hydra they see vanishing farther into the darkness. William scratches his head.

"We're completely dependent on the guy giving us some very real stuff. I mean, it's all about opening the gateways of

Hell for…whatever reason they have."

Serena ponders this for a moment. "Maybe that is the story. People trying to descend down under. What is it to them and for what reasons? I just…" She pauses to consider. "I really don't think we're gonna find any relevance in understanding this as a whole. The real meat is the people. Their mission."

William nods a few times but keeps his silence. Then, he gives her a sudden smile. "Glad to have your producer brains back in the game."

"Hey! You're damn lucky for not having to go through *this*." She rubs her stomach.

William reaches to her, gives her a kiss, and brushes her stomach with his hand. "Glad to have you with me."

The baby kicks thrice. The little rest Serena had been given seems to be over. Then, William's phone beeps again. He taps the message open and reads it.

"We have the address for the night."

"Finally. Tonight, or *the* night?"

"The night…" William sighs. "Satanists."

They spend the afternoon finding a place to eat and getting some food supplies and spare batteries for flashlights. Then, they reserve the room for another evening, realizing the stupidity of the initial plan to drive home at night.

After taking an hour-long nap, William loads their essentials into the trunk of their red SUV and checks the camera, batteries, and flashlights for the last time. "Ready to go?" He bangs the car's rear shut.

Standing a little aside, Serena stares into the darkening woods. The treetops stand black, like spears in offense against the red sky.

"Everything okay?" William comes to her side.

"Just troubled." Serena gives him a brief look and presses her head against his shoulder.

"We'll back away the second anything goes wrong, okay?" William reaches his arm around her and gives her hair a stroke. "Love you, babe."

"Love you too."

They kiss before entering the car.

The contrast between the woods and their headlights increases for the whole forty-minute trip. Upon reaching the destination, they park by the dark roadside, the address but a little gravel drive separating from the main road.

They exit the car to have a closer look at a rusted barricade blocking the road from vehicles—"private property" in black letters on a yellow, flaked paint.

"Yeah, right." Serena sighs, looking at the road's leaf-laden shapes and branch-eaten space snaking into the woods beyond the barricade.

William unloads their stuff from the trunk. He hangs the Canon by its strap around his neck and places extra batteries into his pockets. Then, he turns on both of their black, sturdy flashlights, giving the other one to Serena. Pulling his phone out from his pocket, William reads the message he received during the drive. "Yep, this is it."

As they lock the car, an absolute darkness falls upon them at the death of the SUV's headlights.

Serena aims her flashlight at the trail that seems to suck the power out of the light. "God, should I like this?"

"I suppose it's not too far. We got this."

They circle the barricade and enter the trail. As they walk, Serena looks into the darkness on her side, outside the immediate halo of light. That void in the photo wasn't far from this. Could she even realize the difference, if they were the same? Serena shivers and takes a side step, making sure she walks the exact middle of the trail. The baby kicks twice, sounding suddenly like knocks on a door within herself. For a moment, it seems they are walking to a dead-end, but then the trail takes a tight left turn.

They arrive at the upper end of cracked concrete stairs leading down a hillside for at least ten yards. Misplaced and separated from the surrounding forest, the naked stairs seem robbed from skeletal remains of some other place and time. But that's how the ruined foundations always looked to Serena—brutal hints of gone presences among the landscape.

"Watch out," William says, reaching his hand to Serena as they descend.

At the bottom, the trail continues only a little further, and red-bricked formations begin to shape into their sweeping halos from beyond the boughs. They see at least two floors and numerous small windows with black iron frames coming visible from the dark, with bright reflections flashing back at them from the glasses that seems largely whole. Black ridges grow pointed into the darkness beyond the reach of their lights. They approach the building from behind, the trail escorting them to a gaping stairway leading to the level below the ground.

"Okay…I'm not going in there." Serena points her light into the cellar, seeing but a coarse concrete floor below.

"This is the place." William looks around. "Hello?"

"Shush, God!" Serena hisses from between her teeth.

"Hey, we're supposed to meet the guy here. Don't get too hyped yet. Hello!" William calls out even louder.

A crack echoes from the cellar, and they both turn their lights toward the stairs. A black shape appears at the bottom and looks up at them. A man in a dark hoodie, a ski mask covering his face, stares straight into their lights.

"It's almost the time. Come."

"Stay cool," William whispers through tightened lips, popping off the lens cover of his camera and turning it on to a video mode.

They walk down to the man, who immediately starts to pass further in. William and Serena follow him across two empty rooms, where the darkness escapes their lights only at a direct hit and creeps back the moment they turn aside. Damp, moldy smells increase at every step, and in the third room—a large main space with rooms growing out of it—the smell is horrendous. Something completely other than mold and damp.

At first, a concrete pillar hides the center of the space

from the doorway. But as they step further in, they see a strange pile assembled in the middle. Brown, dirty, blackened fabrics and dry heaps among them. Two sockets and a line of teeth. Muscular, shriveled forms attaching into bones, partially wreathed in torn, dry pieces of skin and clothing, all gone past the embrace of the grave.

"Oh God." Serena gasps.

William's breath is now audibly shallow. Rapid. He focuses on the screen on the back of his camera. A little red dot blinks in the corner. He is filming.

The man walks to the center, reaches his hand toward the remains, and grasps a handle pointing from it. He pulls, and the handle grows into a machete emerging out of the pile. Keeping the blade on his side, he begins to circle the pile, uninterested about their presence in the room.

"Open wide, O' Gates of Hell!" he shouts, thrusting the blade toward the other end of the space. "Zazaz, zazaz!" he spits out repeatedly. "Zazaz, zazaz." His voice turns into a guttural, feverish bark that leaps along with his blade, piercing the air in all four cardinal directions around the sickening pile. His militant pacing is now but a bewildered dance. "Turn them off!" he shouts, pointing the blade toward them.

"What?" William startles from behind the screen and looks at him from the side of the camera. "Camera?"

"Lights off!" the man yells again.

Serena looks at William, then behind them. They could make it. Four steps toward the wall, then straight from the doorway.

"Off! Now!" The man rushes at them, his blade raised in manic defiance.

They turn the flashlights off. Now that the light shows no space nor distance, Serena feels the sickening thickness licking her skin. She gags. Her skin crawls. Revulsion leaks over the boundaries of her senses and attacks her body through her nerves.

The man's breath roars in the dark. His steps back away, and everything is silent for a moment. Serena's pulse pounds in her ears, and strangling sensations build in her throat. She must move. Now. Serena slides her feet across the floor behind her. She reaches toward William, grasps his sleeve, and pulls.

William doesn't move. He hushes at her, but she pulls again, harder. They have to leave. William pulls back.

"I'll stay," he hisses.

The darkness is quiet, a thick, brooding presence without a form. Serena steps back, slides her feet across the concrete, sweep after sweep. A rough wall stops her. She follows it to her right, sensing it with her arm until the crude door pane. She turns to it and walks, keeping her hands ahead of her. She looks back without stopping. William's little screen light is but a ghostly spot far in the dark.

On the outside, the little wind gives an immediate sense of distance. Treetops wave above, and the ground is steady below. She can breathe. Serena turns on her flashlight and starts to run.

After the uphill stairs, she can see her lights reflecting

from the surface of their SUV beyond the trees. She keeps running all the way until she slams against the car, gasping for air. Serena pulls the passenger side door handle with both hands.

Locked, the door rumbles without opening. She yells and grasps it even tighter, pulling again in vain. Serena reaches for her phone and taps it with her shaking hands, barely managing to open the locked screen while gasping for crisp, open air. She calls William. The line beeps once. Twice. It shuts. She calls again, quakes on her trembling knees and crumbles down by the car, crying.

The call goes straight to voicemail.

After some time, Serena sees light in the woods. Bright white light approaches her slowly along the trail, and she cannot see anything but a black figure behind the light.

"William?" Serena shields her face with her hands.

The car lights flash, and the locked doors snap open. William walks past her and opens the trunk.

She stands up and walks to him. Slaps him, yells, and pounds her fists against his chest.

William stands tall, receives the blows without a word. When Serena stops, he turns his back to her, packs the camera, and slams the trunk shut. Then, he walks to the car's side and sits behind the wheel.

Serena stays behind the car for a moment, shivering. Then, she follows and sits on the passenger side, still trembling out of hate, fear, and relief she cannot tell apart. The engine begins to roar, and William steers the car around. Dark woods begin to sweep in their headlights. They drive back to the motel in silence, neither of them saying a single word along the road.

Instead of working in the shared space downstairs, William spends the following two weeks shut inside his upstairs "studio," which he had now set up in the spare guest room. Every night, Serena comes in to tell him goodnight, or otherwise visit the room. She sees stopped frames of blur, still darkness opening in the size of two full monitor screens. William tells her he has to work, asks her to shut the door upon exiting. Every time she leaves, she hears that man beginning to yell behind the door, repeating those sickening litanies that echo through the upstairs hallway.

William's bedside remains cold and untouched for most of the nights. In the daytime, Serena eats alone. The morning nausea she'd been lacking for the whole pregnancy has now begun. Each morning, she vomits for the first two hours, and usually, the nausea relieves only long after midday.

On a Sunday morning, Serena's phone rings on the dining table. She's eating her breakfast downstairs and looks at the phone, not recognizing the number. "Serena. Hello?"

"Hi, it's Richard. William's..."

"Oh, yeah, hi." She looks up at the spot in the ceiling

corresponding to where William supposedly works upstairs. "Umm...what can I do for you?"

"Just called in to...First, congratulations for the new episode."

"Oh, thanks. Um..." She swallows the last bits of bread in her gums. "William shown you some footage?"

"Well, yeah. I mean, it's going viral."

"Ah, okay..." She looks up again. What does he mean about going viral? "Why didn't you call him, by the way?"

"That's the...problem. I...haven't heard from him in a while. Just wanted to make sure, you know, that everything is fine. I mean—"

Serena sighs. "To be honest. Quite the date you hooked us with."

"What you mean?"

"That sick dude he filmed. You passed the message, right?"

"No, I...never passed anything. Just mentioned to him once that there was this guy online, talking about the stuff he looked for. But that's, like, what, three months ago?" Richard's voice staggers, and he rasps his throat. "Haven't heard of him since, to be honest. I'm sorry."

"Umm, hey...thanks for—" Serena's stomach twists. "I need to go."

"Hey, could you—"

Serena hangs up and rushes to reach over the kitchen sink, vomiting with the full force of her upper body. After three rounds of puking, Serena sits down by the table again and scratches its top with her fingers. She takes her phone and opens their channel. There is a new upload—"The Descent to Hell."

"God." She sighs and swallows a bitter lump from her throat while looking at the video information. That's the title he really came up with? Uploaded last night, duration 13:54, 23k views. "What a—?" In six hours. *Holy shit*. She taps the play icon and opens the video on full screen.

It begins at the first screams. "Zazaz, zazaz." The masked man circles around the pile of desecrated remains in their bright spotlights. There are no cuts or effects. Editing seems non-existent. She taps the time line forward.

Both camera and lights shake.

"Off! Now!"

The image goes dark. This is when she began to move away, with William's, "I'll stay," audible on the soundtrack. He really left that there?

The image remains dark, its black static cracking. The soundtrack is but humming and distant scratches. She turns the volume up and hears gasps and hissing, indecipherable litanies in the booming silence. Then, dragging sounds of the masked man moving in the distance. William moves too, and the litanies increase in volume. The light turns back on. The camera hovers over the desecrated remains in a sharp spotlight. Gets closer. Glides across the disgusting vistas in horrible, continuous close-ups. The man's hands dig into the pile, and the remains turn and move as he handles them with bare hands. He grabs a brown limb, an arm that is still partially gowned in torn, dirty shrouds.

The camera gets closer. The man raises the arm to his lips and rips a sinewy strip out of it with his teeth in a painful close-up, his half-outed eyes blazing from the mask's holes like scattered bonfires.

Serena looks aside and covers her mouth. She almost turns it off but sees the light turning its angle suddenly, and the flashlight is placed on the floor. William's hand stretches out from behind the camera and digs into the remains. The camera's focus rolls in and out, blurring the motion for a moment. Then, it settles, showing all too well his hand ripping and clawing dry pieces out of the flesh and raising them behind the camera.

Tears compress into Serena's eyes as she hears the chewing of two mouths eating. The camera falls down, hanging loose by its strap. The man stands up and steps closer in blur motion. Serena hears clanging sounds, like belts opening. The camera glides from side to side along with heavy breathing and fabrics rustling. The image drops almost to the floor level and focuses into dusty nothingness outside the sphere of light. The image begins to swing. Back and forth toward the blurred wall, with gasps and painful groans following the motion.

Serena cries, gasps, and tastes blood bleeding from her bitten tongue.

The rocking motion, the wall going in and out of focus, groaning and dry thudding, continues for minutes. Serena cannot but look through her tear-shed eyes until the motion stops. Focus returns, and the camera turns around, still loose on a strap. Gasping, painful breaths cover all other voices. Camera focuses on pale feet standing by the wall at the far edge of darkness. Apart from his feet, this third person remains in shadows, barely existing at all. Creaking litanies rise in feverish crescendo until the replay icon fills the screen in Serena's shaking hands.

She hears a door opening upstairs. Sounds of footsteps approaching along the hallway. She cries and shivers, bites her lip again and presses her face against her hands. "What hav—" she screams and turns around on her chair, facing the empty stairs. "William?" She jumps up, shivering violently and screaming his name without an answer. "William!" She runs into the stairway and hastily past the hallway toward the studio.

William steps out from the doorway and faces her.

"What have you done?" she screams, her spit flying across William's face. "Why?" She pounds her fists at his face and chest.

"We agreed, it's about the people."

"What are you talking about?" She shivers, in tears, seeing the mounted camera pointed toward them inside the studio. "You—"

"About our own account." William turns his eyes away from her face, looking now at the hallway behind her back.

The pounding sounds start again, coming closer and closer. William gasps. Smiles.

She whimpers and tries to turn around to face the

intruder, but William grasps her shoulders and pins her against his chest. Locked tight to her place in his embrace, Serena cannot but close her eyes in desperate prayer.

"Don't worry," William whispers to her ear and grasps her throat with relentless force. "We'll have so many stories to tell."

Serena fights back, struggles to breath, wails like a drowning dog.

"So many..."

Everything blackens as her eyes turn backward, little veins exploding on their wide, open whites.

"Deals to seal for the sequels."

THE END

MR. CHEW

BY ANGELA SYLVAINE

Mr. Chew isn't real.

He's a monster from an old nursery rhyme, a myth passed from the big kids to the little ones.

Mr. Chew, all dressed in black,
His jaw unhinges with a crack.

An older girl at the playground scared me with the rhyme so bad I'd cried when I was younger. The other kids laughed. My brother, Jason, is eight now, so I passed the rhyme down to him, like any good big sister would. Maybe I wanted to give him a scare too.

But I'm the one who's scared.

Mr. Chew wears a too-small black suit, with cuffs stopping mid-forearm, leaving his spindly hands dangling. Liver spots dot every patch of pale, exposed skin on his oversized bald head, long neck, and bare feet. But it's his eyes that betray he's a monster—bulbous, white orbs with blood-red irises pitted by black pupils and no eyelids I can see. He doesn't blink, only stares.

Watches you with blood-filled eyes,
Grabs with fingers sharp as knives.

I sang Jason the rhyme a week ago, and I've seen Mr. Chew every day since. He comes closer each day. At first, he was just a hulking figure standing at the end of the block. Today, he's posted on the sidewalk in front of our house. I walk past him to wait for the bus and feel a rush of hot air, smell a hint of rotting fruit.

"You're not real," I say, still watching him.

"Who?" asks the skinny, shaggy-haired boy just ahead of me on the sidewalk, waiting with the others for the middle school bus. He's a year younger than me and new, or else he wouldn't be talking to me.

"Him." I point at Mr. Chew.

"There's no one there." The boy cocks his head to the side.

Heat climbs up my neck. "I know."

Late at night, the man will creep,
Eats the bad ones while they sleep.

"Crazy Cammie." Drew, the coolest of the cool girls, sing-songs my nickname and bumps me from behind, earning giggles from her friends. She eyes my threadbare gray T-shirt and stained, ill-fitting jeans. "Crazy *Crusty* Cammie." She pushes me, knocking me into the boy.

"Watch it," he says, grasping my arm.

At the press of his fingers on my skin, my pulse swells to fill my ears like a crashing wave, and I shove him to the ground.

His face reddens, and he scrambles back to his feet. He won't look at me.

I should apologize, but my teeth are clenched too tight, my throat closed off against an anger I can't let escape.

Drew snickers, and my fists itch to find her face, but I jam my hands in my pockets instead. Remember what the counselor said. I control my temper. It doesn't control me.

The bus pulls up, and I'm the first to climb the steps, slumping into a seat at the very back. As we pull away from the curb, I watch Mr. Chew.

There is no chance to run away.

Mr. Chew will make you pay.

His eyes swivel in their sockets, and the black pupils settle on me, bore into me.

See you soon, his eyes seem to say.

I get off the bus after school and stand frozen on the sidewalk.

Mr. Chew has moved again.

He waits on the front porch, his bare toes poking over the edge. My heart thumps hard enough to crack my chest wide, but I force myself to walk up the stairs. I'll get the belt if I try to climb in through a window. I ease past him, closer to him than I've ever been. The black pupils at the center of the red irises aren't pupils at all, but holes which want to suck you in. His sweet stench wafts by, and those black pits follow me. He doesn't move, doesn't even seem to breathe.

The worn porch boards creak, alerting Mama Theresa to my presence, and the door swings open. I rush inside and close the door behind me, though I know very well doors can't keep monsters out.

A lipstick-stained cigarette clasped between her lips, she dumps baby Trev into my arms.

His full diaper smooshes against me, sending a whiff of crap to sting my nose.

"He needs changed," I say.

She removes the cigarette from her mouth and swipes it past my bare arm, laughing when I flinch.

I should know better than to think she'd burn me where someone might see.

She heads back toward the living room, her ass swishing back and forth beneath purple velvet sweats.

Trev gives a whiny cry, and I smooth back his fine hair. "Shh, shh. It's okay."

He's only been here a month, hasn't learned yet not to cry.

I prop the baby on one hip and enter the kitchen. The linoleum floor is almost as cracked as the front walk, a definite tripping hazard. And still, the foster care people think this is a good place for kids.

Jason stands on a wooden milk crate at the sink, doing dishes. He's just tall enough, even with the boost. I haven't gotten used to this yet, seeing him every day. After our parents died in the accident, he was taken in by a real nice foster family. He almost made it out. But they sent him back. Four years he was with them, and they returned him.

He won't tell me why.

I place a peck on his cheek.

"Ewww." Having recently learned about girl cooties, he rubs at his face with one hand, leaving a trail of soap suds.

I lean back against the counter. "How was school?"

"Stupid," he says, avoiding my gaze.

"Did something happen? You can tell me. Maybe I can help."

"I can take care of myself." He scrubs at the frying pan with a Brillo pad, and I notice the scrapes marring his knuckles.

He's turning out just like me. "Fighting isn't the answer. You know that."

"Whatever."

I sigh. "I'll dry after I get Trev cleaned up." I bump Jason's shoulder with my arm, my chest tight with the knowledge I'm the reason he's here. Sitting next to me in the backseat, he just wouldn't stop bawling. So, I had grabbed his arm and twisted, like the kids at school did to me—a snakebite, they called it. Dad only looked away from the road for a few seconds. By the time Mom screamed, it was too late.

Maybe that's why Mr. Chew is coming for me.

I make my way down the hall and into the room the three of us kids share, furnished with a mattress and playpen. Trev wiggles in my arms and his face scrunches, a sure sign he's about to let loose.

"Shh, shh." I close the door to drown out his cries so Mama doesn't hear.

After grabbing a towel from the laundry basket, I place it on the mattress and plop Trev down.

I tug down his shorts, and the sight of the sickly yellow and purple bruises marring his chubby little thighs turns my stomach. I try to take the brunt of Mama's anger, but it's not enough. She hurts the boys, and I can't stop her.

Maybe dying won't be so bad. A little pain and then nothing but relief.

Mr. Chew can't be real, but he's here, standing at the foot of the bed. Jason snores beside me, his tattered blanket wrapped around him, and Trev is passed out in his playpen.

A tremor starts in my bones, works its way outward until I'm shaking so hard I might shatter. I want to burrow under my own blanket, but there's nowhere to hide, nowhere to run from the things I've done to deserve this.

At least I can protect the boys from *him*.

I force myself to creep across the room and step into the hallway. The house is dark, except for the sliver of light from the television spilling out in strobe-like flashes from beneath Mama's bedroom door. The voices from one of her idiot reality shows screech through the wall.

Mr. Chew follows and walks a slow circle around me. The smell of him clings to me—decay with a hint of syrupy sweetness.

My legs are too wobbly, too weak, to try and run.

"It was just a snakebite. No one was supposed to die," I

say before fear steals my voice. I should beg to be spared, say I'm only a kid. I'm trying to be better. But maybe I'm really bad deep down inside, and maybe a little piece of me wants to die.

He stops and faces me, gnashing his teeth.

His jaw snaps open with a crack, and I flinch. Too many teeth, too sharp to be human, line the gaping hole which has become the lower half of his face.

I press my hand to my mouth and swallow back a scream. No, no, no. I don't want to die. Not like this.

"Mr. Chew," Jason says.

I gasp and look over my shoulder to see him peeking from our bedroom doorway. "Go back to bed. Now. And close the door."

"It's okay, Cammie. I called him."

"What are you talking about?" I ask in a harsh whisper.

Mr. Chew inclines his head toward Jason, then turns to Mama Theresa's door, reaching one clawed hand out to grip the doorknob.

Jason creeps up next to me and takes my hand. He's riveted, eyes gleaming with excitement. "He's going to help us hurt them all."

Rasping breaths seize my lungs. I watch Mr. Chew twist the knob, and Mama T's door swings open with a creak. Flickering light bathes Mr. Chew, bleaching his already pale skin, and he steps into the room. Jason tugs me forward until we can see inside, where Mama T lies naked, sprawled atop her blankets, with an empty bottle of whiskey beside her. Drunken snores saw from her throat.

Mr. Chew slams the door, cutting off our view, and I sob in relief. I have to drag Jason away, back to our room, but even there, even with the blaring of her television, I can't block out Mama's screams.

Mr. Chew is real. Jason called and he came.

Mama Theresa lies splayed across her bed, her mouth a grimace of pain, even in death. Her body is covered with bites, jagged wounds where the man chewed off soft-ball-sized chunks of her flesh. Blood covers almost every inch of her skin, soaks the sheets, and drips onto the floor in great, red, shining pools. There must be buckets of it. The room stinks like the worst of Trev's diapers mixed with copper and sweat.

Bile surges up my throat, and I turn away to puke on the floor.

She hurt me, hurt the boys, but she didn't deserve that. No one deserves that.

I stumble down the hall and into the bedroom to scoop Trev from his playpen. "We'll go to the neighbors', call the police. Say we found her like that." I swallow hard, taste the vomit coating my tongue. "It's going to be okay. We're going to be okay."

Jason sits on the edge of his mattress, tying his sneakers. "Don't worry. No one can hurt us anymore. Or else Mr. Chew will get them."

"You can't call him again, Jason. Not ever."

Jason grabs his backpack from the floor and slings it over his shoulder, like it's morning and he's off to school. "Mama Theresa tried to tell me what to do too."

My knees buckle, but I catch myself with my free hand, bracing it against the door frame.

Jason runs down the hall, his shoes squelching on the vomit-soaked shag carpet.

I stagger after him with Trev cradled in my arms. My vision jumps and blurs, but I manage to make it through the house and outside. I suck in a deep breath, but that horrid smell of pain and death sticks inside my nose.

Jason skips along the sidewalk, singing.

"Mr. Chew, all dressed in black,
His jaw unhinges with a crack.
Watches you with blood-filled eyes,
Grabs with fingers sharp as knives."

The glow of the full moon does nothing to wipe away the image of that room, of what Mr. Chew—what *Jason*—did to Mama. I shuffle along, the concrete scraping my bare feet.

Jason continues, his voice cutting through the quiet calm of the night.

"Late at night, the man will creep,
Eats the bad ones while they sleep.
Sing this song, again and again.
Say his name, invite him in."

Jason stops at the neighbor's walk and looks back at

me. "Hurry up, Cammie. We need help." His lip quivers and he sniffles. "Someone hurt Mama Theresa. Please, help us. There's so much blood."

His face changes, shifts as the monster he's become resurfaces, and he actually *giggles*.

Directly ahead of Jason, on the sidewalk, Mr. Chew appears, the pale skin of his face and hands smeared red.

I lurch to a stop, clutching Trev to my chest. Spiders of panic crawl up my spine and across my scalp. "Go away. Leave us alone!"

The man is inches away from Jason, but my brother doesn't react, doesn't even seem to see the man.

"Who're you talking to, Crazy Cammie?" Jason turns down the neighbor's walk, humming that horrible rhyme.

Mr. Chew looks at me and raises his long, clawed, index finger to his mouth.

Shh.

Gnashing his teeth, he watches Jason race up the steps of the front porch. Watches his next victim.

The final verse of the song lilts through my mind.

Careful, careful, what you dare.

Not all survive his bloody stare.

Tears blur my eyes, scorch my cheeks. "You can't be real. You're not real!"

Trev starts to wail, and I fall to my knees on the sidewalk.

"I just wanted to scare him a little," I say, my voice choked by sobs. Mom. Dad. Now Jason.

And it's all my fault.

Mr. Chew drifts after my baby brother, leaving a trail of rotting fruit wafting in the night air.

LET'S BE SUBMARINES

BY DANNY NICHOLAS

His brother would have been thirty-three today. The same age Jesus died. *Unlike the bearded one*, Kyle thought, *he isn't coming back*. But if he were to, he wouldn't be coming back as pretty as Jesus. Kyle made sure of that, didn't he?

No, no. It wasn't his fault. No one to blame but cruel fate, which was as useless as blaming the ocean for being wet.

Or a rubber ducky for being cute.

Kyle squeezed the rubber duck in his hand. It squeaked like a constipated fart.

Under him was the Atlantic Ocean. Above his head were stars. Below deck there was a beautiful girl, naked, lying in bed. His head was swimming in sea salt and alcohol.

The ocean lay as still as glass. Kyle stared at his reflection and wondered if his brother would've looked better than him at his age—which was thirty-three also.

Perhaps his brother might've looked slimmer, healthier, wouldn't have the beer belly Kyle had. Although, Kyle would rather his dead brother have been fatter than him, with a balding scalp dotted with only a few dangling strands of hair, making him look sadder than if he just went completely bald.

Kyle laughed, choking on the cool Atlantic air. He stopped laughing when he remembered he was holding the rubber ducky.

Where did it come from, he wondered. On the bottom, it said the duck was made in China, but that wasn't the answer he wanted.

Over the years, the duck's yellow surface had faded white in places, like patches of skin where the flow of blood had bypassed. The orange paint of its beak flaked at the tip and smeared into the edges of its cheeks, like drunkenly applied lipstick.

Kyle assumed the duck was nearly as old as he was, and in the same crummy shape he was in. Funny thing, Kyle knew the duck would out live him, just as it had his brother.

Sometimes, he thought about chucking it into a garbage deposal, savoring the sound of overworked metal blades chewing and barfing out rubber ribbons like paper streamers blown from a party horn. Other times, Kyle would've liked to toss the duck into the fireplace, dose it with lighter fluid, spark a match, and smell that rubber burn.

Yet Kyle kept the duck because he enjoyed hurting himself. Simply, he had grown used to the pain and was afraid of losing it. As awful as that sounded, the grief supplied him comfort. Despite how gut-wrenching and cancer-ridden it was, Kyle couldn't bring himself to amputate.

However, tonight he felt different.

Partly since he was drunker than normal, and maybe it was the calmness of being alone at sea, or possibly because it was his and his brother's birthday tonight, thirty-three years was enough time to live with all that guilt.

Kyle kept gazing at his refection, hypnotized by the smooth glassiness of the watcr. The surface of the ocean was streaked with sparkles of sliver from the stars and the moonlight above. A perk about being one half of a twin, Kyle supposed. If you ever missed your brother, all you had to do was find your reflection, and there he be.

He homed-in on the refection of his eyes, his brother's eyes. It all began with water. It made sense that it would end with it.

He could still remember hearing the bath running, the gurgling purr of water meeting water, mixing with bubble bath, birthing suds. And then the hiss deep in the neck of the faucet as the flow of water was cut suddenly by his mother twisting the knobs.

Many doctors claim one can't recall memories from when you were three years old, that you'd be far too young to shovel up any faithful recollections. Simply, one doesn't possess the awareness to maintain such early memories. For the most part, Kyle believed that was true, in terms of say, remembering that particular He-Man cartoon episode, and what brand of cereal he was munching on as he watched it.

However, if you experienced the same world-shattering episode as what followed in that bathtub, in a sleepy subdivision in West Illinois,—Kyle would argue you'd remember that milestone, even if you were a speck of floating sperm baking in your daddy's testicle.

Although, to counterpoint that, Kyle wasn't sure how much of what happened inside the bathtub had been embellished over time, or was edited unconsciously from himself to make things easier to live with.

He knew without any corruption of gray echoes—since here he stood more than thirty years later on a sailboat—that Kyle was the only one out of the two to come out of that bathtub.

The rubber duck was the sole toy in the water, idly riding the currents the brothers made as their mother washed them. Sometimes, the duck would bump into the boys and swirl about, hitting a wall of the tub, eventually slowing its spin and resuming its lazy drift.

The brothers were getting along just fine without him. The bubbles in the bath were more intriguing than any wafting lump of rubber. How could it compare to a handful of suds that could be blown into the air and drop back on you like flakes of snow? It hid in a corner, bobbling, waiting for bath-time to be over.

Kyle wasn't sure why his mother left. Maybe the telephone rang, or she forgot something burning on the stove?

What mattered was, she stepped away for only a minute. And it took exactly that long for Kyle's brother to die.

This was where memory became fuzzy.

Kyle couldn't tell you how his brother wound up dead. When his mother returned to the bathtub, Kyle was as surprised as she was to find him deceased, and he had been sitting next to him.

Somehow, his brother, Jacob, had drowned. The water wasn't deep. It nearly touched their petite kneecaps. While his mother was away, Jacob had managed to belly flop over the tub, take a face full of bubbles and bathwater, and remain facedown against the porcelain. There wasn't enough water for him to float in. His body simply stayed lying, like a drunk who had wound up passed out over a puddle in the street.

The duck crawled out of hiding, and circled the body in the tub in the same way a starving dog would do when it smelled something it liked in your pocket.

Kyle couldn't remember if there was any thrashing. He assumed there had to have been some kind of struggle against the soapy water stuffing his brother's lungs, but he couldn't recall any tussling. As incredible as it seemed, Jacob went out without a fuss, as though he had planned it.

That was trickier for Kyle to accept, that a three-year-old could be suicidal.

What else was much harder for anyone, predominantly for his mother, to bear was that a child—dead, soaking, beginning to bloat and gradually turning blue—was happily alive for one second, and in the next moment became another bath toy, no different than the rubber duck.

One other thing Kyle remembered, despite the experts' assurance he was far too young, was the trail of trickling water his bother left behind, leading from the bathroom, across the living room, and through the door as the coroner wheeled his body out of the house. The body bag was soppy with water, like a half-filled water balloon. The material at the corners must have been very thin. Water seeped from a weak spot, and the dewy mix of coagulated blood and bubble bath dripped throughout the house, each drop sounding like a penny landing on the floor.

Kyle could still hear the dripping—regardless of what the experts refuted—when he was in his bed, alone in the dark, and the room was nothing but a block of uncompromising blackness. Kyle would hear:

*Drip...Drip...*and a *drip...*

It wasn't his leaky kitchen faucet, Kyle knew. His brother was leaving a mess again, stains which would last for a long time, no matter how often you mopped it over.

Understandably, his mother lost her mind. You can stamp "Accidental Death" over all the reports and news articles you wanted, but it wouldn't alleviate one's conscience, especially if the misfortune happened on your watch and you could have prevented it by only letting the phone ring or the toast burn.

Kyle didn't fare any better. Slightly more so than his mom who, after suffering from fifteen years of guilt, decided to drown herself. She picked a nearby canal, parked her car at the edge, and just walked in. His mother was fished out two days later on his birthday.

Happy birthday, kid. Here is your bloated, drowned, fish-nibbled mother to go alongside your bloated, drowned-by-bubble-bath brother. Still want to play Pin the Tail on the Donkey or more fitting, Pin the Tail on the Ducky?

Kyle's father remarried shortly after Jacob's death, and Kyle never saw him since. Fashionably late, he got the news at age twenty-five that his father died on Kyle's seventeenth birthday. Maybe the news would've stung much harder if he received it when he was younger. His father also drowned. He was driving over a bridge, a distracted driver passing the opposite way swiped him, and his father's vehicle cartwheeled over the side and fell into a shallow creek.

His father might've made it if his car hadn't landed upside down. He hung, buckled in his seat, face dunked into the creek, and he slurped up the muddy water.

His mother and father drowned on his birthday, and his brother, also, drowned on both his and Kyle's birthdays. So why, with that track record combined with some bad *juju*...Oh why did Kyle decide to celebrate his birthday on the goddamn Atlantic Ocean?

To be honest, he felt a bit self-destructive.

The waiting had finally worn him down. And Kyle believed he would never be as relatively healthy as he was now to compensate for his sheer drive of recklessness. So why not take the shot? He wasn't going to wait for this sadistic destiny to catch up with him later on when he was an old man crippled by shame.

You want me? Kyle thought. *Come take me when I'm too screwed up to care. I made it easy for you! Enough already! Come on by and take your damn duck back*!

Then again, why should he be afraid, Kyle wondered.

He was nothing more than a bystander. And what could he have done to save his brother? He was just three years old at the time, couldn't tie his own shoelaces together, let alone employ any lifeguard training.

Yet the guilt was there like some inflamed hair follicle which kept resurfacing, regardless of how certain you were you had yanked it out the last time.

There was one more thing Kyle had trouble grappling with. He never even discussed it with any therapist, since he believed it would get him thrown behind bars or locked inside a padded room.

Perhaps his brother's death wasn't accidental after all. Nor was it suicide.

If it wasn't either of those two, it had to be only one other choice—old, bloody *murder*. And no one else could have committed the crime besides Kyle himself.

No, I couldn't have, Kyle would discredit himself.

Then who killed Jacob?

Easy, Kyle thought, *it was Professor Plum, in the bathroom, with a rubber ducky*. It made more sense than a three-year-old drowning his twin brother in the bathtub.

Although, Kyle couldn't reject the possibility he was capable of such a deed. And that was the hard part.

Somewhere over the fizzy laden hurdles of memory before and after Jacob's drowning, there was a spanning wasteland of unbefitting threads where the margins were so thin yet so tangled, like a dry crumbly ball of yarn beginning to disintegrate when you unraveled it too fast.

Could it be his hands were red, even at that early age?

Kyle couldn't deny it. Perhaps what transpired in that bathtub was the classic *Cain and Abel* scenario. Kyle wasn't positive what fed the hate. That rubber ducky could be to blame. Baby Kyle might've wanted to play with it, and baby Jacob wouldn't share. So instead, Kyle found another game to play with his brother—Let's be Submarines.

Enemy vessel approaching, dear brother.

Dive! Dive! Dive!

And his brother didn't dive deep enough, so Kyle thought he could help him out. After all, what are brothers for? According to the Bible, plenty of murder.

He might have blocked the killing out of his mind. His hand reaching out to grab a handful of his brother's fine sandy hair and pulling him down to the suds of the bath, holding him against the bottom of the tub until his foot stopped twitching.

It would be nice for Kyle to know without any doubt that he had murdered his bother. Such a relief to identify that one reason, the cause for everything disastrous.

It'd be so simple to say, "Uh huh! I know why my world stinks. It's because I killed my brother, and he wants to get even! It wasn't my bad choices or because of ill-fated timing. It was all my dead brother's doing." Since one of the privileges you're graced with when you're dead is the ability to control the universe, like it was a marionette show.

There weren't any other damn logical justifications. Only that his brother's ghost was sore at him for what he did to him when they were three. *For Chrisshake, Jac,* Kyle thought, *let it go already*!

Kyle knew most of that was him being silly, yet a tiny shred of him couldn't help but to take it seriously.

He looked into the water and saw the man his brother could've become. His guilt had faded, burnt to a thin haze by the anger rising from his belly.

"You want the stupid duck, Jakey boy?" Kyle said to his reflection. "All right, you can have the son of a bitch!"

He pitched his hands behind him, drunkenly imitating a major league pitcher setting up a fast ball, and then he let the duck fly. Kyle watched it soar away, becoming a teeny yellow dot in the night, until he lost sight of it and heard distantly the satisfying *plash* as it landed yards away.

"Darwinism, motherfucker. I was the strongest to survive!" Kyle shouted into the darkness. "Eat it, you stinkin' bastard. If I didn't drown you, I really wished I did!"

Immediately, he wanted to take it back. For a moment, Kyle sobered and felt horrible at what he had said, even when he said it to no one besides the Atlantic Ocean. And what did it care?

Still, there was an ugly tug at his heart. He knew it was pathetic, yet he was beginning to feel better. With the rubber ducky truly, completely away from him, Kyle was free of the handcuffs of his past. The smear-coated window looking upon that tragic bath-time was miles away and stretching after every second.

Kyle felt as if whatever was owed had been squared away. His brother's dead body, which had floated around him since Kyle was a child, had finally taken enough water and sank under.

He glanced back at his reflection. The water wasn't as calm as it was a moment ago. Waves started to chop, splitting Kyle's perfect image. He stood a while longer, breathing in the salty air, and then Kyle went below deck where the girl was waiting for him.

She was a hooker who was paid extravagantly well to join Kyle, alone, out on the ocean. The girl was young. Kyle suspected she was nearly eighteen. Although, with the boat sitting on international waters, he didn't have to worry too much about the statutes of U.S. laws.

"I thought you'd be back to bed sooner, baby," she said. "What were you doin' up there that took you so long?"

"I was talking with my brother."

"Your brother?" the girl asked. She knew there was no one else on the boat. At least, she probably hoped there wasn't. "Well, honey, if he wants to party, too, it's going to cost extra."

"You don't have to worry about it."

"What were you talking to him about?"

"We were swapping jokes," Kyle said. "Between me and my brother, we know the funniest jokes."

"Tell me one."

"What did the duck say to his doctor when he didn't like his diagnosis?"

"What did he say?" she asked.

"He told him he was a '*quack*.'"

There was a delay to her giggle since she laughed out of politeness. As much as Kyle was paying her, she'd even laugh at an awkwardly delivered "knock-knock" joke.

"Tell me your brother had a better joke than that one."

"That was the problem," Kyle said. "He didn't. So, I tossed him overboard."

Now the girl laughed without hesitation. "Did he float like a duck?" she asked.

"No. But he kept clucking like a chicken."

The girl was the only one laughing.

He heard the dripping in his sleep again, the undying rhythm of his brother's soppiness tapping across the floor. Each patter louder than the last, deafening his ears, splintering his mind. Kyle could still smell the sweet bubble soup soured by the copper taste of blood. Then, he heard the pounding, like the calls of a doomed, trapped crew of a submarine, knocking on the steel hulls, praying anyone would hear them before the air dried up. When Kyle awoke, he realized what the pounding was—it was his heart thudding against his chest.

The cabin subtly wobbled with the ocean, and he could feel the shifting in his gut. Kyle's heart kept jackhammering under his shirt, visibly pushing against his skin and chest muscles as if it was punching it way out. He tried breathing deeply to slow it down. Kyle needed a drink, maybe even a couple? The problem was, the bottle was sitting on a desk nowhere near arm's reach.

The girl was cuddled on his side, and he had to untangle her hands and feet away from him. She squeaked a tiny, cute murmur from her lips but remained asleep as he climbed out of bed.

Kyle drank three full glasses, straight up, one after another. His heart quit hammering but still shuddered. He had to breathe better air, Kyle reasoned. Below deck was stuffy, too closed off and sealed up. Once more, he thought about the trapped submarine crew, hammering against their tomb.

Let's be submarines.

He went up and stood on deck, breathed fresh air once, and stifled the next gulp with cigarette smoke. Kyle hacked out a glob of phlegm and took a deep long drag. His heart slacked some. It wasn't comfortable, but Kyle knew he was going to live.

Suddenly, something occurred to him, something he should have given some thought to before, yet Kyle assumed there wouldn't be a tomorrow after tonight. He had blown plenty of money on this sail-boat, and on the girl. His financial future seemed destined to be a blasted heath where no green would grow. And unless Kyle decided to become a full-time sailor, his next living quarters would be a cramped, tiny box, consisting of four soggy walls of thin cardboard.

His heart started drumming again. He took another drag and told himself to worry about it in the morning.

Kyle peered into the ocean, looking for his reflection again, but couldn't find it. Clouds had settled over the moon. It was as if Kyle was floating in a well of ink. Frustrated nature had ruined his habit to pass the time, Kyle stared off the bow of the boat into the murky black sea.

He caught a glimpse of a shape bobbing through the surface of the water, drifting toward him. Kyle wanted to believe his eyes were playing tricks, too much alcohol, not enough good sleep, and bleary eyes trying to glaze through cigarette smoke. What he saw couldn't be there.

Enemy vessel approaching, dear brother.

His cigarette dangled from his lip, slipped off, and extinguished into the water below.

"Oh, fuck you!" Kyle yelled at the rubber ducky. "You can't be fucking serious!"

The duck zipped through the ocean. Kyle saw the yellow speck so clear in the dark water, like it was a dab of mustard on a charred slab of beef. It was drawing closer to the boat. Kyle watched it with the unsteady eyes of a terrified sailor tracing a torpedo's course, propelling directly at his ship.

The rubber ducky reached the rear of the boat, brushing against the hull, twirling unevenly, bumping along, working itself down toward the left side of the boat, and hugging across it.

It's gonna go away, Kyle told himself. *Let it pass. It's going to go away. Keep it together, and just wait it out.*

Kyle waited, and the duck circled the boat, like a shark waiting for a mortally wounded victim to bleed out.

You're kiddin' me, Kyle frantically thought. *It's never ever going to leave me! It will follow me. Even if I hide on top of a mountain, it will sprout wings and hunt me down.*

He closed his eyes to shut out the yellow nightmare.

The night was so still Kyle could hear the rubber skin of the duck rasping beside the hull, like a fingertip scratching across a balloon, and it sounded ungodly loud. Kyle felt as though it was rubbing alongside his head, a kneading sensation, his brains being fondled by unkempt hands.

Kyle brought a net up from a side compartment. It was wide enough to help haul in a healthy sized bass. He was going to hoist this son of a bitch back, and this time, Kyle was going to throw it into a fire and piss on the ashes.

He dipped the hoop of the net into the water and waited as the duck passed by. It seemed it would drift right into the trap. Instead, the duck veered off and floated away.

"Oh no, you don't," Kyle said, sending out a plum of ice. "Come to poppa." He clenched a hand on the railing, which went around the rim of the ship, and reached farther out, skimming the net through the water, agitating ripples and stirring up...bubbles. Kyle couldn't get out of that goddam bathtub.

The duck was inside the net for a moment. When Kyle scooped it up, the toy hung on the steel rim of the hoop, overbalanced, and then teetered over the side into the ocean again. Kyle growled at the night, icing up his throat.

It wasn't going to make it easy.

Kyle pulled a leg over the railing, then the other. One handed, he hung over the side of the boat, like he was a scurvy pirate. With net in the other hand, Kyle reached out. The net hovered over the rubber ducky, eclipsing it within its shadow.

The net dropped over the duck, trapping it completely. Kyle swiveled the handle, snatching up the load.

It felt as if the duck had gained a pound or two. Lifting the net wasn't effortless. Kyle clenched his teeth and grunted to pull the hoop up to his head.

Let's be submarines.

Swinging in the netting, dribbling water, was Kyle's three-year-old twin brother. His skin had wrinkled and turned a pale green as if he had been pickled in a jar. Baby Jacob rolled his colorless eyes at this brother. He yawned at him like he was awaking from a nap, his gums making a wet, smacking sound. An eel skidded from the baby's mouth and wiggled in the slack of the net.

Dive! Dive! Dive!

Kyle slipped, and the water was much colder than he thought it'd be. Since he had been afraid of the water for so long, Kyle never bothered learning how to swim.

He thrashed in the Atlantic Ocean, feet kicking helplessly, his head slowly sinking under the inking dark. It had been thirty years, and finally, Kyle was in the water with his bother again. It was likely he was tugging at his foot, dragging Kyle down deeper.

The moon had broken through the clouds, and it was becoming fainter in Kyle's vision, blurry by the splashing of salt and seas in his eyes.

It was going to end the way Kyle always knew it would.

Let's be submarines.

Fuckin' bath-time, Kyle thought. Then, he was hit on the head, hard. He heard another splash in the water. Something rapped at his hands, and Kyle seized it.

The girl was shouting from the deck of the boat, waggling a pole at the water. She pulled, and Kyle was heaved away from his destiny.

He didn't bother with a glass. Kyle drank the liquor straight from the bottle.

They were below deck. He sat on the bed, wrapped in a towel. Underneath it, Kyle was only in his underwear. His pile of wet clothes drenched the floor near a rug.

The girl sat in a chair in the corner, watching him cautiously as he drank. She was shivering, yet she hadn't had a touch of water on her nightdress. Kyle thanked her for saving his life.

"My pleasure, handsome. If you drowned, then who the hell else is supposed to sail this boat?" she said without any humor behind it.

Kyle was nipped with a pinch of depression. He had no one else to love, and the girl—as much affection as she gave him—couldn't care less about his well-being. Kyle wondered what her name was. He never asked. It seemed it would be easier for the both of them if they remained nameless.

"How did you wind up off the boat, sweetie?"

"My brother," Kyle said. "He wants me dead."

"Baby, there is no one out here other than you and me."

What could Kyle tell her? That a rubber ducky was the harbinger of death, and the soggy corpse of his baby brother wanted to finally tie up some loose ends? She was shivering now. How hard would she shake if he told her that?

Kyle simply said, "I know," and left it at that.

"If you excuse me, I have to use the ladies room. I almost pissed myself while I dragged you back onboard." The girl stood and gave Kyle a wide berth as she crossed to the restroom, shutting the door behind her.

Kyle finished the bottle and felt the ocean under him, teeter-tottering the boat. He heard the girl flush the toilet and run the water in the lavatory to wash her hands.

He let the bottle slip from his fingers and tumble to the floor. The bottle whispered and jangled as it was caught in the throes of the rocking seas, rolling back and forth over the floor.

Let's be submarines.

I beat him, Kyle finally admitted to himself. At least, for tonight. Tomorrow and the battles after that, Kyle would have to wait and see. One thing was for sure, he wasn't going to go near the water again.

The girl screamed. And Kyle knew his baby brother was back for round two.

He rushed to the bathroom door and threw it open. She stood at the sink, turned away from him, but in the mirror, Kyle saw her reflection. Her face was white, and her hands were raised as if she was ready to claw her eyes out. A flow of thick blood poured from the faucet, filling the basin.

"What is going on...What is going on!" the girl screamed over and over, like a looping audio recording.

"A long-overdue family reunion," Kyle said, watching the blood reaching the plateau of the washbowl, overflowing, and dripping to the floor. Besides in his dreams, he hadn't heard that dripping sound in thirty years, but now it had returned with a vengeance, splattering all over his feet.

The flow cut suddenly, and the pipes below them grinded, as if they were choking, struggling to bring up something too nasty to handle.

Out of the mouth of the tap, a tiny orange wedge peeked out. It looked like the tip of a piece of candy corn was cramming its way out of the plumbing. The chunk of orange grew fatter, and it took Kyle another moment to realize what it was. He knew what was worming out to say "hi" once he saw the yellow trim at the end of the orange.

The rubber ducky popped its head out of the faucet, upside down. Its cheerful, blue painted-on eyes bent and turned to look at Kyle, and those happy eyes forced his heart to halt for a beat. When the rhythm came back, it was a constant hammer. Kyle's ears were pounding with it.

The rest of the duck fell out like it was a sliver of jam slipping from the two pieces of bread you pressed together to make your sandwich. The duck dove into the basin of blood and disappeared under it for a moment before shooting back up, yellow stained with red, and settling, floating on top of blood, appearing quite at home.

Let's be submarines.

The girl pushed Kyle aside and puked on the floor of the cabin. Kyle stayed in the bathroom, staring at the duck relaxing on the pool of blood like it was a nice warm day. His eyes glanced up at his reflection in the mirror, once more seeing what his brother would have looked like if he lived past three.

Yet this time, Kyle understood that what was staring back at him *was* his brother. What was reflected in that glass was completely monstrous—his own face, yes, but warped and changed as if it had been rearranged by a demented surgeon. Nose mushed out of alignment, eyebrows budging from his forehead, the irises of the eyes swooshed in and elongated as though they belonged to a goat. What smiled back at Kyle had rotten, crooked teeth.

Kyle shattered the mirror with a punch. Glass rained over the rubber ducky, breaking its peaceful holiday cruise.

Enemy vessel approaching.

When Kyle walked out of the bathroom, he believed, after everything he saw, nothing else would surprise him.

Kyle froze when the girl aimed the gun at him. She

must have had it hidden in her purse. It was understandable, really. Kyle would pack heat, too, if he was in her line of work, or had to accompany a madman at sea by herself.

"Stay back," she ordered.

Kyle slowly raised his hands, defenseless. "I know you're scared," he said. "I'm scared, too."

The girl steadied the gun, locking both hands over the grip. "Your brother wants you dead, huh?" she asked. "What about me? Does he want me gone?"

The boat rocked, corners swaying. The sound of the rolling empty liquor bottle whispered through the cabin.

"I don't know," Kyle said.

She took a step closer. "If you're dead, do you think he'll just go away?"

"I guess there is only one way to find out, but do you want to risk your life on that?" Kyle said. "With me dead, how are you going to captain this boat? Are you going to whistle into the sails?"

"Where's the fuckin' radio?"

"No radio. No phones."

"You came out here to die, didn't you?"

"It was one of things on my mind, sure."

"And you brought *me* along?" the girl shrieked.

"Well? Now that you put it that way...," Kyle said evenly. "It all sounds like a terrible idea."

The gun spat fire.

A chip of his shoulder exploded with red.

The girl fired again.

Dive! Dive! Dive!

Kyle rolled to the floor.

Another loud shot rang within the cabin. It was like standing near a church bell when the hour ended and the next one started.

A hole appeared in a patch of floor where a second ago Kyle had stood.

More shots. Kyle hid behind the bed. Stuffing and feathers sprang into the air where bullets hit.

It was pure luck the bottle tumbled into his hand when the boat rocked with the waves. Kyle doubted how well it would fare against a pistol. Although, what did he have to lose? A bullet would be quieter to endure than death by rubber ducky.

Maybe the girl hesitated because she was surprised by the unexpected madness, foolishness, of Kyle rushing at her in the open, totally unshielded. That sort of recklessness gives your mind pause to process it, since it contradicts against the very nature of self-preservation driving us all.

She squeezed off another shot. It was too late.

Kyle swung the bottle at her head. It didn't shatter on the first blow, nor the second or third. On the fifth, the bottle smashed to smithereens.

There was plenty of blood spurting from her head, but Kyle wasn't sure if she was dead or dying. Certainly, he felt awful about hurting her, but honestly, her death wasn't the utmost concern Kyle had at the moment.

For one, there were the bullets which had punctured

the floor and gone straight through the underside of the boat.

And two, water had started to bubble up through those holes.

Third, unintentionally, the girl had made Swiss cheese out of the packaged life raft when she randomly doled out the bullets.

Fourth, the water coming from the floor wasn't stopping.

Fifth, and most importantly, Kyle knew what waited to meet him out there in the water, and the ocean was sliding him closer and closer toward it.

Kyle was screwed, but he still had one more concern left, and it wasn't the blood spilling from his shoulder.

Six, Jesus Christ, he needed a cigarette. He left a pack near the bed, but the silly girl had to blow that away too.

The water touched his toes...

Sitting crossed-leg on the deck, Kyle waited.

The boat hadn't capsized yet. It was simply lowering itself like an elevator going down. A thin layer of water lay over the deck. The bottom compartments were flooded. The hooker was either trapped against the ceiling of the cabin or had someway floated off into the sea.

Kyle was freezing. Doubly cold since he was still wrapped in a bloodied towel with only his drawers on, along with sitting in the frigid Atlantic water, but this was only a taste. Once the ocean took the boat over, he'd be talkin' about a really bitter, icy drink. The same death the unfortunate passengers on the *Titanic* had.

Kyle could only hope for that kind of death.

What seemed to be in his cards was something much uglier.

Let's be Submarines.

Fifteen minutes passed. Kyle remained sitting. The water had reached up over his kneecaps and up to his waist. The entire deck was underneath ten inches of water. He could feel the boat wavering beneath him, being sucked further down.

The moon was out, and the sky was clear. Kyle could see the horizon, and it reached on forever.

Enemy vessel approaching.

He felt something bump against his knee, and Kyle knew what it was before he grabbed it.

Kyle held the rubber duck. Even through the thick salt-drenched air of the Atlantic, he could still smell the sweet bubble bath scent that brought him back in time.

He squeezed the duck, and it squawked like a cheap kazoo. In the stillness of the night, Kyle bet one could hear its call from miles out.

There he is again, Kyle thought. Bathing in water up to his knees, playing with a rubber ducky...Only one tiny ingredient would make the whole recreation complete.

The boat momentary lurched underneath him and rocked back as the guest of honor climbed aboard.

Little Jacob flopped on the boat. His body slushed against the deck, the sound of a soaked wad of pulpy moss plonking on the hood of your car. Then, the dead baby waddled across the boat like a desperately pregnant sea turtle, ready to dump a batch of eggs.

It reeked of squirmy underwater smells, rotten fish and dying sea kelp, dozens of algae and fungoid growths that keeps things either floating or decaying.

Kyle silently thanked the girl one last time—she left one last bullet. From inside his towel, he brought out the pistol in his hand, and as his brother wormed his way closer, Kyle squeezed the trigger. It became daytime for a fraction of a second. The top corner of the scuttling thing's head was blasted off. Tiny flakes of brain matter scattered in the night as if it was candy being beaten from a piñata.

Then, instantly, Kyle wished he would've used the bullet on himself instead. The horror kept coming, unfazed by having most of his skull gone.

Defeated, Kyle tossed the gun into the ocean, sat quietly, and waited.

It crawled to Kyle's feet and sat up, mimicking his cross-legged sitting position. Jacob simply waved a hand up to greet his brother. His arm was waterlogged and bloated. The wiggly fat of the underarm drooped, dripped, and hung like a rag taken out of the wash to be wrung out to dry. The palm of his hand was as white as a fish's belly and smelled twice as nasty.

Kyle waved back, feeling soaked to the bone himself.

In his other hand, Kyle played with the rubber ducky, twirling it around with his fingers. He was so cold now he could barely feel his hands.

"All righty, Jacob," Kyle said. He let the ducky drop from his hand, plopping it into the water. The duck returned to the dead boy's side like a faithful dog. "What sort of game do you have rolling inside of that head of yours? Even when there is barely anything left of it to call a head."

The boy with lips as blue as the ocean on warm undercast mornings spoke with the speech impediment most three-year-olds have, where the R's veer off into W's and the T's went "twah" instead of "tah."

"Let's be submarines."

"I knew you'd say that," Kyle said. "Are you sure you want to play that with me, kid?"

Jacob said, "Wes," but Kyle knew he meant, "*Yes*."

"All right, brother," Kyle said, teeth clattering. "You'd be surprised how good I am at this game...I might even last longer than you."

The night was set ablaze with the giggling of a little boy, his vocal cords long drowned so his laugher sounded bubbly and staticky.

Another fifteen minutes later, the ocean was up to Kyle's neck. The boat had sucked away from his legs. The only remnant of his sailing career was the lone tip of the mast of the boat, which still stood straight, but in another minute it'd be gone too.

The rubber ducky danced on the water at the side of

Kyle's ear, almost pecking at him.

Eye level with Kyle's face was his brother. They floated next to each other, as close as lovers.

Fighting to keep his head above water, Kyle tried to stare into that putrid face, it skin weak and soggy from being in water for decades. It was so spongy one could almost reach out, and it would be as though you'd be touching a layer of Play-Doh, and you could mold a new funny face for the monster. Kyle tried to do just that, but his hands came back covered in green goop and black pus.

Jacob's tiny hand seized Kyle by his hair and began to push.

"Dive!" Jacob tittered, sounding as wildly monotonous as the trill of piano keys. "Dive! Dive! Dive!"

Dimly, Kyle thought, *It took long enough, but we are finally going to resemble one another, as twins should. In another hour, I'll look as gross as my brother. Hopefully, I'd look nastier, since I have to win at something.*

THE END

PLAYLAND

BY C.M. FOREST

The smell—a stale combination of grease and sweat—
wafted through the open door as Robert followed his
daughter into the playland. Beyond, a cacophony of
gleeful screams mixed and mingled into a banshee's song.
The glassed-in room located off the side of the fast-food
restaurant housed a jumble of brightly colored tubes and
slides. A dozen children swarmed over the garish plastic like
fleas on a stray.

"Take your shoes off!" Robert yelled after Lily.

The little girl flew toward the structure like a for-
ty-pound cannonball, erupting giggles as she went.

A series of tables surrounded the architectural acid-trip
that was the playland, forming a semi-circle. Most of the tables were occupied by tired-looking adults. The telltale signs
of bags under eyes and unkempt hair, of stained clothing
and defeated slants to their mouths, said they were parents.
Robert could sympathize with them. Before the divorce,
when he was still a full-time parent, he found taking care of

Lily to be a near overwhelming proposition.

Now, only having the five-year-old one weekend a month, he longed for those tired days. Lily's absence in his life created an unfillable hole, a void in his very guts. The kind of absence that should kill him, but didn't. Somehow, even with a vital piece missing, life went on.

Spotting a table in the corner, Robert tightened his grip on the brown plastic food tray and wandered through the chaos. Although the fun was theoretically supposed to be contained to the plastic octopus-like playland, the children—not only free from constraint, but outright encouraged to use up all their energy—would spill out with abandon all across the room.

Two boys, both decked out in neon-colored garb, zigzagged around the tables, hooting and hollering. A chubby girl, who looked like she was pushing the limit on what was an acceptable age to be crawling through the tubes, bounded off the bottom of one of the slides and charged across to a table with appropriately obese adults.

A little girl in a stripped dress stared at what Robert could only assume was her twin sister, looking back at her from just within the entrance of the structure. The twin was singing some sort of eerily tuneless lullaby. The girl outside was so preoccupied by her sister's song, she was nearly bowled over by the chubby girl as she darted back, mouth full of chicken nuggets.

Robert shook his head. It was amazing, the places he found himself since having a kid. Under any other circumstance, wading into the stink and noise of such a place would have been about as appealing to him as a back-alley vasectomy. But if it made Lily happy, somehow it transcended the part of his brain that cared about himself.

Robert sat so he was facing the play area and slid the cardboard box containing Lily's kids' meal, complete with small plastic toy, across from him. He knew it would have been a fool's errand to try and get the girl to eat before playing, but if he arranged her meal—a cheeseburger, fries, and an apple juice—just so, she would return like a carrier pigeon every so often to take a bite.

A sudden vibration issued from his pocket. Robert pulled out his cell phone and groaned at what greeted him. It was a message from his ex-wife, Nicole.

When are you dropping Lily off? Geoff wanted to see her before he goes into work tonight.

"Geoff. Fucking Geoff," Robert grumbled under his breath.

When Nicole had dropped the news on Robert that her new guy, Geoff, would be moving in with her and Lily, it made Robert want to scream. It wasn't Nicole dating again after their divorce that bothered him. In fact, in that regard, Robert felt sorry for the chap. Nicole had been a hard person to live with. No, what really hurt about the whole situation was that, in terms of day-to-day life, Geoff was now effectively Lily's father.

Robert's anger began to spike. His fingers flew across the screen.

I really don't give a fuck what Geoff wants! I'll bring her home when I'm ready to!

Robert looked at his reply for several seconds, his thumb hanging like a guillotine over the send button. Before he could blast his nasty response toward the nearest cell tower, something caught his attention. Lily was calling for him.

One of the true miracles of parenthood, Robert discovered, was the almost superhero-like ability to hear your child call out to you. It didn't matter if it was coming from a nightmarish structure filled with the lunatic glee of a dozen other children who, by all accounts, sounded almost identical to each other. Some corner of the parental brain could pull apart the audible layers and pick out that solitary voice, as if it was the only sound in existence.

Lily, a cherub's grin splitting her tiny face, waved energetically from a clear plastic bubble protruding like a tumor from the side of the playland. The observation window, which was easily fifteen feet off the ground and larger than the portholes peppered throughout, was a hot spot for the tiny people skittering around within.

Robert laughed, as honest a response as he had ever had, and waved back at his daughter. Apparently satisfied that her world still existed below, she ducked away, her rainbow-colored socks waving comically behind her before she was gone.

God, I love that kid.

He looked down at the unsent message and blew out

a sigh, lost to the din around him, before slowly erasing it.

Robert stared at the blank screen, shook his head, and typed. *I'll have her home soon. It was a fun weekend!*

With Nicole placated, Robert plopped his phone down on the table and eyed his daughter's food. The pull of her fries, a grease-soaked gravity that would give the tug of a black hole a run for its money, was too much to resist. He snatched one of the golden sticks from its paper sleeve and quickly gobbled it down. *Heaven!*

"Daddy! Daddy!" Lily came sprinting over to the table. "There's a boy in there." She momentary paused as she breathlessly took a bite of her burger. "He's crying."

Robert laughed. "Oh no, why?"

Lily looked back at the playland, her pigtails bobbing through the air. "He said there's a monster in there."

Robert leaned across the table and rested his hand on his daughter's slender shoulder. The little girl radiated heat, a tiny engine running at full capacity. "What! Not a monster!"

"Yes, a monster!" She nodded excitedly.

He laughed again and rubbed Lily's head. "I'm sure he's just playing, honey."

She seemed to weigh this reply before finding it to be adequate. With the update on the crying boy delivered, she inhaled two French fries, a second bite of burger, and a swallow of juice before tearing back across the padded floor. She dodged the rowdy neon boys, dove into one of the openings along the base of the structure, and vanished from sight.

Robert resisted the urge to reach across the table and devour the rest of Lily's food, instead scooping up his phone. He tried to connect to the building's Wi-Fi, but the signal was spotty at best. After several attempts, he was granted access. Robert had a whole suite of game apps on his phone. Nothing too complicated—just simple time killers. Something he was eager to do in that moment.

As he waited through an ad for a better, more expensive game, he became vaguely aware of one of the parents, a woman in beige capris, peeling away from the viewing area and approaching the playland.

"Zachary? Is that you crying?" the woman asked, her voice not quite loud enough to compete with the parade of noise streaming from within the tangle of plastic and steel.

A small boy, all tears and snot, burst from the end of one of the two slides. "He looked like me!" he squealed as his mother scooped him off the foam-matted floor surrounding the playland.

Robert was mildly amused by the boy's hysterics. He always felt like his parenting skills were lacking, until he saw how messed up other people's children were.

He returned his attention back to the screen and began sliding his thumb across its surface to get a series of colored columns to line up before time ran out.

A distant rumble pulled Robert away from his phone.

He stretched his arms, slipped his cell into his pocket,

and looked around. Outside, the clear blue sky had been taken over by a collection of storm clouds. They extended—pulled, dirty cotton—as far as he could see. A slight patter of rain was already hitting the glass. Dozens of tiny specks of water appeared like freckles on the panes. Another deep, bass-filled boom of far-off thunder echoed through the sky.

Not only had he been oblivious to the change in weather, but had also apparently missed what was happening directly around him as well. The tables, which had previously housed the tired-looking parents, were all empty. Various cups and used food wrappers—crumbled and encrusted with mustard and finely diced onions—cluttered the tabletops. A single kids' meal box was overturned on the padded floor. The restaurant's mascot, a furry creature who loved hamburgers, stared at Robert from the side of the cardboard.

He stood up, his back popping, and noticed Lily's food still sat across from him. The cheeseburger, minus the two bites she had taken earlier, remained otherwise untouched. A fly wandered lazily across the bun-landscape.

Damn it, Lily. He shook his hand, shooing the insect away. His knee-jerk reaction was to scold the child, but then he realized he was the one to blame. Instead of making sure she ate her dinner, he'd been on his phone.

Robert scooped up the wasted food and placed it onto the plastic tray before walking over to one of the trashcans and dumping it in.

"As long as you don't tell your mom you didn't eat

dinner, we'll be okay."

The playland was eerily quiet. Robert thought the place must be downright terrifying when the lights were off. He moved over to the purple cube with the hole cut into it and said, "C'mon Lily, we have to get you home."

Her running shoes still sat where they fell. They looked comically small to him in that moment. Like no human could be so tiny as to wear such things. Lily had such a big personality, Robert sometimes forgot how little his daughter was. He bent over and collected them before returning his attention to the entrance.

"Lily! Your mom is *not* gonna be happy with Daddy if I don't get you home, honey."

Robert drummed his fingers on the lip of the plastic rim entrance to the playland. He leaned into the opening and listened for any sound at all.

"Lily?"

A terrible thought came to him. *What if someone's taken her?*

He shook his head to dislodge the idea from his brain. But a growing level of unease, like some dank fungus flourishing in the darkest of places, kept the horrible possibility present in his mind.

"Lily, this isn't funny, baby." Robert stuck his head farther into the hole, and his voice immediately echoed back at him, a dozen clones parroting his words.

Panic, the likes of which Robert wouldn't have thought possible—certainly not so quickly anyway—arced through his body. He yelled again into the structure.

Nothing.

Not even the smallest knock or scratch to indicate there was anything alive in the playland at all.

He stood back up, spinning in a half circle, expecting to see the child hiding in a corner, hand over mouth, giggling at how good a trick she had just pulled on Daddy. But the room was empty. In fact, in that moment, it felt more than just empty. It was abandoned, a mausoleum made of colorful materials and cartoon decals. Even the stench of food was absent.

Robert blasted through the glass door leading back to the main seating area of the restaurant and darted toward the counter. He knocked into a group of teens mixing various flavors of soda into their cups at the fountain machine. A nasty comment, followed by snickering, was left in his wake. Robert barely heard them, though, as his own breathing, short and rapid, filled his ears. He felt like maybe he was having a heart attack.

Why can't I breathe?

A girl, not yet seventeen—if her acne-covered cheeks were to be believed—smiled at Robert from the other side of the counter. The plastic badge on her chest revealed her name to be Edith, a name completely at odds with her apparent young age. "Welcome to—"

"My daughter!" he cut her off.

The unexpected response caused Edith to rock back slightly on her heels, like his voice had physically pushed her. Her eyes darted for a second, in search of what, Robert couldn't say.

"Is everything okay, sir?"

"No!" He could barely get the word out. "I can't find her! My daughter!"

Edith visibly swallowed and glanced around a second time. "Um, where was she, sir?"

"She was in the playland. We were eating, and I looked down at my phone for a minute—" Only, it hadn't been a minute. His attention had been off his daughter for longer than that. "And now I can't find her!" He was aware he was twisting and bending Lily's shoes as he spoke.

Edith, eyes wide, called over a young man wearing a black shirt. Robert realized this fellow had been the source of her wandering gaze. His nametag identified him as Timothy and that he held the coveted position of shift manager. She relayed the message.

"Have you checked the bathrooms?" Timothy asked. His tone hovered between concerned and annoyed. It was as if he wanted Lily found so he wouldn't have to fill out the paperwork that would almost certainly be involved with a lost child.

Robert flushed with embarrassment. He hadn't thought of the bathroom. Although he doubted Lily would venture off to the restroom without informing him, she *was* constantly trying to prove how much of a "big girl" she'd become. It wasn't completely out of the realm of possibility that she would attempt the trek alone.

"No...I haven't."

"Okay, Edith, go check the ladies' room for..."

"Lily," Robert blurted.

"Go check for Lily."

Edith hurried around the counter and headed for the bathrooms.

The shift manager, his dark hair stiff with too much product, leaned across the counter and smiled at Robert. "Don't worry, sir. I'm sure your little one is in the building. Did you check the playland thoroughly? We've had kids play tricks on their parents before." He rolled his eyes and made a clucking sound with his tongue. "They don't understand how upset it makes their folks. But kids will be kids. Maybe go take another look. If she isn't there or in the restroom—which she probably is—then we can check the cameras."

The cameras? Jesus Christ! This can't be happening.

Robert nodded. His body had grown numb.

As he rushed back to the glass door leading to the playland, a single thought corkscrewed through his mind.

She's already gone.

He had visions of a car—probably something non-descript, a Toyota Camry, or Honda Accord, the kind of vehicle nobody looked twice at—driving farther and farther away from him. A car that had his daughter in it.

Don't fucking think that! he scolded himself. But he couldn't help it, his mind had become something else, a gray matter Mr. Hyde, tormenting him with visions of his baby in the most horrible places possible.

"Lily," he yelled as soon as he cleared the door.

Nothing. The room was still empty. Robert wasn't sure if he would have felt better or worse with an audience. One thing was certain, he wanted to cry but felt like it wasn't the time for such a thing. As if the act of crying would make his nightmares a reality, as if it would cement his daughter's fate.

The playland, looming like a many-armed leviathan, seemed to grow, breathe, as Robert rushed toward the black maw yawning open along the front.

"Lily! Please, Daddy is not playing anymore. If you are in there, it's time to come out."

She's not in there. She's crying in the backseat of a forgettable car heading toward the highway, as a man with dead eyes tells her to shut up before he gives her something to really cry about. Robert let out a frustrated groan at the thought.

A small, playful laugh, born from deep inside the plastic innards of the playland, bounced off the tubular walls until it reached the circular hole Robert leaned into.

It was Lily. He was sure of it.

A great wash of relief flooded through him, a deluge he was happy to drown in.

"Lily!" he shouted, dropping her shoes and squeezing through the hole.

Damp heat greeted him upon entering the structure. It was easily ten degrees warmer within the confines of the plastic tubing.

How can kids stand to be in here? he wondered.

Besides the temperature, which was already causing small beads of sweat to burst forth along his hairline, there was also the stench—a pungent aroma of dirty feet and filthy clothing mixed with an underlying stink of vomit. Robert gagged with the first lungful of air he sucked in.

It didn't take long to realize he was far too large to be navigating the thing with any sort of ease. The plastic underneath him was hard and unforgiving. Each crawling slide forward sent a rake of fiery pain through his knees. The sides of his jacket brushed along the interior of the tube, and his head grazed the ceiling.

"Lily, come out, now!"

He stared into the length of pipe before him. The shaft ended at a ninety-degree turn a half dozen feet ahead.

"I'm stuck." Her voice wafted down from somewhere above.

Robert sighed. "All right, honey, I'm coming."

A giggle, like the jingle of a delicate bell, was the only reply.

The bend was too sharp and narrow for Robert to make the turn on his hands and knees. Shifting onto his side, he formed his body around the curve and then pulled himself past. He was dismayed to find the tunnel on the other side much tighter than what he was already used to. The only way to continue on was to worm his way through until it opened back up.

A surge of primal panic filled him as he felt the pressing hardness of the colorful tube on all sides. He tried to reassure himself that, even if he became stuck, he was hardly in an unreachable location. Still, the sensation of being pinned was enough to make his limbs jittery, his heart race. Just as he was sure the tube was starting to constrict around him, slowly crushing him like a plastic boa constrictor, he shimmied over a lip and fell into a small room.

The walls of the space—approximately the size of a compact car—where bright yellow, the ceiling just high enough he could rise to a crouch. His knees popped angrily as he took up the new position. Decals decorated every available surface. They depicted a gaggle of cartoony-looking pirates—a mess of peg legs, eye patches, and shoulder-mounted parrots—chasing a dashing buccaneer. Three nautical steering wheels jutted from the wall like perfectly round mushrooms. The wheels were made of the same yellow plastic, but the grips had been permanently stained black from countless dirty hands groping them. An upended box of French fries stood in the corner. The golden sticks had turned dark, almost gray. Lines of green mold sprouted from them. The food had to have been there for days.

"Don't they ever clean this place?"

He wondered how many children poured through the playland on a daily basis. What horrific things must grow in its nooks and crannies, just waiting for small hands to rub across them. The idea that, even after the restaurant closed, there was a plethora of life continuing to expand, fester, within the place made him nauseous.

Robert put aside the thought and continued to survey

the area. In the far end of the room was a series of indented rungs, which led up through an opening in the ceiling. If he was picturing the playland correctly in his mind, the ladder would ascend upward, bringing him to the plastic observation bubble Lily had waved from earlier.

He started making his way forward, when a sudden dizzy spell caused him to stop. The heat was starting to get to him. It made his head spin. His thoughts took on a molten, sticky quality, and he felt like reality was pulling away. As if beyond the yellow walls of the room he crouched inside, the world had begun peeling back like the layers of an onion, revealing something new and terrifying underneath. He rubbed the palm of his hand across his forehead. It came back soaked with sweat.

He'd read a book once, a war story, and in it, the protagonist had been locked in a metal box in the middle of a field on a hot day. The narrator had described the situation as being as close to hell as a person could be while in the land of the living. As Robert blinked away the heat-spots filling his vision, he thought it was very likely the author had never crawled through a playland before.

A shrill beep issued from his pocket, causing him to jump, which resulted in a painful bump on the head when he hit the ceiling. Robert reached into his pocket and pulled free his cellphone. Lit across the screen was a message from Nicole.

Where are you!? I expected Lily home an hour ago! Is everything okay?

"Great." Robert sighed.

Nicole already thought him incompetent as a father, and now, he might have to reveal to her he had lost their child at a fast-food restaurant.

We got sidetracked (having too much fun!). We'll be there soon. His reply grew fuzzy in his sight as the salt from his sweat stung his eyes. He shoved the phone back in his pocket.

Somewhere around—above?—him, there came a knock. It was sudden and light. Just faint enough that, when Robert leaned forward, he was convinced it hadn't been there at all. But then it came again, this time with more conviction.

"Lily, are you still stuck? Daddy is having some trouble here. It would be really helpful if you could just come back out." Robert fell absolutely still in anticipation of a reply as soon as the words left his lips.

A soft, whispering sound began to waft through the plastic innards of the structure. It was almost melodic, but Robert couldn't make out any clear words. Even the source was hard to identify. It might have been a child, or it might have been a loud radio from a car pulling from the drive-thru.

"Is that you, Lily? Where are you?"

The girl didn't answer—not even a giggle. Instead, he heard a wild clatter of small hands and feet scurrying over plastic.

So much for being stuck!

Something about the sound paralyzed Robert. It was frenzied...crazed. The kind of racket an animal would make—a racoon breaking free from a trap—not a little girl.

He hurried over to the hole in the ceiling and stood up. Robert imagined the ladder must be quite the obstacle for the playland's usual population, but for him, it only went up to his shoulders. Standing allowed his head to pop through to the next level.

"Lily, enough's enough! Come to me right now!"

Nothing.

A long section of purple pipe stretched off in both directions. To the left, he could see the edges of the clear plastic bubble Lily had waved from. The bright, fluorescent lighting of the room beyond blared through the membrane, supercharging the violet hue of the plastic. To the right, the tube broke off into three paths—an oblong-shaped blue tube, an orange shaft, and a green tunnel with pink polka dots. He thought at least two of them led to slides.

"Lily?" Sweat dribbled down his face. He wasn't sure how much longer he could stand to be within the confines of the playland.

"Daddy." Lily's voice, barely above a whisper, wafted around him.

"Where are you, baby?"

Robert hefted himself up through the hole. In the depths of the green tunnel, he caught a glimpse of movement and crawled forward. A pair of feet wiggled away, feet wrapped in rainbow socks.

"Lily! Come back here right now!"

Robert launched himself into the green tube with the pink polka dots. She was playing with him. She wasn't stuck at all. Anger began to flare inside him.

"You are in big trouble, missy!"

The thick miasma of funk filling the air made him gag as he took in deep, sucking lungsful of air. He could feel the entire structure shift and sway under his weight.

"Come get me," Lily whispered again.

Robert paused in his forward crawl. Something was not right about his daughter's voice. He couldn't place it exactly, but it sounded fake. Like an impersonation. Close to the real thing, but not quite. A slight stretching of words, a barely perceived stutter.

That's not Lily.

It was a ridiculous thought, of course, and one Robert was quick to dismiss. He was stressed out, over-taxed. The heat was playing with his mind, the acoustics of the playland distorting Lily's words.

There was another burst of movement. This time, it seemed to emanate from the exterior of the playland's walls. An image of a huge spider scaling the plastic innards of the place flashed through his mind before he could stop it.

What was that?

"Lily?"

Robert held his breath, waiting for a reply. His heart pounded ferociously in his chest. Just when he thought there would be nothing, a delicate voice began to sing.

"The sweet little children all like to play. The sweet little children all want to stay. The sweet little children will live forever this day." The tone abruptly changed to something deeper, but still Lily. "We are hungry and must be fed. We are tired and want to sleep in their bed. We will take their faces and go in their stead."

The sweat coating his skin turned cold, sending a shiver across his body. He realized he had heard the tune before.

The twin girls.

The one inside the playland had been looking at her sister, singing the same rhyme.

"Honey?" He found himself crawling forward once again but this time at a much slower pace.

The green tunnel looped around a wide bend before joining the orange shaft. As Robert continued forward, he noticed deep gouges and scratches in the plastic. Little hard, orange curls stood out along the floor, like somebody had taken four knives and dragged them along the walls.

"What could do this?" He had no answer to his question.

"You're getting so close, Daddy!"

Robert looked ahead, and there she was, right in front of him, scurrying away. Her rainbow socks, loose and saggy on her feet, bounced and bobbed as she crawled. The girl rocketed from the orange shaft, back into the purple tube, and continued toward the observation bubble.

"Lily, stop!" Robert shot forward, snatching at her. His fingers gripped the floppy toe of one of her socks, pulling it free.

Just before she disappeared around the corner of the bubble, he saw the newly exposed appendage. Instead of his child's small, delicate foot, the limb was wrinkled and splotchy.

Slowly, Robert crawled along until he was fully bathed in the light of the clear bubble. Ahead of him, he could see the huddled form of his daughter where the tube terminated in a dead end.

His breath came in ragged, whistling bursts as he stared at the child. She sat hunched, her face hidden behind her hair.

"Lily?"

Movement through the observation dome pulled him away from the child. It was the shift manager, Timothy, entering through the glass door into the room. The man walked with a cocky swagger which affected his entire body, except for his stiff hair. Behind him came Edith. The young woman smiled proudly. And next to her, gripping the cashier's hand, was Lily. The little girl had a strip of toilet paper hanging out of the side of her pants.

Lily's eyes lit up when she noticed Robert inside the playland. She waved and laughed, her small finger pointing. He couldn't hear what she said, but her words drew the attention of the two employees. Edith appeared to chuckle at the sight of a grown man wedged inside the children's play place, while Timothy rolled his eyes.

Slowly, hesitantly, Robert returned his attention to the child he had been chasing, his mind suddenly making connections he had no idea existed until that moment. The twins, the little boy crying about a monster trying to take him, a monster that looked just like him. And of course, the lullaby.

"Robert." The voice coming from the thing before him was much deeper that it had been the other times it spoke.

And, with a growing fountain of horror filling his body with icy terror, he saw why. It no longer looked like Lily. In fact, it was not a child at all. In the purple haze piercing the plastic of the playland, the thing he had been pursuing now looked exactly like him.

Robert tried to back away, but it was too fast. It grabbed him and pulled him away from the observation bubble.

Away from the Lily.

Away from the light.

THE OILY

BY TRISH WILSON

Winwood House stood on the high hill butting up to Strangeman's Swamp, a five-mile pit reeking of desolation on the island of Caleb's Woe, located off the northeastern coast of Massachusetts. Spiders lived in the corners, and all manner of creaks and pops had kept Lara Winwood awake at night when she was a little girl. Whatever lurked in the swamp crept through the yawning hallways at night, seeking any entrance into a weak mind.

Lara's family had resided in Winwood House for three generations after her great-grandfather won the house in a bet. The Winwood's were interlopers, and the house made it clear from early on they were not welcome, but being stubborn folk, they wouldn't leave.

This hot summer day, she mopped the hardwood floor where Nate had found her father's body only three months prior. Those damned blood stains wouldn't come out, no matter how hard she scrubbed. She wished bleach and detergent would wash away the long years of pain and neglect, but she knew neither would give up the house without a fight.

"Thanks for helping me clean up this hell hole, Lara." Nate tossed tattered *Life* magazines into a box. He held one to his face, sniffed, and recoiled in disgust. "Cat pee. Damn it. Some of these magazines were worth money."

"Helping is the least I could do. I just wish I could have spent more time with you when we were kids."

"It's not your fault Mom and Dad sent you to a boarding school."

She remembered why, and a chill rippled down her spine. "You had to stay here with them. I'm surprised you're not a raving maniac by now."

Heartache lurked beneath his good-natured grin. "How do you know I'm not? Why don't you head upstairs and clean up that dresser you want in the guest room? I'll be up in a bit to help you carry it down. Gotta get the hand truck out of the car."

"I'd rather wait until you went with me."

He stopped in mid-toss and gaped at her. "You aren't scared to go up there, are you? After all these years?"

"Maybe."

"How old are you now? Forty-three?"

"Forty-two. Don't age me prematurely."

"So sorry, sis! I won't make that mistake again. What could possibly be up there that has you so spooked, aside of spiders the size of dinner plates?"

"Scotty Shaw."

There, she said it. She hadn't spoken his name in years, and voicing it called his ghost from the deepest recesses of the marshes beyond the house.

"Little Scotty Shaw? I haven't thought of him in thirty years. You don't believe that silly story, do you?"

"Of course, I do because it's true. I used to babysit him, remember?"

"What happened to him wasn't your fault."

Scotty Shaw had wandered into Strangeman's Swamp one hot summer day, and all the rescuers found were saddle shoes and his *Howdy Doody* doll that never left his side.

"He went to the worst spot."

"Yeah. The Oily."

The Oily was the wettest, most desolate marsh in Strangeman's Swamp. Pet dogs wandered in there. Jake Southern's wife, Nancy, hadn't left him for another man and moved out of Massachusetts to live in Florida. Everyone in Caleb's Woe suspected he had dumped her body in The Oily.

No one had the guts to search for her there, though, just as they didn't search much for Scotty Shaw. Once rescuers found his shoes and that doll on the edge of The Oily, the search was called off. No point in losing more locals to that miserable swamp.

"Look, Lara, I have to get the hand truck. It's broad daylight. Nothing is going to get you. Stop being a sissy, go upstairs, and clean up that dresser so I can help you drag it downstairs. And you want the Oriental rug. Roll it up, and I'll haul it down for you."

I'm being a scaredy-cat. This is stupid. Go upstairs and get that dresser.

There was nothing to be afraid of. Nothing at all.

Lara climbed the steep staircase until she reached the second floor, the tapping of her shoes echoing off the wood. Four bedrooms stood on the right side of a narrow hallway. She wanted to put as much distance between herself and the second floor as quickly as possible. *Clear out that dresser, roll up the rug, and get the hell downstairs as fast as you can.*

As she passed her old bedroom, she heard a sigh from behind the closed door.

She stopped dead in her tracks, listening, her heart thumping so hard it hurt.

Nothing.

She turned the knob and opened the door that creaked so loudly she jumped as she stepped into the room. *Stop being so skittish! There's nothing to be afraid of.*

Believe that if you wish, Lara. You know you have good reason to be afraid.

Dirty, yellow lace curtains that had once been white hung from the windows like loose flesh. Sunlight illuminated clouds of dust floating about the room. Stale air hung around her, like a dirty blanket covering a quaking child. Memories lurked in the shadows, on the walls, and in the floorboards, painful snippets of times past.

Storm clouds roiled in the distance, casting shadows on

Strangeman's Swamp. Wind blew strong and hard, tossing the tree branches that danced a frenzied tango. Gnarled branch arms reached into the afternoon sky, grasping at ravens steering clear in fear. As the sun hid behind cloud skirts, shadows lurked in the underbrush a few thousand yards away in The Oily. Lara raised the window to let out the stale air, and a gush of marsh wind blew into the room, rustling the flesh curtains. Dust coughed up around her, making her sneeze.

She leaned against the windowsill and stared out into the dank afternoon, watching Strangeman's Swamp as if demons lurked in the bramble far below.

No demons lived in Strangeman's Swamp. No ghosts either. Only creatures born of rock and wood, sticker bushes, vines choking the life out of trees, mud, water, and wild flowering shrubs. Nothing human lived in Strangeman's Swamp or The Oily. Whatever lurked there felt nothing for humanity and only wanted to end mankind's encroachment in its territory.

Lights flashed in the distance. What were cars doing on the road so close to the swamp? Especially during a thunderstorm?

Then, she remembered. No road ran along the swamp's edge.

Lights blinked on and off like fireflies, but there were no fireflies on Caleb's Woe. She watched the glowing pinpricks and wondered what they were. Will-o'-the-wisp? Saint Elmo's fire? Swamp gas? Phosphorescence?

Corpse candles?

They migrated from the edges of the swamp to meet in the center, circling each other like cats around a carcass. The lights danced and twirled, some only inches above the muddy waters and others high in the trees. They met in the center of the swamp. Once they reached The Oily, they stopped moving.

Then, they crept toward the house.

Lara stood riveted to the window, unable to move. Dread coiled at the base of her spine, whispering to her in a voice harsh with terror. She could only watch the spectacle taking place below, worrying what intelligence moved those lights en mass like a swarm of angry bees.

The lights floated on the breeze until they disappeared beneath the covered porch. Lara waited until the glow from below crept up the screen. Heart thumping and mouth dry with fear, she froze to her spot, unable to lower the window despite her desperate urge to slam it down. Knowing something horrid was about to happen, eyes wide and unblinking, she stared out the window at the growing glow, waiting. Fetid air hung around her, smelling of low tide and dead fish. The stink clung to her skin, absorbing into her pores. In disgust, she scratched her arms to scrape it off, but its grip only tightened.

The wizened hand creeping up the screen, shriveled in a dirty, tattered sleeve. Fingers crawled along the screen like a gnarled pale spider, seeking entrance. Mesmerized, Lara could only watch as the hand felt along the edges of the window, long ragged nails picking at the wood to break through.

Below the arm was a small body capped with a head full of matted brown hair. Mud clung to the tresses and caked on the shoulders. The body of the boy gripped the side of the house, clinging like a spider on a wall. Spiders terrified Lara. Those hairy limbs and those eyes...

The boy lifted his head. When Lara saw the face, she recoiled in horror, backing up enough so if it reached that arm through the screen it wouldn't touch her. Scotty Shaw's skin shrunk against his skull like shrink-wrap. A hole gaped from where the nose should have been. His mouth contorted into a gruesome frown devoid of tongue and teeth, a gaping maw of cracked, blue lips. The anguish in that battered face tore at her heart.

I'm sorry...I'm so sorry I left you alone up there when I was busy downstairs with my boyfriend...

Worst of all were his eyes. Where Scotty Shaw's blue eyes should have been were two gaping sockets, seeing nothing yet watching her intently, blaming her for not catching him sneaking out the window the night he disappeared. Mud tears poured from those sockets to fall down high-jutting cheekbones.

Lara fled, not once looking back as Scotty Shaw picked his way past the window frame and into the room. She ran outside through the hot afternoon haze, not knowing her brother stood in the cellar beneath the house, battling his own demons.

Nate chugged from his bottle of water after hauling in the hand truck. Refreshing cold fluid flowed down his throat, cooling his overheated body. He wiped sweat from his brow with his T-shirt. This hot day was going to be the death of him yet.

I have to get those bags out of the cellar. No point in putting it off. Might as well do it now. Nate finished his water, grabbed his flashlight, and headed for the fireplace. He opened the door to the left of the hearth. Moss and mildew stink belched from the stairwell, clinging to his clothes. *I'm going to need another shower after I get done in here.* He brushed past cobwebs overhead and aimed the flashlight beam down the steep steps as he walked.

The brick-hewn cellar stretched out for several hundred yards, disappearing into blackness a few feet ahead of him. Nate picked up the flashlight from the floor and flicked it on, illuminating the dank, long room with soft light.

The six plastic garbage bags loaded with old clothing and children's toys must have sat in the cellar for years. His father intended to take the bags to the local thrift store, but he never made it there. With a resigned sigh, Nate grabbed the bags two at a time and hoisted them up the stairs, dumping them on the floor in front of the fireplace. He returned to the cellar, walked the long distance to a large room, and grabbed another two bags of trash. He turned to return to the stairs when he heard a sigh, hidden in blackness.

Nate aimed his flashlight into the distance, illuminating the walls and reflecting off dust motes floating in fetid air. The sound was most likely an underground breeze creeping along the bricks.

At least, that's what he hoped it was.

He aimed the flashlight toward the edge of the room, light shining on the walls, revealing running water and moss adhered to the bricks. Nate walked into the darkness cut by his flashlight beam, listening to the dripping water and the faint sound of the surf in the distance. Concave gaping boxes blackened with mold and wet stood against the far wall.

The wispy sigh floated in the darkness ahead of him, closer than it sounded the last time.

"Lara you won't believe this mess. I don't think anything here is worth salvaging. You roll up the rug?"

"Rug."

"Lara? Hello?"

"Lo."

He turned around. "Lara, I—"

He was alone in the room. The hair on the back of his neck stood on end.

"Anyone there?"

"There."

It was a feminine voice. Not Lara's. Heart banging hard and legs aching to flee, he aimed the light ahead of him and crept along the wall, his back to the bricks. His teeth chattered in fear, the chill sinking into his skin from the cold bricks.

"Who is it?"

"Nate."

The woman who stepped into the room hunched over as if in great pain. Torn stockings hung from legs covered with deep, bright red scratches. Blond hair matted with mud hung in a sheet, obscuring her face. The Indian wrap-around skirt ripped in places, revealing shapely milky-white thighs. Handkerchief sleeves provided weak cover for the welts and angry gouges on her stick-thin arms.

"Who are you? What do you want?" His voice trembled with fear.

What stood before him was not his sister. The woman wore the same clothes Nancy Southern had worn their last day together—the day she disappeared.

She stumbled toward him on legs jutting out at odd angles as if broken. Arms reached for him. Withered fingers with long, ragged nails tensed into claws that would scrape his eyes out if she touched him.

"Stay away from me."

As her outstretched arms reached for his face, his heart raced so hard he couldn't breathe. Pain shot through his chest and into his shoulders. Panic set in, but he couldn't get away from her.

"I'm so sorry. We never should have hooked up. I was only seventeen..." He backed up against the wall, creeping sideways to get away from her, but she only changed her direction, reducing the distance between them. "Please, leave me alone! I didn't mean to hurt you." He cowered in the corner, whimpering in terror. "What do you want from me?"

Frozen in place against the wall, he stood helpless as her claws brushed against his cheeks. He squeezed his eyes shut, fearing those ragged nails would dig his eyeballs out. At her touch, he opened his mouth to cry out but only managed a deep, frightened moan, the type he often made while in the midst of a nightmare from which he couldn't awaken.

Nate opened his eyes but looked down, not wanting to meet her gaze. He gripped her by her upper arms and tried to push her away, but her thickened flesh felt like water balloons filled to the bursting point. Nate was afraid to squeeze her arms too hard lest he rupture them, and he didn't want to see what would come pouring out of her if that happened.

She lifted her head, eyes and mouth closed, and turned her face toward his. Without thinking, he glanced at her. He gaped in horror at her shriveled face, skin stretched taut over jutting bones that could not hide her rage and despair. Fear overcame him, and his chest hurt at her assault. He couldn't breathe, pain jolted down his left arm, and panic froze him in his tracks.

She moved her face toward his. When she opened her eyes, deep caverns yawned where her brown eyes should have been. Black widows crawled out and skittered across her forehead. Nate whimpered, trying to shove her away, but her strength overpowered him.

When she opened her mouth for her kiss, she was only a breath away from his lips. Mud poured from her lips' cracked corners, oozing down her chin to drip onto his T-shirt. With one swift kick, he kneed her in the stomach, and she doubled over, giving him time to get out from under her grasp.

"Nate? Where are you?" Lara's voice came from the stairwell.

"Here!"

Heart racing and adrenaline pumping, he ran out of the claustrophobic room and took three steps toward the stairs when he stopped.

A pasty body the size of a child crept toward him, illuminated by his flashlight's flickering glow as the batteries failed. It crawled on all fours, moving in jerking motions, head twisted around and facing the ceiling. It opened its withered mouth, groaning a menacing cry of anguish as it crept toward him.

He turned and dropped the flashlight, which sputtered out, leaving him in inky blackness.

"N-Nate? Come up here. You know I hate going down there."

Stumbling into the darkness in the opposite direction, he headed for the rear of the house, not knowing how or if he would make it to safety.

Lara couldn't leave her brother alone in the house with whatever it was that lurked in the silent rooms. Steeling herself, she strode into the living room, only to find herself alone.

When she saw the open door by the fireplace, she suspected where he went.

"Nate? Where are you?"

"Here."

His voice came from the cellar. Lara walked to the open door but did not go down the stairs. Cold air blew past her, bringing forth a bone-chill so intense she wrapped her arms around her body, but she shivered in spite of herself.

"N-Nate? Come up here. You know I hate going down there."

"Lara, come down."

Against her better judgment, she gingerly tiptoed down the steps, taking it slow until she reached the bottom. As her eyes adjusted to the darkness, she looked into the distance of the tunnel, but she didn't see her brother.

"Nate? Where are you?"

"Here."

She walked across the cellar, feeling along the wall as she approached the storage room, the one Nate used to take his girlfriends to, although he wasn't aware she knew. Did he come down here to chase old memories?

"Nate, I can't find you."

"I'm here."

His voice called from the blackness further down the cellar, going toward the back of the house. Kicking the flashlight as she fumbled in the darkness, she picked it up and turned it on. The weak beam lit her path only a foot ahead.

"Don't leave me here alone. Stay where you are. I'm coming to you."

She walked slowly through the cellar, one hand shaking as she held the flashlight ahead of her and the other hugging the wall. Despite the soft beam of light, she could not see well. The deeper into the cellar she walked, the darker her surroundings became until the flashlight flickered and went out. Panicked and whimpering, she smacked the flashlight against her palm to no avail. She stood in the pitch blackness, terrified and crying, feeling along the cold bricks and hugging the wall as if blind.

"Dammit, Nate! Get over here! Don't leave me alone like this, you shit!"

A cool hand grasped hers and led her along the cellar. She stumbled to keep up, nearly dragged in the dark.

"Don't walk so fast. I can't see, and I'm going to fall. And don't hold my hand so tightly. You're hurting me."

The only response was to drag her faster, panting and grunting all the way. He must have been as scared as she was. Her hand holding the flashlight scraped the wall, tearing her flesh, and she winced at the pain, but she used her mangled hand to keep a grip on something solid so she wouldn't lose her balance. In the darkness, she lost her sense, not only of direction but of up and down, as if she were a diver lost deep in a black sea, thinking she was swimming toward the surface only to swim deeper and deeper until she drowned, exhausted and out of air.

Her head spun with confusion and fear, and her stomach lurched, bile-churned by dread and dizziness. She fought off vomiting as Nate dragged her further through the cellar. Lara shook the flashlight a few times, but it wouldn't light. After what couldn't have been more than a minute or two, Nate released her grip, and light from her flashlight illuminated her path enough to make her squint her eyes at the sudden brightness.

Nate lay on the ground a few yards ahead of her.

She raced over, fearing he lost his footing in the darkness, but when she touched him, his skin, slack and pale, nearly slid off in her hand. He lay on his back, a wild grimace marring his handsome face, one hand clawed over his chest. *Damn it, his heart finally gave out.*

Who was holding my hand...

"N-Nate?"

Her voice echoed in the darkness behind her and was answered by a soft sigh and a rustling as if a small body dragged across the floor.

Lara Winwood ran screaming from the cellar and out the back door, her mind and soul shattered and torn. She was the one who got away.

The Oily claimed its own.

The Well

By David-Jack Fletcher

Now

The old wooden stairs of the lighthouse creak as I hold onto the railing and climb the spiraling staircase. Through clouded vision, I look at my feet and wonder how far I'll get before the stairs shudder and collapse under my weight forever.

I can't think about that now. I can't worry myself with the blisters and the splinters of wood digging into my raw feet, or the open wounds all over my body. I can't think about the black oil seeping from me where blood used to be.

I have a job to do.

"You can't stop me!" My voice echoes through the stairwell. "I will end you!"

The silence that follows is broken only by my breaths and the adrenaline of my heart thumping through my skull.

Gasoline is slick on the wood, the stench consuming my nostrils. I'm satisfied I poured enough and choke on the thick vapors working their way through my lungs. The gasoline splashes around my toes as I climb another stair.

I hear the whisper through the pounding of my heart. That terrible sound carries on a wind that doesn't exist, audible only to me.

"Miiiichaeeeel." The slow drawl of my name grates like nails on a chalkboard. Like a hand wrapped around my soul.

I shrink at the sound, and with each step, the presence grows stronger. It whispers my name again, the invisible hand squeezing tighter. The blackness inside me bubbles to the surface, frothing at my lips and splashing against the gasoline.

"Is that the best you can do?" I hurl again and scream into the empty lighthouse.

Slipping in the black muck from my stomach, I grip the railing again, ignoring the squish as my foot sinks through the liquid. It doesn't matter. None of it matters—not the oil seeping from my eyes or the weight pressing my soul into nothingness. None of it.

I just have to get there.

To the Watch Room.

I'm almost there. Right where this started. Right where it'll end. The door at the landing is open, swinging on its hinges. Beckoning me into the darkness beyond.

"Miiiichaeeeel."

I fumble through my pants pocket for the lighter and

hold it in front of my face. The presence sneers as the orange flame pierces the darkness.

I smile and close my eyes.

Drop the lighter and laugh.

THREE MONTHS AGO

The realtor had used the word "derelict" when I first inquired about the lighthouse. The emails said the place had burned down eighty years earlier and its original use as a lighthouse abandoned long before that. The realtor, Shelley, seemed reluctant, muttering about a sordid history, but agreed to take me out to see it.

"I must warn you, though," she said in a hushed whisper on the phone, "the place is worthless. Any price will be too much."

"Sounds perfect," I said and hung up, lighting a cigarette and puffing with a deep sigh.

My phone vibrated in my hand to tell me I had four missed calls from Ted. He was a bear of a man, rugged and thickset, with a manicured beard. But he acted more like a terrified cat, clinging to me for dear life. I wasn't surprised at the missed calls. Or the texts.

I sighed and pocketed the phone. He wanted space. Fine. He wanted me to move out. Okay. I told myself I'd do whatever he needed to keep this marriage alive. But I couldn't take the incessant phone calls and the stream-of-consciousness text messages relaying his every thought about everything at any given time.

I promised myself I'd call him after the inspection. He wouldn't want me living in a burned-out old lighthouse, but he didn't have a say in that. Not at the moment. Not anymore.

The lighthouse was right near the beach—an obvious statement, but one worth mentioning. This particular beach was also abandoned. Huge signs advising people to stay off the sand and the obscure "falling rocks" warnings had been plastered around the place. It was abandoned all right.

I stood outside the lighthouse, taking in its shape and the visible burn marks discoloring the once-white tower. According to the listing, the lighthouse was 101 meters tall, the same as the tallest lighthouse in Yokohama. It was situated 300 meters above sea level, overlooking the Pacific Ocean, with glimpses of the aurora when the light was just right. It was no surprise, then, that the slightest breeze felt like a hurricane.

Ted would have hated it.

I smiled.

Shelley appeared flustered as she approached the lighthouse, juggling keys, a folder, and her phone while trying not to slip out of her high heels. Brushing hair out of her face, she greeted me with a smile. Forever professional.

"Professor Myers?" she called over the wind.

We shook hands for a brief moment until the delicate balance of folder, phone, and keys started to slip. Shelley was jittery, uncomfortable being there. She ushered me to a building around the back, almost invisible from the road leading up to the lighthouse.

It turned out to be the living quarters—a quaint little two-bedroom cabin like you might see in a seaside town in Italy or Spain. Unlike the lighthouse, the living quarters had not been burned down. They hadn't been maintained by any stretch, but at least there were no piles of charred wood lying around. Shelley mentioned the boathouse a few hundred meters away.

"So, as you can see..." Shelley started the tour of the living quarters.

Despite myself, I tuned her out. There was nothing Shelley could say to me I couldn't already see. The stained glass windows filtering blocks of color onto the wooden floors. The gas stove and cooktop from the early 1900s, never updated. The exposed brick interior and the families of spiders nesting in the wooden beams streaming across the ceiling.

It was perfect.

I tuned back in at the mention of the government fence and the history of disappearances in the area.

"It's quite infamous. I'm surprised Council listed it," Shelley said.

"Infamous?" I raised my eyebrows.

"The caretaker and his whole family—wife and three kids, even the dog—just vanished one night. Gone, like they never even existed."

"That's a bit disturbing," I said with a frown. Still, something about the place spoke to me.

Shelley nodded. "Very disturbing. The next fellow, a real loner according to all sources, also disappeared, but not before shutting the lighthouse lamp down in the middle of a storm. A ship carrying families from England smashed right into the cliff-face. Everybody drowned."

"What happened to that caretaker?"

Shelley shrugged. "He was never seen again either."

I opened my mouth but was shushed as the story continued.

"That was in 1912. Since then, two other caretakers vanished. The lighthouse was abandoned in 1940 when the last caretaker set fire to the place. Newspapers at the time said he was found wandering across the beach with first-degree burns, muttering about a well. He died a few hours later in hospital."

"Spooky." I fought the urge to roll my eyes, knowing the game she was playing. Sell the mystique, not the property.

"It's been a historical site ever since. Closed to the public. That's why I'm surprised Council would list it. But here we are."

"What's your best price?" I asked.

"Professor, uh…" Shelley paused to look over the folder in her hand. "Michael, is it?"

I nodded.

"Michael, there is no price that would be fair. The lighthouse must be maintained as part of the sale, and as you can see…" She pointed out the window and let the evidence speak for itself.

"Well, whatever the price," I said, a thin smile spreading across my lips, "I'll take it."

Shelley protested as much as someone who didn't want to lose commission would. That being said, I was in her office thirty minutes later, organizing the paperwork for a purchase.

Walking to my car, I felt my phone buzzing in my pocket again and swiped to answer.

"Ah, he picks up," Ted said, with *that* tone.

"I was busy. I just bought a property," I replied, swallowing my frustration and lighting a cigarette.

"A property?" Ted asked and fell silent.

I sighed. "Ted, this is what you wanted. You asked me to move out, so I'm going."

No response, just a whisper of sharp breaths.

"Look, Ted, I have to go."

The phone, along with my excitement, went dead.

As I drove in the direction of the motel—my home until the settlement of the property—I found myself gazing toward the lighthouse. A beacon in the distance, my new home.

Somewhere beneath the hum of the engine, a voice whispered my name.

Moving day

Ted had promised to help with the move but had developed a cough at the last moment. As usual. Yet somehow, I was the one with communication problems. I had told him it was fine and helped the movers with some of the lighter boxes as he watched from the kitchen, sipping an herbal tea. Moments like that made the move feel like the right thing to do. Other moments, the ones where his arms were wrapped around me and his lips caressed mine, the move didn't feel so right.

I thought about that as the truck was emptied into my new home. Jason, the removalist, pushed some papers under my nose and asked for a signature, peering out the window toward the lighthouse.

"Place gives me the creeps," he muttered as I scrawled my signature. "Make sure you review us on Yelp." He waved on his way out.

I nodded, knowing full well I was never going to leave a review.

Ted tried to phone again, and I silenced the call, letting the screen dim into black. I knew unpacking would be the only sure-fire way to push him from my thoughts, so I got to work.

As I tore packing tape from the closest box and threw it to the messy ground around me, a shiver ran down my spine.

"Michael." A whisper, like the one I'd heard that day in my car. Just audible in the silence, but low enough to be my imagination.

292

My tingling spine told me my mind was not playing tricks.

The voice came again, just behind my shoulder. I spun around. The room was empty. I listened to my body, to the crawling of my skin, the knot in my stomach, and walked outside. It was as though a rope was tied to my heart, leading me through the property grounds.

To the lighthouse.

The whisper echoed around the vacant land. It came from inside the lighthouse, somewhere near the lantern at the top.

The door was just a charred plank, a feeble barrier between the inside and the outside. I reached for the brass handle, somehow unscathed in the fire long ago, and pushed the door open with a long, steady creak.

Thin strips of light filtered through cracks in the walls, illuminating the mess inside. The floors were black with ash and what looked to be some kind of dried black gunk—coagulated and gelatinous, all these years later.

I knelt and touched the goo, rubbed it between my thumb and forefinger. It reminded me of moldy custard. I wiped my hands on my jeans, stood up, and looked around. Beams of wood had crashed to the ground, and the winding staircase lining the walls was missing a few steps here and there, the brass railing, like the door handle, untouched. I could smell smoke, felt it stinging my eyes, as I moved through the lighthouse toward the staircase. There was something familiar about the stairs. They reminded me of something. Of some*where* I'd been before.

The walls were rotted, littered with holes, like wounds half-eaten by rats and other vermin.

"Michael."

The whisper rose again, twisting down the staircase toward me. The breath hit my face, washing over me like the detritus of a dead animal. Whoever was calling for me was just upstairs in the Watch Room.

The railing buckled under my grip as I climbed the stairs. I felt the rope again, tightening around my heart, willing me to follow its desire. It pulled me to a place I'd never been, yet which felt so familiar.

Like home.

The Watch Room was dusty. Patches of mold spread across the crevices in the corners of the ceiling. The fire had reached the door but not the room. Save for the dust and the mold, the room was untouched. I noticed some canisters of gasoline sitting in one of the corners, undisturbed and waiting.

Behind the gasoline, an old white sheet hung over something hiding in the corner. The rope around my heart squeezed again, and I went toward it and pulled the sheet away to reveal what lay beneath.

A painting.

A faded golden frame made the interior seem even darker, casting light away from the image in the painting. I stared into it, wishing the gold away until I could no longer see it. All that remained was the painting, fumes of the oil still strong after years of abandonment.

It was a well—large, gray cement bricks of different

sizes and shapes. Jagged edges spiked at my eyes as I took in the well. It sat within a patch of brown, dead grass. Inside the well was nothingness, a deep, inky blackness, leading into the depths of the Earth. As I looked upon the painting, absorbing each brick in the well and staring into the abyss contained within, the ashen staircase began to heal, restoring itself to a former glory nobody had seen for two generations.

"Miiiichaeeeel." The whisper turned into a sneer, closer than before.

It came from the well.

Every inch of me wanted to turn and run, but the force around my heart gripped me, pulled me to my knees. I stared into the well, unable to speak or breathe or blink. Unable to move.

All I could do was listen.

Something in the well spoke to me in muffled whispers, nonsensical sounds forming ancient knowledge. Words I'd never heard, but which I knew. It reached out of the darkest depths of the earth, penetrating my ears.

A message.

My mind sank into the well until everything around me vanished. Everything but the whispers, the message entering me, filling me with words I didn't understand. Words I didn't want to hear.

The darkness surrounded me, immersed me in an abyss of nothingness. I tried to breathe. My lungs moved, but only because it was their nature to do so. No air came in, none escaped. But it didn't matter. In this space, this eternal black,

I didn't need to breathe. I didn't need to see or think or feel. The abyss did it all for me.

My skin broke out in goosebumps, shivering up my arms first and down the back of my neck, caressing the tiny hairs on my upper back. The cold nothingness sunk into my bones, stabbed into my heart and brain. My mind seized.

I reached through the freezing emptiness, unable to see my fingertips. It called again, the whisper groaning in a language I'd only heard once before. In the lighthouse. Groaning through the depths of the abyss, each syllable like an ice pick jabbing at my brain.

The darkness closed in around me. I opened my mouth to scream, but the sound was stolen, captured by the darkness. The silence felt heavy, like a presence drawing closer. I couldn't shut my mouth. I couldn't do anything.

The cold black sunk into my open mouth, reaching into me like a bony hand scraping at my insides. It explored my body, twisting through my organs. As the blackness spread through me, I knew I belonged to it, and I disappeared into the abyss.

In the next moment, the whispers were gone. I was alone in silence. The grip around my heart was gone. I clutched my chest, drew in deep breaths, and fell to my backside. After my breathing settled, I rose to my feet and reached for the painting.

It needed light. It needed me.

I headed back down the stairs, only just noticing the holes in the walls were gone, the staircase renewed. I moved through the lighthouse toward the charred front door, painting tucked under my arm, and paused to take in the sight of the ash rising into the air, healing the burns and the scars and the rot of the last eighty years. Rubbing my face in disbelief, I felt the same gunk from the floor leak from my eyes and ran back to my new home.

I awoke the next morning, scrambling for air as I fell out of my unmade bed. My lungs burned, my head heavy with sharp pains. On my hands and knees, I wretched, coughing and choking on a black oil drizzling out of my throat. I heaved again, trying to urge the thick ooze out of my body. It crept along my esophagus for a moment but slid back down toward my stomach. I shoved fingers down my throat to force a reaction, to expunge the black bile, but it was no use. It had settled in me now.

Clutching my stomach, I somehow knew the blackness was inside all of me. A life force, pulsating around my body. Sharing my oxygen and blood and cells. Taking what it needed.

Across the room, the painting of the well lay dormant, uncovered, facing me. The blackness in the well comforted me. It made me feel something. It made me feel at home.

I ran to it and pressed my face against the oil paint, my head surrounded by the opening of the well. As I leaked tears onto the canvas, the sick feeling dissipated. My headache vanished, and the almost inaudible whispering became like soft rhythms of my favorite song.

In the days that passed, the lighthouse continued to

heal itself. The land, too, had begun to prosper—the grass a bright green, the sand on the beach below a crisp gold, unlike anything I had seen before. I had unpacked most of the house, my new painting taking centerstage in the living room. In any other house, the living room was where I would put the television. But the well gave me a sense of peace.

On the fifth day, as the sun drowned into the horizon, I gazed through the burnt oranges and golden yellows from the top of the lighthouse. Waves crashed against the shore below. The salty water bubbled and fizzed as it was absorbed back into the ocean. Losing myself in the moment, I forgot about Ted and the reasons I was living there.

A figure moved on the sand.

The small entity, a man, ran across the shore with a surfboard, leaving faint footprints as he rushed toward the ocean. The waves lashed at him as he pushed his board further into the water, past the break line. My serenity dissipated with each of his paddles. His hands fishing through the water were like punches to my skin.

He was on my beach.

"Bring him to me." The whispering rose from within me as black ooze leaked from my ears.

I made my descent through the lighthouse. The pores in my skin felt heavy with coagulated oil, and I wondered how long before I started to split open. I dragged my fingertips along the walls as I shuffled through the building, feeling the warmth of its energy, the subtle vibrations from the wind outside like soft heartbeats.

The bleeding sunset fell into shades of black as I waited by the fence at the entrance to the beach. With the light fading away, the surfer made his approach back to dry land, shaking water from his long, wavy hair. He threw his board over the fence, climbing the mesh cage with impressive skill.

"Hey." He waved at me and extended a hand.

I shook his hand and smiled. "The beach is closed, isn't it?"

The surfer lifted his eyebrows up and down with an excited, childish glee. "Yeah." He stifled a laugh.

"You come here often?" I asked, releasing the man's hand.

He frowned in contemplation and tilted his head. "A few times a week. Are you from around here?"

I thumbed over my shoulder toward the lighthouse. "Just moved in a few days ago."

The surfer gave a confused smile as he looked at the lighthouse.

"I've always wanted to go in there, but Council never let me," he said. "You did all that in a few days?"

I nodded and pretended to wipe sweat from my brow. "You should come and have a look. Feel like a coffee, or maybe a beer?"

"Absolutely," he said, following me past the lighthouse to the living quarters. "I'm a historian, so this is like all of my Christmases coming at once. I don't care how terrible the history."

I ushered him inside and closed the door behind us, the

surfer already sitting on the lounge, glancing around at the outdated features.

As I headed to the kitchen to get the beer, unsure of what I was supposed to do next, the surfer called out, "You an art collector or something?"

"Professor of engineering, although I am taking some time off," I called back. "Why?"

I handed him the beer, wiped bottle sweat on my jeans, and sat next to him. He motioned toward the painting displayed on the wall.

"That painting is rare," he said. At my silence, he continued. "As I said, I'm a historian. I specialize in rare or collectible art and jewelry."

"Good timing that you showed up just after I moved in," I said, suspicion clear in my tone.

The art historian surfer adopted a sheepish grin. "I must confess, I saw you moving in. I was going to come knocking in the next day or so, anyway." He pointed to the painting. "Most people think it was lost in a shipwreck, but I've seen old photos of the Watch Room, and lo and behold, there it was, hanging on the wall. The main reason I've been dying to get inside the lighthouse."

I remembered the realtor, Shelley, telling me about a ship sinking just off the coast and asked the surfer if there was any connection.

He took a swig from the bottle and nodded. "That ship carried more than families. It had a bunch of possessions from some wealthy Spanish family. Jewels, furniture, art. All lost in the shipwreck, of course."

"Except for this," I said.

"Except for this," the surfer agreed. "This painting is one of a kind. *The Well*. Artist unknown."

We sat in silence for a moment—him sculling down more fermented yeast, me contemplating the origins of the painting.

"Do you mind?" he asked, interrupting my thoughts. He pointed to the painting. "Can I have a closer look?"

"Of course." I smiled and watched him approach the painting.

The surfer wiped strands of damp hair from his face and stood in front of *The Well*, hands clasped behind his back as though afraid to touch. He muttered amazement under his breath and paused a few times to tell me he thought it was genuine, asked where I found it. I told him it came from the Watch Room in the lighthouse.

"Another beer?" I asked.

But the art historian surfer wasn't listening. He stared into the well as if in a trance. The whispering began again, though I sensed it was not for me. Not this time. The surfer stepped closer to the painting, held out a hand to touch it. His finger seemed to penetrate the canvas, sinking into the oily abyss of the well.

He pulled back, stunned, and wiped oil from his finger. The surfer looked at me for an explanation but received none. I shrugged and pointed back to the painting. Black oil overflowed from the well and dripped from the bottom of the painting.

"What is that?" The surfer stumbled backwards.

As if compelled, I caught him, held him close to the painting as the oil seeped into the carpet and snaked toward us. The blackness inside me stirred in unison with the oil, now shaped like a hand, thin fingers stretching toward the surfer as he screamed.

The oil crawled across his skin, clutching at his limbs, dragging him toward the canvas. The muscles in my body disobeyed my desire to help the man. My efforts to pull him away from the painting were all but nonexistent, and I found my hands pushing the surfer further toward *The Well*.

He begged as the oil reached from the depths, wrapping around his face, flowing down his throat. His head disappeared into the canvas, his choked screams echoing in the darkness against the jagged grey bricks. His body melted into the painting, swallowed by the oil as whispers of gratitude sank into me.

The surfer was gone, dragged somewhere into the abyss, as though he'd never existed. My stomach lurched, though the blackness inside me refused to surface, and I fell to the ground, cussing my weakness. Consciousness felt impossible, and I closed my eyes to sounds of chewing and slurping coming from the well.

Something at the bottom was hungry, and I had provided its first meal.

Through the grinding of teeth against bone was the greedy hiss of one word: "More."

Last Week

The following two weeks were a blur of oil and black gunk and the sounds of an unseen entity feasting on the surfer. I'd woken up the morning after the incident, with an itch all over my body, to find the painting gone—a patch of black oil in the carpet the only evidence of its presence in my house.

My skin crawled as though ants had found a home under the surface. Thin and papery, the skin tore as I scratched to reveal not human blood, but a thick black substance.

The painting was inside me, and despite my surprise that it no longer hung in the living room, I knew without a doubt it had taken itself home.

The Watch Room.

I had tried to move it back, to be close to it, but each morning, the painting was gone. Back in the Watch Room, in the dark, hanging on the wall facing the door. I stood alone in the living room and scratched the skin on my left forearm, clumps of skin melting beneath my blackened fingernails.

As the oily bile seeped down my arm and onto my hand, *The Well* called to me. The surfer had kept it at bay, whatever it was that lived at the bottom of the well. But it was hungry again. I had helped it feed, and it was counting on me to bring more sustenance.

"More." Its orders were relentless.

"I can't," I sobbed, tasting the thick black ooze rolling

from my tear ducts into my mouth.

I cried harder as my legs buckled, giving in to an overwhelming urge to scour the streets for meat. The darkness thrashed inside me, willing me to the door. I punched at my legs until I fell, bringing my knees to my chin and wrapping myself in a ball. I rocked back and forth, scratching at the unending itching in my limbs.

Earlier Today

With the intensity of recent events and the burning desire to bring food to *The Well*, I hadn't called Ted for weeks. I couldn't endanger him. He, as usual, called every hour or so, and by the time I picked up my phone, there were dozens of voicemails clogging up my digital cloud. The first few were filled with undertones of annoyance and upset and by the fifth had progressed to a combination of anger and remorse in typical Ted fashion.

That had been my mistake—giving in to my selfish desire to hear from my husband. *The Well* sensed the weakness, leaped at its chance.

My fingers dialed his number, automated extremities disobeying my will.

Don't pick up, Ted. Please, don't pick up.

"Hello." Ted sounded distant, moody.

"Hi," I said. "I missed a bunch of calls." I wanted to scream at him, tell him to stay away. I didn't want him to see the wounds on my arms and legs or the dark rings under my eyes from crying thick black liquid all the time.

I said nothing.

Ted scoffed under his breath but loud enough for me to hear. I told myself not to react, to let it slide.

"You could say that," he said, and I imagined him biting his lower lip in frustration. "How's the new place?"

The blackness swelled inside me again, pushed words from my mouth. "You should come over. It would be nice to see you. To talk."

No!

"Really?" The note of excitement in his voice was charming. "When?"

No, Ted, stay away.

"Now." I hung up and clasped a hand over my mouth.

He arrived fifteen minutes later, fiddling with his shirt collar as he approached the lighthouse. Ted's nerves always appeared as fidgets or a bouncing knee. I watched from the front door, now no longer charred at all, but a beautiful brown oak. He breathed into a cupped hand and smiled, unaware of *The Well's* plans for him.

We hugged at the door, my head buried in his chest. The beat of his heart felt like home. I felt the strength of the darkness inside me falter, and I tried to tell him to leave, to never look back. But I wasn't strong enough.

I kissed him on the cheek, letting his stubble scratch at my lips. Then, I ushered him inside with a firm hand on the back, telling him we'd have plenty of time to chat after he asked about my bruises and wounds.

"I want to show you something very special." I smiled, scratching my forearm.

I lit a cigarette and pushed the lighter into my pants pocket. Ted followed me to the Watch Room, saying something about the place looking brand new. I couldn't hear him over the whispering, the snide voice taunting me for being weak, luring my husband to an eternity inside the canvas.

As I reached the door, I managed to grip the frame, using all my energy. Splinters of wood fell to the ground. The stairs behind us creaked as I strained harder against the doorframe, unwilling to let Ted fall victim to the eternal abyss. The splinters disintegrated into ash.

The lighthouse, I thought. *Hurt the lighthouse, hurt the painting. That's its weakness.*

I remembered Shelley's warnings, the stories about the fire and the other caretakers. The last one, burnt beyond repair, walking around the beach. He'd known too.

Ted put a soft hand on my shoulder. "What is it?"

His touch sent a warm energy through my clothes. These were the moments where I knew moving here was wrong, that I knew I needed to be with him at home. Our home.

I have to get him out of here.

I tried to turn around, tried to face him and explain, but *The Well* squeezed around my heart again.

The jolt of pain made my grip loosen, and I spilled through into the Watch Room. *The Well* greeted us, the dusty gold frame grabbing Ted's attention.

"Ted!" I cried, unable to move from the floor. "Don't look at it!"

It was too late.

He glided toward the painting, mesmerized by the darkness inside the well. The whispering grew into a laughter hissing around the room. Ted lifted his hand to touch the canvas.

"No!" I cried and strained with all my might to get up from the ground, the black gunk inside me like stones weighing me down, drowning me.

But I was up, on my feet. That's what mattered.

I reached for Ted and pulled his arm toward me. He lost his balance, slipping backward into my arms.

"Ted?" I caressed his cheek, but he was still entranced. To the painting, I yelled, "Let him go! You can't have him!"

The laughter pierced my ears once more, the painting spewing the word, "Hungry," again and again in an ancient language. As I dragged Ted toward the door, my stomach heaved black bile, the evil inside me splattering across Ted's shirt and the wooden floor. When I was emptied, it spread across the room with a will of its own. It raced to the door behind me, building itself into a barricade.

I felt lighter as the black goo left my body, but I sensed it wasn't all gone. My veins still pumped remnants of the evil into my heart.

"Hungry," the voice spat again.

In the corner of my eye, the canisters of gasoline gleamed through the dark. I rushed toward them. Pouring the clear liquid across the room and over the barricade, I begged for Ted to wake up.

As the gasoline splashed against the wooden floor, the laughter stopped. *The Well* had a weakness, and I'd found it. With that knowledge, I smiled, tipping gasoline onto the gooey barricade. It melted away as the liquid rushed down its surface, revealing the exit once more.

Dragging Ted through the doorway, I looked at the painting, the oil dripping as it had before. The well overflowed. I felt the evil now, pouring through the Watch Room toward us.

"Come on, Ted," I yelled at him, eyes unblinking.

I stepped backward toward the stairs, pulling his body with me, slipping over the gunk encircling us.

It crept up Ted's legs and torso, bony fingers clawing at his clothes and skin. I pulled as hard as I could, but the liquid was stronger. Ted began to wake, confused but alert, and struggled against the strength of *The Well*.

It was no use.

It dragged him toward the canvas, his feet disappearing into the midnight black of the well. I begged for it to let him go, told it I would find ten others in his place, but *The Well* had tasted him now.

"Michael?" Ted looked at me, his upper body sinking into nothingness. His eyes, those beautiful brown eyes, begged me through their terror and confusion.

I rushed to him, grabbed at him, but I was too late.

He was gone.

Through my screams, *The Well* purred with satisfaction,

grinding Ted's flesh and bones in its teeth.

Black bile snaked toward me. *The Well* knew its control over me had ended.

"I have nothing now," I said to the evil surrounding me.

Grabbing the remaining canisters of gasoline, I began to pour. I tossed the gasoline in every direction, heading down the stairs. No inch of the lighthouse could be spared. The last drops of gasoline splashed onto the ground of the first floor.

The remnants of the evil substance leaked from my eyes as I made my way through the lighthouse. It groaned and creaked in anger with each step I took up the staircase.

In defiance, I shouted, "This is how you die."

Now

The flames lick at my body, melting skin from bone. I tear *The Well* from the wall, clutch it against my chest as the fire envelops us. I cry as we're devoured by the fire, oil leaking from the frame once more. From the depths of the well, painful screams fill the lighthouse as the fire burns the building from existence.

A tear escapes my body. In the heat and pain, I am glad it is salty water. I close my eyes, letting the fire devour me as the oil melts into my skin, merging me to the painting.

Taking me to my new home.

Inside the well.

MIDNIGHT VISIT

BY CONSTANTINE E. KIOUSIS

Marcus walked down the dimly lit corridor, fingers clenched around the handle of his toolkit. He threw wary glances left and right, eyes wandering across the shoddy apartment doors as he made his way toward the end of the hallway. The man flinched when a lightbulb flickered, its amber light wavering. The whole place sank into darkness for the briefest of intermittent moments, enough for his mind to rush back to its initial flight response from ten minutes ago, when he first pulled the truck up the side of the road and gazed upon the dilapidated building.

Seeing it towering toward the dark, starry sky, an edifice bathed in the pale, argent light of the midnight moon, his knee-jerk reaction had been to turn around and drive back home, leaving this godforsaken neighborhood in his rearview mirror. But Marcus couldn't do that. With Laura recently laid off from the diner and a second baby on the way, he couldn't afford to be picky. That's why he'd started making late night visits again. She'd been there for him in his times of need, and he'd done the same for her. *Till death do us part.* That was the oath.

Thus, instead of bolting, he got out of the vehicle and into the frosty night, stepped onto the trash-littered sidewalk, walked up to the ramshackle entrance, and eyeing the rusted buzzer, forced himself to ring. He waited a good minute before ringing again since no one buzzed him in and another thirty seconds before frustration reared its ugly head, prompting him to try the iron door, which slid open with one push, its locking mechanism broken. It hadn't really come as a surprise. Nothing around there worked properly. He knew that much from experience. Having shot one last glimpse up and down the empty street, Marcus had entered the shadowed entrance hall.

And so here he was, second floor, standing outside apartment 2-G in his blue denim overalls, shivers creeping down his spine. He scanned for a doorbell and was met with a darkened frame upon the peeling gray surface of the wall to the right of the door, in place of where the button casing was once screwed in. With a sigh, Marcus raised a hesitant hand and knocked, his mind drifting to his little girl, Trisha, as it always did when he needed some cheering up. He'd tucked her in before he'd gone out, and she'd made him promise to wake her up when he returned, to make sure he'd gotten back safely. She was the most wonderful six-year-old in the world, and he was going to make sure she had everything him and his wife never had as kids. Same for his unborn boy.

The sound of muffled footsteps pulled him from his

thoughts. Someone approached from the other side of the door. A *clank* tore at the silence of the hallway, followed by the jingling of keys as the door was unlocked and opened a crack, its hinges creaking and releasing a cold, sickly light from within. He was midway to forcing a smile when he paused as the half-concealed face of a guy emerged between the gap, head slightly bowed, a weary eye locked on Marcus.

"Yes?" the man asked, whisper-like.

"Uhm, hello," Marcus replied, managing a lopsided grin. "I'm Marcus. Marcus Barrows."

The man kept staring at him, pulling the door back a bit more, his whole form coming into view. Marcus caught a glimpse of a television somewhere in the background, the source of the pallid glow, the stranger's shape cast ominously against it. He was barefoot, sporting a set of ragged, baggy brown pants and what used to be a white tank top, now tainted by smears of various hues and origins. And he was thin. No, not thin. Emaciated.

His whole body looked withered, his arms almost entirely skin on bone, veins engraved across them. Ribcage fully visible above the slack neckline of his stretched shirt, his cheeks pulled in. Gray, darkened eyes sunken in their sockets beneath his bald scalp.

The hair at Marcus's nape stood on edge. There was something eerie about the guy's gaunt form, the screen's luminosity radiating around it, giving him an almost other-worldly, skeletal quality.

"Are you Mr. Simons?" Marcus asked after an uncomfortable amount of silence.

The stranger's eyes narrowed. "I am."

"We spoke on the phone a couple of hours ago," Marcus said, the tenant frowning. "I'm here about the bathroom sink."

Simons averted his gaze momentarily before returning his attention back to his visitor. "Oh," he said, realization flashing across his fatigued visage. "The plumber?"

"That's me," Marcus replied jovially, tugging at the straps of his overalls.

"I'm-I'm sorry," Simons said, rubbing his forehead as he chuckled feebly. "I had dozed off. My brain's still half asleep," he continued, wincing as he swallowed.

"Don't worry about it. I tried ringing downstairs but got no response, so I let myself in. Hope that's all right."

"Sorry about that. The buzzer has been malfunctioning for the past few months. I should have mentioned that during our call," he explained, swallowing once more. "It slipped my mind. I'm truly sorry," Simons went on, cringing.

"No worries," the plumber reassured him, his forehead creasing as he observed the man's countenance. *When was the last time this guy slept?* he wondered. He looked beyond exhausted.

The lean man looked at him, pursing his lips. Marcus's brows converged. There was something odd about the way Simons stared, his gray eyes giving off a discreet intensity. They glinted against the warm light of the hallway, despite his tired visage. The orange glow of the lamps contrasted the one coming from the television. Simons must have caught him looking because his eyes went wide abruptly.

"P-please, come on in," he said hurriedly, opening the door and stepping to the side, extending a bony arm toward the inside in invitation.

Marcus looked ahead, his gaze traveling down the length of the apartment. The sharp shadows cast by the blue radiance of the screen were as uninviting as the building itself. His thoughts gravitated toward his daughter yet again, sleeping soundly back home, her little arms wrapped tightly around Fluffers, her favorite teddy bear, the one he'd bought her for her fifth birthday. *Remember what's at stake here.*

"Thank you, Mr. Simons," he said, nodding.

"Arthur," the man retorted. "Just...just call me Arthur, please."

"Arthur it is," the plumber obliged with a smile.

He passed the threshold, and a faint, sour smell assaulted his nostrils, a mix of dampness and probably rotten food. The tang intensified as he moved further in, finding himself in the living room. Marcus glanced back in time to see Arthur shut the door, the last sliver of the hallway's light disappearing from sight. The man locked it with his keys and pocketed them, before securing it further by sliding an iron bolt attached to the entrance at about head height. The plumber's mouth tightened, and beads of sweat started forming on his forehead.

Maybe visiting this part of the city at this hour hadn't been wise.

"Can't be too safe around here," Arthur stated as if reading his thoughts. "There's been a string of break-ins in the area, and I'm on my own on this floor." He pouted, crossing his arms over his chest. "I can't afford to lose anything more," he concluded with an awkward chortle.

Marcus detected a hint of shame coloring the man's words, a tinge of pity tempering his feelings of unease as his eyes wandered across the apartment.

Arthur wasn't kidding. This place was barebones. The short, empty entrance hall led to the living room he currently stood in—a brown, old recliner sitting in its middle, the chair's leather upholstery frayed and flaking, the television positioned close to it at an angle, broadcasting late night news on mute. Aside from numerous snack packages strewn across the floor, there was nothing else in the room. No additional furniture, no portraits, no photographs. Just a closed, single-hung window located on the other end, traces of lunar light shedding through the foggy panes, and a rusty radiator, which, judging from the temperature, was probably off. Glancing left and right, Marcus saw two more doors, both closed, facing each other from opposite sides.

"Excuse the mess," Arthur's voice came from behind, and Marcus turned to meet him. "I work long hours, and I'm usually drained by the time I'm back home." He bowed his head.

"Hey man, you don't have to tell me," Marcus said, trying to sound cheery. "I'm here at this hour, aren't I? I know a thing or two about burnout. I mean, by the time I'm home, I barely have enough strength to take a shower, let alone clean the house."

Arthur returned a frail smile, nodding. The plumber examined him, top to bottom. There was something genuinely sad about that man, about the way he carried himself, like he was constantly on guard, expecting to get jumped at any moment.

"So," Marcus started, trying to nip the advent of another stretch of awkward silence in the bud, "shall we take a look at that sink of yours?"

"Of course, please," Arthur replied, motioning toward the door to his right. "The bathroom's right there." He rubbed his nape. "Just…It-it's a bit messy…"

"Arthur, I've been doing this for eighteen years. Trust me, I've seen it all." The plumber reaffirmed his grip on the toolkit and moved to the door, its knob chilly against his palm as he turned it and pushed.

He struggled against his gag reflex. A vile stench overwhelmed him, pouring out of the dark opening like the plague and adding to the already near-unbearable reek permeating the apartment.

"The light is to your left," Arthur said.

Discreetly switching his breathing from nose to mouth, Marcus flipped the switch. Bluish, fluorescent light flickered to life from above.

First thing he noticed was the tiled, white floor, its surface smudged by spots and smears ranging from dark brown to black. There was a cast-iron, dirtied white bathtub crammed to the right, a fracture spiderwebbing part of its exterior. Its interior was veiled by a moldy, jaundice-colored plastic curtain. To the left was the lavatory, the lid lowered over the bowl, a used-up toilet paper roll sitting atop the tank. Right across the entry was the sink, wall-mounted, a cracked cabinet mirror directly above it. Marcus couldn't help an eyebrow raise. Turns out, he was wrong. He'd been to some disgusting places, but this one took the cake.

"On the phone, you said something about dirty water, right?" he asked as nonchalantly as possible while he walked up to the basin, observing a few dark-reddish rings circling the inner surface of the bowl. The faucet was corroded by rust.

"Yes, that's right," Arthur replied, appearing at the door, his reflection split across the shattered mirror's fragments.

The plumber turned one of the handles. Pipes vibrated behind the wall, and the faucet sputtered brown water, spraying the bowl.

"Shit," Marcus mumbled, leaning toward the drywall, noticing faint traces of a blackened line snaking across it.

"Is it bad?" Simons asked.

"Looks like it," he replied, kneeling and placing the toolkit by his side as he kept examining the wall's surface. *Bad* was an understatement. "We definitely have a problem here."

"Yeah, sounds about right. Not much works as it should around here," Arthur continued with a chortle of defeatism.

"Oh, I know. I actually used to live around these parts myself."

"You did?"

"Yup." The plumber opened the toolbox and pulled out a screwdriver. "Back when I was a kid. About three blocks from here, actually."

"No kidding. How far back is that, if I may?"

Marcus pondered a bit. "About twenty-five years, I think," he answered, eyeing the dark line across the wall. "Me and my folks left when I turned ten. One of the happiest days of my life."

"Wise choice," Arthur said.

"I don't think *choice* is the right word," Marcus replied, beginning to jab at the darkened surface with the tip of the tool, flakes of rot scraping off. "I doubt anyone lives here because they want to."

"You're probably right," the tenant concurred dejectedly. "Was it like this back then?"

"Yeah, it was bad. Not sure how bad it is now, though. It's been more than a decade since I last visited. Had a grandma that still lived here, refused to relocate," Marcus explained as he kept digging into the wall. "What about you? How long you been here?"

"About a year or so," Arthur replied. "I lived in a small town in Massachusetts before that."

Marcus paused and glanced back with a frown. "Massachusetts?" he muttered. "That's a really long way from here."

"Yeah," the man said, looking toward a random spot in the bathroom, seemingly far away.

"Don't take this the wrong way but...how'd you end up

MIDNIGHT VISIT

here? Was it that bad where you lived?"

Arthur chuckled good-naturedly. "No offense taken," he said and took a deep breath. "It wasn't bad. I actually was quite content there."

"Then why leave?"

The lean man made to speak but paused. His head twitched noticeably, face cringing as he pressed one hand against his temple.

"You all right?" Marcus asked.

"Y-yes," the man replied with a clearly forced smile. "Just a small migraine. I get them from time to time."

It wasn't even a moment after he finished his sentence that a rumbling sound boomed. A wincing Arthur folded a bit as his skinny fingers clutched at his stomach. Marcus's eyes widened.

"I'm really sorry," Arthur managed as he swallowed hard, apparently struggling to stand straight. "I'm so sorry."

A pang of pity stabbed at the plumber's heart. He knew that sound all too well. Starvation. He tried to find something to say but couldn't settle on an appropriate response that would allow the guy to save some face.

"You know, I got a sandwich packed with me," he finally blurted awkwardly, immediately regretting it. *Way to help him keep his dignity...*

"No, no, no, it's quite all right," Arthur rambled. "I just forget to eat sometimes. It's really nothing." He finally straightened himself, his hands still clasped over his abdomen. "I'll get something once we're done here." He lowered his head, face reddened, lips trembling faintly. "But...thank you, for the offer."

Marcus sighed and kept staring at the tenant. He pitied him more and more by the minute. The worst thing was, he couldn't come up with anything to say in order to make him feel better. Marcus wasn't even sure if there *was* anything to say. Back in his destitute days, no words ever made the hunger pangs go away. Only actions. Food. It's why he'd offered Arthur the meal Laura had prepared for him in the first place. You can't eat words, no matter how well-meaning.

"So, what about your hometown?" the plumber asked in a not-so-subtle attempt to change the subject. He returned to the task at hand. Hopefully, there was some pride left for Arthur to salvage.

"Excuse me?"

"You were about to tell me why you left and came here."

"Oh, of course," Arthur said. "That wasn't my hometown, actually," he corrected. "I was born elsewhere. I just relocated there to tend to the community's parish after a sudden opening. Stationed, to be more precise."

For the second time today, Marcus glimpsed back incredulously. "You are a priest?" he asked, sounding a bit more surprised than he intended. If he'd been given a hundred chances to figure out this guy's profession, man of the cloth would have never made the cut.

Arthur opened his mouth to say something but stopped as his eyes gravitated to the ground, his face twisting. "I...I was, yes..." He rubbed the nape of his neck. "Feels like a lifetime ago, really," he mumbled, his tone tinged in hints of nostalgia.

"Sorry, man, I didn't mean for it to sound like that," Marcus said, genuinely apologetic. The last thing he wanted was to kick the poor guy while he was down.

"It's all right. My appearance doesn't exactly scream 'member of the clergy' now, does it?" Arthur quipped with a chuckle.

Marcus sighed and returned his attention forward, resuming his work on the wall. "So, what happened?" he asked, trying to steer the conversation away from his disbelief at the man's vocation.

His question was met with silence. Marcus pursed his lips. Perhaps he had pried deeper than was appropriate.

"Work-related incident," Arthur finally replied, his tone level.

Marcus frowned as he tried to determine what could constitute a work-related incident for a pastor, especially one that would force someone to leave a life he called 'content' for this shitshow. A couple of disgusting ideas popped in his head. Maybe Mr. Simons wasn't so deserving of pity after all. He deliberated on whether he wanted to ask another question on the subject but decided this was a rabbit hole he'd rather not go down.

"Do you still practice here?"

"No," the thin man answered. "I don't practice anymore."

"How come?"

Another stretch of silence, the only audible sound being the screwdriver jabbing at the wall.

"Are you a religious man, Mr. Burrows?"

Marcus paused and wiped a few beads of sweat that had formed on his forehead. "Can't say I am," he replied. "My folks were. Never missed a Sunday sermon." He huffed. "It didn't rub off on me, I guess."

"Why?"

"Well," the plumber started with a sigh, "growing up here, all the crap I saw…I guess it clashed with the idea of the existence of an almighty, benevolent God looking over us."

"What about the Devil?"

"That I find much more plausible," Marcus said with a sneer. "But still, I think we are all the Devil we need. People have probably done stuff that have made Lucifer blush. I don't think we need demons to make our lives hell. We're just as capable of doing that ourselves."

Silence once more. Marcus breathed deep. A philosophical conversation on religion was definitely not one of the things he had expected from a visit here.

His tool-holding hand vibrated as the screwdriver's tip dragged across a hard surface, a metallic scratching noise tearing at the quiet. Marcus pulled back and saw the wall had completely scraped away to reveal a rusted pipe, its corroded exterior giving it the look of a cancerous, malignant vein.

"S-so, uhm." Simons cleared his throat. "Are-are you… uhh…a-a family man? Anyone waiting back home?"

The plumber raised an eyebrow and glanced back toward Arthur, who was now resting against the doorframe, arms crossed, head bowed. He didn't know why the question had struck him as odd.

"Nah," he answered, surprising himself with the lie. Maybe he wanted to keep his family away from this place, even in reference. "Too busy surviving to settle down, you know?"

"Yeah, I know," Arthur replied, voice low.

"How about you? You got anyone?"

"No, no one," the tenant answered. "There was a… uhm…a wife, once, but she left around the time I was ordained," he continued with a chuckle, but Marcus discerned pain through the mirth.

"Sorry to hear that."

"No, it's all right," Arthur muttered. "In hindsight, it was for the best."

The plumber sighed. He wasn't very good at offering comfort, or receiving it, for that matter.

"Well, Arthur," he said, rising to his feet, "I've got good news and bad news." Marcus was eager to change the subject and bring this visit to a much-desired conclusion.

That's when he noticed the man's reflection.

Simons stared at him intently, his eyes boring into his back. Marcus instinctively tightened his grip around the screwdriver's hilt, his heartbeat spiking abruptly. There was something primal about Arthur's expression, almost predatory. The plumber turned and faced the thin man. Simons lowered his head, eyes closing as he swallowed hard.

"The...uhm...the good news is I've found the problem," Marcus said, trying to keep a steady tone. "The bad news—"

"He's real, you know," Arthur interrupted.

Marcus cocked his head faintly. "Who's real?"

"The Devil," came the reply in a hushed whisper. "He's very real. His minions too."

The plumber's lips parted. "Okay..."

"They're there," Arthur continued, mouth shuddering. "Always lurking, always waiting. And they're much, much worse than us, trust me."

Marcus swallowed. "Well...The-the pipes in the wall are rotted through, so—"

A loud grumbling sound reverberated once more. Arthur's face contorted, and he hugged his lower torso, arms fastening around his belly.

"I-I'm so sorry," he uttered, the strain in his voice palpable.

Every muscle in Marcus's body tensed. "Y-you know, I still have that sandwich," he said, but this time it was something more than pity that guided his words. He sensed the shadowy fingers of fear scratching at the back of his head. Something felt completely off.

Arthur shook his head, face twisting in agony.

"Listen, I'll need to get replacements to fix this, so I'll just get out of your way for now," the plumber rambled, making to leave the bathroom.

Simons shifted, blocking the exit.

"I-I'm sorry," Arthur whispered. "I'm so sorry." He

gritted his teeth. "It's just...it's this thing, this fucking thing in here," he said, tapping his fingers against his temple. "It won't leave me alone, won't let me sleep, won't let me die. It just whispers incessantly, always hungry." His voice broke, sobs infecting it. "And nothing sates it," he exclaimed. "It just feeds and feeds and feeds and I can't stop it. I've tried. I've really tried, but nothing's enough. It just wants more. And those fuckers, they just sent me to that town like a lamb to the slaughter," he raved. "They knew something was lurking there. The signs were everywhere. I mean, how the fuck did they think my predecessor devoured himself to death?"

Marcus gawked, dumbfounded. He didn't have the faintest clue what was going on.

"And then the girl happened," Arthur carried on, pain chiseling his face. "Jesus, that girl. She was all skin and bone by the end...And I tried to save her. I really tried, but that thing had latched onto her soul like a parasite. And all those teachings of theirs? Nothing worked—not that holy water nonsense, no prayers, nothing," he cried out, tears streaming down his cheeks, spittle flying from his lips. "I had to release her. That thing would have dragged her down with it." He paused, glistening eyes gravitating to the floor. "And instead of thanking me for saving her and taking on her burden, those holier-than-thou bastards just fed me to the wolves." The sides of his mouth tilted down.

Marcus took a step back. "Arthur," he started, his throat catching, "I'm-I'm sorry, man. I'm...I don't understand."

Arthur raised his attention to him. He made to say

something, but no words made it out. Instead, he arched his head back and bellowed a bloodcurdling scream.

The man shrieked, and his body began to twist and bend in unnatural ways, like a wooden puppet manipulated at the hands of a wicked child. The sound of bones cracking and muscle going taut filled the room. Marcus felt shivers travel down his spine, his mouth drying as he watched the gangly form contort. Arthur cried and pleaded for his ordeal to end.

And then his body just stopped, freezing in a weird, grotesque pose, like a marionet hanging from invisible strings. He suddenly grew quiet, his head stooped.

The plumber felt every beat of his heart throb in his ears. Time stood still. Against the backdrop of the television's sickly light, Arthur stirred. He slowly raised his head. The blood ebbed from Marcus's face as the tenant's eyes met his.

There was nothing there.

Nothing. Just deep, complete darkness, pitch-black, the kind that consumes all light, an endless, empty void.

Marcus backtracked once more, and the ebony eyes locked onto him. No pupils were visible, but he knew they were glaring right at him. Arthur's body shifted, and his back hunched slightly forward, his arms resting at his sides, his spindly fingers twitching. He just stood there, right at the threshold between the bathroom and the living room.

"Arthur," Marcus said, raising his free hand defensively, "I just want to go, man."

"Arthur's not here at the moment," the lanky man declared in a sonorous, outlandish voice. "Nobody likes a chatterbox, so I sent him to his room," he said, cocking his head. "There's really no point to blabbering with the takeout order." His thin lips pulled back, baring yellowed teeth. His smile extended impossibly in a grimace, stretching his skin tightly over his skull. "But I got to give it to the guy, he lasted longer than any of the previous ones. They'd made the jump to human flesh within the first week of my joyride. Never thought I'd find a meat-suit who'd last nearly a year."

Marcus swallowed hard. His mind raced as it tried to rationalize what he was seeing. There had to be a logical explanation behind this. *Drugs*. It had to be drugs. This guy was probably hopped up on something that had widened his pupils so much they'd turned to black holes. That had to be it.

And then the plumber's brows knit.

"Takeout order?" he echoed.

A part of his brain couldn't help but find the humor in the fact that, out of all the weird crap he had seen and heard, that's what he'd chosen to inquire about. The rest was too busy managing every survival instinct that had gone on high alert to find anything about this situation funny.

Arthur's toothy grin began to fade. His expression segued to an ominous blank. Saliva began to drip down his chin and onto the smudged tank-top. His breathing turned heavy, and he leered at Marcus. His bony digits curved as his body arched forward, giving his form an animalistic quality.

The plumber's eyes widened, and his instincts warned him about what was coming.

"Arthur," Marcus managed, his heart pounding against his ribcage. The screwdriver's handle dug into his palm. "Don't do this, man."

A guttural growl thundered, and Arthur lunged at him. Marcus made to dodge but, restricted by the narrow space and close proximity, met him head on. The tenant clutched the sides of his shoulders. The plumber barely managed to bring his forearm against his attacker's chest as the rabid man's jaws snapped close to his neck. Momentum sent both tumbling down the bathtub, the plastic curtain tearing from its hooks. Ache radiated throughout Marcus's head as it struck the rim of the tub, his back landing on something squishy.

"Stop!" the plumber shouted, but Arthur kept growling. His maw was wide open. He pressed against Marcus's resistance, nearing the soft of his throat, his black eyes still wet from his previous outburst before everything went to complete shit. "Please, stop!"

Simons was gaining ground. Marcus wasn't sure if it was the hit he had sustained or their position, but it felt as if the lean man was unreasonably strong for his stature. His gaping jaws were closing in, his foul breath dizzying.

Marcus's ears began to ring. His daughter's smiling face flashed across his eyes.

"Arthur, stop!" he screamed in vain, his defending arm beginning to go sore. His hold on the screwdriver strengthened. Images assaulted him—visions of his pregnant wife and daughter standing over his grave, weeping, all alone in the world. Marcus screamed. Arm flexing, he thrust the tool at the man's side, feeling the spike burying in flesh.

Arthur wailed but kept pushing. Marcus roared, stabbing at his ribs repeatedly, warm liquid wetting his hand. The teeth were almost upon him. Muscles clenching, Marcus let out one final cry and buried the shank in Arthur's neck.

The tenant jolted, eyes widening as he pulled away violently, ripping the weapon away from his prey and pulling the screwdriver out with a trembling hand. Crimson blood gushed from the puncture. He stumbled to the toilet, his cries morphing to gurgling sounds as he fell down.

Adrenaline coursed through his veins. Marcus clambered out of the tub and rushed through the door. He darted across the living room and toward the entrance. Reaching it, he turned the handle and pulled, but the door didn't budge.

His heart sank in his chest—the exit had been locked upon entry. Terror rose when he recalled where the keys were.

Breathing deep, he turned and skulked to the corner of the small hall, then peeked at the bathroom entrance. He couldn't see much of the interior from there, but Arthur's feet were visible. Mustering every ounce of willpower he could find, he began his approach, his courage draining with every step he took until, finally, he was back at the threshold. Arthur's body lay still on the floor, eyes open, a pool of blood forming next to his neck. Marcus frowned. His eyes looked normal. They were no longer black, just bloodshot.

Whimpering, he neared the corpse and rummaged frantically through the dead man's pockets. Moments later, he fished out the keys. He was about to move away when the bathtub caught his attention. Buzzing. The bathtub was buzzing. Had it been buzzing before? Swallowing hard, he approached, pulling the torn curtain off it.

Marcus gagged, covering his nose and mouth with the inside of his elbow as flies scattered haphazardly from what looked like the half-devoured remains of a dog. Maggots feasted on its carcass.

Whiteness began to crown his vision, and he felt his stomach churn. He turned tail and hurried back toward the apartment entrance door, struggling to keep himself from retching. When he reached it, he fumbled with the keys for what felt like an eternity before finally managing to slide the right one into the keyhole. Relief overwhelmed him as the door unlocked with a *clank*. He let go of the key and was halfway to grabbing the iron bolt when fast approaching footsteps came from behind.

Marcus turned just as a gangly arm reached out. Fingers clenched around his neck like a vice. The plumber was smashed against the door and raised from the floor, his feet dangling. Below him stood Arthur, his blood-stained visage cast in harsh shadows, his face a mask of pure hate, his eyes black once more.

"You insolent piece of shit," he roared in a resonant tone, tightening his grip. "You dare to raise your hand against me? Do you know who I am? I have commanded legions!" he spat.

Marcus gurgled and tried to breathe. His eyes watered, and his back pressed against the exit, the chokehold absolute, blocking all attempts for air.

"Oh, I'll make you last for days," Arthur continued. "I'll start with your arms and legs and work my way to the top."

"Ar...Arth...Please...K-kid..."

The tenant smiled. "The meat has famous last words?" He brought the plumber close to his face as if the man's weight meant nothing to him. "Let's have it."

Marcus felt the grasp lighten just a fraction.

"I-I lied...I have a kid...Please...," he managed.

"You have a kid?" Arthur repeated. "Well, that's grand news. There's always room for desser—" His sentence interrupted, and his face winced. "Wh-what—"

Marcus found himself dropping on the floor as his attacker's grip released. He coughed and drew air in hungrily. Arthur stumbled back, his hands grasping at the sides of his head, and he grunted.

"What are you doing?" the tenant hissed through his teeth. "Stop, you imbecile! I said—"

He was brought to his knees.

"He has a kid," Arthur shrieked, but this time his voice sounded normal. "We had a deal! No famil—" he screamed.

"Shut up and go back to sleep, you useless piece of—"

"No," Arthur's voice returned, darting his attention toward Marcus. "Run! Please, run!"

Marcus sat frozen, watching the man have a discussion with himself in two different voices.

"I said run!" Arthur repeated. "Just leav—" His words were cut short as they turned to full-blown guttural screams.

The plumber watched in horror as the man's arms began to mangle. Crunching sounds accompanied each twist and bend, mixing with his chilling pleas for the torment to finish.

Marcus's body jolted awake. The horrifying scene snapped him from his paralysis. He rose as fast as he could and quickly unbolted the door before pulling it open. Rushing the corridor, he flew down the stairs. Arthur's cries faded in the distance. He burst out of the building and jumped in his truck, pulse racing.

As the vehicle's door closed next to him, Marcus paused. He opened it again, leaned over the asphalt, and heaved his guts out. Whole body trembling, he wiped at his mouth, tasting copper. He looked at his bloodied hands as if seeing them for the first time.

"Fuck," he murmured as something began to well up inside him. He clenched at the steering wheel and bowed his head. "Fuck, fuck, fuck, fuck," he repeated, sobbing. Images of the upstairs carnage mixed with his daughter's and wife's faces in his mind's eye.

He glanced at the passenger seat and realized he'd left his things behind. His attention drifted toward the dark building. He wasn't sure, but he thought he could still hear Arthur's begging.

Weeping, he switched the ignition on and drove away, the vehicle disappearing into the night.

HUNTED

BY RACHAEL BOUCKER

We're alone. The shop girl jolts as the buzzing tube-lights flicker.

"They keep doing that." She shudders, looking up at them like they'll stay on if watched.

I glance over my shoulder, down the two-aisled store. Gaps in the shelves mark where I've bought more than my fair share, but I can't come out often. I adjust my mask. A burden to some, but I couldn't be happier, considering mine and Aamon's faces are plastered all over the newspapers stacked next to me. They're meant to be compulsory, these masks, but I'm not going to pull the shop girl up for letting hers dangle from one ear.

The girl hands me another full bag and starts ringing up and packing items into the next. "You were in a few weeks back, weren't you?" she asks.

"Yeah, this was just supposed to be a short rambling holiday while our contract went through on a house, but the pandemic hit, and we'd already moved out of our place when the new one got taken off the market." *Dream house, should've said dream house. Sell the lie, moron.*

The girl behind the Perspex smiles at me. "So, Connie let you stay?"

Of course, she knows where we're staying. Small village like this, everyone's a gossip.

"Worked out for both of us. All her holiday bookings were canceled, and we have nowhere to go until lockdown's up." A bead of sweat trickles down my forehead. I look at the paper. It's not the best picture, but is the mask and bad dye job really enough to stop her from recognizing me? A bunch of bullshit is tucked between those pages. They can make up all the charges they want. Something far deadlier than the police is trying to flush us out.

"That'll be eighty-nine-sixty-seven. Cash only, I'm afraid. Never had good enough service around here for a card reader."

"Internet's terrible as well," I say, hoping it sounds like a complaint, not one more benefit in choosing this place.

She nods her agreement and passes over my change. The lights flicker again, staying off longer this time. "Could you..."

I grab the last bag as she hands it over, but she keeps a grip on it.

"Could you stick around? Just while I lock up, I mean. I don't scare easy, but..." Her voice trails off, and she looks back up at the lights.

"Not afraid of ghosts, are you?" I snigger. Worse than that out there, things that don't belong in this world, things that crawled straight out of Hell, but I'm not about to add to her fear.

"No." She laughs it off and lets go of the bag, but the fear beneath the smile sways me.

"If the power goes out, you'll need someone to hold a flashlight." A small kindness, the decent thing to do—even though every fiber of my being is screaming to leave the girl and get back to the cottage. I've been gone too long already.

The girl closes up shop like she's on speed. Never seen anyone move so fast, and when we're both standing outside—me with a flashlight and her with the keys rattling in her hands—that fear of hers leaks into me. I'm urging her to lock the door in my head, but when the key clicks, there's this awkward moment. She's staring wide-eyed over my shoulder, down the lane I need to travel. *Is she trembling?*

"Well, goodnight then," I say with a half-hearted wave.

"Be careful," she replies.

I go to ask her what she means by that, but she's already jogging away. "Huh? Strange girl."

Probably knows the ghost story Connie told us the day we moved in.

It were dark that night, darker than a bottomless hole, and that's what it felt like being on that lane alone. You'll call me an old fool, but I felt like I'd fallen into the night, and no one or nothing were ever gonna find me. Most folks got a tale about that lane, but I lived here all my life and never heard or saw anything till that night. The wind seemed fit to pick me up and be away with me. Fought me every step, it did. Then it vanished. Gone. Thought it'd battered my ears deaf, it were so quiet, but then I heard the crying. Coulda been a girl or boy, but a child no less, wailing in the dark. Tried telling myself that it were a lost lamb bleating, but it weren't lambing season. So, I keeps on.

Didn't have the farmhouse back then, just this cottage— born here, if you can believe it—and the only way home was down the lane. It's a long old walk in the dark, can't say why, but that lane's twice the walk at night, always has been. Anyway, the crying gets louder, and I sees her, a little girl, crouched by the bushes, hugging her knees and rocking, long fair hair falling over her hands. I says something like, "You lost?" Or, "Where's your mother?" But she don't say nothing back, just cries the same set of sobs over and over like a stuck record. That shoulda been clue enough, but I didn't pay much mind to the strangeness of it. Even a child were welcome company on that road, so I reached for her. The crying stopped, and her head shot up. She got no eyes, just bottomless holes, looking and feeling the same way as that lane. Rest of her face was sweet as can be, so I were thinking, the poor wretch had 'em scooped out. "Gonna be okay," I says, and I take my coat off and drapes it over her. Damn thing falls to the ground. The girl ain't there no more, and the wind came back in force like it never left.

A bottomless hole. Not a bad way to describe this lane, I suppose. The cottage advertisement listed ghosts as well as scenic walks. Figured it was just part of the spiel, but I've got to hand it to Connie, that story of hers was pretty convincing. Still, I'd take Connie's ghost girl over what's hunting us any day.

Can't carry the flashlight and the groceries, so I turn it off, stick it in my coat pocket, and organize the bags so the weight is even. I start down the lane, winding between high hedges. The few lights still on in the village fade to nothing, not extending down the muddy one-car track. It's not like I have to worry about traffic. I'd see their lights a mile off, and I can make out the hedge rows well enough to stop from walking into them. No, cars and bushes don't concern me. It was always a risk, coming out after dark. Fewer people around to recognize me and call the tip line, but the night's filled with the things hunting us. Figure they won't have caught up with us just yet, though. Everything's paid in cash, fake names, no phones or internet access. We used public transport to get here, so no car GPS to tap into. We've made ourselves damn near impossible to track.

I swear I can feel eyes on me, a voice whispering on the wind. Can almost hear a child's repetitive cry, but I know that one's in my head. Focus, on one heavy step after the next, on the plastic handles sawing grooves in my palms.

An expanse of empty lane stretches before me, and I'm beginning to think there's something to it being longer at night. Started calling it the death run. Said to Aamon before I left, "Better limber up for the death run", and he laughed. It doesn't feel funny anymore. He's not been well, stress of it all, I think, and—no, he's going to get better, just a bit homesick.

Damn, the stars are bright, and so many of them. I know people say city light pollution kills the night sky, but I never expected it to look so otherworldly. Every time my eyes drift to the shadowy bushes on either side of me, I focus back on the stars because they are worlds away from here. Far from this never-ending corner. Once I've rounded it, I'll see the porch light of the cottage and won't feel so alone, so exposed. It'll be dim from this distance, but with no other light for miles, it's a beacon, leading me to safety. Aamon will have the kettle boiling ready, and the fire lit and—

The bushes rustle to the side of me, and ice slides through my veins. I almost drop the bags and run, abandon three weeks' worth of rations in the road. A strange grunting noise resonates through my chest, and a chill spreads across my skin. I've stopped dead in the road, closer to the sleeping village than my only ally. I consider turning back.

Wait, silence, the grunting's stopped—because I'm holding my breath. *What a prick! Scared of my breathing?* I could laugh out loud, but that chill hasn't left me. I pull the mask off and let my warm breath mist the air. Was I expecting to be anything other than cold out here?

I drag my feet forward, my overloaded bags seemingly gaining weight with every step. My breathing's still wheezy. Don't need to be silent, I just need to get back to the cottage, back to Aamon and the hot drink he'll have waiting. Need to make it home. The latest home, at least. We've moved so often these past few years, trying to keep ahead of these things.

For a moment, I see the place we last ran from clear in my memories.

That thing skulked down the alley next to our apartment block. It flickered like an optical illusion, walking the Earth while still tethered to its domain in Hell. The homeless guy didn't see it. The cat rummaging in the trash didn't either. But I saw it, and for a second, as I leaned out of the high window, I swear it saw me.

"Aamon, we have to go! They've found us."

Stupid thing to remember now. It's the fear, I think, that shop girl's fear and Connie's triggering my own. Damn close call that was too. If we hadn't taken the fire escape, if we'd met it on the stairwell or the elevator...I shudder. *Great, now I'm seeing shit.* Looks like a figure's emerging in the darkness, blending into the shadows. Could be a farmer out for a star-lit stroll. I practice my greeting in my head, something about the cold. Just need a forgettable hi and bye, but the person says nothing. A man, I'm guessing, from the height. He's lean. I could probably take him if it came to it. Good swing with these bags, and I could take out anyone, I reckon. His clothes, though, they must be skin-tight, almost looks like he's not wearing anything.

"Evening," I call. "Cold tonight, isn't it?"

He's silent, unmoving. I search for the man's features, but they're too dark to make out. Could be looking at the back of a bald head for all I know. *Where's his coat, his layers?* I'm feeling colder just looking at him. I take a few steps and reach for him.

"Hey, you okay?"

The man blurs, and my hand slips through his shoulder. Blinking erases the blur—and the figure vanishes.

I jolt back, heart racing, clutched breath sitting uncomfortably in my lungs. No matter how I angle my head or squint, I can't make the bulges in the bush look like a person. The hedge here grows densely enough that no one could pass through it without making one hell of a noise and mess.

Move, damn it. Can't stay here all night!

Shaking, I shift the dirt with my foot, looking for broken twigs and leaves. It must've been in my head. Still, as I try and push the figure from my mind, the feel of it remains. The slight resistance, air pressure change as my hand met that shoulder. I curl that hand inside my sleeve and stumble on a few lopsided paces with all bags clutched in my left, until I can take it no longer and reluctantly put my swaddled hand back to work.

The bushes rustle beside me. A scream struggles against its snare, trying to claw its way up my throat. Then, a gust tears down the road, shaking the leaves. I take off running, an ungainly hunched charge, trying to control the swinging bags that have travel plans of their own.

Just my imagination, nothing more.

The hedgerow ends on the right-hand side, replaced by a fence, and the porch light shines in the distance. I need to slow down. Can't maintain this sprint for long. Gravel crunching and twigs snapping has me searching the empty lane. Couldn't have seen what I thought I saw. I'm just losing my shit, is all. Paranoid. Not that that's any better. They should let us live in peace. Not like we ever did anything to them. Demonic ugly fucks.

I remember the feel of it, the thickness of air separating this world from theirs, not too dissimilar from that shoulder.

I saw my body, oxygen mask on my face, paramedics pumping my heart. They were going to bring me back. I knew they would, but before I could reunite with it, something tore me from this world. I didn't see it, not then, anyway. Found myself alone in darkness and knew from the distant screams that this wasn't a place I was going to stay.

It felt like years, an eternity of drifting until I bumped into the wall between their world and ours, but time worked differently there. I kept slapping at this wall of air. Just knew instinctively that home was on the other side. Something was close, snorting in my scent, making the air ripple around me. Then came the chill. Temperature must've dropped ten degrees. I found a small tear, not big enough for my body, but then, I wasn't in my body. That was waiting for me on the other side. Only glimpsed them for a moment, the demons guarding my exit, but that was enough to keep me sleep free for months. I tore through that hole like my life depended on it, 'cause no doubt it did, and crossed back over.

Aamon's story's much like my own. We found each other on the internet of all places, a forum for people who'd had near-death experiences, and we became inseparable. Didn't know it at the time, but we'd need to be, to watch each other's backs. You'd think they'd be over it by now. We escaped. It wasn't our time. Let it go. But those things have hunted us for years.

Need to shut my brain off. My anxiety's in overdrive. Just want to get back, have a hot drink, stick a log on the fire, and laugh with Aamon about another successful death run.

The porch light, much clearer now, flickers, and my heart stops. *Bad power lines,* I tell myself. It was like that in the shop. I'm torn between believing it and turning on my heels, fleeing this place. From the corner of my eye, I swear I can see the shadowy figure blending in and out of the darkness. The lane meanders on, but the field provides a straight shot to Aamon. He'll laugh about this when I tell him, call me a twat, and I'll laugh too. But I'm not laughing now.

I mount the fence, dangle the bags over, and drop onto the frost-covered field. The second I'm off the road, I try to calculate how many steps, minutes, seconds, are between me and the warmth of the cottage.

Darkness swallows the long grass. I sense it dragging across my boots and flattening beneath them. I can't see it or the uneven ground that keeps making me stumble. The porch light grows clearer, and I pick out the impression of the cottage. A dimmer light shielded behind a curtain forms the window, and some of that fear I've been clutching slips away. Aamon's home, he's safe, and once I'm behind those walls, I will be too.

My foot bends backward, twisting in a hole. Before I can react, I'm eating field. The ground's solid, like I've just head-butted concrete, not dirt. My nose and forehead smart like hell. Probably hurt even more without the numbing cold. I pull a long blade of frozen grass from my mouth, and it opens a paper cut along my tongue. *Is frozen grass sharper?* I hear cans rolling. A bag must've split. I guess I can come back to get them in the—

I've turned my head to face the blackest black I've ever seen. A pulsating oil spill, thick and rancid and globule. Every muscle, every inch of my skin tightens and contracts. Can't even blink in this panicked stare. Its lack of face is lying next to mine, a congealed head shape. There's no body, just a head sticking out of the ground. We'd be kissing noses if it had one. Hands pull through the earth, and it rises through the frozen dirt, sucking the color, the joy, from the world.

My soul is next!

I'm pushing up, feet scrambling on the mud before gripping, and I'm off. Glancing back, I see it oozing out of existence, that blackest black fading to the darkest color on Earth's palette.

To hell with the bags. They've found us! I need to get to Aamon. We need to get as far from here as possible. Swinging a bag won't stop these things. I'm not unfit, but my god I'm wheezing, running as fast as these barely toned legs will take me.

When I reach the decking, my whole body sighs. We can make it if we're quick, if we go now. It didn't look fully formed, still stuck somewhere between our world and the other side.

The light flickers again. The power cuts out, just for a

moment, and in that bleakness, standing six feet from me, is the same dark figure. Can't take my eyes off it, can't take the last few steps to the door. It's just standing there, but I know if I close my eyes, if I blink, it'll be right up on the porch with me when I open them.

I shield from the light bulb bursting back to life, like it's some kind of aerial assault, and look back to the drive where the figure was. It's not there now.

I shakily open the door and click it shut behind me. Doors don't mean much to these things, but it can't get me yet, not while it's got a foot in Hell.

Can't laugh that figure away, but I almost chuckle when I realize I survived another death run—just. I want to turn back the last half hour, to stand back in that poor excuse for a shop. The girl's company wouldn't save me, though. Nor would handing myself in to the police. They'd come for us in custody, steal our souls, leaving empty corpses in the cell.

My skin prickles again. *Something's not right here.* Everything is as I left it, *exactly* as I left it. No hot drink, doesn't look like Aamon's bookmark's moved the whole time I've been gone, and the logs I asked him to put on the fire still sit beside the dying embers in the hearth. Might as well not be lit, for all the good it's doing fighting the cold in here. Only thing that's moved is Aamon.

I keep my back to the door, the thing I was desperate to pass through and now can't bring myself to leave. An old-fashioned clock ticks on the wall, and the wind whistles through broken window seals.

"Aamon?" It leaves my mouth as a whisper.

Drag marks in the deep shag catch my eye, subtle shades in the carpet, but clear enough to follow from Aamon's chair all the way to the bedroom.

The lights flicker again, and the figure appears, clearer this time—eyes and mouth sewn shut, a rotten hole where its nose should be. I freeze, watching this blackened, mummified demon amble forward. If it weren't for its legs seeping through Aamon's chair, I'd think it'd made it all the way through this time.

Can't move, can't make my whimpered moans erupt into screams. It moves closer, levitating just above the floor. Slowly, I reach my hand back and caress the door handle as the creature reaches me and strokes shadowy fingers down my cheek. They feel like wisps of frigid air. My throat constricts, my chest tightens, and my knees buckle. I grip the door handle, hoping to somehow stop from sliding all the way down.

This is it. All that running and hiding all for n—

The lights come back on, and the thing slips back where it came from.

Need to get Aamon and the box that holds our last resort, our only defense against these things. With it, we have a shot, a slim chance of survival.

I stop.

But if they've got Aamon, then he's—

A scream comes from behind the cracked bedroom door. I'm not sure if it's curiosity, wanting to know what they'll do if they catch me, or some lingering hope that I can free Aamon that drives me forward. Okay, honestly, it's neither, just good old-fashioned self-preservation. The box is under the bed, and if I'm making it out of this, I need that damn box. No squeaky floorboards stand between me and that back room, but the damn door is hinged with mice.

I crawl the last few paces and crouch in the hallway, peering around the doorframe. Gap's just big enough for me to squeeze through without setting off those hinges.

Candlelight flickers on the walls. Four of those things hold Aamon, lifting him above the bed. These ones are about as clear as they can get. Aamon's writhing, wailing, weeping. *He's worth more than this. We're worth more than this!* We escaped these creatures, made a new life together, and now Aamon's soul's being quartered as they peel it from his levitated body.

I crouch even lower, practically lying down now to get a better look, but it's too dark under the bed to see anything. *Fuck! Did they get the box already?* I sure as shit ain't getting out of this one without it.

Aamon wails again. It won't be long before his torture in this world ends and he starts an eternity of it on the other side. Commando crawling forward, I ease into the room and slowly edge under the bed. Feels like I'm sealing my own fate, pinned under here with no way to run if they spot my feet sticking out. Still can't see a damn thing, and sweeping my hands out, I can't feel anything either. I flinch as Aamon's scream crescendos, and his ghostly face plummets through the bed, his misty, glowing form clutched in the hands of these abominations.

"Armchair," he wheezes. "Under my ch—"

Wispy hands paw at me, almost like he's trying to crawl inside my body. The things come through the bed with him, each wrenching away a quarter of ethereal mist. That's all any of us are outside of our meat suits. That's all I'll be if one of these things gets me. A breathless moment later, they descend through the floor, taking Aamon's torn soul with them, and his body thumps onto the bed above me. I stay frozen in shock.

My Aamon, my only ally in the whole world, gone.

My senses returning, I scramble out from under the bed, and the temperature drops. I jerk my head. My old friend from the field is bubbling up through the carpet like ripe tar-colored pus. I jump up and sprint, leaping over the emerging monstrosity. Its icy fingers drag freezer burns across my ankles, and the very touch of it gives me a sharp headache, like brain freeze.

How did it feel for Aamon, four of them, fully formed, holding him like that? Must've been agony.

I don't need to look back to know it's following me. Can feel the cold and growing sense of dread. *Just slip back into Hell, you uncompromising shit, and leave me be.* The short hall and living room seem twice as long as normal, just like the lane. Connie's wrong. It's not the night that does that, but fear. Dread, panic, and fear.

"Place is a dump," I said the moment Connie's car disap-

peared down the drive. The keys were heavy in my hand. Felt more like a chain than freedom, than safety.

"It's rustic," Aamon said. "Dripping with charm."

I wasn't sure about that, but there was something about the way he looked at it. Started to see it through his eyes—the mismatched armchairs by the fire, the uneven beams that made Aamon stoop, the floral wallpaper, carpet almost redundant with all the rugs. It was when I turned back to the window, though, that I could breathe for the first time in months. Fields surrounded us. Nothing was going to find us out here.

I turned to a satisfied groan.

"Oh yeah," Aamon said. "This is definitely my chair."

I smiled as he melted into the cushions.

I picture him in the chair as I race toward it. There's nothing rustic or charming about superfluous rugs now. I skid across them, slow as they shift and bunch, almost tripping me, and reach under the chair's skirting. My hand doesn't immediately grasp it, so I'm left groping for the box, face pushed up against the old fabric. Aamon lazed here often enough for his scent to linger, and I almost take a moment to indulge in more thoughts of him.

I feel it! The box is in my hand!

The dying fire's warmer than I first thought. No, that's not it. The cold has receded. I quickly stand, hoping the demon's gone back where it belongs. It's moved off to bar the door instead, standing taller than it, feet firmly planted on the ground, lumpy, thick oil-like body pulsating. It feels like it's dragged some of that world through with it—the dread, the crushing numbness and vastness of nothing.

I've fought for every moment of this life, and I'm not about to give up now.

The demon turns its head and sidesteps as the front door opens.

"Only me, love," Connie calls, strolling into the cottage without invitation. "Brought you some fuel for the generator. Can't 'ave my favorite tenants freezing now, can I?"

Connie's never been to the other side, never seen what horrors await us when we die, but I have, and I can't unsee, can't untune my eyes to the demons walking unseen in this world.

The carpet discolors in four places. The ones who took Aamon are returning, bubbling up in putrid pools. I don't know how it works, don't know if they can push through quicker having only just left.

I grip the box all the tighter.

"Where's that fella of yours?" Connie asks, still smiling, still oblivious.

I'm not exactly innocent. My soul's not squeaky clean— *is anyone's?*—but I know for damn sure, I don't deserve to die. Not like this.

"You all right? Look like you seen a ghost?"

As Connie puts her hand on my shoulder, the thing at the door rushes me. I twist, thrusting the woman into it at the last second. Connie thuds to the ground. Her screaming soul is disappearing through the floor in the demon's grip, and I run to the door, jumping over two of the oozing puddles.

I'm not looking back, don't want to see how far through those things have managed to get. The door slams, and I tear off into the field. I don't sense them yet, but those things can't be far behind.

I have to force myself to stop, my legs desperate to keep running. Trembling, I open the box. Connie wasn't the first to die so I could live. Hard to say how many people I tortured to get the location of these beauties, how many priests I killed to get our hands on what's in this box. Got easier with time—the hurting, the killing. Pretty sure anyone would do the same in my situation after what I went through. It was life or death, and they wouldn't hand it over. Rather keep the box locked away, preserved.

I can't go back, not ever. I don't know how long I was stuck in Hell for. When I broke through, when I escaped back here, I found my body was gone—cremated—but that didn't stop this place being home.

I pull out one of the two ancient daggers. Can't tell you what's different about these things and your average kitchen knife, only the ritual won't work without them.

Come on, come on.

I shake my arms out, lightly jogging on the spot. I can do this, not that I ever wanted to. Grown attached to this body, may as well have always been mine with the years I've spent in it, but here I am. *Last resort time.*

Under that gorgeous star-studded sky, I blink away tears, plunge the dagger into my belly, and tear it open. Hot blood rushes onto my frigid skin, and intestines slip through. It's strange, their slimy caress somehow still stimulating nerves through the blinding pain. *Please work!* I'm already succumbing to lightheadedness, but I need to push through, need to finish this. Rubbing my fingers on the entrails, I draw a pentagram on my chest. The pain penetrates my being, even after my connection to the vessel severs. I hover above the fallen corpse, no longer weighed down, though I felt freer within it. The guardians of Hell must've been sleeping on the job when I slipped through, but they're not sleeping now. The cottage door slams open, and I fly away before they can catch sight of me.

It'll be a decade before I can possess another body. Takes time for the victim to hear my whispers, time for them to submit and let me in, more time for me to push them out. A decade of living in shadows and avoiding being dragged from this world.

But I was taken too soon. I deserve a chance to live, and there's no way I'll let them take me back to Hell.

SHRIEKING WILLOW

BY AMANDA CECELIA LANG

The legend of Shrieking Willow was old when my grandparents were young. Gran says Willow was a girl like any girl who ever died from a broken heart. At night, she walks the mountain where she fell to her brutal end, searching for the moonlit lover who left her to die alone and shrieking at young couples who dare to be in love. Sometimes, she is the silver mist blowing through the forest where the trees grow crooked like spine-bent girls. Sometimes, she appears as a gauzy, shadow-mouthed specter high atop the cliff beside the Falls, or as a nude, fish-pale body shimmering on the surface of the water below. Some believe she was once a maiden of the native tribes or the wayward daughter of colonial settlers or even a nubile spirit of the Black Hills themselves. But no matter who tells her story, those lucky, happy couples who see Willow always agree on one thing.

If she shrieks at you and yours, it means your love will last forever.

I've waited my entire life to hear her scream.

Adam turns onto a slow dirt road. The desolate scent of pine breezes through the windows, and filigree traces of moonlight glide across my blindfold.

I know where he's taking me—and not just by the sweet-nervous way he lured me into the passenger seat, or the inevitability of it all. It's the mountain's eerie rollercoaster gravity. Not everyone feels it, but I always do. It sweeps over me long before the road runs out. Heavy granite sinks into my bones, and my stomach floats on eddies of vertigo—up is down, inside is out, fantasy is reality. We're finally doing this.

My senses are buzzing on overdrive by the time his tires crunch to a stop. Adam doublechecks my blindfold, then guides me into the brisk open air. My feet feel wobbly, and my first steps tangle on loose rock.

"Careful now." He steadies my hips and walks me forward. His hands tremble, and I wonder if it's from the possibilities of ghosts or our first full night alone together. "Have you guessed where we are?"

"I hope so," I say as the blindfold lifts.

A rocky dead end, darkness, trees. I've never been here after sunset. Up ahead, hanging from a split rail fence, a lantern burns against the evergreen night. Beyond that, a long white shadow floats between the branches, caught wide-eyed in the lamp glow.

Boo.

A shiver of terror thrills through me. I clutch Adam's arm a split-second before bursting with delicious, nervous laughter.

"Gotcha," he says. It's only cheesecloth hanging there, wavering in a slow breeze, cut in the shape of a bedsheet ghost.

"You put that there?" My heart swells. He must've driven up here earlier just to do it.

He shrugs, so full of tiny gestures they're second nature. "Just setting the mood. In case the real thing has the night off."

"Impossible." I stare into the murky dark trees. "She's out there. Probably watching us right now. Don't you think?"

"I think if anyone can make her jealous, it's us." He kisses my hand, concealing his skepticism like a gentleman.

But really, it doesn't matter what he believes. The legend of Shrieking Willow is in my blood. My grandparents saw her when they were our age, and they're the happiest couple I know. It's my favorite bedtime story. Gran says Willow appeared on the cliffs above their campsite, a smudge of white wind shrieking at them to beat the choir. That's how she knew Granddad was her one and only.

Adam sweeps my curls behind my shoulders, and his grin turns ever-serious. "You sure you're ready for this, Annalee?"

The lantern light carves his bookish features with fiery

new angles. Usually so straight-laced, he stands before me, defiant and daring and a little wild—a hero from my own gothic romance. The cheesecloth Willow flutters behind him like sweet surrender, and I wonder what other surprises he has waiting. I glide my arms around his strong shoulders and kiss him until our heartbeats turn primal.

"Never been so ready," I whisper against his lips.

"Me too."

As he pulls our overnight packs from the truck, a nervous warmth blossoms inside my chest. We've whispered about this night since freshmen year. All the candy-flavored kisses in the back row of the Rialto, all those study dates with the bedroom door closed, so many sweet-scary moments where we climbed to the edge of *almost*...

Up ahead, the split rail fence stretches in both directions, and there's a sign: *Danger, Forgotten Falls, No Trespassing.*

The wind holds its breath in the forbidden land beyond, and moonlight, ethereal and swirling, pools in the jagged spaces above the treetops. Water crashes in the distance, calling to us.

I take an unsteady step forward. "Think we'll get in trouble?"

"I think it's worth the risk." Adam hops the fence and offers his hand.

For a guilty split-second, the good girl inside me balks. My grandparents still think I'm spending the weekend marathoning rom-coms at my best friend's house—and I *was,* until Adam appeared at her window, throwing pebbles and holding a blindfold out to me. I never lie to them. I always follow the rules. But it's the summer before college, and this night is long overdue. Besides, I think Gran would understand.

Adam and I exchange rebellious smiles, then I take his hand and cross over.

Before we get started, he doublechecks our gear and trades the electric lantern for a heavy-duty flashlight. The beam cuts a hole through the darkened forest, and Adam chuckles. "Sorry, not as romantic, but it gets tricky deeper in. We should watch our feet."

There's no path, only the distant watery murmur of the Falls. Adam takes the lead, and I trust every step. Even at the peak of spontaneity, he always has a plan. His flashlight washes out the ponderosas and quaking aspens we pass. The branches seem to reach for us, bright and wraithlike. Although the rocky ground has only the slightest incline, my equilibrium tilts, and my stomach floats in giddy knots. That upside-down gravity again.

"Whoa, you feel that?" I steady myself against him. "Getting dizzy out here."

"Yeah, it's spooky." He kisses my forehead. "I think I'm love-drunk."

"You goof." I grab his hand and hold my arms out, walking an invisible tightrope. "You know what I mean. This mountain is...*off-balance*."

Over the years, everyone from physicists to geologists

to paranormal investigators have studied this area and its mysterious gut-bending qualities. They all have their pet theories—optical illusions, electromagnetism, even vortexes. Of course, Gran says it's Willow's forsaken heart hanging heavy in the air here, whetting the stones and twisting the trees.

As we weave between branches, I try to sense invisible eyes on us. Has Willow noticed Adam's strong silhouette? Does she see how he sweeps me up like wings in a fairytale? It's not just his Eagle Scout confidence. It's his purity, his earnest chivalry. Every day with him is a waking adventure, every small moment the next best moment of my life.

Love-drunk indeed.

I yank Adam to a stop, silencing our footsteps, and turn an ear to the cool night, searching for a jealous murmur.

"What?" Adam says. "Do you hear something?"

The night holds silent. Fills with the pounding in my chest. I press his hand against the front of my jacket. "Can you feel my heart?"

"Always." He bows like a knight, and I giggle. Exactly the kind of romantic cheese that makes our friends roll their eyes.

But I live for this. I'll never get enough.

We continue on. Slowly, the air turns heavy with the promise of wet earth. The tumbling thunder of the Falls echoes around us, louder and louder. We're close.

Up ahead, Adam's light brushes the skeletal white arm of something crooked and abnormal. I gasp, delighted, and aim his hand in that direction.

"One of her trees!"

The aspen stands bent at an extreme angle, and the top branches skew sideways, the sparse leaves twitching like fingers.

I flutter my hand, teasing a wave. "Why hello, you sad lonely thing."

"Just wait." Adam chuckles.

We pass dozens more, each tree bent and bowing into the landscape at random, crooked angles. Aspens, ponderosas, white spruce. I've seen these same trees in the daylight, of course, but that doesn't stop the gooseflesh from prickling the length of my neck. Not axe-cracked or staked down, they grow like this on their own. To me, they've always seemed like tragic, forgotten dolls, leaning outward, reaching for something that will never be theirs. Looking at them too long makes me feel as if I'm tumbling off the edge of the sky.

"This place is amazing in the dark," I say. "Feels like the entire forest is float— "

"*Shhh.*" Adam presses his finger against my lips. "Look."

He clicks the flashlight off. The shadows are immediate. My eyes strain against the expanding, jagged darkness. Then I see it.

Something glowing up ahead.

A pathway of lanterns.

They flicker inside a misty silver gloom, leading the way like will-o'-the-wisps.

"Adam?" I don't have to glance sideways to feel him grinning.

I grab his hand—or does he grab mine? We race each other forward, passing lantern after lantern, until we burst from the tree line into open air. My blood rushes like I'm falling, even with a meadow firmly underfoot and Forgotten Falls rising above us. The waterfall reflects the moonlight and pulls my attention to the high cliffs, to the place where the river seems to pour from the sky. I brace myself against Adam, but Willow isn't up there. No lovely, wispy-white shadow glaring down at us from the edge, not even an after-image of all my daydreams.

Not yet.

"Night is young," Adam whispers in my ear, reading my mind.

I turn and take it all in. We stand knee-deep in wild grass and pink fireweed. The meadow reaches all the way to the murky shore. Nearby, more lanterns illuminate a campsite with a stone firepit and a two-person tent. It's perfect.

"You did all this?" I say.

"Well, not *all* this." He admires the view.

The power of the place rushes through me like water. This is it, where they say she died. Beneath the Falls, down where the jagged boulders ring the edge of the waterline like teeth in a jawbone. Willow and her lover used to swim right here. They'd run naked and dive from the cliffs, feel the gorgeous thrill of air and euphoria on their skin as they fell. No one knows if that long-ago girl stumbled or was pushed or simply leapt that final time—only that a luckier fall would've landed her safely deep in the reflecting pool.

"Come out, come out," Adam calls.

The air feels playful but heavy. A ridiculously earnest part of me longs for this. Willow only unleashes her jealousy upon couples who outshine the love she lost. Her voice is the inverse of a curse. I believe in her like I believe in Heaven and *happily ever after*. I *want* her to be true.

The full moon glows bright enough to see by as we bring our little campsite to life. Adam ignites the kindling in the firepit. Humming songs from old movies, I collect the electric lamps from the trees and arrange them around the meadow like set-pieces in a dream. All the while, we trade soft kisses and keep our eyes on the cliffside.

I catch myself smiling slyly, a little cruelly. Are you watching, Willow? Is your envy turning you green?

By the time our campfire burns hot and crackling, the suspense has me ready to burst. I grab the flashlight. "What are we waiting for?"

"What do you mean?"

"Let's climb to the top." I aim the beam at the craggy edges laddering up the cliffside. I hear stories all the time about people climbing up there and living to tell about it. Looks easy. "Don't you want to see what it's like where Willow fell?"

"Annalee, no!" Adam sounds genuinely horrified.

"Imagine the story we'd have."

"No way. I promised your granddad we wouldn't go up there."

Well, *that* stops me. I swing the light his way. "You what?"

He shields his eyes, and his smile turns bashful. "I might've asked your grandparents' permission to take you up here."

Laughter, sweet nerdy relief, bubbles from me—so much for our rebellious streak. "You asked for their blessing?"

"Who do you think packed your sleeping bag? Your grandma called me 'an honorable young gentleman.'"

Sounds like Gran alright. Sappy and perfectly romantic. She and Granddad met in kindergarten, just like Adam and me. They started dating as freshmen in high school, just like Adam and me. They were accepted to the same university, just like Adam and me. And of course, they only have eyes for each other. Gran invites Adam to supper so often I'm convinced she only wants to moon at us over the pot roast and reminiscence about young love. And who can blame her? Young love makes a girl feel daring and electric and wild.

I return my light to the cliff and trace the water to the bottom. "People do it all the time. Jump. The water's deep enough."

"Doesn't matter how deep it is if we break our necks climbing rocks in the dark." Adam squeezes my hand. "Besides, I might know another way up there. But not until morning."

"You promise?"

"Have I ever let you down?"

That's enough for me.

As a backup adventure, we slip off our hiking boots and tiptoe to the shore. The rippling water around my ankles is an icy, exhilarating shock. I shiver and can't stop smiling. A shapeless silver mist hangs over the water where the pool catches the Falls. Even in the shallow end, the spray caresses my face. It should be deafening, but it sinks into the background as if I've always heard it. I marvel at the tranquility, the floating stillness.

Is this the breath before the scream?

"Now what?" Adam wraps his arms around me and scans the rocky cliffside.

"I don't know." I bite my lip. It's funny, actually. I always imagined us being here would be enough. "The way Gran tells it, Willow just suddenly appeared."

"And started shrieking 'to beat the choir,'" Adam says. He's heard Gran's story nearly as many times as I have. "Your granddad thinks it was the wind howling down the cliffs."

"Grandad has no imagination." I stare out at the water, scanning the boulders for a smudge of ethereal white wind. "Which rock do you think broke her back?"

Adam sucks in a breath. "Christ, Annalee, that's grim."

"It's what they say happened."

"They also say her man watched from the shore, then left her to die."

"You really don't believe it?"

He darkens. "I don't believe anyone could abandon someone they love like that."

"Maybe he didn't love her. Maybe he had someone

better waiting at home. Or he just got bored with her..." I lean over and search my moonlit reflection, hoping to find Willow's sunken fish-pale face staring back, pining and abandoned. It's only me there—cherub cheeks, loose blond curls.

I look eerily beautiful.

Where *is* that ghost? I glare at the cliffs, then whirl on Adam and embrace him like he just slayed his first dragon. I drag my damsel fingers through his thick, windswept hair and exaggerate every slow lusty kiss, putting on a show, brandishing him like a weapon. All's fair, right? By the time we stop, our skin is on fire.

"You see that?" I shout to the sky, liking the way my voice cracks and echoes against the cliffside. "He's all mine!"

Adam chuckles. "Be careful. A woman scorned..."

I brace for icy fingers to reach from the water and curl around my ankles, but after several minutes, my feet only turn numb. Willow's a no-show.

"The campfire's getting low," Adam says at last, a sudden shyness adding gravity to his voice, and I agree.

It's time.

We cross the meadow, hand in hand. As we reach the campsite, a new kind of nervousness pulses through me, altogether achy and wonderful.

After Adam tends the fire, we sit together and warm our feet with our shoulders wrapped in an oversized sleeping bag. We have a magical view of the Falls, but all I see is Adam.

"Are you disappointed?" he says.

Am I? Maybe. I was hoping we'd have a story to tell our grandkids one day, but..."I'm not here for a campfire tale." I brush my lips against him, across his mouth, his jawline, his throat. He tastes like first kisses and dizzy mountain air. I don't need a ghost to tell me what I already know. I slide my hand down and undo his top button.

He pulls back, holding me in a solemn burning gaze. "Are you sure?"

"Feel my heartbeat." I press his open palm to my chest. My entire ribcage thunders like the Falls. "Never been so sure."

By the light of the campfire, beneath a blazing sky of stars, this moment is inevitable. A rustle of clothing, then we are bare and warm and trembling inside the sleeping bag. We've never done this before, but it feels like we've been waiting all our lives.

A gentle sting, then sweet.

I gasp, and Adam goes very still, concern and firelight flickering across his face.

"I'm fine," I whisper and fall into the sweetness.

He moves slowly, shyly, hungrily, kissing me deeper as I tighten my arms around him. I never want to let go. I close my eyes and let his body unlock me, let my spirit loosen from my flesh until I am *his*. Completely, wholly, intertwined. I want to whimper, I want to cry out, I want to exhale our love and hear it echo. The mountain tilts with us until we're floating, tumbling deliciously. The wind stirs, cool fingers in my hair. If I open my eyes while gravity is still spinning, I'm certain I'll catch something watching us from the trees, spine-bent and misty and reaching. I smile wickedly. And for a quick, icy heartbeat, I sense the piercing jealousy of a thousand shrieking ghosts.

Then Adam whispers my name, and I'm back with him, and it's just the two of us.

Always.

Cool fingers snake across my shoulders, and I wake to darkness.

My exposed skin prickles, but it's not just the cold—I sense immediately that I'm alone.

"Adam?" I sit up. My head feels loose, my mind swoons, the darkness fills my eyes. I press a hand to my temple, and my fingertips brush a band of cotton.

He blindfolded me?

Slowly, I pull the cloth from my eyes.

Darkness still. Where are the stars? My spirit feels turned around, disconnected. Unfelt wind rustles a thin nylon ceiling above my head—the tent?

I wrap my arms across my naked chest. I remember Adam holding me inside the sleeping bag, my nude body tender and exhausted. We fell asleep next to the fire, beneath the open sky. Sometime during the night, we must've crawled inside the tent. But I don't remember waking up.

"Adam?" I say it louder this time, and my fingers curl

around the blindfold.

Why isn't he answering me? I grope around the gritty empty floor for my clothing. My hand brushes the scattered lumps of my boots and a jacket. I pull them on quickly, then unzip the door.

In the chilly open air, my exposed legs tremble, and my body aches in delicate new ways. My footsteps sound unnatural, scraping and dull. I approach the cold ashes in the firepit. It's not like Adam to let the fire burn out. Our sleeping bag sits nearby—a flattened forgotten husk.

I'm suddenly desperate for the light, but the lanterns I placed around the campsite are missing. This isn't funny, though I can't quite form the words. An icy hollowness spreads inside me. Why would Adam do this? Why would he leave me alone, naked, and blindfolded? After everything we just gave to each other.

The meadow becomes slow-moving shadows. Wild grass sways like seaweed at the murkiest depths. The stars have gone impossibly black, and the moon hides behind the smoky grey arm of a cloud. Without the lunar reflection, the Falls disappear into the cliffside like a phantom lover slipping back into the night. My eyes slide to the top where they say a heartbroken girl fell to her doom. I don't want to look.

There's no one up there.

The emptiness is disorienting. It continues to gut me.

"Adam, please..." I turn in a small circle, tightening my arms around myself. All color has abandoned the night. A soft breeze rattles the tent, creating the illusion of unseen hands groping for the exit. That's *not* Adam. I slink backward into the tall grass while gravity sucks at the meat in my chest. Where *is* he? The promise we made to each other is still raw upon me. I can still *feel* him.

"Adam!" This time I scream it. My voice ricochets off the cliffs. "Answer me!"

Nothing. *Nothing.*

A branch snaps behind me, splitting the night.

I turn to face the trees.

And I see her in the light of a single lantern.

Willow.

I don't know how I missed her before. She must've been floating there this whole time. A white shadow against the murky evergreens.

A sting of sweet relief bleeds through me.

It's Adam's cheesecloth ghost.

The gauzy spirit ripples like a flag, waving to me from the trees. In the dim, I can just make out another light deeper in the forest, and another beyond that. The message is clear: *Follow me...*

"Anywhere." I race to the tree line. The flashlight hangs beside the lantern. With a growing smile, I unhook it and aim the beam between the branches.

Movement, deeper in. A flash of Adam's naked chest blurs through my light. Is he crazy, with the chill in the air? Of course, all *I'm* wearing are boots and a jacket.

I don't waste another second. I chase after him, drunk

on the memory of his touch and the tumbling gravity of the mountain. My quick breath echoes the crunching rhythm of his footsteps. I catch washed-out glimpses of him in my flashlight—pale shoulders and arms slipping behind a white spruce.

"Adam!" My voice ricochets. I can't tell if he calls back. I can barely tell sky from ground. I reach the first lantern. It hangs from a crooked ponderosa. The malformed trunk bows at the waist, sinking deeper even as I watch. Trick of the light, but the drifting sight of it slows me.

A twig snaps. Adam again—almost twenty trees ahead. A bright flash of eyes and grinning teeth. I bolt after him. My flashlight dances jagged lines across the forest. I follow the path of the lanterns, each one suspended from trees with glowing skeletal branches. My legs beat with upside-down adrenaline. The balmy oils of my earlier unease turn to exhilaration. But he's too fast, dashing through the trees ahead.

"Will you wait?" I cry.

The gap between us starts to shrink, closer and closer, until I pass the final lantern. Adam vanishes.

I stop cold and sweep the forest with my light.

Nothing moves ahead. The air is utter silence. I realize I've lost the sound of the Falls. The woods can disorient fast—I know that—but I should still be able to hear the water. I turn around, head spinning. The forest behind me is featureless. The lanterns have gone dark.

"Hello?"

A branch cracks immediately behind me, loud as thunder and intimately close. It could be the sound of my own spine snapping, it's so close. I lurch out of my flesh and pivot with my light. How did he sneak up so fast?

"You goof..." But the words wither on my lips.

The trees are bent.

Every last one.

The massive trunks bow away from me at brutal aberrant angles, every treetop reaching, every branch stretching for a single distant point in the forest...

Adam.

There in the center of the treefall, holding a single flickering lantern, waiting for me. The boy I've known all my life, the only boy I'll ever love.

"Oh, Adam, the trees..."

I stagger toward him—but something slithers around his waist.

I stop cold. To my very marrow, I freeze.

Hideous female hands stroke his torso.

Fingers like water-bloated worms crawl around his hips and his stomach. Muddy and slimy, they glide upward and fondle his naked chest.

Adam tilts his head at me.

His lips curve upward in carnal pleasure as the rest of the creature appears like mist behind him. Her ethereal, malformed torso slumps sideways, boneless and waterlogged. Jagged knobs of spinal cord protrude from her ragged flesh, and her endless, murky hair hangs like a midnight waterfall. Her arms cling tighter around Adam, hideous, horribly long branches bound in bruised flesh. They snap and pop like twigs underfoot. She doesn't let go—and he doesn't struggle.

He just stands there with that gruesome sideways smile.

The thing that is Willow glares at me, and it's rage, not jealousy, gathering in those empty, fish-eaten eyes. Her mouth unhinges, and she sucks the nightmare wind into her wheezing rib-punctured lungs, inhaling the misty gloom deeper and deeper.

Preparing to shriek.

And it's strange—all those starry-eyed years listening to ghost stories. It never occurred to me to be afraid.

For a weightless second, my vision doubles, my spirit tumbles, and I see myself from her angle. Me, a blood-drained husk with limp blond curls and horrified moon eyes, rooted in place by the deity I once worshipped. I never should've tempted her.

She caresses the top button of Adam's jeans.

"Get away from him," I cry, breaking the spell.

I stagger forward, but my vision tumbles again, and I collapse over my own tangled feet, slamming the ground with my lungs. I gasp, try to breathe, try to see past the sudden prickling darkness. My hands fumble across pine needles, groping, grasping for the flashlight. I find the handle and aim the beam forward.

Nothing's there.

Nobody's there.

The trees are normal, tall and upright.

Pushing up onto my knees, I want to laugh but can barely breathe. I press a hand against my pounding head. Was that even *real*? A legend-induced hallucination? Those slimy hands caressing Adam's chest. His savage, euphoric grin. The after images sear my vision. Shuddering to my feet, I try to blink them away.

"Annalee!" Adam's voice echoes from impossibly far away, sending a flock of sleeping birds full feather into the sky.

"I'm here!" I pivot toward the sound with a sob of manic relief. I can't believe it.

The lanterns are there.

They line the woods, showing the way back to him.

I can hear the Falls again. My knees wobble, liquid bones, but I rush toward the lights and the sound of Adam calling. When I break through the trees, he's there waiting.

He tilts his head, taking me in—scratched legs and pale lingering horror. He holds a hand out to me. "Told you I knew another way to the top."

As he says it, the mountain flips upside down, my stomach plunges, and I stagger backward with a gasp.

The Falls are magnificent and nearby.

But we're not at the bottom any longer.

We stand on the cliff, high above the meadow in the place where the river leaves the sky. Two final lanterns mark the edge, lights on a runway.

It's the second most amazing thing I've seen all night.

"Adam, she's out there, I saw...I..." I almost tell him

everything. How Willow broke the trees, how she was horrible and muddy and had her hands all over him—and the
insidiously enthusiastic way he *let* her. But the story withers
on my lips. I breathe it back in. That *wasn't* Adam. Whatever
hideous illusion that was back there between the trees, it
won't be part of our legend.

What's real is right in front of me, standing tall and
cherished on the edge. Flesh and blood and the other half
of my soul.

We haven't been this close since we fell asleep, skin to
skin beside the campfire. We lock eyes, and an ambrosial
shyness overtakes me. We're different now yet still the same.
My body burns with sweet-raw memories. And as I approach
him, my blood beats for our next adventure.

We walk between the lanterns and peer down the welcoming arm of the river. We contemplate the drop into the
moonlit pool below. It's going to be deep. And cold. But this
is Adam, after all. Even at the height of spontaneity, he has
a plan.

"What do you think, Annalee?" His words whisper
chills through me, and I can't believe we're standing here,
even as I know it's inevitable. "Are you ready?"

I take his hand—or does he take mine?

We back away from the edge, giving ourselves a running
start.

Hand in hand, we rush and fly and soar over the side.

Gravity returns and yanks us straight down. Falling
plummeting loving, it all happens in a slow-motion heart-

beat. The air rushes past us, lifting my hair, and I hear my voice on the wind, and I see the meadow and our campsite below.

The campfire still burns.

The lamps still dot the tall grass.

And Adam's strong form is still there in the sleeping bag.

Even as I feel his hand tighten around mine. Slimy and wormy and cold.

I jerk sideways, but there's no time to scream. A bloated muddy creature with whipping dark hair plummets beside me. She yanks me close, embraces me from behind. Her gangly, fish-pale arms squeeze my waist, and we break against the rock.

Our spines split with the crack of a thousand trees.

I crush her, and she slams through me as my spirit tears loose from my fibers.

In the dizzy black seconds that follow, my body slides limply off the rock. Blood and spirit, I seep into the water, dying as Willow once died. My tragedy will twist the trees. With the last of myself, I turn my head toward the shore. I try to call for Adam, but my voice chokes on sorrow and mist.

And yet someone shouts his name. *Someone* does.

Floating beneath the Falls, I hear my voice echo against the cliffside. A heartbeat later, Adam's flashlight zigzags across my face, and he splashes through the water.

"Annalee, are you insane? Did you jump?"

He wades closer, and raw terror darkens his voice—of

course it does. I can feel the split-branch nightmare of my spine protruding from my back.

But Adam's expression softens. His sudden relief disorients me. "You're okay. Just breathe. I'm here. You knocked the air from yourself, that's all. My God, what were you thinking, jumping alone like that?"

He guides me upright and walks me from the water, wet glistening legs and sagging blond curls. Only...

Only the mountain is upside down and misty, and I witness all this from outside myself. My body walks with Adam, possessed, lovely, upright, even as my spirit bobs here on the water.

No no no *no!*

I twist and writhe until my feet sink into the muddy shallows. As I attempt to stand upright, my torso slumps sideways, and my arms stretch outward like branches.

I reach for Adam.

He leads the girl that is not me from the shore and into the firelight. His voice is lush with concern as he drapes her in a sleeping bag. "Are you warm enough, Annalee?"

"Oh, yes." She smiles wickedly and presses his hand against her nude chest. "Feel my heartbeat."

He leans in to kiss her—and I reach and reach but cannot touch him! My mouth unhinges, and the wind rushes from me, a gale force of hollowing despair.

I shriek.

And far, far away, Adam breaks their kiss just long enough to gasp. "*Shhh*. Did you hear that?"

THE END

Rotten Mummy

By Conner McAleese

She choked on her own vomit.

Her son found her the next morning upon carefully entering her room. He had been searching for the keys to unlock the front door to go to school.

Today was LGBTQI+ history day, and he'd written an essay, including pictures—which Janine, who worked in the library on Monday and Thursday afternoons, had shown him how to source, place, and set—on the suspected homosexuality of James VI of Scotland. He hadn't eaten breakfast that morning, though his mum had left out a bowl of frosted shredded wheat when she'd eventually gone to bed.

He didn't want to eat anything. He was so nervous as it was. It was a big day.

He had no idea.

Chunks of half-eaten, half-cooked oven chips lay on her pillow like clumpy petals, chewed up and spat out. Her cheeks were blue, her eyes open and staring at the ceiling. A congealed pool of red wine, more chips, stomach acid, and a curdled skin that floated on top like pond scum lay perfectly still in her gaping mouth.

"Mum?" he'd ventured. He'd understood its futility but felt himself regressing back into a scared child. It was a violent and unyielding pressure on his chest, abdomen, and lower spine that tugged all semblance of maturity from him. It left him scared, vacillating between crying and disbelief. He'd reached for her hand and fell to his knees as he felt the chill on her skin. Even he, eyes blurred, understood that she was dead—and had been since the wee hours of the morning.

A sick, revolting thought pummeled at the doors of his memory. He'd woken up during the night—not because he'd heard anything, but because his pajama bottoms were wet. He'd cum in his sleep. A not-infrequent occurrence. He pulled his pajama bottoms down and kicked them from beneath his Ned Stark duvet—head on the pillow cases in case you wanted to play at King Joffrey and Ser Ilyn Payne—before turning over and resuming his sleep. A putrid, yet clear and reflective as a mirror, thought promised him his mother had been choking to death while he came.

"Mum," he said again, this time gripping her fingers tightly in his own. "Please, Mum."

The chill radiated from her bones. The smell of her insides rotting in her mouth laced the air with a bile-like undertone that rustled his own innards. He was openly weeping now and knew he'd have to phone an ambulance—

and soon. But this was the one secret his mum kept from the world. The one thing he and she shared alone. The one thing in the entire world that was solely theirs. Not the divorce, which traveled from lip to lip of neighbor to neighbor, nor his vandalism of his head of years Mazda, nor the quiet reality that they were the last members of a broken home. Dad now lived in Sunderland. The baby that wasn't born, a bloody lump incinerated in Merrygate Hospital. Only the wine bottles, gin bottles, and beer bottles were their secret alone. And now, in her death, the last thing they would ever share. He couldn't break her confidence now.

Nor could he stomach the thought of scooping the sick from between his mother's teeth and cleaning her up before phoning the ambulance. Some things a son should never do for his mother.

"Come back, Mum, please? Don't leave me here. Not alone."

He willed the heat from his own hands into her fingers, as if he could pass what little life he had lived into her through some perverse osmosis. Leaning his forehead against the back of her hand, he let his sodden cheeks rest on her knuckles.

And then she coughed.

Violently, with a vicious contraction of her body, snapping her spine straight and sending that filth in her mouth flying across her bed sheets, onto the carpet, over her son's hair.

Her stomach contracted over and over again, not letting her catch her breath. More and more bile pummeled from her body, wracking her thin frame with tremors that would have reminded anyone watching of Raegan McNeil being thrown about her bed by Pazuza. Unable to catch her breath, unable to see through the newly invigorated pupils of her eyes, she gripped onto her son's hand like he was her only anchor to the world of the living. Her nails drew blood from his fingers. She pushed them deeper as each convulsion brought up more and more green, thick, viscous bile.

She couldn't smell it—she could barely breathe—but he could. It was burning his nostrils, acidic and potent. He could feel it drooling down his arm. A chuckle reverberated around the room, but his mother was still gasping for air.

As immediately as the vomiting came on, it stopped. Dazed, unable to process the pale pink of her room, the rose lining engraved into the skirting boards, the mini-Venetian crystal chandelier hanging from her ceiling, she lay back in her bed and looked at her son.

"Guy?" she whispered. "Junior, what...what happened to Mummy, baby?"

Junior said nothing. Could say nothing. Her hands were still cold in his. Even though both were slick—spackled almost—with his blood, there was no warmth in her. That same chill from her bones was in her voice now too.

"Guy? Answer Mummy. What did you do?"

"Nothing," he said, looking down at the bile now hardening on his arm. "I came in, and you were...I just needed...a key...but then...and I couldn't...I didn't want to phone..."

"Shh, come on now, hush. Mummy's here." She pulled him into her arms. They were still weak. Only her insistent unrelenting grip on his bloodied fingers showed any lingering strength. She stunk of stale sweat.

As the covers moved, the smell of smeared shit wafted up and made him gag. She didn't notice, though. Or if she did, she didn't let on. Strings of blood, snot, and puke hung from her left nostril and curled around her cheek. It looked to him, in the seconds before he was pressed between her breasts, like the nasal cannula he'd seen her wear right after the baby was no more. Except this one looked to be sucking the life from her, not granting it.

She showered while he stripped the bed. Only the blinding pressure of his teeth being clamped shut kept his own vomit at bay while he pulled the sheets and pushed them into a doubled-up big black bag. He peeled the pillowcase from one pillow but gave up halfway through, seeing how sodden it was. There were spares in the downstairs bedroom. He'd bring them up. They weren't feather like these ones, but they would do.

Once the bed was stripped, he pulled off the mattress protector and doubled-up the new ones he'd brought from the linen closet. By the time his mum came back from the bathroom, her bed looked as if nothing had ever happened. The smell was still there, though, lingering. He hadn't gotten around to cleaning the floor yet, scrubbing the carpet. He didn't know how. He'd Google it.

"Mum, why are you naked?" He covered his eyes while he spoke, but not before seeing the tufts of brown hair.

He'd seen his mother naked once before. Right after his dad had left, his brown stitched suitcase in one hand, his car keys and the baby's blanket in the other. His mum had drank two bottles of red wine and half a bottle of violet gin and smoked a funny cigarette that didn't smell like smoke as much as it did arm pits and crusty socks. Beneath the impassionate eye of the moon, she'd stripped down to her bra and panties and began singing Bon Jovi songs.

Junior didn't know where she was halfway too, but it was a funny kind of prayer she was doing. He was only eight, but he knew that if the neighbors saw his mum out there, there'd be questions, accusations, and maybe he would leave her too. She couldn't survive losing another child. He knew that the same way he knew that if he played football down the M8, he'd be squished by a passing car.

It was instinctual. Powerful. Primal.

And he guessed that's what made her unclip her bra and expose herself to the rhododendrons they'd planted the spring before.

"Take my hand, Junior. We'll make it, I swear!" She'd laughed before tripping over her own feet and landing with a thud on the soft grass.

He'd gone to her, trying desperately not to look at the way her breasts spilled down between her armpits. She was crying and laughing at the same time, and it took four days and endless Google searches before he convinced himself his mother hadn't had a psychotic break.

"Call me Mariana," she said as she stood in front of him, no shame at exposing herself like that.

"Mum?"

"Mariana," she shouted, throwing her hairbrush into the glass of her vanity mirror. Six deep splinters rocketed from the impact zone, and little shards sparkled like rain as they flew upward before landing on the carpet. "Out."

He sat with his back to his bedroom door, holding two marbles, one in each hand, and passed them between his legs along each side of the road printed on his Hot Wheels rug. He hadn't played like this in years, but the urge had overcome him like Jason Voorhees at the twist ending in Friday the 13th. Sudden. Violent. He'd drowned in the need to just be a kid.

Junior could hear her singing. Her voice, once lilting and perfume-like in the air, was coarser, still melodic, but more chant-like rather than true singing. His essay lay untouched in his bag, and the distant chatter of voices somewhere over his garden wall outside told him school must have finished. He'd been in his room, playing with marbles, for over four hours. His stomach rumbled. His bladder ached to be released. But he dared not move.

"Junior?"

He hadn't noticed his mum's voice stop singing. She stood in his doorway, clothed, and smiled at him. The corners of her mouth rose as they always did, but the warmth of her heart was missing. It was perfunctory. He could smell the orange scent of her perfume and the gentle sound of a running bath.

"Junior, would you like a biscuit?"

He nodded. Careful not to anger her again.

She led him down their hallway, pictures of forgotten days staring down at him as he followed his mum.

She'd been dead. He knew it. But here she was...walking, talking, moving with the same simple grace her twelve years at ballet class had taught her. He'd done it. He knew he had. He just didn't know how.

"How do you feel?" he asked her. His voice stumbled over the question, afraid to end it with the word mum for fear of something else being thrown.

"Like death," she said over her shoulder, laughing.

Two cups sat steaming on the breakfast bar, and he climbed onto the stool he always sat on and lifted his mug to his mouth. He still needed to pee, but he was thirsty too. If the day wasn't as weird as it was, he'd feel like a sim that needed to pee, eat, sleep, and puke all at the same time, and instead of doing any of those things, he'd just hop up and down in the same spot. But his mother had made him a mug of tea, so he'd drink it.

"I shouldn't be here," she said simply. "Yet here I am."

Junior, not knowing what to say, stared at his tea.

"You did something, didn't you?"

He shrugged.

"You did. But it's not your fault. You don't know better."

Her face began to bloat on the second day. Deep purple welts blossomed like pogonias across her cheeks. The roots found their way down her neck, burying themselves into the soft flesh of her shoulders. Her ankles ballooned, too, and her wrists. Every few minutes, she wiped the bloody foam congealing in the corners of her mouth.

While he lightly napped on the sofa, his mother sat down beside his head, tussling his hair with her cold fingers. Her fingertips brushed the skin behind his ear, and he shivered, sitting upright, cringing away from her deathly touch. She hadn't stopped smiling since that morning. Each tooth sat rigid between cracked lips.

"You are Mummy's little boy, aren't you?" she said.

He nodded, scared to speak in case he puked. Her touch still haunted the spot on his skin.

"I remember when you were a wee boy," she said, reaching for his arm, and it took all his willpower not to convulse away from her. "Always smiling. Always reaching for Mummy. Always hungry."

He nodded. She grinned.

"Is my little man hungry now?"

He shook his head.

"Sure, he is. Bringing back Mummy from the dead must have made him hungry. Do you want your favorite?"

"Pepperoni pizza?" he whispered. His stomach rumbled.

She hadn't cooked. Hadn't cleaned. Hadn't done anything apart from sit and stare at herself in her vanity mirror, the television playing Buffy reruns behind her.

"No." She chuckled. A deep and dark sound that, until then, he'd thought was only a sound a man could produce. A ghastly, testosterone-filled sound. "Your old favorite."

"Mum…"

"Mummy. I'm your mummy. Aren't I? I'm Mummy."

"Mummy." He corrected.

She stared at him with dull eyes. The brown that had once filled him with such safety, such care, that even when she was drunk enough to puke behind the sofa, she'd still been his mum, that same brown was now charcoal mixed with mud. Dimmer. Lifeless. She didn't blink anymore.

"Shouldn't we take you to the doctor?"

The laugh that came from her throat was more hyena than woman. It was a chorus of diabolical laughter at his expense. A reprimand in chortle. Her eyes never left him.

"After your dinner," she said.

She reached into her pajama top and heaved out her left breast. He closed his eyes, turning his nose from the stench of the dried sweat which had formed a film all over her skin. The soft meat of her armpit gasped a breath of halitosis-like body odor. She cupped her boob in both hands, pointing her nipple at him. Offering him his supper.

"Mummy, no…" he cried, salty tears careening down his cheek.

"Listen to Mummy. She'll make you big and strong."

"No," he said, trying to stand.

Her right hand shot out and slapped him across the

face. He heard something click in her hand as it left his cheek.

"You'll do as Mummy says."

Her fingers curled into his hair and tore at the roots. Still, he fought, pulling with all the might of the muscles in his neck to free himself from her. But her grip was steady, her control tight. His body began to concede precious millimeters, then centimeters, then whole inches, until her areola stared into his eyes like her own once-brown ones had a moment before.

The smell was unbearable. Rotted clumps of cheese, the lingering smell of shit, the sweet scent of the macabre burnt at his nostrils, but he was too scared to open his lips in case she yanked him forward still.

"Suppy time," she trilled, like it was a song.

"Mummy, no," he said, while looking at the one long hair growing from one of the bumps ringing her nipple.

"Yes."

With that, she yanked him forward, mashing his face into her breast. His nose choked on her skin, not being able to pull through enough air to stop the pain in his chest growing. Junior panicked. She was so strong, so determined, but if he opened his mouth, his tongue would never forget the taste of his mother's decaying flesh. He tried to pull his face to the side to get one last gulp of air, but she wouldn't let him. In desperation, his brain overrode his will. Survival opened his mouth and flooded him with disgust.

"That's a good baby," she said, cooing as she forced

herself into his mouth. "Now suck."

He shook his head.

Her fingers from her left hand pinched at the back of his neck and twisted the skin until it turned red. "Suck."

Again, he shook his head. She twisted harder, blood vessels popping and spilling blood inside his skin. The sound of a passing police car tapped at the living room window. A wind grew in their garden, making the tulips planted there sway in the sunset. A barbeque four doors down was drawing to a close, a case of beer by three men and six women's feet filling with more and more empty cans.

"Suck."

A spray of sour liquid coated his tongue. He threw up, but his mother held him so tightly to her that he had to swallow it to breathe again. She twisted the skin on his neck tighter, forcing him to keep drawing the milk from her teat. He wept onto her skin. She rocked him gently with her body, cooing him like he was a child, like she believed she had her baby back instead of a fourteen-year-old son.

He remembered the song she was humming, but not the words. More and more of his mother's milk came onto his tongue. He swallowed. And sucked. Swallowed and sucked. Swallowed and sucked. The stench of her body ravished each breath he took, her humming tainting every memory he had of her. He didn't remember blacking out, nor seeing his mother grin down at him as his body slumped onto the carpet, a trickle of her foul milk falling from the corner of his mouth.

With only a basic understanding of medical knowledge gleaned from CSI and Buffy the Vampire Slayer, he'd have guessed he'd lain with his mother's milk in his mouth for well over a week. Passed out, unwilling to awaken, or whatever it was that had happened, he'd have guessed a week. But the clock said it had only been six or so hours.

His mother rested in the bed, almost at peace. Her arms lay by her body, her eyes closed, her mouth perfectly shut. But the blood had pooled beneath her biceps, her calves, her back, bloating them with putrid black bruises that made her face look to be in the first stages of healing. There was no breath, but the stench rolled from her like a languid tide on a calm summer day.

Once it reached his feet, it climbed his body in a moment and cloistered in his nostrils. It was sweet. Like a hundred packs of rotting mince in the bin all at once. He coughed as it sauntered down his throat, gladly taking his body as his own. It swarmed his lungs, to a gratifying exclusion of all oxygen. He coughed again, choking this time as the smell of his mother's corpse violated him.

"Oh, my poor boy," she said.

His eyes streaming with tears, his fingers clasping at the skin around his throat, he looked up to see Mummy grinning down at him.

He puked.

Not because she was still alive, somehow, but because, as she spoke, a chunk of her lips fell from her face, like the first petal from the cursed rose in Beauty and the Beast.

When all her skin had fallen off, would this be over?

But lurking beneath the chunk of skin, burrowing its way deep into the gums of her exposed teeth, was the arse end of a maggot. Once he'd seen one, he couldn't help but see the rest.

The night was terrifyingly dark outside. The street-lights lighting the little courtyard of their tower block each smashed with exposed bulbs and protruding wires. Youths, Mrs. Gertler upstairs would complain bitterly to the post-man as she sprung her door open like a huntsman spider and dragged him into the depths of a ten-minute moan about the state of the world. Still, she tipped twenty dollars every Christmas. She was tittering down the phone to her daughter as Junior saw the first of the maggots cluttering his mother's mouth.

"Wakey, wakey, for Mummy!" she cooed, while reaching down for his arm to heave him up from the carpet.

"No," he said, trying to pull himself free of her grip. "No, Mum, stop it!"

"What did you say, you little shit? No? You drag Mummy back into her body and then say 'no'? Oh, oh, oh, ungrateful little cunt—just like you always were. Buried the wrong babe that day, didn't we?" she said, clawing at his T-shirt.

He kicked the carpet beneath him, using the friction to propel himself to the window. It was dark, but the moon was bright in the sky. There was no silver in the moonlight, no romantic notions of fantasy—only the hued tones of black and white, the gripping chill of the darkness.

"I didn't mean to. I don't know...how...I didn't mean to."

"You want Mummy dead again, hmm?" she said as she gripped the skin of his shoulder and finally wretched him from the floor.

He could see her fully now. The white was plastered across her face from the moonlight. A chunk of her cheek was missing, the edges of the flesh rotting and fizzing, forcing her breath to whistle from her lungs. The maggots were in more abundance than he'd first realized and had begun to destabilize the foundations of her teeth, pointing them into unnatural angles. Her right eyelid was missing—torn edges alluding to her rubbing it too hard and it simply peeling off like kid-friendly glue after it dried.

"Mum, please. Stop."

"Oh my, Junior," she said, releasing him as she stumbled backward toward the sofa. She landed with barely a sound, and she hunched herself over her knees, burying her face in her hands. "You don't know what you've done. I can feel it."

"Feel what?" he said. His heart wanted to reach out to her—the most human she'd been in the two days she'd been back—but the odor, the still-tingling flesh on his shoulder where she'd touched him, and that crazy brown in her eye all held him by the window.

"My soul steaming from this body. It's not natural, not right. It should have left in a whole, not in bits and pieces, drips and drabs. Ha! Drips and drabs! Drips and Drabs!

Fucking hell. That's a funny word, isn't it?"

"Which one?"

She sat upright, hands folded over her knees.

"Does it matter? I can feel them. The maggots. It hurts."

Before she died, his grandma had shown him only a handful of pictures of his mum and her sisters when they were children, and he could never believe that the weak-smiled little girl she pointed to and proclaimed his mother ever could have been. He could see it now. The way her mouth curved down in humility. Even with missing chunks of flesh, he could still feel the shape of her body language in his mind as he could when he'd seen those pictures.

"And the missing pieces. Why did you do it?"

"Do what? I didn't mean to do anything, Mum. I promise. I don't even know if I did. If I could have. Can anyone?" He remembered the laughter but didn't know if he'd imagined it.

"I'm rotting in my own body. You have no fucking idea what this is like!"

The idea caught her like a stray football to the face on a Saturday morning in the park.

"But you will...," she said.

She lunged like a viper, her fingers venomous and sizzling as they constricted around his throat. The room was cold now, so cold he could see the last few wheezes of his breath puff away toward the living room ceiling. Then, she was moving. He heard something snap as she took his weight in her stride. The crack of it was sickening, but she didn't let it slow her. She was pulling him now, and he'd given up fighting back.

He could still taste her on his tongue, could still smell her, could feel her, could see her. Now, he had heard some unfathomable bone within her break. She was right. He'd wanted her back. He'd drug her back from wherever dead people go, all so he could uphold a promise to never tell the world about her drinking, like she'd have given a damn if he had. She'd been dead. Now, she was witness to her own body curdling around her. Parts of it falling away like leaves from an old oak.

The hallway was as cold as the living room. She dragged him past the bathroom, past his bedroom, past his bag with the essay he'd been so proud only a few days before. She threw him into her bedroom.

The pale pink of the walls seemed to radiate a comforting heat. Here, in her room, the air was sweet and warm. It felt thick, the air almost liquid as it doused around him. The chandelier glistened with muted light that seemed to be passing through a layer of skin before reaching him. He lay his head on the carpet and felt it softly caress each hair on his head.

She walked slowly around him, smiling now as if she hadn't been hollering all the way from the living room. There was something in her hand, something she'd taken from the bedside table. She was breathing in one long inhale and three short exhales, finally sitting down at the crown of his head. The skin of her inner thighs rested on his ears. She kept up the rhythmic breathing.

"Maybe...," she said to the room. She wasn't aware of him now. He knew that. Not really. "Maybe I can trade?" she asked herself. "God." She laughed. "If I take him away, will you give her back?"

Junior didn't hear the answer.

The blade was clean.

The cut was swift.

And he finally understood what she meant about leaving your body whole.

He was the lucky one.

ABOUT THE AUTHORS

RACHAEL BOUCKER

Rachael Boucker doesn't know how she got on this planet, but she sure as celibate, shelved Seans doesn't know how to get off it. She's settled in the Forest of Dean, a hub for peculiar beings, with her human Richard (enslaved in a long term relationship) and three hybrid semi-sentient minatures (the oldest of which has turned grunting into a new language). With a tentative connection to the hive mind, Rachael listens in on strange stories spanning multiple dimensions, and passes these eavesdroppings off as fiction, mostly horror and fantasy. Sci-fi can be triggering, dredging up memories of the spacebound life she left behind, but she does occasionally indulge in this genre. Look out for her upcoming Night Order dark fantasy series, being published by Eerie River Publishing.

www.rachaelboucker.com
www.facebook.com/RachaelBouckerAuthorArtist

HOLLEY CORNETTO

Holley Cornetto is a writer, librarian, professor, book reviewer, and transplanted southerner who now calls New Jersey home. Her debut novella, We Haunt These Woods, is forthcoming this summer from Bleeding Edge Books. Her short fiction has appeared in magazines such as Daily Science Fiction, Flame Tree Press Newsletter, Dark Recesses Press, and anthologies from Cemetery Gates Media, Eerie River Publishing, Dark Ink, and Kandisha Press. In 2020, she was awarded a grant from the Ladies of Horror Fiction. In addition to writing The Horror Tree's weekly newsletter, she regularly reviews for Booklist, Ginger Nuts of Horror, The Horror Tree, and Dark Recesses Press. She teaches creative writing in the online MFA program at Southern New Hampshire University. Find her on Twitter @HLCornetto.

Twitter: https://twitter.com/HLCornetto
 Web: https://www.holleycornetto.com

HENRY BEN EDOM

Henry Ben Edom is a Finnish horror author, cat dad and a lifelong lover of the macabre, whose short fiction has appeared in a number of small press publications during the past few years. His growing list of publications includes anthologies from Hellbound Books Publishing, Black Hare Press and TK Pulp. Beside writing short stories, he is currently working on longer forms of fiction. While travelling, he can be usually found from somewhere dark and underground.

www.facebook.com/HenryBenEdom

DAVID-JACK FLETCHER

David-Jack is an Australian horror author, also writing crime/thriller, humour (including dark, bizarro and romantic), and anything LGBTQI+. His debut horror-comedy released early 2022 titled The Haunting of Harry Peck. He is currently undertaking a Post Graduate Diploma in Editing and Publishing with the University of Southern Queensland and is writing his second novel titled Indentured, a horror-comedy centred around cursed dentures.

Chainsaw Editing: https://www.facebook.com/chainsawediting/ FB: https://www.facebook.com/fletcherhorror/ Instagram: davidjack_fletcher_author https://linktr.ee/djfletcher

C.M. FOREST

C.M. Forest, also known as Christian Laforet, is the author of the novel Infested, the novella *We All Fall Before the Harvest,* the short story collection *The Space Between Houses*, as well as the co-author of the short-story collection *No Light Tomorrow.* His short fiction has been featured in several anthologies across multiple genres. A self-proclaimed horror movie expert, he spent an embarrassing amount of his youth watching scary movies. When not writing, he lives in Ontario, Canada with his wife, kids, three cats and a pandemic dog named Sully who has an ongoing love affair with a blanket.

Website: ChristianLaforet.com
Facebook: Author C.M. Forest
Instagram: @christianlaforet
Twitter: @C_Laforet
TikTok: @christian_writes_horror

RB KELLY

RB Kelly's debut novel, Edge of Heaven, was shortlisted for the Arthur C Clarke Award and the European Science Fiction Society Award for Best Work of Fiction. The sequel, On The Brink, was published in May 2022. Her short stories can be found in publications from around the world, including The Best of British Science Fiction, Aurealis, and Lamplight Magazine. She has a PhD in film theory, and blogs and podcasts on film and popular culture as a founding member of CinePunked.

RB Kelly can be found on Instagram as @rachael.b.kelly and Facebook as RachaelKellyWriter.
Her website is www.rbkelly.co.uk

CONSTANTINE E. KIOUSIS

Constantine E. Kiousis spends most of his time wandering through the worlds he has created, exploring every nook and cranny and constantly discovering new places and stories that need to be told. He is in the company of his fictional characters more often than he likes to admit, sharing in their ordeals and times of joy, and has had some very interesting conversations, as well as legendary arguments, with many of them.

He currently resides in Athens, Greece, plotting new ways to unleash the terrifying stories hiding in his mind upon the rest of the world, one word at a time.

You can keep up with his work by visiting his author page: https://www.facebook.com/KiousisStoryteller

AMANDA CECELIA LANG

Amanda Cecelia Lang is a horror author and aspiring recluse from Denver, Colorado. As a die-hard scary movie nerd, her favorite things are meta-slashers, 80s nostalgia, and the rise of a fierce final girl. Her stories currently haunt the dark corners of several podcasts, zines, and anthologies, including NoSleep, Tales to Terrify, Creepy, and Mixtape: 1986. You can stalk her work at amandacecelialang.com—just don't be surprised if she leaps out at you from the shadows.

Facebook: https://www.facebook.com/amanda.lang.562/

NIKKI R. LEIGH

Nikki R. Leigh is a queer, forever-90s-kid wallowing in all things horror. When not writing horror fiction and poetry, she can be found creating custom horror-inspired toys, making comics, and hunting vintage paperbacks. She reads her stories to her partner and her cat, one of which gets scared very easily.

Instagram - @spinetinglers
Twitter - @fivexxfive
Website - spinetinglershorror.com

COLIN LEONARD

Some grotesque creatures lurk in the ancient countryside of Co.Meath, Ireland. Colin Leonard is one of them. His stories have been published in the magazines Dark Tales, Frost Zone Zine, Fudoki, and The Harrow and are included in the anthologies Eyes from Gravestone Press and Horror Library Volume 7 by Dark Moon Books. His debut novel, Country Roads, is due for release in 2023 from Brigids Gate Press.

website: www.collyleonard.com
 twitter: https://twitter.com/collyleonard

CONNER MCALEESE

Conner McAleese is the author of The Goose Mistress (Dark Ink Press, 2018), a historical fiction novel that follows Eva Braun and her descent into madness during World War Two. More recently, Conner has found his was to writing horror and has several scary short stories published both here in the U.K. and in the U.S. He is currently a Ph.D candidate at the University of Dundee researching how liminal spaces in contemporary horror literature details the modern experience of living with terrorism. He lives in Dundee with his new pup, Circe!

Twitter: @ConnerMcAleese
Insta:@Conner_McAleese

CA McDonald

CA McDonald lives in Portland, OR with her daughter, husband, and two rescue dogs. In her spare time she enjoys running stupidly long distances and dabbling in the dark arts. She has a BA in Comparative Literature and Spanish from the University of CA, Davis. Check out her most recent works at CAMCDONALD.COM

R. L. Meza

R. L. Meza is an author of horror fiction. Her short stories have appeared in Nightmare and Dark Matter Magazine. She lives in a century-old Victorian house on the coast of northern California with her husband and the collection of strange animals they call family. Meza is currently hard at work on her first novel. Learn more at rlmeza.com.

Follow her on Twitter: @RL_Meza
Website: rlmeza.com
Twitter: https://twitter.com/RL_Meza

DANNY NICHOLAS

Danny writes, particularly, stuff involving ghoulies and ghosties and long-legged beasties. When he isn't writing or reading, Danny spends his time painting, drawing, and making comics. He lives in the small, quiet town of Kraemer, Louisiana, just outside the city of Thibodaux.

Social Media Links:
Twitter: @DannyNicholas_j
Instagram: @danny_nicholas_jo
Facebook: https://www.facebook.com/danny.nicholas.37

SHELBY SUDERMAN

Shelby has been writing stories down for almost twenty years, and telling stories even longer. Her short story, Nightmares, was recently featured in the anthology Monsters & Mayhem from Eerie River Publishing.

You can find her at https://linktr.ee/shelbysuderman

ANGELA SYLVAINE

Angela Sylvaine is a self-proclaimed cheerful goth who writes horror fiction and poetry. Her debut novella, Chopping Spree, an homage to 1980s slashers and mall culture, is available now. Angela's short fiction has appeared in many publications and anthologies, including Dark Recesses, Places We Fear to Tread, and Not All Monsters. Her poetry has appeared in publications including Under Her Skin and Monstroddities. You can find her online angelasylvaine. com.

Social Media Links:
instagram.com/angela_sylvaine/
twitter.com/sylvaine_angela
facebook.com/authorangelasylvaine

TRISH WILSON

Trish Wilson's short fiction has appeared in "Zippered Flesh 3", "Wicked Women: An Anthology of the New England Horror Writers", "Teeming Terrors," "The Black Stone: Stories for Lovecraftian Summonings", "Dancing in the Shadows: A Tribute to Anne Rice", "Death's Garden Revisited", "The Horror Zine's Book of Ghost Stories", "The Horror Zine's Book of Werewolf Stories", and more. She has interviewed numerous horror writers for The Horror Zine, including Josh Malerman, Kathe Koja, Ray Garton, and Ramsey Campbell. Her podcast guests include Jack Ketchum, Billie Sue Mosiman, Joe Lansdale, and more. She sometimes writes as E. A. Black and Elizabeth Black. In addition to writing horror, she is the Media Director for The Horror Zine.

Find her on Facebook -https://www.facebook.com/ elizabethablack

Nu Yang

Nu Yang is a writer and editor, residing in Southern California. Her creative works have appeared in several magazines and anthologies. Nu is a graduate of the Odyssey Writing Workshop and Writing Popular Fiction Master's program at Seton Hill University.

Find her online at nuyangwriter.wordpress.com.

More from Eerie River

Eerie River Publishing, is a small independant publishing house that is devoted to releasing quality dark fiction books and anthologies.

To stay up to date with all our new releases and upcoming giveaways, follow us on Facebook, Twitter, Instagram and YouTube. Sign up for our monthly newsletter and receive a free ebook Darkness Reclaimed, as our thank you gift.

https://mailchi.mp/71e45b6d5880/welcomebook

Interested in becoming a Patreon member?
Patreon membership gives you exclusive sneak peeks at upcoming books, early chapter releases, covers art as well as free ebooks and discounts on paperbacks.

https://www.patreon.com/EerieRiverPub.

Coming Soon

Nothus by Drew Starling

Out Now

Infested by C.M. Forest

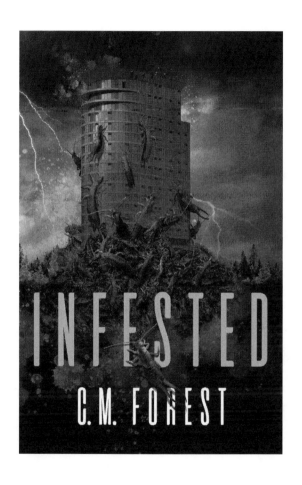

Out Now

It Calls From the Doors

Manufactured by Amazon.ca
Bolton, ON

27312575R00243